SECOND CHANCE OF SUNSHINE

SECOND CHANCE OF SUNSHINE

Pamela Evans

headline

First published in 2004
by HEADLINE BOOK PUBLISHING

10 9 8 7 6 5 4 3 2 1

Cataloguing in Publication Data is
available from the British Library

ISBN 0 7553 0042 4

Typeset in Times by
Letterpart Limited, Reigate, Surrey

Printed and bound in Great Britain by
Mackays of Chatham plc, Chatham, Kent

HEADLINE BOOK PUBLISHING
A division of Hodder Headline
338 Euston Road
LONDON NW1 3BH

www.headline.co.uk
www.hodderheadline.com

To the latest arrivals – in order of appearance – Samuel and Isabella, with love.

Chapter One

The resonant peal of the bell inside the old red-brick building, officially ending school for the day, drifted outside to the group of waiting mothers, who were enjoying a chat and catching up on the local gossip.

'Stand by for bedlam, girls,' joked one of them, looking towards the school. 'Any minute now those doors are going to be thrown open.'

Which they were seconds later, releasing an exuberant torrent of infants making a beeline for the gates, the collective roar of childish voices crescendoing in the West London street.

'Guess what, Mum,' burst out Rosa Hawkins excitedly to her mother, Molly.

'You got a star?'

'Not just a star. A *gold* one for spelling.' She looked ready to explode with triumph. Gold was the ultimate accolade.

'Well done, love.' Molly Hawkins hugged her six-year-old, imbued with warmth and pride in her achievement. Rosa's impish face when she was happy put Molly in mind of a summer's day; sparkling blue eyes, corn-coloured hair – so caringly brushed and tied into neat bunches by her mother that morning – now bearing a distinct resemblance to Molly's floor mop.

'I'll probably get a star for something tomorrow,' declared a pretty, dark-eyed little girl with pigtails, who was Rosa's best friend, Patsy, and the daughter of Molly's bosom pal, Angie. The little girls were fiercely competitive over the much-coveted classroom awards, and Patsy wasn't prepared to be outshone. 'Miss said that my writing was very good today.'

'Your turn will come,' encouraged Angie, giving her a cuddle, glad her daughter wasn't yet old enough to wriggle away from any such public display of affection.

'Don't forget you had a gold star the other day when Rosa didn't,' came Molly's timely reminder, her lively blue eyes resting affectionately on Patsy. Having been close friends with Angie since their own first day at this very same school, Molly was extremely fond of Patsy. 'So I think the two of you are just about even in the star department.'

'Course you are,' added Angie, an elegant woman, tall and slim with dark hair cut and permed in a short, fashionable layered style. She was smartly dressed in a pale blue twinset and black pencil skirt, with

1

high-heeled court shoes, her shapely legs enhanced by sheer stockings.

'So, having sorted that out, let's go home.' A woman of petite proportions, Molly was much less glamorous than her friend, and had on a faded summer frock and shapeless navy-blue cardigan she'd had for years, shabby sandals on her stockingless feet. Her shoulder-length blonde hair had none of Angie's salon stylishness since Molly was forced by economics to take the scissors to it herself. It was thick and glossy, though, and suited a simple style.

Chattering companionably, the foursome made their leisurely way home through streets of predominantly terraced houses with tiny privet-edged front gardens and potted geraniums splashing some front steps with colour, albeit that the flowers were a little wilted this late in the season. Collecting the children from school was something of a social occasion – being at a time of day when the main chores of the day were done – and they stopped every now and then to exchange a few words with people they knew, of which there were plenty because both women had lived around here all their lives. There was only a couple of months between them in age; they were both twenty-five.

It was a warm September afternoon in 1956. Gentle sunshine bathed the homely London suburb of Hanwell – which still had something of a village atmosphere, despite its heavy urbanisation – the air infused with the unmistakable tang of autumn. The rooftops rose to the hazy blue sky in serried ranks, a glimpse of the Wharncliffe Viaduct visible at certain points through gaps between the houses, the distinctive bottle-shaped top of the Beckett Pottery kiln poking up behind the chimneys.

When they reached the corner where they were to go their separate ways, Molly and Angie lingered, chatting.

After a while Angie gave Molly a studied look. 'Are you all right, kid?' she enquired.

'Yeah. Why?' Molly met her friend's gaze steadily, just a hint of defensiveness in her tone.

'You seem a bit . . . sort of preoccupied.'

'I'm fine.' She did, actually, have something particular on her mind but didn't want to go into it until there was something definite to say.

Angie could sense that something was up but was wise enough not to persist. 'That's all right then. As long as there's nothing wrong.'

'There isn't, but thanks for asking.'

'What are friends for?' Angie guessed it was money trouble; that was a permanent state for Molly, but she was too loyal to her husband to make much of it. She was the sort who would put up a front if she was down to her last penny, and no matter how difficult things were for her she always had time for other people's problems. Angie had been on the receiving end of her good nature when she herself had been ill with TB in her early teens and been confined to bed for two years. Molly had visited her every day and encouraged other friends to call. Being poorly at an age when

2

peer-group friendship was paramount, it had been hard for the young Angie, but Molly had made the whole ghastly business more bearable.

She was certainly too good for that idle husband of hers. It infuriated Angie to see her friend so down at heel because of his laziness, but a tacit agreement existed between the two friends. Molly pretended that Brian Hawkins did his best as a provider out of loyalty to him, and Angie pretended to believe her because of respect for Molly's pride.

The building trade was booming at this time of affluence, and builders' labourers were in huge demand. But Brian Hawkins wasn't one to embrace the work ethic and did as little as he could get away with. He would work until he had enough money to meet his basic requirements – his own beer and cigarettes being a top priority – then take a rest, dividing his time between the sofa at home and the local pub. Being self-employed on a cash-in-hand basis, he was paid only for the hours he put in, so Molly was kept short of housekeeping money and had a struggle to pay the bills and clothe Rosa to any sort of decent standard. As for clothes for herself, Angie couldn't remember the last time Molly had had anything new to wear. But she was a proud woman and bristled at so much as a hint of pity or assistance.

Suddenly Molly's problems were pushed to the back of Angie's mind by an ambulance coming round the corner at speed, its bell ringing as it tore down the street in the direction of the main road. It was shortly followed by a motorcyclist, who roared up to the two women and stopped.

'Where are you off to in such a hurry?' Angie asked her brother lightly. 'Are you racing the ambulance or something?'

He looked at his sister with a worried expression. 'It's Dad,' explained Billy Beckett, a good-looking man of twenty-four, black curly hair wind-blown, the dark eyes, usually so bright with liveliness and devilment, now dull with anxiety.

She gaped, turning pale. 'What . . . you mean Dad's in the ambulance?'

'That's right.'

'Oh, my God.' She was now trembling so much her teeth were chattering. 'What . . . what's the matter with him?'

'The doctor isn't sure,' he informed her. 'It's some sort of stomach trouble. He got terrible pains at dinner time so he didn't come back to work this afternoon. He thought he'd be all right after a lie-down, but he wasn't. Mum got the doctor in and he arranged for Dad to go to hospital right away. They're taking him to King Edward's. Mum's in the ambulance with him.'

Seeing every last vestige of colour drain from her friend's face, Molly put a steadying hand on her arm. Angie adored her father and, being the only daughter, she'd always been the apple of his eye.

'Oh, Billy,' Angie breathed shakily.

'Don't panic, sis,' he tried to comfort her. 'It's probably just his

3

gallstones acting up again. You know how they flare up from time to time.'

'Where's Josh?' she asked.

'Skiving as usual.' Their younger brother, who was sixteen, was a bit of a tearaway and a thorn in the side of his elder siblings. 'We sent him to the Broadway to get some milk for our afternoon cuppa and he forgot to come back, as usual.' He rolled his eyes. 'Anyway, I've left your husband holding the fort at the pottery. He'll tell Josh what's happened when the little bugger does decide to show up.' Billy indicated the pillion of his BSA. 'You gonna hop on the back then, sis?' He winked at Molly, managing a half-smile even though he was obviously extremely tense. 'You'll look after Patsy for her, won't you, love?'

'Course I will.' Molly took Patsy's hand kindly. 'She'll be fine with me and Rosa, won't you, Pats?' She raised her eyes to Angie. 'Go on. You go with Billy to the hospital. I'll give Patsy her tea and keep her for as long as you like so there's no need to rush back.'

Her friend gave her a grateful look, big eyes clouded, face taut with fear. 'Thanks, Moll.' She looked at her daughter, who was pale and bewildered, obviously having picked up on the air of sudden drama. 'That's an unexpected treat for you, isn't it, sweetheart?' she said, forcing a positive tone. 'Tea with Rosa, eh! What a lucky girl you are. Be good for Auntie Molly. I'll be back soon.' She hugged her daughter and smothered her with kisses, then – with an uncharacteristic lack of modesty – hitched up her skirt and straddled the pillion.

'Is my grandpa gonna die?' asked Patsy, as the three of them headed for the council estate where Molly and Rosa lived, Molly holding each child by the hand.

'Whatever makes you say that?' said Molly.

'Mr Johnson next door went away in an ambulance and he died,' she informed her in the matter-of-fact way children sometimes have at times of gravity. 'He's in heaven, Mummy said.'

'People don't just slip off up to heaven that easily,' encouraged Molly, deliberately keeping her tone light. 'Hospitals make people better.'

Patsy wasn't to be fobbed off. 'Why didn't they make Mr Johnson better then?'

What did you say to a six-year-old? 'Well, I suppose they can't always manage it,' she suggested. 'But they do lots of times, and your grandpa will be well looked after.'

This seemed to satisfy the child, and she and Rosa walked a few steps ahead, chattering about the fact that Rosa didn't have a grandpa, leaving Molly to her own thoughts. Despite her ostensible confidence, she was actually very shaken by this turn of events. She'd worked for Angie's father, George Beckett, in the office at their family pottery from the time she left school until she'd had Rosa. He'd been an exemplary employer

4

and a kind man, and she thought a lot of him. Maybe it was just his gallstones playing up, as Billy had said, she thought hopefully. George had had trouble with them for years.

Beyond the bay-windowed terraces, the architecture changed to the newer, scruffier buildings of the Peacock Council Estate of houses and flats that had been built just before the war. Molly's thoughts lingering on the Beckett family, she found herself comparing Angie's circumstances to her own. Angie had a happy marriage, a lovely home and financial security. The Becketts were by no means rich or posh – you'd go a long way to find more down-to-earth people – but they were in business and George had been able to give his daughter the deposit on a small house when she'd married Dan Plater, who was now a partner in the pottery.

Angie and Dan's house wasn't grand – just a three-bedroom terrace – but they were buying and not renting, and that was immensely special to Molly, whose council flat felt like a palace after a stint of living with her mother when she first got married. Being at the mercy of her mother's constant criticism had been hellish, but she and Brian had had nowhere else to go, the housing shortage being so bad in London at that time. Their flat – in a three-storey block – was small and basic, but at least they had their own front door, and it was on the ground floor.

Envy wasn't in Molly's nature and she certainly wasn't jealous of her friend's good fortune. She reckoned Angie was due some happiness after the long illness that had struck her in her early teens. She had it all now but nothing could make up for the youth she had lost then.

Thoughts of Angie were banished by the sight of Brian's pushbike leaning against the wall by their front door. Her spirits plummeted because this meant he'd finished work early, which would leave her short of housekeeping money again this week. Even more worrying was the thought that there wouldn't be a site manager left who would employ him soon, the amount of times he skived off. That settled it. She was going to make him listen to what she had to say later on, after Rosa had gone to bed. Tension knotted her stomach at the thought. He wasn't an easy man.

He was lying on the sofa in the living room reading the newspaper and smoking a cigarette when she and the girls went in. A strong, thickset man of twenty-seven with abundant brown hair and small grey-brown eyes, he was good-looking in a rough sort of way, being muscular and square-jawed with tanned skin from working out in the open. He greeted Molly and the girls absently and carried on reading.

'You're home early,' Molly remarked.

'Yeah.' He didn't go in for explanations.

'Did work finish for the day for everyone at the site?'

'No.' He never tried to justify or hide his laziness. 'The others were still there working. I'd had enough for one day so I made up some story about not feeling well and came home.'

'I see.'

The girls went through to the kitchen.

'What's Patsy doing here?' he demanded.

'Angie's dad's been rushed into hospital so she's gone to see him,' Molly explained. 'Patsy will stay with us until her mother gets back.'

He dropped the newspaper and sat up sharply. 'George Beckett in hospital? Blimey, that's a turn-up. It must be serious.'

'Not necessarily. He's only had stomach pains. It might turn out to be some minor thing.' It was important to her to stay positive and it would help if he did the same. But no such luck.

'They don't rush you to hospital for something minor,' he pointed out in a doom-laden voice.

'No. But not all bad pains turn out to be life-threatening either. Anyway, I'd rather look on the bright side.'

'That's up to you.' He looked towards the door. 'I hope those kids aren't gonna make too much noise.'

'They're not usually too bad.' She was always on the defensive with him. 'But I'll give them some tea and then they can play outside in the street. Might as well make the most of the good weather while it lasts.'

He gave an indifferent shrug. 'I could do with a cuppa,' he told her.

The smallest household task, even something as simple as boiling a kettle, he refused to do on principle because he considered it to be out of his male domain. But Molly stifled her irritation and said, 'I'll make some tea in a minute.'

Having settled the girls at the kitchen table with fish-paste sandwiches, a jam sponge she'd made earlier, and a glass of milk each, she made a pot of tea and took a cup into the other room for Brian. The room was cheaply furnished but cosy, with a red three-piece suite, and various other items including a sideboard with a wireless sitting on top, the floor covered by a square of patterned carpet bordered by lino. Molly kept the place spotless. Every surface that could be polished, gleamed.

'Well, I've got no sympathy for old man Beckett. That's what good living does for you.' Brian was envious of the Beckett family almost to the point of hatred, and resented Molly's friendship with them. 'These well-off types always get ulcers from eating too much rich food. Serves 'em right an' all.'

'They're not the type of people to go in for fancy living,' Molly pointed out.

'With all their money? Don't make me laugh.'

'They're not filthy rich, you know, Brian.'

'Ooh, not much,' he scorned. 'If they're not well off how come your best friend's father gave her the deposit on a house, and Rosa is always going on about their lovely garden and the fact that they've got a television?'

'I said they weren't filthy rich, I didn't say they weren't comfortable,'

Molly pointed out. 'Anyway, lots of ordinary families have a television set now. Even people on this estate.'

'Only because they get them on the never-never,' he stated categorically. 'The Becketts wouldn't have to do that. They'd be able to pay outright for theirs.'

'I've no idea what their arrangements are. That's their business,' she said curtly. 'Anyway, they work very hard for their money.'

'Call what they do work?'

'I certainly do,' she replied. 'It takes years to learn to be a good potter. According to what I've heard, George Beckett built his business from nothing. He and his wife took a derelict house and made it into a home for the family, and he built the kiln and the workshops in the garden. He didn't exactly have anything handed to him on a plate.'

'Even so, pottery is a doddle compared to working on a building site.'

'Being a potter is quite physically demanding, you know,' she informed him. 'I've worked there; I've seen what goes on. It's very hard on the shoulders and arms, sitting at a potter's wheel all day moulding clay.'

'It's a holiday compared to what I have to do: digging bloody footings and humping heavy stuff like drainage pipes and fittings about all day,' he complained.

'Obviously it isn't as strenuous as that,' Molly was forced to agree. 'But maybe you should do something else if you hate the work that much. There are plenty of jobs about.'

'Fat chance of me learning anything new when I've got you and Rosa to support.'

The remark had the desired effect, prodding the aching guilt already deeply embedded within her. 'There are plenty of vacancies for unskilled workers in the factories,' she mentioned. 'You could earn good money straight away.'

'Nah. The building trade is what I know,' he dismissed her suggestion. 'I'm just saying that those Becketts have an easy time of it compared to someone like me. They wouldn't last five minutes on a building site.'

'I expect they would if they had to, once they got used to it,' she defended.

'You would say that, wouldn't you?' Brian's eyes flashed with resentment. 'You've always been thick with that family, even though you know I can't stand the sight of them.'

Realising where this conversation was heading, Molly swiftly brought the subject to a close. 'Well, I can't stay here chatting. I've got to go and peel the spuds,' she said.

'What are we having?'

'Sausages.'

'Not bangers and mash again?'

'No. Bangers and chips,' she said, and departed hastily to the kitchen. She'd resisted the temptation to say that he couldn't expect rump steak

7

on the money he gave her, because she didn't want a row to break out while Patsy was here. Anyway, there was bound to be a slanging match later on when she told him what she intended to do to make things easier for them. That would be more than enough for one day.

It was getting late and Molly was wondering if she should put Patsy to bed with Rosa, as both the girls were tired and it was past their bedtime. She could just about squeeze the camp bed into Rosa's tiny cupboard of a room.

. She was going to find some pyjamas for their visitor when there was a knock at the door. It was Dan Plater, Angie's husband, a tall fresh-complexioned man with warm, shandy-coloured eyes, thick brows and rich brown wavy hair.

'Sorry to be so late coming for Patsy,' he apologised with a quick anxious smile. 'I should have come to get her straight from work but I decided to go to the hospital. Thought I needed to be there for Angie. She's having a tough time, the poor love.'

'Patsy's no trouble to us,' Molly assured him warmly. 'I told Angie not to worry about the time.'

'Thanks, Moll.' Dan shook his head, puffing out his lips. 'Phew, what a day.'

'Cuppa tea?' she offered.

'No, I'd better not stop, thanks. I need to get Patsy home to bed.' Just then they were interrupted by his daughter, who tore towards him and leaped up, throwing her arms round his neck and wrapping her legs round his waist. 'Hello there, princess,' he said, kissing her head.

''Lo, Dad.'

The love flowing between them was so tangible it brought a lump to Molly's throat. Nothing like that existed between Rosa and Brian. He rarely spoke to the child, let alone touched her. Molly instinctively put her arm around her daughter's shoulders.

'Sorry I'm late, poppet,' said Dan.

'S'all right.' Patsy continued to hug him. 'Isn't Mum with you?'

'No. She's still at the hospital with Grandpa and the others,' he explained. 'So she's put me in charge and it's bedtime for you, young lady. You go and get your things while I talk to Auntie Moll for a minute.'

'How is George?' enquired Molly as the girls trotted out of earshot.

'He's stable now after surgery and they seem to think he'll make a full recovery. He was sleeping when I left, still drowsy from the anaesthetic. It was a burst appendix, apparently.'

'Poor old George,' she said sympathetically. 'Still, he's going to be all right. That's the important thing.'

'Ooh, I'll say. He's given us all a scare, I can tell you,' he went on. 'Poor Angie has been in a terrible state. You know what she's like about her dad. But she managed to keep a grip for the sake of her mum.'

'Are they both staying at the hospital all night?'

'No. They'll be home later. Angie's mum wanted to stay for a while longer so Angie stayed on to keep her company. Billy and Josh have gone off to get some fish and chips. They've got their appetites back now they know that their dad is going to be all right.'

'If there's anything I can do, you only have to say.'

'That's kind of you,' he told her. 'You've been a great help already, looking after Patsy.'

'Any time at all,' she assured him. 'If you want me to take her to school in the morning, or collect her, just let me know.'

'I think we'll be back to normal tomorrow, as far as that's concerned,' Dan said. 'Now that George is off the danger list we'll go to the hospital during normal visiting times.'

They were talking in the tiny hall and Brian appeared from the living room. Molly knew from the suspicious gleam in his eyes that there would be a post-mortem about her conversation with Dan after he'd gone. Fortunately, it was such a personal perception no one else would have noticed. Dan certainly didn't.

'Wotcha, mate,' greeted Brian. 'I hear you've got a bit of trouble. How are things?'

Dan put him up to date.

'So you'll all be able to sleep easy in your beds tonight then,' said Brian, 'knowing George is going to be all right.'

'We all feel better than we did earlier on, and that's a fact.'

Patsy appeared wearing her blazer and carrying her navy-blue school shoe bag. After a little more polite conversation she and Dan left.

'What were you talking to him about before I appeared on the scene?' came Brian's predictable enquiry when Rosa had gone to get ready for bed.

'George, of course.'

'And the rest,' he accused. 'I'm not blind, yer know. I saw the way he was looking at you.'

Molly sighed. Brian had only a tenuous grip on reality when it came to her and other men, and would suspect her of fancying Hitler himself if the mood took him. 'Don't go down that road, please,' she entreated. 'Dan is the most happily married man I know. He only has eyes for Angie.'

'Don't make me laugh,' Brian snorted. 'Everyone knows he's the biggest womaniser in the borough.'

'That just isn't true.'

'It is,' he persisted. 'Even her parents were against the marriage because of his reputation.'

'You're going back a bit, aren't you? He was a bit of a lad when he was in his teens,' she admitted. 'But that was just wild oats and he was only a boy. He's come a long way since then, and is a real family man and absolutely devoted to his wife. Since he and Angie got together he's never so much as looked at another woman.'

'Trust you to take his side.' Brian looked sulky now. 'You always go against me.'

'What do you expect when you say such horrible things about people; things that just aren't true?' The sound of Rosa calling from the bathroom ended the conversation. 'Coming, love,' Molly shouted, and hurried from the room.

As soon as she was certain that Rosa had gone off to sleep, Molly turned off the wireless, sat down in the armchair and broached the subject that had been on her mind all day, needing to discuss it before Brian departed to the pub. He certainly wouldn't be in any state to listen when he got back.

'There's a part-time job going at the school,' she announced. 'In the office. Someone's leaving unexpectedly so they need a replacement in a hurry. I was talking to one of the other mums when I was shopping in the Broadway this morning. She works as a dinner lady there, which is how she knows about it.'

Reclining on the sofa, Brian looked across at her, brows raised. 'So, what are you telling me for?' He feigned innocence. 'I can't type.'

'There's no need to be sarky.' Although she was putting on a bold front, Molly was actually very nervous. Brian had a powerful hold over her that made her feel permanently vulnerable. 'You know exactly what I've got in mind.'

His features tightened and his tone became harsh. 'Yeah, and you know exactly how I feel about your going out to work. So why bring it up?'

'Because this job would be absolutely ideal,' she tried to persuade him. 'It's only a few hours a day, and only on school days, so it would fit in with Rosa perfectly. I'd get all the school holidays off.'

'No, Molly, you're not doing it.' He was adamant.

'But it wouldn't inconvenience you in the slightest,' she assured him. 'The household wouldn't be disrupted. I wouldn't neglect my responsibilities here.'

'I'm not having people think I can't support my family.'

'What does it matter what people think?'

'It matters to me.'

'Quite a few mothers go out to work these days when their children start school.'

'You're not gonna be one of them,' he insisted. 'A woman's place is in the home.'

'Women did all sorts of jobs during the war,' she reminded him. 'Driving ambulances and buses; they even flew planes and did precision engineering.'

10

'So what? The war's been over for eleven years and women are back where they belong – in the home.'

'Not all of them, not now that jobs are plentiful,' Molly disagreed. 'Anyway, I'm talking about a little part-time job not a full-time career. I would never do anything to interfere with Rosa or you; you know that.'

'You're not going out to work, Molly, so there's no point in your keeping on about it.' He was seething with irritation. 'I'm not having it and that's that.'

'I see.' She took a deep breath in an effort to calm her nerves, forcing herself to continue. 'In that case you'll have to give me more housekeeping money every week,' she told him. 'I simply can't manage on what you give me at the moment.'

'You'll have to try harder then, because I'm not giving you any more.'

'Let me get a job then, for heaven's sake.' She was trembling, partly with anger and exasperation but also from the profound sense of failure Brian instilled in her. 'At least then I could provide decent meals for us and get my daughter the things she needs without having to ask you for extra money. I wouldn't earn a fortune at the school but at least I'd feel as though I was doing my bit. God knows, I don't want to keep on at you but I can only make the housekeeping money stretch so far.'

She could have reminded him that he never went short of beer or cigarettes and that he could earn double what he did now if he were to work normal hours. But because of the circumstances of their marriage she didn't feel able to do that.

'Instead of complaining you ought to think back to where you'd be now if I hadn't married you,' he said nastily. 'In the gutter, that's where.'

Even though he reminded her about this on a regular basis, it still hurt. 'I haven't forgotten and I'm very grateful to you, you know that,' Molly said, her manner more subdued.

'Not grateful enough, obviously, or you wouldn't be giving me all this earache about going out to work when you know it's something I'm dead set against,' he grumbled, lighting a cigarette, inhaling deeply and coughing as a result.

'I can't see what's so terrible about it when it will make life easier for you.' He was infuriating. 'Some men would be glad to have a wife who's prepared to get out there working to bring in extra money.'

'Some men might but not me, and you know that because you've talked about getting a job before and I've told you how I feel about it,' he raged. 'If you thought anything of me at all you wouldn't upset me by suggesting it.' His deep-set eyes pierced into her. 'Still, you don't, do you, Molly?' He paused, his steady gaze not leaving her face. 'Think anything of me.'

A feeling of hopelessness swept over her. She was no match for his emotional blackmail. He made the rules in this marriage and there wasn't a thing she could do about it because she was so much in his debt. 'Don't be silly, Brian, of course I think a lot of you,' she told him. 'Don't start all that again.'

'I'm not starting anything,' he said angrily, rising with a purposeful air. 'You're the one who started this.' He paused, looking down at her perched stiffly on the edge of the armchair. 'I've done everything a man possibly could for you and Rosa. No one could have done more.'

'I know, I know,' she agreed.

'Then the least you can do is respect my wishes over this.' He drew hard on his cigarette. 'I'm going down the pub and I don't want to hear another word about any job. As far as I'm concerned the subject is closed.'

And with that he left the flat.

In the kitchen, making a cup of Camp coffee, Molly found her hands were trembling. Sitting down to drink the coffee in the living room, she mulled over the impasse she found herself in. Brian had an aversion to work so kept her short of money. She was willing to work to get the cash they needed to keep the household running to a decent standard, and Brian, paradoxically, forbade her to do it. It was ridiculous! But then his judgement was impaired by bitterness. And she was to blame. She should never have allowed herself to be panicked into marriage to a man she didn't love.

She thought back to a time when she and Brian had been friends. He'd lived just round the corner from her and they'd played together in the street with the rest of the kids. They'd always got on well, even though he'd had a crush on her that wasn't reciprocated. Naturally they'd drifted apart as they'd grown up and spread their wings. He'd gone away to do his national service; she'd met new people and started dating. When she was just nineteen – after an intense and reckless love affair with a boy called Ray, whom she'd adored and who had asked her to marry him – she'd found herself jilted, broken-hearted, pregnant and alone. Ray had run off to start a new life in Harlow New Town with a greengrocer's daughter from Shepherd's Bush.

One day, driven by despair, she'd poured out her heart to Brian when they'd happened to meet in Churchfields, soon after he'd come back from a stint in the army in Germany. He'd offered to marry her and bring the baby up as his own; had claimed it didn't matter that she didn't love him because her friendship would be enough. Entirely motivated by the opportunity of respectability for her child, she'd agreed. Her mother knew the truth; Molly had also confided in Angie. Everyone else had been encouraged to believe that Brian had got her in the family way and done the decent thing by marrying her.

So Molly was hugely in his debt. Because of his generosity, Rosa was being brought up in a family, instead of as an outcast. And Molly herself had a place in the community rather than the isolation she would have endured as an unmarried mother. Not many men would be willing to take on a woman who was pregnant with another man's child as Brian had.

Despite claiming to need only friendship from her when he was persuading her to marry him, it had soon become obvious that her affection wasn't enough. Molly did her duty to Brian in the bedroom, but never enjoyed it, and he sensed this, despite all her efforts to hide it. She had hoped she would grow to love him in the way he wanted; had tried to hard to make it happen. But gratitude simply wouldn't turn into love. Brian was no Einstein but he wasn't fooled. His disappointment made him bitter and imbued him with a perpetual sense of grievance. As he became increasingly jealous and possessive, even her fondness for him began to fade and they lost the companionship they'd once shared.

Plagued by compunction and a sense of having failed him, Molly had tried to make it up to him by being an exemplary wife; had pandered to his every need and accepted the double standards that allowed him pocket money and the freedom to come and go as he pleased but forbade her the same privilege.

It was the same gratitude and guilt that made her feel she couldn't defy him and go out to work, even though it would improve life for them all. She couldn't give him love but she could give him the loyalty he deserved after all he had done for her. He wasn't an affectionate father to Rosa and stayed very much on the periphery of her upbringing, but he was never actually unkind to her beyond being irritated by her youthful ebullience. That meant a lot to Molly. Rosa was her life and she'd put up with anything to keep her safe.

Sometimes, though, the longing to be free of Brian was almost a physical pain. It was as though he hadn't matured; had retained his adolescent mentality. She wanted to be away from the poison of his constant jealousy and the relentless strain of living on the verge of an argument. But she would never leave him; that would be too cruel. He was rough and small-minded but he was emotionally fragile where Molly was concerned.

She finished her coffee, took the cup out to the kitchen and washed it. The mess she was in was of her own making so she had no right to indulge in self-pity. She just had to continue to do what she'd been doing ever since she married Brian: making the best of things. She really didn't know how she was going to get Rosa the new clothes she needed for school, though, or the winter shoes that would soon become urgent.

Oh well, she'd just have to beg Brian for more money if he wouldn't let her earn it. Although he complained, he enjoyed making her grovel. It confirmed his power over her. Still, she supposed that was a small compensation for her lack of love.

Brian ordered a pint, speedily emptied the glass and asked for another. He needed it to cheer him up; to lessen the fear of losing Molly that

13

haunted him and had been exacerbated by talk of her going out to work. If he allowed her to do that, it would be the beginning of the end. Once she got a taste of freedom and wasn't totally reliant on him financially, she'd have no reason to stay. She certainly didn't stay with him because she loved him.

He'd wanted her for so long, the thought of losing her terrified him. He'd sooner have her under any terms than not at all. Of course, the extra money she would bring in would be handy, especially as he hated work and liked plenty of pocket money, but he daren't risk it. If she got so much as a glimpse of independence there was no knowing where it would end. She certainly wouldn't have any trouble finding another bloke, saddled with a kid or not. He'd seen heads turn when she walked into a room. She wasn't smartly dressed – he made sure she couldn't afford to be – but she was a very attractive woman with her blonde hair and slim figure.

Ordering yet another drink, he found himself longing to be free from the all-consuming passion he felt for her that caused him so much pain. The constant feeling of insecurity exhausted and depressed him. He didn't enjoy being struck with panic every time she so much as spoke to another man, or the agony of wondering when she went out of the door if she would ever come back.

It would be nice to be with someone who returned his feelings and thought he was wonderful. How good it must feel to be in a relationship where both parties enjoyed each other's company like he and Molly used to be before they got married. It wasn't as though he was repulsive to women. He'd had his chances, and taken some of them too, married or not. Women liked a man with plenty of muscle.

But it was Molly who stirred his blood, and there was nothing he could do about it. He felt compelled to keep her in whatever way he could. She claimed she would never leave him, but women couldn't be trusted. As his own mother had run off with another man when he was a boy, he could speak with authority on the subject. The only way to make sure of Molly was to keep her grateful and at home. Of course, the ultimate safeguard would be to get her pregnant but that wasn't possible because there had been damage to her womb during Rosa's birth.

'Wotcha, Bri,' said a man of about his own age, whom he knew vaguely from the building site. 'You look as though you've got the worries of the world on your shoulders.'

Brian shrugged.

'Woman trouble, I bet,' guessed the man. 'When a bloke gets that defeated look about him, there's bound to be a woman in the picture somewhere.'

'Yeah, well, that's what they do to you, innit?' Brian agreed matily. 'I reckon they were put on earth to make us men suffer.'

14

'Peculiar creatures, women,' consoled the man, becoming philosophical. 'You've more chance of swimming the Channel with bricks tied to your feet than understanding any one of 'em.'

'You can say that again.'

'Have another drink, and forget all about her for an hour or two,' invited the man.

'That's very civil of you,' replied Brian, considerably cheered. 'I'll have a pint of bitter, please.'

'We could have a game o' darts, if you like,' suggested the man. 'The dartboard's free.'

'Yeah, OK.'

By the time he'd thrown a few darts and made inroads into his next pint, the last person on Brian's mind was Molly. He was far too engrossed in his own enjoyment to give her another thought for the rest of the evening.

'You must put all ideas of getting a job out of your head if your husband's against it,' pronounced Molly's mother, Joan Rawlings, the next morning. Molly had called to see her at the tiny flat the council had moved her to when both her daughters had left home. 'You can't afford to rock the boat there.'

As soon as the words were out Molly realised it was a mistake to have mentioned the school job to her mother. It had slipped out when she was off her guard. Even now, after twenty-five years of criticism and unfavourable comparison to her elder sister, Molly still lived in hope that one day her mother might support her in something.

'I know that. It just seems a bit daft for him to object when we need the money,' mentioned Molly.

Joan poured hot water on to bottled coffee in two cups, added milk and sugar, put the cups on the kitchen table at which Molly was sitting and sat down opposite her. 'That's men for you. They have these notions about being the breadwinner even if they don't do a decent job of it. Anyway, you should be pleased he's willing to support you,' lectured Joan, who was small like Molly, and had similar features though none of her charm. Her hair had once been honey-coloured but was now white and tightly permed, which emphasised her wrinkled skin, her waistline eradicated by the passing years and a passion for sweet things.

'So he keeps telling me.'

Joan sipped her coffee. 'Just remember where you and Rosa would be if he hadn't married you,' she warned.

'Between you and Brian, I never get the chance to forget,' Molly replied.

'That can only be a good thing. It doesn't do to take things for granted,' Joan continued, missing Molly's point. 'Brian's a bit of a rough diamond and not the sort of man I'd have chosen for either of my daughters, but he was your ticket to respectability and you should be grateful for that.'

'Yes, Mum.' Without wishing to pass blame, she sometimes wondered if she would have rushed into marriage with Brian so readily if her mother had been more understanding. But Joan didn't have the mettle to cope with the disgrace of an illegitimate baby in the family and had all but dragged Molly to the register office.

'Anyway, it isn't right to go out to work when you've got a young child,' Joan went on.

'You did.'

'I didn't have any choice, did I?' Joan was quick to point out. 'Seeing as I had to bring you and Peggy up on my own, after your father was killed in action. I'd much rather have been at home but my army pension doesn't go far.'

'Neither does the money Brian gives me.'

Her mother sighed heavily, her thin lips setting in a hard line. 'You made your bed, Molly,' she reminded her. 'It's no good coming to me for sympathy.'

Molly wasn't that self-deluded. 'Actually, I came to see how you are as you thought you were going down with a cold yesterday,' she explained. 'I only mentioned the job out of interest.'

'Oh.' Joan sniffed. 'Well, all I'm saying is you can't go against your husband on this one.'

'I'm not going to.'

Joan stared thoughtfully into space. 'You could have done so much better, if only you'd behaved yourself,' she said.

'It wasn't like that, Mum.' Her mother always made it seem as though Molly had been some cheap tart who'd slept with all and sundry, and she never seemed to realise how painful her insensitivity was.

'You can dress it up any way you like: it was different for you, he was the love of your life and he promised you marriage, and all the rest of it,' she went on, 'but it doesn't alter anything. If you'd shown some restraint—'

'Then I wouldn't have Rosa, would I?' Molly cut in. 'And no matter how stupid I was, I can *never, ever* regret it because she's the best thing that's ever happened to me and I thank God for her every day of my life.'

'Your sister had the right idea.' Molly might as well not have spoken. Her mother was unstoppable when she got into her stride, pride creeping into her tone at the mention of her favoured child. 'She waited until she'd found a man who meant it when he said he'd marry her, a man who could provide well for her. You won't hear Peggy talking about getting a job, oh no. She's perfectly content to let Reg earn the money.'

'She works on the cash desk in Reg's shop,' Molly pointed out.

'Only a few hours a week,' said Joan, immediately on the defensive.

16

'Anyway, it isn't like going out to work when it's your own business.'

There was no point in arguing with her mother when she got on to the subject of Peggy's achievements, so Molly just said, 'I suppose not.'

'Reg's business is doing ever so well,' Joan went on proudly. 'They've got a car now.'

'They'll be able to come and visit you more often then, won't they?' said Molly pointedly.

'Well, yes, and I'm sure they will.' Joan seemed oblivious to Molly's hint. 'But they're very busy, what with the children and the business.'

Reg was a butcher and had his own shop in Wembley. Peggy was one of those people on whom fortune seemed to shine. She had a good husband who provided well for her, one child of each sex, just as she had always wanted, a lovely home and a stable family life. With all of that, Molly thought she might find it in her heart to show a bit more interest in the woman who had brought her up.

But she only occasionally visited or invited Mum there. But Mum still appeared to worship her. Molly called in on a regular basis and was rewarded with criticism. If she dared to say a word out of place about Peggy, she was accused of jealousy. It was impossible not to feel an occasional twinge of envy for Peggy, who could feed and clothe her children decently, but Molly tried not to let it take root.

However, she was too tired to pursue the subject of Peggy today, and give her mother cause for accusation. Molly had barely slept. What with the worry of how she was going to find the money for Rosa's winter clothes, and Brian being drunk and aggressive when he'd got home from the pub, sleep had eluded her.

'Yeah, I expect they are,' she agreed now with a weary sigh.

Mercifully her mother changed the subject. 'George Beckett's going to be all right then?' she said.

Molly nodded. 'I saw Angie at the school this morning. She said he'll have to stay in hospital for a few more days but the panic's over.'

'Thank God for that. We don't want him popping off at this early stage,' she said. 'He's not much older than I am – early to mid-fifties, I should think.'

'Something like that.' Molly paused thoughtfully. 'Which reminds me, I must call in at Angie's on the way home to see if she'd like me to collect Patsy from school this afternoon. She might want to go to the hospital to see her dad and be worried about getting back in time.'

'She'll appreciate that.'

Molly finished her coffee and stood up. 'I'd better be off then,' she said.

Joan looked at the kitchen clock. 'It's time I was getting on anyway. I want to give the place a going-over before I leave for work this afternoon.' She worked in a draper's store in Hanwell Broadway. 'I'm starting at one o'clock.'

17

'I'll leave you to it then,' said Molly, heading for the door. 'See you tomorrow.'

Angie and Dan lived in Darley Avenue, a tree-lined street of well-kept terraced and semi-detached houses not far from the canal. The street was quite ordinary but had a nice feel about it, being clean and quiet.

There were very few cars parked in the road at this time of day, and Molly was surprised to see Dan's old Ford. He must have popped home from work for something, she thought idly. The pottery was within easy walking distance.

She was about to knock at the front door when it opened and Dan and Angie appeared, obviously on their way out. From the stricken look on their faces it was obvious that something awful had happened.

Molly looked from one to the other, shaking her head slowly, not wanting to believe what she saw in their eyes. 'No . . .' She was breathless with shock. 'Oh, Angie, no . . .'

'Mum's just phoned from the hospital,' her friend explained shakily.

'But he was going to be all right,' Molly muttered almost to herself.

'There were post-operative complications, apparently,' explained Dan through dry lips, his arm round his wife supportively. 'He died about ten minutes ago.'

Molly's head spun and her heart was pounding. 'Oh, Angie,' she said at last, holding out her arms, 'I'm so very sorry.'

Angie went into Molly's arms but she was stiff and tense, her eyes dry, her body trembling. 'Yeah, I know you are, kid,' she said, her voice high and tight.

'I don't know what to say . . .'

'Don't worry . . .'

'We'd better get going, love,' said Dan tenderly. 'Your mum will be needing us.'

'Yeah, of course.' She drew back from Molly, looking vague as though trying to gather her wits. 'Could you take Patsy home from school with you, Moll, if I'm not there when they come out? Just in case we're held up.'

'Sure.'

'God knows what sort of a state Mum will be in.'

'Give her my love,' Molly managed to choke out.

'Yeah.'

With Dan's arm round his wife, they walked out to the car. The love between them was palpable. Molly didn't know of a more devoted couple.

As she walked home, her own eyes were brimming with tears. George Beckett had been a lovely man and very well liked in the area. It would be a sadder place without him. Poor Angie must be devastated. Thank goodness she had a husband like Dan to comfort her.

Chapter Two

'I'll have to go soon, Mrs Beckett,' Molly mentioned to the newly bereaved widow. 'It's almost time for me to collect Rosa from school.'

'All right, dear,' Hattie Beckett replied amiably. 'You slip off as soon as you need to.'

George Beckett's funeral wake had been underway for some time and the two women were busy in the kitchen of the Beckett home. Aptly named The Hawthorns, it was a rambling old house with rear gardens extending to the towpath of the canal. As well as apple trees, straggling blackberry bushes and wild roses, it also contained the pottery workshops and brick-built kiln of the family business. The eponymous hawthorns – that filled the garden with the sweet scent of May blossom every spring – were in abundance at the bottom.

Molly was at the kitchen sink washing glasses; Hattie was making more tea for the guests.

'Sorry I can't stay to help with the clearing-up when the guests have gone,' said Molly.

'Don't apologise, dear. You've done more for us today than we had any right to expect of you.' Hattie was a tall woman in her fifties, with a round, softly featured face and warm brown eyes currently shadowed by grief. A mushroom pallor was visible through the liberal application of powder and rouge intended to conceal it. A heavy peppering of grey in her dark permed hair seemed to add to the look of frailty that had descended upon her since her husband's death. 'You've been a godsend to us today. I don't know what we would have done without you. Thanks ever so much.'

'I was glad to help.' Brian had refused to go to the funeral with Molly – he hadn't been prepared to forget his savage dislike of the Becketts for a few hours for her sake – so she'd gone on her own. Sensitive to the fact that it was very much a family occasion, she hadn't planned on going to the wake but Angie had seemed so keen for her to be there she'd let herself be persuaded. Being the practical type, she'd made herself useful by replenishing the stocks of rolls and sandwiches as they ran out so that Angie and her mother could mingle with their guests. The Beckett brothers were in charge of the booze.

'It was very much appreciated anyway, and I'm so glad you were with us today,' Hattie went on. 'George was very fond of you, you know. As well as being a good friend to Angie, you were the best office assistant he ever had – he always used to say that.'

Taking a tea towel from a hook and starting to dry the glasses, Molly looked wistful. 'He was a smashing boss and I enjoyed working for him. I was sorry to leave . . .'

Hattie leaned towards Molly and spoke in a confidential manner. 'I'm pleased you came today for Angie's sake too. You've always been such a calming influence on her. I'm sure your being here will have helped her get through the ordeal.' She paused, her sad eyes resting on Molly's face. 'Dan's an absolute dear and a great comfort to her, but at a time like this you need your friends as well, and you two have been so close for such a long time.'

'Indeed.'

The older woman moistened her dry, cracked lips and Molly noticed how tired she looked. Her eyelids were puffy and the lines around her mouth seemed to have deepened this past week. 'I'm worried about my daughter, actually.' She shook her head, drawing in a loud breath. 'She hasn't let go and cried yet and she needs to. Keeping it all inside is doing her no good at all. You know how much she adored her father.'

'I'm sure she'll be fine, Mrs Beckett. Nature will take its course eventually,' Molly reassured. 'Try not to worry too much. You've enough to contend with; you don't need to add to it. Angie's tough. I think her illness strengthened her character; gave her added resilience. She'll cry when she's ready.'

Hattie nodded, her eyes filling with tears. 'I expect you're right.' She paused, struggling to compose herself and failing completely. 'I'm too much the other way,' she choked out, mopping her tears with a handkerchief. 'I've barely stopped weeping since it happened. I can't seem to stop.'

'The best thing for you.' Molly knew it sounded like a platitude but didn't know what else to say since nothing could ease the other woman's pain.

The conversation came to a sudden halt as Billy sailed into the kitchen with a tray of empty glasses. Always an attractive man, with his swarthy looks and dark eyes, he looked strikingly handsome today, Molly thought, in a black suit, wayward hair combed neatly into place. Noticing that his mother was distressed, he set the tray down on the table and put his arm round her.

'Aah,' he said sympathetically. 'Getting too much for you again, is it, Mum?'

She blew her nose, composing herself 'I'll be all right,' she told him thickly.

'It's hard for you, I know. But you're doing really well. We're all gutted. But we're a family and we'll get through this together,' he

20

comforted, his own eyes moist. 'You've got two strong sons and a daughter. We'll look after you.'

Agonisingly touched, Molly lowered her head, swallowing hard. She looked up when a lanky youth of sixteen dressed in a teddy boy suit came in carrying some used crockery, which he put down on the wooden draining board. He filled a glass from a bottle of light ale and made short work of it.

'Hey, go easy on that stuff, Josh,' admonished Billy, moving towards his brother. 'You're too young for heavy drinking.'

'A drop won't hurt him today.' Hattie's youngest child could do no wrong in her eyes. 'We all need a little something at a time like this.'

'He's had a lot more than a little something already,' stated Billy. 'He's really been knocking 'em back. We don't want him making a fool of himself and showing us up.'

'Leave him alone, Billy, there's a dear,' urged Hattie, sounding weak and exhausted.

'That's right, Mum,' approved Josh, slipping a filial arm round her. 'You tell him what's what. You're the best mum anyone could have, do you know that?'

'Crawler,' accused Billy.

'Now, now, boys,' rebuked Hattie wearily. 'All three of my children have been a tower of strength to me since your dad died and you've been especially wonderful today, helping me to host the funeral and I'm proud of you. Don't spoil it now by bickering.'

'That isn't bickering; it's just normal behaviour for us. If I wasn't having a go at Josh, he'd think I was ill or something, wouldn't you?' grinned Billy, looking at his brother. 'I'm just trying to keep some sort of normality about the place; make it a bit less morbid.'

'Keep it friendly then,' warned his mother. 'I don't want any rows, not today.'

Billy ran his eye over his brother's black drape jacket and drainpipe trousers, which he wore with a white shirt and bootlace tie. 'Bloody yob,' he tutted. 'Still, at least the suit's respectfully dark. That's something, I suppose.'

'I think he looks rather smart, actually,' chipped in Molly, who sometimes thought Josh's siblings were a little too hard on him. He was lazy, unreliable, ill-mannered and full of his own importance, it was true. And he certainly milked his mother's tendency to spoil him for all it was worth. But he always seemed to be the odd one out of the Beckett children, somehow; outside the warm mateyness that existed between his brother and sister. There was only a year between Angie and Billy, and they'd always been good pals. Josh was nine years younger than Angie, which was a barrier in itself. Added to that, he didn't have the striking good looks of his siblings, which would naturally cause jealousy in him. The fact that he always got his own way with his mother didn't do much for his popularity with the others either.

'Well said, Molly,' responded Josh, thin face suggestive of a grey-hound. 'I'm glad there's someone around here who recognises good taste.'

'If that's good taste, my name's Elvis Presley.' Billy's gaze rested on his brother's mouse-brown greased hair, quiffed at the front and cut into a DA at the back. 'You'd better make the most of your flash hairstyle, mate,' he advised. 'The army'll soon have it off you when you get called up for national service. Good job too. You might look somewhere near human without that poncy bird's nest on your bonce.'

'I shouldn't think he'd have to go in the army as he's got a weak chest,' mentioned their mother.

'That was only when he was a nipper,' Billy pointed out.

'He's still got it even though he doesn't get sick much now. He's always a bit chesty in the winter,' Hattie told him. 'It'll show up at the medical.'

'Trust him to get out of it,' was Billy's response. 'The jammy little sod.'

'Language, Billy . . .'

'Sorry, Mum.'

Billy's banter had an extremely false ring to it, observed Molly. He was doing his best to raise their spirits and failing miserably because their own grief was still too raw.

'Well, folks, I must go,' she told them. 'But first I need to find Angie to see if she'd like me to collect Patsy from school.'

'What's this, a meeting of minds?' This was Angie from the door. 'You boys need to get out there, mingling and looking after our guests.' She looked at her mother. 'You bearing up, Mum?'

'Yes, dear, I'm all right.'

'I was just coming to find you, actually, to ask if you'd like me to pick Patsy up and bring her home,' put in Molly. 'I'm going to get Rosa now.'

Angie looked thoughtful, then gave her mother a questioning look. 'I wouldn't mind a walk down to the school with Molly, if you'll be all right here for half an hour, Mum,' she said.

''Course I'll be all right,' Hattie assured her. 'A breath of fresh air will do you the world of good. Me and your brothers will cope here.'

'I'll just go and tell Dan where I'm going,' Angie told her friend. 'Shan't be a minute.'

Molly gave Hattie a polite peck on the cheek, said goodbye to the others and went to get her coat, an awful old black thing she'd borrowed from her mother for the occasion. She slipped it on over a dark jumper and skirt and waited at the door for Angie.

'I think we did the right thing in sending Patsy to school today.' In contrast to Molly, Angie looked extremely elegant in a tailored black suit

22

and white blouse. 'A funeral's no place for a child of that age. Dan and I were agreed on that. Some people like them to be there but not us. She can spend some time with the guests when we get back. That's enough for a little girl.'

Molly nodded.

'Honestly, Moll, I don't know how Mum's going to get on without Dad,' Angie confided. 'She'll be like a lost soul when everything settles down and gets back to normal. It's been like Paddington Station at her place this past week, with everyone calling to pay their respects. But it'll go quiet now that the funeral is over, and she'll have to get used to everyday life without him. I'll be calling in to see her every day but even so . . .'

'It will be hard for her, there's no doubt about that,' agreed Molly. 'But people seem to find the strength somehow in this sort of situation, don't they?'

'I suppose so, but Mum's always been so dependent on him,' Angie continued. 'She's never been one for women friends even. The family has always been her life. Even apart from the emotional side of it, there are the household practicalities that she's never had to deal with before. Dad always looked after the finances – paid the bills and so on. She looked after the home and family, he took responsibility for everything else.'

'I suppose that's the way it is in a lot of marriages,' commented Molly, though she herself had to pay all the bills out of the housekeeping money Brian gave her.

'Mum was particularly reliant, though. I don't think she'd ever even written a cheque until she had to pay the undertakers.'

Neither had Molly. She and Brian didn't even have a bank account. But she said, 'Billy and Josh still live at home – maybe they can take over?'

'They could do but I'm not so sure if that will be such a good idea because they'll leave home eventually and she'll be back in the same boat. Maybe it's best if she gets used to it now, to give her confidence,' Angie suggested. 'Dad will have left her well provided for so there's no problem there, but she's never had any financial responsibility before.' She paused, looking worried. 'We're all behind her to give her support but we can't replace him. Life is going to be very different for her from now on.'

'How about you?' enquired Molly. 'I haven't seen much of you this past week with you having so much family business to attend to. You seem to be coping but I know how fond of your dad you were.'

'I don't think it's sunk in properly yet,' Angie confessed. 'I'm hurting but I feel a bit numb too – sort of knotted up inside. Mind you, I've had to keep a hold of myself because I need to be strong for Mum, and Patsy. I didn't want to be blubbing all over the place in front of a six-year-old.'

'You did really well today,' praised Molly. 'You were very dignified and a great backup to your mum.'

'I just went through it automatically, as though I wasn't actually there. I felt as though it was all happening to someone else.'

They fell silent as they walked along by Elthorne Park. Although Molly's thoughts had been with the Becketts all day, now that the funeral was over, a problem of her own began to nag, making her tense. But before it had time to develop she was distracted by her friend grabbing her arm. Turning, she saw that Angie's face was twisted with anguish as she let out a strangled cry.

'Shush, shush,' soothed Molly, putting her arm round her and guiding her gently into the park, away from the curious looks of passers-by.

'The children . . .' Angie choked out. 'We'll be late. They'll be waiting for us.'

'We've got a little while yet,' Molly assured her, easing her down on to a bench and sitting beside her. 'You just let it all out.'

With Molly's arm firmly round her, Angie sobbed until she could cry no more. This would be the first of many tears she would shed for her father, Molly knew, but hoped they would come easier after this first outpouring.

When Angie was feeling calmer, they got up and made their way to the school. Molly was aware that – as so many times in the past – they had weathered an important moment together.

'I suppose there was a big turnout for George Beckett,' remarked Brian that evening when Molly went into the living room, having just put Rosa to bed and cleared up in the kitchen. He was in his usual position, prostrate on the sofa, smoking a cigarette and reading the paper. There was dance music on the wireless, turned down low.

'I'll say there was. Most of Hanwell seemed to be at the cemetery,' she told him.

'He was well known, that's why.' No mention of him being well liked too, Molly noticed.

'Well, I'm very glad it's over, and I bet the family are too. Awful things, funerals.'

'Not necessarily,' he disagreed mildly. 'They're all right once the burial is over. People soon relax when they've had a few drinks. They turned my gran's into a party.' He put the paper down and sat up. 'And talking of drinks reminds me that it's time I wasn't here. There's a darts match on down the pub.'

Molly went over to the door and closed it quietly to make sure they couldn't be heard by Rosa. She took a deep breath and said, 'Before you go, I need to talk to you.'

His eyes narrowed suspiciously. 'What about?'

Another calming breath. 'Money,' she told him shakily.

24

'Oh, no! Not again,' Brian objected. 'You're always on my back for money.'

'Only because you don't give me enough in the first place,' she informed him, anger making her bold.

'Rubbish!'

'Every single thing we need to live has to come out of what you give me, and I've barely enough for food and rent, let alone anything else,' she informed him. 'Rosa needs clothes for school. The weather's getting chilly now and she's got nothing warm to fit her. She's grown out of all her winter things from last year.'

'You should save a bit every week out of the housekeeping money,' he suggested.

'How can I save anything when I don't have enough for basics?' she wanted to know.

'Can't you get a Provident cheque?'

'No. I have enough of a struggle keeping up with the payments on the one we already owe money on,' she told him. 'I daren't add to it.'

He tutted. 'It isn't good enough, Molly,' he complained. 'You should manage the money better. It's your job.'

She knew that he was getting a perverse feeling of pleasure from this. He was her only means of income and he loved it. 'I do my best,' she defended. 'But I can't work miracles and I need clothes for Rosa.'

'Drain me dry, why don't you?'

'Come off it,' she retorted. 'You don't go short of anything.'

'Oh, so you begrudge me a few beers and some ciggies, do you?'

'You know me better than that,' Molly replied, determined to stand her ground. 'But I'm not going to let my daughter go around in rags and catch cold because she doesn't have a warm coat to wear.' She gave him a steely look. 'And before you remind me, yes I do know what you've done for us and I am *very, very* grateful. But you wanted to take us on. You knew what you were letting yourself in for.'

'But you always want more . . . on and on and on.'

'And I've just told you the reason why,' came her spirited response. 'Clothes don't come cheap. Nor does food or anything else that I have to buy. God knows how much a week you spend on beer and fags.'

'Bloody hell, can't a man even go down the pub without feeling guilty?'

Would anything stir his conscience, she wondered, but said, 'If you were to put in more hours it would help. You've only worked a few days this week.'

'There hasn't been the work about.'

He was either lying or the site manager had finally decided he was too unreliable and found another labourer. She knew for a fact that there was plenty of work in the building trade. But to say so would serve no useful purpose. So she came up with another suggestion. 'OK, if you can't earn more and you don't want to cut down on your own spending money, why not let me get a job? That would solve the problem.'

'No.'

'But it just doesn't make sense, Brian.' She drew in an exasperated breath. 'You say you can't give me the money I need to make ends meet, so for me to get a job is the simple solution.'

'I'm not having it, Molly.'

She gave him a hard look. 'And neither will I allow this awful situation to continue,' she said firmly. 'Either you give me the money I need to clothe my daughter and run this home properly or I'll go out and earn it.'

His beady eyes met hers in a challenge. There was a silence. Then he stood up and dug his hand into his trouser pocket, sighing irritably. 'Here, have this,' he said grudgingly, handing her three pound notes.

'Thanks very much.'

'You're not going out to work, Molly – *not ever.*' His tone was threatening.

'I shall have to ask you for more money again then, won't I?' she told him. 'Because this won't last for ever.'

'Oh, I've had enough of this. I'm off to the pub to get some peace,' he snapped, and marched from the room.

Molly took her purse from the sideboard drawer and put the notes inside. Despite her brave stand her hands were shaking and she felt sick. The constant rows about money had her nerves in tatters; made her feel at fault and belittled, as though she was failing in the running of the home, and not pulling her weight in their partnership. The guilt of burdening Brian with the financial responsibility of another man's child never really left her. He made sure of that. It was an ongoing problem too, because the money he'd given her wouldn't go far for Rosa's clothes so was merely a temporary reprieve. In a matter of weeks they'd be at hammer and tongs again over the same issue.

Molly and Angie were shopping in Hanwell Broadway one morning a few days later, having just taken the children to school. There was a smoky mist in the air, the sky a hazy grey dome, but a hint of warmth in the air suggested sunshine later.

'Those apples look lovely,' Angie remarked as they waited in the queue at the greengrocer's, which was bright and colourful with autumn vegetables, oranges and pears, the sweet tang of fresh apples in the air. 'You can't beat a nice Cox's Orange Pippin, can you?'

'They do look nice,' agreed Molly.

The shop was crowded and the queue slow to move on. 'Oh, by the way, I ran into Betty Miller in the Broadway yesterday,' mentioned Angie to pass the time, referring to one of the other mothers from the school. 'She was saying that she's got herself a little job.'

'Good for her,' said Molly. 'Doing what?'

'Office work.'

'Nice. Does it fit in with her family commitments?'

'Perfectly. It's only a few hours a day.'

'She was lucky to get that.'

'That's what she said. She's thrilled to bits.'

'What firm is it?'

'It's at the school, that's why it's so ideal. School hours only.'

'Oh, she got that job, did she?' burst out Molly, her own disappointment stirred. 'I was going to apply for that myself, actually.'

'Really?' Angie was surprised she hadn't heard about it. 'You didn't mention it.'

'I would have done if I'd gone ahead and applied, but Brian was so dead set against it I gave up the idea,' she explained. 'Didn't think to mention it after that.'

'Why was he against it?'

'Male pride, I suppose,' replied Molly. 'You know what some men are like about their wives going out to work.'

'Some men don't like it, I know, but it's often a case of when the devil drives,' her friend opined. 'I must say it's never been an issue between Dan and me. The subject has never even come up.'

'It wouldn't, would it? I mean, you don't need to work, with Dan having a partnership in the pottery. But we need the money.' Molly didn't usually confide her marital problems, and wasn't going to give much away now. Ever loyal to her spouse, she was only prepared to go so far with the truth, even to her best friend. 'Building work is so irregular, and what with the winter coming and the bad weather, which means periods when Brian can't work, it'll be even worse.'

'All the more reason for you to get a job then, surely,' Angie said logically, 'especially like the one at the school, which would have fitted in so well with Rosa.'

'Exactly. But he was adamant about it so there's nothing I can do.'

'Pride's all very well,' Angie blurted out impatiently, 'but it doesn't pay the bills.'

'I know, but he just won't have it,' Molly told her. 'So I'll have to abide by what he says. We'll manage, we always do.'

It was obvious from Molly's tone that she didn't want to pursue the matter so Angie dropped the subject. She wished she could help, but Molly was a proud woman so Angie was powerless. Neither of them was to know then that help was at hand from a most unexpected source . . .

'I just can't believe it,' gasped Molly, pale with shock. 'You must have got it wrong.'

'I haven't,' Angie assured her with confidence. 'You'll be hearing

27

from the solicitor officially but I just couldn't wait to tell you the good news as soon as I heard about it. I just had to come round here right away.'

It was a few days later and Angie had called at Molly's flat unexpectedly around midday. They were talking in the kitchen.

'But I don't understand,' Molly was bemused. 'Why would your father leave me anything in his will?'

'The solicitor will give you all the details, but apparently it's mainly in recognition of your kindness to me when I was ill.' Angie thought for a moment, remembering. 'There was something about your being such an asset to the firm when you worked for him too. Over and above the call of duty. But the solicitor will tell you everything when you see him. You would have been invited to the reading but the solicitor decided that only the family should be present as it was such an emotional occasion. I expect you'll hear from him in the next day or two. I was so excited I came tearing round here as soon as the reading was over.'

'A share in the pottery, though . . .'

'That's right.' Angie was still full of grief but her eyes were warm and moist with happy tears as she said, 'Good old Dad. He always did have a soft spot for you.'

'But I'm not family. I have no right—'

'Of course you've a right.' Angie was adamant about that. 'It's what Dad wanted. He's entitled to leave his share of the business to whoever he wants and he wanted you to have a small part of it. You deserve it too.'

'But the others . . .?'

'They're all thrilled for you. We've all been well looked after so nobody begrudges you a small share in the business. I think he said it was ten per cent. It's just what you need right now, Moll, it'll help with some of your problems, anyway. I don't know what sort of an income it'll give you. You'll find out more about that later.'

The emotion Molly felt at the generosity of the gesture was overwhelming, and had nothing to do with money. 'Oh, Angie,' she said thickly, her eyes shining with tears and excitement, 'what a wonderful thing for anyone to do for me. I never thought anything like that would ever happen to me, I'm so touched.'

'And I'm absolutely delighted for you,' confirmed her friend, hugging her. 'Now get that kettle on, kid, for goodness' sake. I'm gasping for a cup of coffee.'

'Coming up,' Molly smiled.

Brian was delighted with the news.

'A part owner in a business, eh?' he approved. 'That'll be worth a few quid.'

'I don't know anything about that side of it yet,' Molly told him. 'I'll have to wait until I see the solicitor. The money's a minor consideration, anyway. I'm just so very touched to have been remembered in this way.'

'There's nothing minor about the money as far as I'm concerned,' he declared.

'Obviously I'm pleased about that because we need it so much but the main thing for me is the fact that George thought well enough of me to do something like that,' she told him. 'I want to weep every time I think about it.'

'You wanna weep about a thing like that? You must be off your head,' Brian said, having no perception of the true value of the legacy to her. 'Cor, that's the way to do it, Moll. Copping an income without having to lift a finger. You'll get a share of the profits.'

'I don't know how it will work,' she told him again. 'But I suppose I'll get something at some point.'

'You've played a blinder this time, love,' he praised, as though she had orchestrated the inheritance in some way. 'All we have to do is sit back and wait for the dough to roll in.'

As it happened, it wasn't as simple as that.

'You're telling me that you've got to work at Becketts to get any benefit from the share in the business you've inherited?' blasted Brian one evening a few days later.

'It isn't as cold-blooded as you're making it sound,' Molly corrected, having been to see the solicitor who had written to her asking her to call into his office. 'A condition of the inheritance is that I take an active part in the office at the pottery, for which I'll be paid a salary plus a share in the profits.'

'They can't do that,' he roared, his eyes hot with rage. 'You've been left something fair and square. You're entitled to have it.'

'Apparently not, if I don't meet the terms of the will,' she explained.

'That can't be legal.'

'It is. The solicitor was quite definite,' she confirmed. 'Let's face it, Brian, until now this sort of thing was completely outside of our experience so we don't know the ins and outs. But I've read about people inheriting on certain conditions.'

'It's all wrong.'

'But it'll be even better than just getting a share of the profits because we'll have a regular income coming in – my salary.'

'But you'll be going out to work.' He looked pained. 'It'll be the same as if you'd got a job.'

'Of course it won't. I'll own part of the firm. I'll be management,' she reminded him. 'I'll be able to do the hours to suit myself. It'll make life better for all of us and I won't have to keep coming to you for extra money.'

'You know how I feel about your going out to work,' he scowled.

'But it wouldn't be going out to work as such, would it?' Molly pointed out. 'I mean, it would be no reflection on your ability to support your family because I'd be a part owner of the business. It's a different thing altogether.'

'Tell them you can't do it.'

'But, Brian—'

'You're not doing it.'

'Then we'll get nothing,' she burst out. 'George made it a condition that I take part in the running of the firm because he liked what I did when I worked there. He probably did it also because he thought that it would help us and knew I would enjoy doing it too, which I would.'

'Just tell the solicitor that you can't do it,' he commanded. 'You'll still be entitled to what's yours.'

She shook her head. 'No, I can't,' she tried to make him understand. 'If I don't meet the conditions the legacy will be null and void.'

'You must have got it wrong,' he insisted. 'People can't do that.'

'Of course they can.'

'In that case we'll have to do without the money because I'm not having you working there.'

'You're being ridiculous.'

'You can say what you like but I'm not letting you do it,' he stated uncompromisingly.

'But I can't let a chance like this pass us by, Brian.' Molly was equally firm. 'It wouldn't be fair to any of us because the extra cash would benefit us as a family. Everything I earn would be for us rather than me personally so you'd be better off.'

Brian gave the matter thought. Some extra dough would be handy. He could do with more spending money, and he could certainly do without having Molly on his back for more money every few weeks. If it were to come without the ruddy conditions, he'd welcome it with open arms. Who wouldn't fancy a spot of easy money? As it was, there were too many disadvantages. She'd get above herself if she was swanning about on the management at Becketts, and soon want to spread her wings. She'd have the means to do so too. More worrying still, she'd be working with Billy Beckett. How long would it be before something developed between the two of them? She'd always been friendly with him, ever since they were kids. He probably fancied her rotten and what was to stop him instigating an affair? He was a free agent. No, it simply wasn't worth the risk. He'd sooner put up with her coming after him for money. At least that way he was in control.

'No, Molly, I absolutely forbid it,' he declared.

'I can't believe you would be that stupid . . .'

'You'd better start believing it because it's the way it's going to be.'

'But you can't—'

'I bloody well can, and I'm going to,' he pronounced. 'I wear the trousers in this house and there is nothing more to be said on the subject.'

With that, he did what he always did after a row: went to the pub, leaving Molly angry and upset.

'It really isn't on,' was Angie's reaction the next morning when the two of them went to her house for coffee, after taking the girls to school, and Molly told her what had happened. 'You'll have to take a firm stand on this one, kid. I've never heard of anything so ridiculous. You can't let him get away with it.'

'He's my husband,' Molly reminded her, sipping her coffee at the red Formica table that matched the Formica-topped units in her friend's modernised kitchen. It was all done in contemporary style with cream-painted cupboard doors and red and cream floor tiles. 'I'll have to abide by what he says.'

'But this legacy is such a wonderful opportunity for you all,' Angie went on. 'It doesn't make sense to throw it away just because he can't bear for you to do anything outside of the home.'

'I know all that but what can I do if he's dead set against it?'

'Stand up to him.'

'He'll make my life hell.'

'Reason with him, then.'

'I've tried but he won't listen. His mind is made up.' Molly thought she probably shouldn't be discussing this with Angie, but her disappointment was so great she just had to tell someone. The Becketts would know that she couldn't join the firm soon enough anyway.

'But his objection doesn't make sense,' persisted Angie, her voice rising angrily. 'Apart from anything else, he's got no right to stop you doing something you'd enjoy and that would benefit you all. You'll be depriving your daughter of a better life, apart from anything else. It isn't as though you wouldn't be able to fit your hours around your household, and I'd help out with Rosa if on the odd occasion you were ever stuck.'

'Everything you say is true but when it comes down to it, Brian is my husband – and he has been good to me,' Molly said.

'And you've been good to him,' Angie pointed out forcefully. 'How much longer are you going to go on being beholden to him for saving you from disgrace?'

'I do have good cause . . .'

'Originally, yes. But you've been a fantastic wife to him,' Angie was quick to remind her. 'You've paid him back a million times over for what he did for you, and you're still doing it every single day of your life.'

'Maybe.'

'Maybe nothing.' Angie was adamant. 'It's a fact. Anyway, he wanted to marry you. He knew the score. You talk about your duty to him, what about his to you? As his wife you're entitled to some consideration.'

'I just don't feel that I can go against him,' confessed Molly. 'Rightly or wrongly I feel in his debt.'

'Well, it isn't my place to interfere in someone else's marital affairs but I don't think you should let a chance like this pass you by,' stated Angie. 'I think you should go for it anyway, whatever he says.'

'Not so easy . . .'

More's the pity, thought Angie, but knew she mustn't interfere further. It was a private matter between husband and wife. She could have wept with disappointment on Molly's behalf, though. 'Oh, well, Moll, it isn't for me to say what you should do,' she said in a softer tone. 'It just seems such a waste to let a chance like this pass you by.'

'I'll just have to live with it,' was Molly's last word on the subject.

A week later, however, when Brian cut her housekeeping money dramatically because he'd had a short week, she was forced to reconsider the matter. Having done so, she told him she was going to accept the inheritance after all.

'You're not,' was his angry response.

'I am, you know. I have to,' she insisted, forcing herself to stay strong. 'You've left me no choice.'

'Don't you dare—'

'I'm going to see the solicitor tomorrow,' she cut in bravely. 'I shall start work at the pottery as soon as possible.'

'No, Molly—'

'Yes, Brian.' She tried to reason with him. 'Look, the last thing I want to do is upset you, but someone has to keep hearth and home together for us and I can't do that on what you've given me this week.'

'You'll have to rob Peter to pay Paul and I'll get some extra hours next week,' he told her.

'I'll have to do that this week anyway but that's all about to come to an end, thank goodness,' she informed him. 'There'll be no need in the future, thanks to George Beckett.'

They were in the kitchen and she was waiting for the kettle to boil for tea. He'd just got in from work and, as Rosa was at Angie's playing with Patsy, Molly had seized the opportunity to tell him while they were on their own.

'You wouldn't defy me.'

'Not normally I wouldn't, no,' she confirmed. 'But I will do over this because I know it's the right thing and your objection just isn't valid.'

Finally realising that she wasn't going to change her mind, he proceeded to make his position clear. 'Well, don't expect me to co-operate in any way whatever,' he announced nastily.

'I'm not that much of a fool . . .'

'There'll be hell to pay if my life is affected to the smallest degree by your going out to work,' he growled.

'I'm prepared for that.'

'Don't expect me to help in the house because you're not here to do what you should be doing.'

'The household will be affected but only for the better.' Molly looked into his hard, craggy face, his small eyes burning with resentment. 'I would have liked your blessing and co-operation, Brian,' she said, 'but as you're not prepared to give it, I'll do it without any help from you.'

He shrugged, looking at her coldly.

'One thing I will say, though,' she added determinedly. 'I'm going to do everything I can to make a success of the job, no matter how many obstacles you put in my way.'

'Really?'

'That's right.' She poured boiling water on to the tea in the teapot, slipped the tea cosy over it and moved towards the door. 'Give the tea a minute or two to brew before you pour it. The milk and sugar are in the cup. I'm going out.'

He looked at her with a mixture of astonishment and fury. 'Where are you going?' he demanded.

'To collect Rosa from Angie's. I won't be very long.'

Leaving him gaping speechlessly after her, she left the flat and walked down the street, her eyes swimming with tears. She'd managed to stand up to him but she'd hated doing it and it had left her emotionally drained. The sad thing was, they should be celebrating this unexpected good fortune together, not arguing about it. Why did Brian have to spoil things, for himself as well as for her? There was a self-destructive side to his personality that would destroy her too, she knew, if she wasn't very careful.

Chapter Three

The Beckett coal-fired bottle kiln was built of sand-coloured bricks and stood a short distance from the pottery workshops towards the side of the back garden of The Hawthorns. The house had been barely habitable when George Beckett had bought it for a song some thirty years previously, but its refurbishment had had to take second place to the building of the pottery as that was to be his means of earning a living. Even when money had begun to trickle in from the sale of his hand-made earthenware, improvements to the house had had to be done very gradually because at that time George had yet to establish himself as a commercially viable potter.

The breakthrough he'd needed for the success of his business had come about because of a new but lasting friendship with a man called Joe Gunter, an enthusiastic patron of the arts and keen admirer of George Beckett's unique pieces, each one meticulously crafted and hand-painted. Joe Gunter owned a shop in the Portobello Road area of London, which he offered to rent to George at a peppercorn rent on a friendly basis because of his passion for Beckettware pottery. Situated in a busy cosmopolitan area – much visited by collectors, and adjacent to a leathergoods shop – the place was the perfect retail outlet for George's work, and the normal rent would have been well beyond his means.

The convenient location of the pottery on the edge of the Grand Union Canal at Hanwell meant that the finished work could be transported into Central London by barge. Although commercial traffic on the canal had been in steady decline for the past few years in favour of road transport, Beckettware was still carried in the old-fashioned way because George had been a traditionalist, nervous of change and impervious to the argument for modernisation.

Molly was to be in charge of the office, working closely with a young woman called Paula, who now had the job that had once been Molly's and which consisted of typing and general office duties. They were to work in adjoining offices separated only by a glass partition and a sliding door, which was left open permanently so that the two offices were virtually one. Molly's had previously been used by George, who'd spent more time supervising in the workshop than at his desk.

Excited by the challenge but deeply apprehensive too – since she'd not been out to work for several years, and her new status as a partner meant serious responsibilities – Molly approached her first day with more than a little trepidation. A baptism of fire, however, soon cured her of that. She'd barely had time to take her coat off when she was faced with a major crisis. It seemed that the business was under serious threat because they were about to lose the shop.

'We haven't said anything to Mum about this yet.' Looking grave, Billy had come into the office from the workshop and handed her a letter. He was followed by Dan. Both were wearing brown potter's aprons over their clothes and had their shirtsleeves rolled up. 'The poor dear has got more than enough to cope with at the moment, trying to come to terms with Dad's death. She'll have to be told eventually, of course, if we can't find a solution, but we want to spare her for as long as we can.'

'Angie doesn't know yet either,' added Dan. 'I don't want to worry her with business problems, not while her dad's death is still so new.'

'But now that you're on the team, Molly, you need to know right away,' Billy said.

'Of course.' Molly turned her attention to the letter that was causing such concern. It was from the son of Joe Gunter, who had inherited the shop after his father's death a few years before. He'd allowed the token rent to continue when his father passed on in respect of the friendship between the two men. Now that George had also died, he no longer felt obliged to honour the agreement. He wanted vacant possession of the shop to use for his own purposes. As it was just a friendly arrangement with no agreement in writing, he pointed out, there was nothing to stop him reclaiming his premises.

'I suppose we shouldn't have taken it for granted,' admitted Billy ruefully. 'But Dad always looked after all the administration so we never gave that side of things a thought.'

'The arrangement has been in existence since long before I came to work here,' Dan mentioned.

'Same here,' said Billy. 'We had no reason to believe it would come to an end.'

'Joe Gunter Junior knows he can make a fortune trading around there in ordinary retail, which will be much more profitable than a specialised craft like ours,' Dan pointed out. 'Then there's the thousands of punters who come from all over the world to the Portobello Market. The shops do a roaring trade as well as the stalls, especially now that the antique trade is beginning to arrive.'

'Losing that site is going to be a crippling blow to us,' Billy went on grimly. 'There's no way we can afford to pay the sort of rent other shop landlords around there are charging. It would be different if we were a factory, mass-producing the pottery. But with every single item being individually hand-made, we can only produce a certain amount in any given time. Joe Gunter understood that and kept the rent low so that we could continue to make unique things to a high standard and not have to sell them at prohibitive prices in order to live decently. His son is obviously more interested in business than the arts.'

'He's quite within his rights, though,' remarked Dan. 'We shouldn't really expect to pay a lower rent than other traders.'

'Of course not. But we're craftsmen; we don't buy and sell, and I don't see how we can stay in business without it,' was Billy's response. 'If we were to rent a shop out here in the suburbs it would be cheaper but there wouldn't be the volume of business we need to keep things ticking over. The only way we could afford a shop in Central London would be to double our prices, which would probably price us out of the market. Anyway, Dad would turn in his grave at the idea of Beckettware being expensive.'

Molly stayed silent, deep in thought.

The door opened and Josh breezed in. 'Right, I've seen the stuff on to the barge . . .' He paused, looking curiously from one to the other. 'Blimey. What's the matter with you lot? You've all got faces like wellington boots. Has Hitler come back from the dead or something?'

'We're just discussing the business and the possible loss of our livelihood,' Billy informed him.

'Oh, not that boring old stuff again,' dismissed Josh, who took no interest in the fortunes of the pottery whatsoever.

'Yes, that boring old stuff again,' confirmed Billy. 'Losing the shop could mean the end of our family business.'

'So what?'

'So, it'll mean your getting a job somewhere else,' Billy informed him. 'You'd have to work for your living then.'

'As if I don't do that already,' Josh objected sulkily. 'You lot see to that. Anyway, you'll have to sort it out. I'm only the boy around here and I'm going for a break.'

'You've only just had one.'

'That was ages ago so now I'm having another.'

'Not until later, you're not,' Billy said with authority. Josh was still learning the job so was expected to do the menial tasks such as sweeping up and making the tea, as well as small pottery jobs like making and sticking on handles. Both sons had gone to work with their father on leaving school. Billy was now a skilled potter, a brilliant designer and had been taken into the business as a partner when he'd proved himself worthy. Dan had received a partnership when he'd joined the family as Angie's husband, having worked there since he was a boy and made a huge contribution. He too was a talented potter and had an imaginative eye for colour. 'If you've nothing sensible to add to the discussion, you can go and get some clay from the store.'

Muttering a string of complaints, Josh slouched from the room.

Billy turned to Molly. 'Anyway, Moll, I know it isn't much of a welcome to the firm, getting news like this on your first day, but we couldn't leave it.'

She nodded in agreement. 'But while you've all been talking, I've been casting my mind back and I don't think Joe Gunter Junior can actually do this to us.'

Both men stared at her enquiringly.

'Oh? Why is that?' asked Billy.

'Because there *is* actually something in writing about the arrangement,' she informed them. 'I remember seeing it when I worked here. I'm pretty certain too that the low rent is to pass on to George's descendants for as long as Beckettware pottery is being marketed through the shop. Only handcrafted Beckettware, nothing else.'

The men were astounded. 'It would be brilliant if there is something on paper,' said Billy. 'It's the sort of thing Joe Gunter would have done.'

'Are you sure, Molly?' Dan sounded wary.

'Positive.' She looked into space, pondering. 'It used to be in one of the filing cabinets. Although it was just a friendly arrangement, there was an actual agreement signed by Joe Gunter to make sure that Beckettware continued to be made and marketed. I'm sure it would stand up in court.'

'Molly, you're a little belter,' said Billy, hugging her.

'I'll second that,' added Dan, beaming.

'Hey, hang on, boys. Don't get too excited,' she warned, exercising a little caution. 'It's a few years since I worked here, remember. I've no idea where the agreement is now.'

'We'll find it,' said Billy. 'We'll turn the place upside down until we do.'

It didn't prove easy. A thorough search of the office turned out to be fruitless. The missing document – handwritten on ordinary notepaper – was finally located in the most obvious place of all: the family solicitor's office. As it had just been a casual arrangement, no one had thought of that. Joe Gunter Junior had written to the pottery direct so the solicitor knew nothing about the problem until, as a last resort, Molly had finally suggested that they ask if he knew anything about it. The written agreement had been given to him for safekeeping at some point after Molly had left the firm, apparently. Anyway, it was legal and there was nothing Joe Gunter could do about it.

After that first dramatic day, Molly settled into the job at a more ordinary level. There was far too much for her to do, though, especially as she couldn't work full time. But with a willing heart and plenty of application, she managed.

'So, how do you like being a working woman?' enquired Billy lightly, one morning when she was passing through the workshop on her way out. She was going to the London shop to collect some paperwork and take the assistant's wages. Billy was working at his wheel, moulding the clay and keeping his fingers moist by dipping them in the bowl of thrower's water placed beside the wheel. He was making jugs and there were rows of them with handles lined up on the shelves that flanked the workshop walls; the handles would be attached with liquid clay known as slip when the jugs were leather hard. Molly enjoyed watching the potters at work and admired their deftness. She liked the smell and the feel of the place; the earthy scent of clay and a faint acid tang of chemicals.

'I'll have you know that I was a working woman before I came back here,' she replied with spirit. 'Housewives don't just sit about all day doing nothing.'

'Yeah, yeah, I know. I've heard all about it from Mum,' he said jokingly.

'But – seriously – I do like being back here,' she added. 'Very much.'

'I bet Angie misses you now that you don't have so much time to spare,' chipped in Dan, with a twinkle in his eye. He was wedging some clay with his fingers to remove the air bubbles. 'All those hours you used to spend drinking tea and nattering together. Don't think we don't know what you women get up to while we're out at work.'

'Cor, that's rich coming from you.' She raised her eyes in mock disapproval. 'You men take some beating in the nattering department. You two never stop. Every time I come in here you're at it. And you could win prizes for tea drinking.'

'Ah, but we can talk and drink tea while we work,' defended Dan, kneading the clay. 'Well, we can talk anyway.'

'You're a couple of old gossips,' she teased.

'Billy's the one with plenty to say. He keeps me well entertained.' Dan and Billy had been pals for many years and were always ribbing each other. 'His love life produces such colourful stories, I can't help but listen.'

Molly looked at Billy. 'So who's the current flavour of the month then?'

'A little blonde from Ealing,' he told her, cocking his head and making a double clicking sound with his tongue. 'A real cracker. Met her at the Hammersmith Palais the other evening. I'm taking her to the pictures tonight.'

'It's time you settled down, mate,' advised Dan. 'You can't beat married life.'

'Don't encourage him to do that.' This was Paula, who'd come to join in the light-hearted discussion. She was a plump, brown-eyed brunette in her early twenties, who'd recently got married. 'What would we do for entertainment if Billy went out of circulation? We rely on his hectic social life to keep us amused.'

He grinned at her. 'Don't worry, I've no intention of settling down for a long time yet. I'll still have a tale to tell for many a long year.' He gave her a saucy look; he was a terrible flirt. 'I'd show you a good time if it wasn't for your old man.'

She fluttered her lashes at him, enjoying the attention but knowing him too well to take him seriously. Billy was an appealing man. Molly was very fond of him herself, as a friend. They'd always got on well, ever since they were children. She enjoyed the working atmosphere at the pottery in general; there was no shortage of camaraderie.

'Anyway, it's time I wasn't here,' she said, looking at her watch.

'Off you go then.' Billy looked around, tutting. 'Where's that boy of ours got to?'

No one seemed to know where Josh was.

'He's never here when you need him,' Billy complained. 'I've never known anyone as cute at disappearing as Josh is. I need him to start putting the handles on. Some of the jugs should be ready. Don't say he's bunked off again. We're firing tomorrow so there's plenty for him to do.'

'He'll turn up,' said Molly, turning to leave. 'I'm off. See you all later.'

Josh was ambling towards the pottery from the house when Molly made her way along the path that led to the street across the garden and alongside the house. He'd obviously been home for a break and didn't seem in any hurry to get back to work.

'Oh, there you are,' she greeted casually.

He scowled at her. A most unprepossessing youth, he had sharp features, a spotty complexion and long greasy sideburns. 'What's it got to do with you?' he asked nastily.

'Nothing at all. You're wanted inside, that's all,' she said in a pleasant manner since it wasn't her job to discipline him.

'I'm not taking orders from you,' he made clear.

'I wasn't thinking of giving you any.'

'You'd better not try it either,' he growled. 'What I do is none of your business. Don't think you're above me just because the old man went funny in the head and left you a bit of the firm.'

'It would never occur to me to think that.'

'You're nothing,' he said through gritted teeth, becoming angrier with every word. 'You're not family.'

'Have I ever behaved as though I am?'

'No. But I wanna make sure you don't start getting any ideas,' he told her. 'So you can take this as a warning.'

Suddenly the reason for his hostility became clear. Josh didn't actually get to own any part of the firm until he was twenty-one, when a share would be allotted to him if he'd proved himself to be sufficiently

40

committed to the business; the same rules had applied to his brother before him. 'I don't need warning, Josh,' Molly said in an even tone. 'I would never try and pull rank over you. You may not believe this but I'd like to be your friend.'

'Well, I don't wanna be yours,' he sneered. 'It ain't right that you've been taken into the firm and I haven't.'

'I can understand how it might rankle,' she said, remaining reasonable, 'but your turn will come. Until then we may as well try and get along.'

'Get stuffed,' he told her, and stomped off towards the workshops.

There goes one very angry and troubled young man, thought Molly. He was difficult to get on with and a disruptive influence at the pottery, but for some reason she felt sorry for him.

Hattie took some small currant cakes out of the oven and put them on a wire tray to cool, with the intention of taking them across to the workers for their teabreak; if she could pluck up the courage. Going to and fro to the pottery with her home cooking and for a chat had been a part of her life, a small everyday pleasure; now that George wasn't there she couldn't bear the place. He'd built it with loving care; it had been his pride and joy. Now his absence filled every corner. She seemed to feel his loss even more intensely there.

The effort of trying to appear brave in adversity was exhausting, but it felt vital that she didn't show how enfeebled she was by George's passing, dreading each day and dragging herself through it. The ageing process seemed to have accelerated out of all proportion too. She was only in her fifties but she felt old, frail and frightened. Having always been so robust, it was a new and bewildering experience. Was it normal to feel so weakened after a bereavement, she wondered.

Sitting down at the kitchen table, she reflected on the family discussions they'd had gathered around this long carved piece of solid wood; the laughter, the rows, the chitchat. The kitchen had always been the nucleus of the house. More time was spent here than in any other room. It was a large area with quarry-tiled floor, a walk-in pantry and big sash windows overlooking the back garden, the pottery and kiln visible to the side.

She got up and wandered into the wood-panelled sitting room, then the dining room with French doors opening on to the garden, and the room leading off the hall known as 'George's den', to which he'd retreated at times when the noisy exuberance of a growing family had got too much for him. The house wasn't furnished in grand or fashionable style but it was homely. Most of the furniture they'd had for years, but it was comfortable. Hattie thought back to the ruin the place had been when she and George had moved in. Every improvement had been made with loving care and hard work. They'd planned it together and done most of the work themselves to save money. She couldn't yet look back on that time without pain. His death was still too new.

Of course, she wasn't the only widow in the world, she realised that. And she was luckier than some in that she had her sons still at home and her daughter living just around the corner. She wasn't short of company. Josh often popped over during the day. He would forage in the larder and put his feet up and have a cigarette. She was always warning him of the trouble he'd be in over at the pottery but he never took any notice. Josh was the most difficult of her brood. He was sulky, cheeky, awkward, bad-tempered, an ugly duckling compared to his good-looking siblings, and always out of things with them somehow.

Maybe that was why she tended to take his side – because he was a loner within the family. He'd never got on with his father, who wouldn't take any nonsense from him. The others accused her of spoiling him and she supposed she did sometimes. She didn't do it intentionally. It was just that he had a knack of getting his own way with her. He'd been a sickly child, plagued by bronchitis, so had needed more attention from an early age.

She reminded herself that she mustn't become too reliant on her children now that she was on her own. It would be the easiest thing in the world while she was in this vulnerable state. Going back to the kitchen, she set the cakes out on a plate, put a cloth over them and headed to the door. Outside, she took a few steps, hesitated for a moment, then came back inside and put the cakes in a tin. The boys could have them when they got home. She just couldn't face that damned pottery today.

Molly got off the train at Notting Hill Gate station and walked briskly along Portobello Road towards Westbourne Grove, where the shop was situated. It was a weekday so the Saturday market crowds weren't around but there were plenty of people on the streets just the same.

She was struck by the vigour of the area and the diversity of the people, the downtrodden and dowdy alongside the sharp dressers in tight skirts and mountainous heels. Beatniks with pale faces and back-combed hair wandered by, and student types in duffel coats. The Caribbean community was a strong presence here now too.

'Hello, Peter,' she said, going into the shop. 'How are things with you?'

'Mustn't grumble, love,' he replied. 'How's yourself?'

'Fine. Any problems?'

'No, just a few queries.'

Peter was a dapper man of about fifty, with small dark eyes, greying hair and a neatly trimmed moustache. He'd been running the shop for the Becketts for many years and kept it looking a picture. It was such a treat to see colourful designs after the drab plain earthenware pottery that had been produced during the years of lingering wartime restrictions, thought

Molly: spots, stripes and squiggles, sleek contemporary shapes as well as the more traditional floral lines.

All the current Beckett ranges were on display: Autumn Blaze – a pattern of autumnal colours; Spring Lights – all fresh pastel shades; Aquamarine, which was myriad shades of blues and green with fish superimposed on to the pattern. Then there were the oriental designs. One of each item from every range – decorative plates of several sizes, mugs, jugs and goblets, lamps, vases, pots of various shapes – all were arranged to make a stunning display.

Someone from the pottery needed to visit the shop on a weekly basis to deliver Peter's wages and collect the sales slips and other paperwork. Sometimes they sent Josh or Paula; other times Molly did it, if she had the time. The potters never did; they were always too busy. Molly rather enjoyed the outing and valued this small connection to the retail side of the business. She liked the busy cosmopolitan atmosphere on the streets around here too.

Now she said, 'Let's go through to the office and sort out the queries then, shall we?'

Peter gave her a look. 'Before we get started on that could you do me a favour and hold the fort here while I pop down the road? I need to see a bloke about something.' Peter didn't have an assistant. If he needed to go out for a short time he simply closed the shop. 'It'll save me shutting the shop and I'll only be a few minutes.'

'Sure,' Molly agreed.

No sooner had he gone than she had a customer, who bought a large oriental-style urn.

'For the wife's birthday,' he explained. 'She loves Beckettware.'

'It's quality stuff,' she enthused.

'Beautiful.'

The man stayed chatting for a while. Molly enjoyed the conversation and was thrilled with the sale because it was one of the more expensive items. But she began to feel anxious when Peter didn't return because she needed to get back to Hanwell to collect Rosa from school. He eventually turned up, but by the time she'd given him the details of the sale, and gone through his queries, she was so late getting away she had to run all the way to the station.

When she'd finally decided to accept the inheritance and all that went with it, she'd promised herself that she would always be at the school gate to meet her daughter and she would *never ever* let the job interfere with that. This was the first time there had been a problem, and she felt terrible.

At the station there was a notice about a delay on the westbound line. Now she really was distraught. Sweating and breathless, she dashed into a call box and phoned Angie to ask her to pick Rosa up from school and take her home with her until Molly got back. Angie didn't mind at all.

Unlike Angie, Brian minded a great deal. By the time Molly and Rosa got home, he was already in and not at all pleased that Molly wasn't there to hand him a cup of tea the instant he walked through the door. He didn't need an excuse to complain about Molly's working, and her being late home meant he could have a field day. He exploited it to the full.

'About bloody time,' he rebuked as she rushed in, out of breath and full of apologies. 'Nice of you to turn up at all.'

'I'm really sorry, Brian.'

'Where have you been?'

'I got held up at the shop,' she explained, puffing and gasping from hurrying. 'Then there was a delay on the tube. I rang Angie and she collected Rosa and gave her her tea.'

'You should have been at the school to collect her yourself,' he objected, his voice rising to a shout.

'I know but—'

'But nothing, you should have been there . . .'

'Don't shout at Mummy,' came an unexpected intervention from Rosa, her face flushed and eyes hot with tears. 'I like it at Patsy's. I don't like it here when you shout. You're always cross, always shouting.'

'Oi, that's enough of that,' rebuked Brian with a fierce look.

'Daddy doesn't mean to shout,' said the ever-loyal Molly, putting a protective arm around her daughter. 'Why don't you go and get changed while Daddy and I have a chat?'

As soon as Rosa was out of earshot, he really went for Molly. 'I knew this sort of thing would happen,' he blasted. 'All that rubbish you fed me about the household not being affected by your going out to work. Phew, not much. Nothing's been the same around here since you started at that pottery. You ought to be ashamed of yourself, leaving someone else to collect your daughter from school and your husband to come home to an empty house.'

'Rosa was perfectly happy playing with Patsy—'

'That isn't the point,' Brian interrupted, his eyes dark with rage. 'You're the child's mother. It's your responsibility to look after her, not your mate's.'

'It isn't Rosa you're worried about, is it? It's yourself,' Molly suggested.

'So what if it is?' he returned. 'A man's entitled to expect his wife to be at home when he gets in after a hard day's work.'

'And I usually am.'

'You weren't today, were you?' he reminded her. 'It's the slippery slope.'

'No it isn't, I promise,' she told him. 'I'll try not to let it happen again.'

'I should think so too.' He picked up a packet of cigarettes from the

44

coffee table and took one out. 'Well, now that you are here you can get that kettle on sharpish. I've waited long enough for my cuppa tea.'

She threw him a look. 'Don't tell me you didn't even make yourself a cup of tea.'

'That's your job.'

'So you've sat here without something to drink rather than make one yourself.'

'That's right.'

'Honestly, Brian, you are the limit—'

'Don't try and put me in the wrong,' he cut in. 'You're the one at fault here.'

She decided it was time to remind him of a few things. 'I didn't hear you complaining when we had best steak for dinner last week, which we can only afford because I'm working,' she said. 'You didn't seem too upset about the cigarettes I bought for you either.'

'If it's there, I'll take it, the same as anyone would,' was his argument. 'If it isn't, I'll do without. Because I eat steak and smoke the fags you buy for me doesn't mean I agree with you going out to work.' A pause, then right out of the blue, he said, 'God knows what you get up to with that Billy Beckett.'

'What on earth has Billy Beckett got to do with anything?' Molly was astounded.

'You've always been a bit too pally with him for my liking.'

'He's my best friend's brother – of course I'm friendly with him,' she said. 'I've known him since I was five years old. Angie and I were always together. I spent a lot of time at their house.'

'Well, I don't like it, Molly. Any of it.'

She sighed. There was no point in trying to reason with him in this mood so she said rather wearily, 'I'll go and make some tea,' and left the room.

Not only did Brian make a point of not lifting a finger to help, he'd also put every obstacle he could find in her way since she'd been working, complaining about every little thing. He hit the roof if she had to catch up with the ironing at a weekend because she'd been too busy all week to finish it. There was also a terrible fuss if she so much as ran the duster over the place when he was in, saying it should have been done when he was out of the house and would have been if she'd been there to see to her duties like any decent wife.

But for all that he made her life hell – and she was also in a constant state of turmoil making sure that Rosa wasn't put out – she didn't regret accepting the inheritance. As well as the relief of being able to pay the bills and clothe her daughter, she actually enjoyed the job, even though Brian did his level best to make her feel that that was sinful in some way.

Smoke rose from the bottle-shaped chimney of the kiln then wisped and

45

scattered, curling down on the garden and the canal and the buildings in the surrounding streets.

'There she goes,' said Billy as the men watched the smoke rise some sixty feet up. 'The Becketts are firing so all's well with the world.'

'I'm not sure that everyone agrees with you about that,' said Dan with a wry grin. 'Judging by the amount of complaints we get from the neighbours about the smoke.'

'There is that,' admitted Billy.

'I really think we should get electric ovens,' Dan suggested, not for the first time. 'I heard that the Fulham pottery are having them put in soon.'

'It is the general trend among potters now,' agreed Billy. 'We've never done anything about it because Dad kept putting it off. He was very set in his ways, my dad.'

'I'll say he was,' reflected Dan. 'He always reckoned that a coal firing was the best method, even though it's energy inefficient, hard work and dirty.'

'That's a load of rubbish about it being the best method,' put in Josh, who was standing with the others, watching the smoke rise. 'We need to move with the times. Coal firing is well out of date. It's nothing short of misery, shovelling all that filthy coal. No one but a fool wants to spend time loading coal into a kiln and messing about with dampers to control the temperature when you can get the same effect with a flick of a switch.'

'You know what Dad was like about the old way of doing things. Anyway, he was sentimental about the kiln, having built it himself,' Billy reminded him. 'He built his reputation on coal-fired pottery. Naturally he would think it's best.'

'Dad isn't here, though, is he?' was Josh's harsh reminder. 'Everything has its time, and coal firing has had its day, everyone knows that. It was different when Dad built the kiln. There was no alternative then.'

'You're a heartless little bugger,' admonished Billy. 'Don't you have a soul?'

'I wouldn't know how to recognise it if I had. But I do recognise pain and I get aching shoulders from shovelling all that coal,' was Josh's answer to that.

'I agree with Josh on this one,' put in Dan. 'It's time we seriously looked into going electric. We'll have to do it eventually anyway. Now that the Clean Air Bill has come in for domestic fires, it's only a matter of time before smoke restrictions will apply to us. Electricity will be much more efficient, anyway.'

'Yeah, yeah, we'll have a chat about it sometime.' Whilst not as adamant as his father, Billy had been brought up with the old ways, and some of George's views had rubbed off on him.

Just then Molly came out of the workshop and walked over to them,

46

having finished work for the day. 'What do you think, Moll?' asked Dan. 'Is it time we seriously thought about having electric ovens installed instead of continuing to use this monster?'

She looked up at the kiln, considering the matter. 'The Beckett kiln is a tradition around here, a local landmark and part of the skyline. I can't imagine it not being there,' she said. 'But there's a lot to be said for electric ovens. I had someone on the phone just now claiming that the smoke is making her washing sooty.'

'People are far too fussy these days,' was Billy's opinion. 'This pottery's been here for thirty years; they ought to be used to the smoke by now.'

'They are, but it doesn't mean they have to like it,' Molly pointed out. 'Times have changed. When your dad built the kiln people didn't worry so much about smoke in a residential area. But since the Clean Air Bill, people are more aware of smoke pollution, especially now that electricity and gas are beginning to take over from coal generally.'

'She's got a point, Billy,' agreed Dan.

'But we're just a little pottery with one kiln,' Billy reminded them. 'It isn't as though we're a factory with several chimneys belching out great clouds of smoke every day of the week.'

'That's true,' said Molly. 'Anyway, I'm not really qualified to give an opinion on this one as I'm not a potter. You'll have to go into the pros and cons and make up your own minds. The first thing to do is get an idea of how much it'll cost.'

'A fortune, probably,' said Billy.

'Not necessarily,' Dan disagreed. 'Not for a small firm like ours. We wouldn't need many ovens. Firing will be much quicker and more energy efficient.'

'All right, all right, I know,' sighed Billy. 'But there's nothing urgent about it. We can carry on as we are for a little while longer.'

'I'll leave you to it then, boys.' Molly half turned to go, then remembered something. 'Oh, by the way, one of the teachers at the school waylaid me this morning and asked if she could bring a party of children along to watch the potters at work some time soon. Some sort of a craft project they're doing, apparently. I said I'd let her know when I'd spoken to you about it.'

'It's fine with me,' said the amiable Billy.

'Me too,' added Dan.

'We'll be like blooming monkeys in the zoo,' came Josh's predictable objection.

'No change there then, in your case,' teased Billy.

The youth scowled. He'd never been able to take a joke.

'I'll take that as a yes then,' said Molly lightly. 'See you tomorrow, boys.'

'See you, Moll,' they chorused.

She hurried along the path towards the road, smiling in anticipation of collecting her daughter from school.

'That was smashing, Mum, thanks,' said Billy, finishing a large portion of syrup pudding and custard. 'Do you mind if I rush off? I've got a date with an angel.'

'You and your women,' she tutted good-humouredly. 'You're always in a hurry.'

He grinned. 'I'm young. I've got to make the most of it while I can.' He looked at his brother. 'You going out?'

Josh nodded.

Billy frowned, looking at his mother in concern. 'Will you be all right on your own, Mum?'

'Course I will,' she replied. 'Angie will probably pop round later on for a chat.'

'As long as you're sure you won't be lonely.' Billy liked a good time but he loved his mum and was always very considerate towards her.

'I'm positive,' she assured him, ever careful not to become too clingy. He still looked uncertain.

'Go on, Billy,' she urged him. 'You get off and meet your lady friend.'

'If you're sure, I'll go and get ready then.' He left the table and went upstairs whistling.

Josh departed soon after and Hattie washed the dishes, then went into the living room to watch *The Billy Cotton Band Show* on television. Billy left for his date. Josh went out to meet his mates a few minutes later but not before removing some money from his mother's purse, which was in her handbag on the kitchen dresser. It was handy her leaving it there and providing him with a regular boost to his spending money. It wasn't as though she missed it. He wouldn't take it if she didn't have plenty of dosh, and he didn't get too greedy in case she started to notice. Anyway, he didn't get paid a fraction of what he was worth at the pottery. So why shouldn't he help himself now and again?

'So, shall we settle on that pair, then, Rosa?' asked Molly, as her daughter paraded up and down the shoe shop in a pair of black patent shoes with a strap and silver buckle. 'Are those the ones you want?'

'Cor, yes, please, Mum.' She was gazing with admiration at her feet.

'Take them off then, love, and the assistant will put them in a box for us.'

'Can I wear them home?' she asked predictably.

'All right then.'

'Can I have a pair like that, Mum?' Patsy asked her mother.

'No.'

'Why not?' she pouted.

'Because you don't need new shoes.'

'Oh,' she whined. 'Please . . .'

'Absolutely not.'

'It isn't fair.'

'Oh, you poor hard-done-by little thing,' said her mother with good-humoured irony. 'You're not having new shoes today and let's not have a drama about it, please.'

It was a Saturday afternoon in October, and Molly and Angie and their offspring were in Ealing Broadway, shopping for clothes for Rosa, a real treat for both mother and daughter. The footwear purchase complete, they headed for Bentalls where Molly bought Rosa a jumper. They had a leisurely browse around the store in general, then went into the cafeteria and ordered tea and toasted teacakes.

'I'm really enjoying myself,' enthused Molly, relishing her snack. 'It's such a joy to be able to get things for Rosa.'

'I can imagine.'

'Shopping's better than playing when you get something nice,' put in Rosa, who was wearing a red winter coat Molly had bought for her recently.

'I've got lots of new things,' boasted Patsy.

'So have I,' retaliated Rosa.

'All right, you two,' admonished Angie. 'No need to make a competition of it.'

'Competition is as natural as breathing to kids,' smiled Molly. 'I expect we were just the same.'

The girls lapsed into a dialogue of their own and Angie switched to another subject. 'I wish I could persuade Mum to come out on a Saturday afternoon,' she said.

'Doesn't she feel like it?'

'No, not now. She used to enjoy a wander around the shops with me but she doesn't seem to go out anywhere since Dad died, except to do the household shopping,' explained Angie. 'She just stays at home running about after those brothers of mine. She spoils them rotten.'

'It's probably a comfort for her, having them to look after,' suggested Molly.

'I expect it is but I don't like to see her turning into a skivvy for them.' She looked worried. 'Billy's a dear and would never knowingly put on her but you know what Josh is like. He's always taken advantage of her good nature but he's even worse now that Dad's not around to put his foot down. Dad didn't stand any nonsense from him.'

Molly nodded in an understanding manner.

'I'm concerned about Mum in general, to tell you the truth,' her friend went on. 'She seems so sad and lost, even though she puts up a front so that we won't worry about her. It turns my heart over to see her like it.'

'She has to grieve,' Molly reminded her.

'I know. I just wish there was something I could do to help,' Angie

49

sighed. 'We're all grieving, of course, but obviously it's much worse for Mum. She's always been the domesticated type, which is probably where I get it from. But some sort of an outside interest would do her good now that Dad isn't around as the focus of her life.'

'She'll find something when she's ready, I expect,' said Molly reassuringly.

'I hope so.'

They talked some more on the subject, then Molly turned her mind to practical matters of her own. 'I think I'll get off the bus at West Ealing on the way home to get a sweater for Brian from Marks and Sparks,' she decided. 'He could do with a new one now that the weather's getting chilly.'

'I'll come with you,' said Angie. 'I'm bound to see something I fancy from there.'

Molly was reminded that spending money was no novelty to Angie, whereas frugality was a habit to Molly, having been hard up for so long. She really appreciated being able to get some of what her family needed, though, and looked forward to choosing a sweater for her husband. She wanted him, as well as Rosa, to enjoy the fruits of her labours.

It was Sunday afternoon. Rosa was playing outside in the street, Molly was ironing in the kitchen and Brian, wearing the new blue sweater Molly had bought for him yesterday, was asleep on the sofa after a session in the pub before lunch.

Molly was feeling tense; she was anxious to finish the chore before he stirred because he would fly into one of his rages at the sight of the ironing board. Her heart sunk when she heard him flush the toilet, indicating that he was up and about, and likely to come in here asking her to make tea.

'Oh no, not ironing again. How many more times must I tell you, Molly?' he complained, appearing as expected. 'I don't want to see sight of that bloody iron on a Sunday.'

'I got a bit behind with things . . .'

'You're always getting behind,' he admonished. 'If you can't manage your responsibilities, you should stop all this going out to work nonsense.'

'You'd soon notice the difference if I did,' she couldn't help pointing out.

'Too true I would,' he agreed, deliberately misunderstanding her. 'We might have some sort of normality about the place.'

'Our standard of living has shot up since I've been working.' It drove her mad: the negativity; the selfishness and refusal to see anyone else's point of view. He was wearing the expression she hated the most: one of cold arrogance, his eyes bright with defiance. Her patience was wearing thin. 'Anyway, I can't see how my ironing interferes with you in any way

50

at all. You'd have cause for complaint if I asked you to do the job for me. Most of the items I'm ironing are yours anyway.'

'It's your job to do them so don't start complaining.'

'You're the one doing that. Why get into such a state about when the ironing is done as long as your clothes are ready for you to wear when you need them?'

'Because Sunday is for relaxing, and I want to relax without tripping over an ironing board.'

'How can you trip over it if you're asleep in the living room and I'm ironing out here?'

'It's the principle of the thing. I don't like to see it going on,' he said moodily. 'Cooking, yeah. The rest should all be done during the week. Surely a man's entitled to have a say in what goes on in his own home.'

She noticed he didn't mention anything about being the sole breadwinner now. He'd have been skating on thin ice if he had, since every penny she earned went into the family budget, and he'd had another short week this week so even the rent had come out of her salary. 'But it isn't just your home, is it?' she reminded him. 'We both live here so I suppose that gives me certain rights.'

'Oh, here we go. I knew you'd start banging on about women's rights once you started going to work,' he said accusingly.

'I'm not banging on. I just think I'm entitled to a bit of consideration, that's all. If I want to do a bit of ironing on a Sunday afternoon, I should be allowed to without getting a load of aggravation from you.'

'And I should be allowed some consideration after all I've done for you, taking you on when no one else would.'

'And I've done nothing for you since then, I suppose,' she said with irony.

'I didn't say that.'

'Look, I want to do things for you and Rosa – for all of us,' she said, desperate for him to understand her motivation. 'I'm working so that we can have a better life.'

'You're working because you're a selfish cow who doesn't give a damn about her husband's views about anything.' White with temper, he pulled off the new sweater and threw it on the floor. 'I can do without your rotten presents and everything else you bring into the house to make sure I never forget that you earn money.' He gave her a hard stare. 'If I see that iron in use in this house on a Sunday again, I'll wrap it around your neck.'

And with that he stormed out of the room, leaving her inwardly trembling. He didn't mean his parting shot literally, of course – she knew that. For all his faults he wasn't a physically violent man. But this constant browbeating over her going out to work put a shocking strain on her. At times she felt ill with dread about what he would erupt about next. Not a day went by when he didn't cause an argument over some aspect of her job. Being a working mum was a difficult balancing act for any woman. With a husband like Brian, who spent his whole life trying to make it impossible for her, it was enough to drive her into resigning. But Molly was determined not to let him break her.

Sadly she picked the sweater up off and the floor and folded it, knowing he would wear it again when he was over his tantrum. She finished the last of the ironing, turned the iron off and put the clothes away.

She was thinking that they'd been blessed with the gift of a part share in the pottery, and Brian was doing his level best to wreck it for them all. The constant rows that wore Molly down couldn't be good for Rosa either. The marriage had never been a happy one but lately it was purgatory. There had been many times over the years when she had regretted marrying Brian, but never more so than now.

They were wrong for each other and he was as miserable with her as she was with him. But he would never let her go because what he felt for her was an obsession, not love. And that wasn't something to be shrugged off. Neither was the gratitude that kept her in his debt. She would continue to defy him about the job because she was certain it was the best thing for them all, but she wouldn't desert him.

Chapter Four

'So, how are you getting on over at the pottery, dear?' Molly had popped over to the house to visit Hattie during her break. 'Settled in to the job by now, I expect.'

Molly nodded. 'It didn't take long to get back into the swing,' she said. 'Having worked there before made a difference.'

'Are you managing to fit the job in with Rosa's school hours?' It was a friendly enquiry.

'Just about.' Molly gave a wry grin. 'It gets a big fraught at times, though, trying to get everything done in the office in the hours I'm able to put in. But I get by.'

Hattie looked thoughtful, as though remembering something. 'Angie was saying that the half-term holiday is coming up soon. So if you need anyone to look after Rosa then, I'll be happy to help out,' she offered.

Molly was enormously warmed by her generosity. 'It's very kind of you to offer, Mrs Beckett, but it's only a short break and I'm trying to organise things so that I won't have to go into work during that time. I'll get right up to date beforehand and the rest will have to wait until I get back.'

'Sounds as though you've got it all worked out,' Hattie remarked. 'It can't be easy, going out to work when you've a young child to care for.'

'It takes some organising,' Molly admitted. 'But when I took the job on I vowed not to work when Rosa was home from school unless it was absolutely unavoidable. I like to be with her, you see. Obviously the longer holidays will be more of a problem but I'll cross that bridge when I come to it.'

'Well . . . you know where I am if you need me.'

'Thanks ever so much. Angie offered to help out too. It's very good of you both.' They were sitting at the kitchen table drinking tea. Knowing how worried Angie was about her mother, Molly had made a point of visiting her. 'Anyway, I didn't come here to talk about me. I came to see how you're getting on.'

Hattie shrugged. 'Not too bad,' she said bravely. 'I'm taking it one day at a time. It's all I can do, really.'

Molly nodded sympathetically. 'We don't see anything of you over at the pottery now,' she mentioned. 'I remember when I worked there before, you often used to pop over for a chat and a cup of tea.'

The older woman made a face. 'I find it too upsetting now that George isn't there,' she found herself confiding. 'I know it's silly because I miss him just as much here in the house. But over there . . .' She paused, trying to find the words to express her feelings. 'It's hard to explain . . .' She gave it more thought. 'It seems so dreadfully odd with him not being about the place. He was such a strong presence there. He *was* the pottery, if you know what I mean.'

'I know exactly what you mean,' Molly told her. 'But we'd love to see something of you when you can face it. You might start to enjoy coming over again once you get used to it.'

'Yes, I really must start doing it again.' Hattie sighed. 'Sometime.'

Molly didn't pursue the subject but hoped Hattie would soon find the strength. It was just a small thing but it might help to ease her loneliness. Losing that sociable connection after so many years must make her husband's death seem like a double blow.

'Well, I'd better get back there, anyway,' said Molly, finishing her tea and rising. 'Or I'll be all behind.'

'Thanks for coming over, dear,' said Hattie.

'A pleasure,' was Molly's sincere response.

Joan Rawlings had been invited to her daughter Peggy's for the day on Sunday and was full of it.

'I'm dying to see their new furniture,' she enthused to Molly, who called to see her one evening, leaving Rosa at home with Brian. Molly was very aware of her filial duty; if she didn't get time to call on her mother during the day now that she was working, she made a point of doing so fairly often in the evening. 'They've got a new three-piece suite. Did I tell you?'

At least a dozen times, Molly thought, but just said, 'You did mention it.'

'Uncut moquette, apparently,' Joan continued, pouring water into the cups over bottled coffee. 'I bet it'll be really lovely. Peggy's got such good taste.'

Molly unwrapped the flowers she'd brought for her mother, who'd barely seemed to notice. 'Which vase would you like me to put these in?' she asked.

'The one on the sideboard'll do.' Joan might just as well have told her to put them in the dustbin. 'You're coming up in the world, aren't you? Being able to afford to buy your mother flowers. Chocolates last week, flowers today.'

'Things are easier now that I'm working.' Molly was defensive, having picked up on a critical note in her mother's tone. 'They looked so nice on the flower stall in the Broadway, I thought you might like them.'

'I do, of course,' she was quick to point out. 'But you shouldn't be wasteful with your money.'

It seemed an odd comment since she was so full of praise for Peggy's extravagance. 'I hardly think that treating my mum now and again makes me a spendthrift,' responded Molly, keeping her tone light.

'It isn't that I'm not pleased with them – I am, of course – but you don't want to get reckless just because you've a few extra quid coming in.'

Molly was cheered by this small sign of appreciation.

Then: 'It's different for Peggy. She can afford to be extravagant, with Reg having a well-established business.'

'I have a part in a well-established business,' Molly felt compelled to remind her. 'Not a big part but it does give me an income.'

'It's hardly the same sort of thing, though, is it?'

'I don't see why not.'

'It isn't solid,' Joan stated in a unequivocal manner. 'People must have meat but they can do without fancy pots.'

'The Beckett Pottery has been established for a long time, Mum. I think you can safely call it a stable business,' defended Molly.

'Mm, there is that, I suppose.' It was a half-hearted acknowledgement. 'But all I'm saying is, meat is an essential commodity. It's part of our staple diet. A priority. Whereas fancy goods like pottery are the last thing anyone would buy if they were a bit hard up.'

'That's like comparing jewellery with Brussels sprouts,' argued Molly. 'Obviously food is essential but that doesn't mean there isn't a thriving market for hand-made pottery. There will always be people who appreciate craft and are willing to spend money on fine things.'

'I know which trade I'd rather trust,' snorted Joan. 'The food on people's plates.'

At this point Molly decided to drop the subject and accept what she already knew; that her mother was, for some reason, incapable of offering encouragement to her younger daughter. She arranged the chrysanthemums in a vase and put them on the sideboard in the other room, then sat down at the kitchen table to drink her coffee.

'So you're getting on all right with the job then?' At least Joan had the decency to ask, but Molly suspected that it was just a token enquiry.

'Yeah, it's going really well.'

'Good.' A pause. 'I hope you're not expecting me to look after Rosa when she's off school for half-term.'

'Of course I'm not.'

'Good, because I'm working myself so I can't help out.'

Molly couldn't help comparing her mother's attitude with that of Hattie Beckett, who was so keen to help. Mum did have a job, it was true, but did she have to be so abrasive when pointing it out? Hattie's warmth made Molly feel liked and valued, a feeling her own mother had never evoked in her. What hurt even more was knowing that if Peggy were to ask Joan to look after her children, she would consider it a privilege.

'I've got that all organised.' She didn't go into detail because she doubted if her mother would be interested.

The weather was kind to them in the half-term holiday. Cold and misty early mornings gave way to hazy sunshine so Rosa was able to play out in the street while Molly whizzed through the household chores. In the afternoon, she and Angie took the girls to Churchfields, stopping for their daily bits of shopping in the Broadway en route. The girls also amused themselves collecting firewood for the bonfire Dan was planning to build in the Platers' back garden for Guy Fawkes night.

One night during the half-term holiday, Brian came home from the pub with some interesting news.

'I've got the chance to earn some decent money,' he informed Molly.

'Ooh, that sounds promising.'

'There's a snag, though.'

'There usually is,' said Molly. 'Is it a big one?'

'Big enough,' he replied. 'I'd be working away from home.'

'Oh? Where?'

'Norfolk.'

'That's a long way off,' she remarked. 'What is it? A housing estate?'

'It's more than just that,' he told her. 'It's one of these new towns they're putting up in the sticks to ease the housing problem in London. They're building housing estates, factories, schools, shops, everything a town needs, and they want builders' labourers urgently. That's why they're offering good money – to encourage building workers to go. Some bloke I know came looking for me in the pub to tell me about it.'

Being only human, Molly's spirits soared instinctively at the idea of a respite from her husband's vile temper, a reaction that once again emphasised the wretched state of her marriage. 'So, are you going?' she enquired.

'Dunno.'

'Sounds like a good opportunity to me.'

'Not sure if I fancy it, though,' he said. 'It'll mean living in lodgings.'

'Mm, there is that.' As much as she wanted him to go, she wouldn't influence his decision.

'Some of the digs are all right, though, according to my mate,' Brian went on. 'A pal of his is already working there. He came home for the weekend and was full of it.'

'Is your mate going?'

'Yeah. Several blokes I know are.'

'You could come home at the weekends if you're missing your home comforts,' Molly suggested.

'Not every weekend, though,' he pointed out. 'It would cost too much in train fares.'

'Mm, I suppose so. You'd have to come every now and again. See how it goes.'

'I'd have to send money home every week.'

The more she thought about it the more enthusiastic she became. A break from each other was exactly what they both needed but if she so much as hinted at this he would take umbrage. 'Well, it must be your decision, Brian. You're the one who'll have to live away from home,' she told him. 'Obviously, some decent money would be nice but if you don't fancy going, don't feel you have to.'

But he did fancy it; *not half*. An adventure away from home was the best thing to come his way in ages. The chance to live like a single man would create all sorts of possibilities. Blokes he knew who'd worked away from home on building jobs had told him all the tales. Birding and boozing every night of the week. They had a whale of a time.

So why didn't he grab the opportunity with both hands? The answer was simple. Because it would threaten his control over Molly. He couldn't keep a tight rein on her if he wasn't here. There was no knowing what she might get up to.

On the other hand, could he afford to lose such an opportunity? Plenty of dough and the freedom to do as he liked. 'I think I might give it a try,' he said casually, as though he didn't care one way or the other. 'If I don't like it I can always give it up and come home, can't I?'

'Course you can,' Molly agreed, trying to conceal her elation. 'When would they want you to start?'

'Right away,' he replied. 'My mate is going tomorrow so I might as well go with him.'

'But you've got no lodgings fixed up,' she pointed out, mindful of his wellbeing.

'We'll find something when we get there,' he said, eager to get away now that he'd decided. 'The blokes who are already there will know all the places.'

'I'd better make sure you've got some clean clothes to take with you then, hadn't I?' Molly said, habitually dutiful.

Back at work after the break, Molly was in a flap. The phone didn't seem to stop ringing, the typing was piling up, Dan wanted an order for materials chased up and it would soon be time for Molly to go and collect Rosa from school. Tomorrow would be even worse. There was a party of schoolchildren to be shown around, the wages to be done and filing all over the place. The reason for the chaos was the sudden departure of Paula, who had left without giving notice because she'd been offered another job. The agency didn't have a temp available for them to use until they found a replacement.

Molly looked at her watch. There were still things she needed to deal with today but she was determined to be at that school gate for Rosa. She could ring Angie and ask her to collect her but she wanted to do it herself. So she'd just have to go and get her daughter and bring her back here while she finished off. But the fact of the matter was, there was simply too much for her to do. She needed help. Tomorrow was going to be unbearable unless she had some assistance.

With a sudden flash of inspiration, she hurried from the office and tore across the garden to the house.

'No, Molly, I can't do it,' stated Hattie firmly. 'I'd like to help and if it was anything else I would do so willingly but I know nothing about office work.'

'I'll do all Paula's work, the typing and wages and so on, if you could just answer the phone, keep the filing under control, chase up the suppliers and help look after the party of school children we've got coming tomorrow. It's all basic stuff, nothing that needs any special training. I'll tell you what to do.'

'Sorry, Molly. The answer is no.' Hattie was most emphatic.

'It's only temporary, just until we get a replacement for Paula,' Molly coaxed. 'I just can't manage both jobs on my own – not without working until about eight o'clock at night, and that wouldn't be fair to Rosa.'

'I'll look after her if you need to work late,' Hattie offered.

'So would Angie if I asked her, but I don't want to farm Rosa out.' Molly was adamant. 'It's help in the office I need, Mrs Beckett. I really would be so very grateful.'

'No.'

Observing the determined set of Hattie's mouth, Molly changed tack slightly. 'Look, if you'd really rather not fill in until we get someone, I won't twist your arm.'

'Good.' Her relief was obvious.

'But please could you just come in tomorrow to help out?' Molly entreated. 'It'll be chaos with the school kids coming on top of everything else.'

Hattie was in a state of turmoil; she really couldn't face working at the pottery. The longer she avoided going over there the more afraid of it she became, almost to the point of obsession. Anyway, she'd be absolutely hopeless, having no experience of clerical work. It had never been expected of her. Before George could afford to employ someone in the office, he'd looked after it himself. Her role had always been in the home. Damn and blast Molly for forcing her into this frightening position.

'Oh, all right then,' she agreed reluctantly. 'I'll probably make a complete hash of it and things'll be even worse for you, but I'll do what

I can.' She paused then added firmly, 'Only for tomorrow, though. I mean that, Molly.'

'Thanks, Mrs Beckett, you're a pal,' beamed Molly, who had Hattie's interests at heart as well as her own. 'I'm ever so grateful to you.'

'This process is called throwing,' said Hattie to a group of schoolchildren who were standing near Billy's wheel watching him mould a vase.

'He doesn't look as if he's throwing anything to me,' said a saucy boy of eight or nine, producing giggles from the others. 'If he threw it we'd be able to catch it.'

'It's a potter's term,' Hattie told him patiently. 'It's called throwing because the clay is initially thrown down on to the revolving wheel head.'

'I'd like to have a go at that,' said another lad. 'I'd love to get me hands in all that sludgy stuff.' He turned to the little girl next to him. 'I'd dollop it all over your face.'

The other children found this hilarious and were reprimanded by the teacher, a fierce woman with enormous teeth and thick horn-rimmed glasses, her hair taken back into a bun.

'That sludgy stuff is called clay,' Hattie continued, trying not to be flustered by the rowdier element in the party.

'What's it gonna be when it's finished?' enquired a little girl with plaits.

'A vase,' replied Billy.

'Can I have a go, mister?' asked a boy.

'Not until you're a bit older, son,' said Billy amiably. 'You can come and work for me then, if you like.'

'What's that pot of water for?' someone else wanted to know.

'To dip my fingers in it to stop the clay sticking to them,' he explained.

'Where does the clay come from?' asked the boy.

'Out of the ground.'

'Do you dig it out?'

'Not personally, no,' he replied. 'We buy it from the wholesaler, who delivers it to us.'

The children began discussing this among themselves. 'Pay attention to what Mr Beckett is doing, please, children,' commanded the teacher in a peremptory manner, 'and don't pester him with so many questions.'

'They can ask as many questions as they like,' Billy assured her. 'It shows a healthy interest, and that's something I like to see in youngsters.'

Turning his attention to Dan, a boy asked, 'What are you making, mister?'

'A plate,' came the reply.

'To eat your dinner off?'

'No. Not this one. This one's going to be a very special commemorative plate,' he informed him. 'It's for a cricket club, and will have special writing on it.'

'Who's gonna do the writing?' asked a little girl with bunches.

'I am,' said Dan.

'Is it hard?'

'Not when you've been doing it for as long as I have,' Dan told her. 'But it does have to be done carefully.'

The questions continued thick and fast until Hattie said, 'I think we should leave the potters to get on with their work now, and go outside and have a look at the kiln.'

There was a roar of approval. 'I've always wanted to see that tall chimney close up,' said someone.

'Yeah,' the others chimed in.

The teacher formed her charges into a crocodile and, led by Hattie, they left the building.

'Little horrors,' said Josh, who was packing finished pottery into wooden crates with straw. 'All those questions. It's enough to drive you nuts.'

'I like to see youngsters with an interest,' remarked Dan. 'They're the potters of the future. It's when they don't ask questions the craft is in danger of dying out.'

'Exactly,' added Billy.

'It's different if you're doing interesting stuff when visitors come, I suppose,' grumbled Josh. 'You can show off your skills. But no one takes any interest in what I'm doing because I'm just the boy around here.'

'There's one thing you really are good at, mate,' said his brother. 'You're a world champion whinger.'

'Your turn will come,' Dan reminded Josh in a kinder tone. 'We've all had to do what you're doing when we're learning. Patience is of the essence.'

'That's something he has very little of,' opined Billy. 'Cheek and laziness in spades. Patience, no.'

At that moment Molly appeared to ask if Josh could be spared to go to the shop because she didn't have time herself and some urgent paperwork needed to be taken.

'We can manage without him as long as he isn't going to take too long,' Billy told her.

'I do have to get a bus and a train, remember,' Josh chipped in. 'So don't expect me to get there and back in half an hour.'

'Don't make a day of it, that's all,' warned his brother. 'I know what you're like.'

'Well, Mrs Beckett,' began Molly as she prepared to go home, 'you've played a blinder today and that's a fact. I don't know what I'd have done without you.'

'You're exaggerating,' was Hattie's modest reply. 'I only answered the phone and cleared up some of the paperwork.'

'And showed a party of kids around and managed to get the suppliers to shift themselves with the delivery we're waiting for and other things so that I could get on with the typing.' She gathered up the outgoing post. 'I'll put these letters in the box on my way to the school. You can go home and put your feet up now. You've done your bit. One of the boys will have to answer the phone.'

'I thought I'd stay on for a while longer,' Hattie said unexpectedly. 'Just to see if I can get the hang of the filing. I'm very slow.'

This sounded extremely promising. 'Are you sure?' enquired Molly.

Hattie nodded. 'I popped home earlier and put a casserole in the oven for later on,' she told her. 'So everything's organised there. If I stay for a while and have a go at the filing, it'll give us a nice fresh start in the morning.'

'You're going to help out again tomorrow then,' Molly was delighted.

'Someone's got to give you a hand until you get a replacement for Paula, haven't they?'

Molly could have hugged her but restrained herself because they weren't on those sort of terms. 'I'll see you in the morning then,' she said, and left smiling.

Watching her go, Hattie mulled things over. Despite her fears and a nasty attack of nerves when she'd first arrived, she'd found a sense of fulfilment working here today; being involved in the world created by her beloved husband, helping his business, showing it off to the children. Much to her amazement, the work had soothed her and created its own energy, regenerating her and carrying her along.

All the fine work that went out of these premises, giving pleasure to buyers and creating employment, existed only because George had had the courage to start the pottery with nothing more than his talent to go on. It felt good to be part of his creation. Anyway, she needed something to do besides cooking and cleaning, and it was so handy being just across the garden.

Looking out of the window, she could see a barge gliding by on the canal beyond the apple trees, almost bare of leaves now, an autumn mist rising above the water. She wanted to weep with love for the place that she and George had built together: the house, the pottery, the garden. The place where they had raised their children. Tears meandered down her cheeks with the pain of knowing that he was never going to walk across the garden to the house again. Nothing would ever be the same.

But for the first time since his death she felt something resembling hope. She felt able to face tomorrow; a different sort of tomorrow to those they'd had together but she knew, somehow, that she was strong enough to take what came.

She would tell Molly that she need look no further for a replacement for Paula. She herself couldn't type but she could learn other jobs so that

61

Molly would be free to do that, and they could share the other duties. Hattie certainly felt capable of learning how to get to grips with the PAYE system and the ledgers. Together they would run this office as a team.

She turned away from the window and looked at a pile of invoices on the desk.

Now where the devil do these go? she wondered.

There was a series of loud popping noises and a shower of golden rain exploded into the night sky.

'Oh, look at that, Rosa,' gasped Molly. 'Isn't it pretty?'

'It's lovely,' breathed Rosa, big blue eyes shining. 'Cor, there goes a rocket. Uncle Dan's setting them off ever so fast.'

'We don't want you to get bored, do we?' Dan was in charge of the fireworks at the Platers' Guy Fawkes party, enthusiastically assisted by Billy. 'Not to mention the fact that we get to have some food when the fireworks are finished, and I'm starving.'

'Can we have some sparklers to hold, please, Uncle Billy?' requested Patsy.

'Course you can,' said Billy, lighting two sparklers and handing them out.

Fizzing and sparkling, they were twirled and twisted to cries of delight, while jumping crackers leaped noisily about on the edge of the bonfire on which the last of the poor beleagured guy was turning to ashes. Dressed in old coats, woolly hats and scarves, Molly, Angie, Hattie and the children stood in the glow of the flames, their faces flushed from the warmth. Dan had a hose pipe and shovel on hand to keep the fire under control.

'Last one,' he said, and let off something that zoomed skywards and burst into a shower of myriad colours to a great communal burst of approval. 'Right. That's your lot for this year, folks.'

'I'm glad we didn't have any bangers,' remarked Patsy.

'They're too loud,' added Rosa.

'Bangers are great,' Billy told them. 'We'd have had lots of them if I'd had my way, but seeing as you two kids are scared . . .'

'We're not scared,' came the joint protest.

'It's just that we like the pretty ones best, don't we, Rosa?' Patsy wanted to convince him.

'There's no fun in bangers,' supported Rosa. 'But we're not scared of them, though.'

'I believe you, thousands wouldn't.' Billy had a way with children. He teased the life out of them and they couldn't get enough.

The women went inside and a cheer rose up when they re-emerged with trays of baked potatoes, sausage rolls, mugs of tomato soup and cheese straws still warm from the oven. There was lemonade, beer and spirits for those who fancied something stronger. It was a real family party.

'Well, I'm off to meet me mates,' announced Josh, after devouring a sizeable portion of everything.

'Aah, so soon.' His mother was disappointed because she enjoyed having the whole of her brood around her. 'Surely you can stay for a bit longer.'

'Sorry, Ma. I've done my duty and stayed for the fireworks. It's time to find some grown-up entertainment now.' He headed for the garden gate before anyone had a chance to object further. 'See you.'

'What about you, Billy?' enquired his sister. 'Are you off on a hot date tonight?'

'What? And miss my skin and blister's bonfire party. No fear.' This little shindig's a tradition and I'll stay until the end.'

'We are honoured,' she grinned.

Brother and sister fell into conversation. They were very close, almost like twins. The children went inside, followed by Hattie, leaving Molly to chat to Dan, who was watching the fire and shovelling back any hot firewood that fell forward, while trying to eat a baked potato.

'Enjoying yourself, Moll?' he asked in a friendly manner.

'I'm having a lovely time, thanks.'

'You usually have to rush off, don't you?' he remarked, remembering. 'The minute the fireworks are finished, you and Rosa are gone.'

'That's only because I have to get home to Brian,' she explained. 'But as he's working away from home there's no rush for me to get back.'

'Of course, I'd forgotten he was away,' Dan said casually. 'Norfolk, isn't it?'

'That's right.'

'So, you get to stay out late,' he said jokingly. 'While the cat's away, eh?'

'Well . . . only in the most innocent sort of way,' she grinned. 'I've no wild parties planned.'

'I'm glad to hear it.' He turned away from the fire to look at her. 'Seriously, though, Moll, are you getting on all right without him?'

'He hasn't been gone long enough for me to tell yet but so far so good.' She couldn't possibly tell him, or anyone, the truth: that she hadn't been this happy in years; that the absence of Brian and his constant criticism had given her a new lease of life. Just her and Rosa at home – it was wonderful. No walking on eggshells, no arguments or tension knots in her stomach. His being away had made her realise just how abysmal the atmosphere had been in the flat. Rosa was already blossoming in the more peaceful environment.

'You seem like the strong, capable type even though there's not much of you,' Dan remarked lightly.

'Ooh, I don't know about that, but I manage.'

He turned back to the fire, looking thoughtful as he finished his potato. 'I think Angie would be absolutely lost if I had to live away from home for any reason and I don't mean that in any critical way.'

Molly believed Angie would too. Not because she was too feeble to cope but because she would be bereft without him. Theirs really was a marriage made in heaven.

'So would you,' she laughed. 'You wouldn't last five minutes without her.'

'I would not,' he readily admitted, 'and I don't care who knows it. I couldn't bear to be away from her.'

'Fortunately you're not likely to have to be,' she pointed out. 'Going away doesn't feature in your line of work, does it?'

'Not often, no. There's the occasional demonstration at a craft fair or exhibition that might need an overnight stay, but nothing more than that.' A lump of red-hot wood fell out of the fire, creating a burst of sparks. He scooped it up with the shovel and threw it back into the flames. Wearing a thick navy sweater, his face smudged with smoke dust from the fire, there was a boyishness about him, Molly noticed. He and Angie made a handsome couple.

'How's Brian getting on in Norfolk, anyway? Missing his home comforts, I expect.'

'I haven't heard from him yet.' Molly added quickly, as though needing to defend her husband, 'We don't have a phone and he isn't much of a letter writer.'

'I don't suppose he's had time, what with settling in and work and everything,' Dan said as if to reassure her, as though she had a normal marriage. 'Us men aren't as good about that sort of thing as you women. Communication isn't our strong point, or so they say.'

Brian never had any trouble communicating his feelings to her, she thought sadly. He was extremely eloquent in his disapproval of practically everything she did but she just said, 'Yes, they do say that.'

Brian and his mates were having a wonderful time. All pleasantly plastered, they were having a singsong around the dying embers of the bonfire on the common at Boxham in Norfolk, a small town in the process of becoming a very large New Town. They'd started off with 'Rock Around the Clock' but had slowed down to a punishing rendition of the first line of 'Unchained Melody', which they kept repeating because no one knew any more.

What a belter of a Guy Fawkes party it had been, Brian thought. There had been hot potatoes and sausage rolls and a good selection of alcoholic drinks. All put on by the local pub for a couple of shillings.

He had his arm around Beryl Brown, his landlady, Flo's, daughter, whom he'd clicked with the minute they'd clapped eyes on each other. She couldn't get enough of him. Twenty-one years old, long legs, big brown eyes, a tiny waist and a chest you could get lost in. Every sane man's fantasy, and she fancied the pants off him.

She didn't know he was married, of course. He wasn't dim enough to wreck his chances by telling her a thing like that. All privileges would immediately be withdrawn if she got so much as a whiff of that. Women were funny about that sort of thing. The lads would keep shtoom. It was an unwritten law among them. Several of the married men had got themselves fixed up with local girls, anyway.

Working away from home was the best thing that had happened to him in years and he was enjoying every single minute, apart from the actual work, that was. That was just as hard to take wherever he was. Still, his spare time advantages made it slightly more palatable, especially as Beryl wasn't one of these possessive women who tried to come between a man and his mates. He'd taken her to the pictures a couple of times to keep her sweet, and the other nights she'd been quite happy for him to go out on the beer with the lads.

It was a great life, and to make it even better he had an absolute dream of a landlady who served good wholesome meals: steak and kidney pudding, beef stew with dumplings and other such favourites to satisfy the appetite of a hungry working man. All his washing and ironing was taken care of and included in the price. He was the only lodger so he didn't have to share the attention. Flo rented out the room, apparently, to subsidise her income from a part-time job in a shop.

Brian certainly had no intention of going home at weekends; not very often anyway. Not while life was this good here. There were years of building work ahead in the area too, so he could stay for as long as he liked.

Beryl and her mother had come here to live from London a year or so ago because of the cheap housing. Flo's husband had walked out when Beryl was a baby so there was no protective father to cramp Brian's style.

Of course, his hectic social life took a bit of funding but he was earning good money and if he sent Molly less than he should, she couldn't do a damned thing about it. Not from this distance. Anyway, she was earning money. She'd insisted on going out to work against his wishes so now she could help support herself and the kid. The idea of her working still infuriated him but while he was away and not affected by it he could try to forget it. The fact that it suited his pocket helped in that respect.

Despite that, lingering thoughts of Molly dampened his mood as the old paranoia crept in. Almost against his will, he began to wonder if she would cheat on him while he was away. The fact that he had already been unfaithful to her didn't lessen his anxiety about her doing the same.

'Let's all go down the pub to finish the party off,' suggested one of his mates.

'Good idea,' said another.

'We'll be just in time for last orders,' added someone else.

'I'm game,' said Beryl.

Not half she is, thought Brian, which was why she appealed to him.

'Come on then, everybody. Last one to the bar pays for the drinks,' he challenged.

Talking and singing, they headed rowdily across the common. With one arm around Beryl's shoulders and the other hand planted firmly on her bottom, Brian moved with the others to the local pub, all thoughts of Molly now pushed firmly to the back of his mind. The bachelor life with the security of a wife at home was the perfect combination. Long may it continue.

Chapter Five

Life continued to be pleasant for Molly in Brian's absence as she and Rosa enjoyed the more relaxed atmosphere at home. The job was going well too. As she and Hattie settled into a working routine, Molly perceived a change in their personal relationship. Until recently she'd always regarded Hattie from the rather formal perspective of a best friend's mother. Now that they were working together there was a chummier feel between them.

Hattie must be having similar thoughts because one day she said, 'I think it's about time we dropped the Mrs Beckett, don't you? Hattie will be better.'

Although they were very much a team, they each had their own responsibilities, though were flexible about some things. If Molly had the time, she kept the books up to date; if not, Hattie did it. Molly did all the typing and Hattie took over the wages on a regular basis. Other daily duties were shared. The fact that Hattie stayed later than Molly helped her to be on time for her afternoon dash to the school.

At the beginning of December their routine was thrown into disarray when Peter went down with flu and someone had to cover for him at the shop during opening hours. Hattie preferred to stay close to home so Molly went to Notting Hill every morning and stayed until Josh came to take over from her in time for her to get back to collect Rosa.

'Such beautiful things,' enthused a female customer one afternoon, hovering over a range of pottery with a seasonal pattern; bunches of red berries and green leaves on a light background. 'I love the design.'

'Yes, I like that one too,' said Molly. 'We've only produced a limited amount of that range for Christmas.'

'A lovely idea for Christmas presents,' the customer remarked. 'That's what I want it for.'

'Someone will be lucky then,' said Molly sociably, careful to hide her anxiety, which was growing by the second. While the customer's attention was focused on the pottery, she glanced at her watch. Where was Josh? He should have been here ages ago. It was time for her to leave. She'd have to close the shop if he didn't come soon.

'Do you have six of these?' asked the customer, holding up a mug.

'There are only four on display and I'd like six to make up a set for my mother.'

'We may have some more outside in the stockroom,' Molly told her. 'I'll have a look.'

At that moment there was a flurry of customers arriving. Damn, now she'd have to stay and serve them unless Josh turned up. Where was he? She hurriedly found the mugs to make up the set, completed the sale and had to ask the waiting customers if they could bear with her for a few moments, whereupon she dashed into the office to call Angie to ask her to collect Rosa from school. There was no way she could get back to Hanwell in time now.

By the time Josh did arrive she'd cleared the queue and was incandescent with rage, especially as she'd phoned the pottery to find out if he was on his way and been told that he'd left two hours before.

'What happened to you?' she wanted to know.

'None of your business.'

He'd changed out of his workshop clothes and was wearing a suit; standard procedure when he was working at the shop. 'I've told you before to keep your big nose out.'

'It is my business when you let me down,' she stated categorically. 'You know perfectly well that I need to get away on time to collect my daughter from school. Instead of which I've been stuck here because you weren't here to take over.'

'You shouldn't go out to work if you're not free to do the job,' he said rudely. 'You can't expect other people to rush about just to fit in with your domestic arrangements.'

'I never expect that of anyone,' she pointed out, 'but I do expect you to be here on time for your stint in the shop while Peter's away.'

'Oh, shut up, you moaning old cow.'

'Don't you dare speak to me like that.'

'I'll speak to you however I like,' he declared with a sullen expression. 'I've told you before, you're no one special. I don't have to take any notice of you.'

'You don't take any notice of anyone,' she pointed out.

'So what if I don't?'

'So one of these days it's going to land you in big trouble,' she warned him. 'You'll find yourself out of a job, if you don't buck your ideas up.'

'Don't make me laugh,' he scorned. 'I'm family. They can't get rid of me.'

'I wouldn't be so sure about that,' she disagreed. 'People can only take so much, family or not.'

'All this fuss just because I was a bit late,' he objected, puffing irritably. 'Look, I had to wait ages for a bus to Ealing Broadway station, and then there was a hold-up on the tube. You know what London Transport is like.'

She didn't believe a word of it. He'd probably spent a happy hour in a coffee bar drinking espresso and listening to the juke box. But to say so would provoke more lies and she didn't have time.

'Anyway, I have to go now.' Molly turned at the door and added, 'Don't forget to put the takings in the night safe and make sure you lock up properly.'

'I'm not an idiot, you know.'

'Just making sure you remember.'

'Bossy cow.'

Ignoring his parting shot, she left the premises without reminding him to be polite to the customers. Oddly enough, she didn't need to. Although he was thoroughly rude and objectionable to everyone at the pottery, with the exception of his mother, he was charm itself when serving in the shop.

The next morning when Molly arrived at the shop, there was a shock in store for her. There had been a burglary and most of the pottery on display had gone. Even before she called the police, she could see how the thieves had got in. The back door was open, though there was no sign of it being tampered with.

'You careless young bugger,' ranted Billy to his brother later on, back at the pottery, when they were all there having a post-mortem. 'How could you be so stupid as to leave without locking up?'

'I did lock up,' he blustered.

'So the door unlocked itself ready for the robbers to get in, did it?'

'There's no need to be sarky,' objected Josh. 'I'm just saying that I'm sure I locked up, front and back.'

'Well, you couldn't have done because there was no forced entry,' Billy ground out.

'Perhaps they were so good at it, it doesn't show,' Josh suggested hopefully.

'Nice try, but it won't work,' Billy told him. 'You don't pay attention to the job, that's your trouble. You're too busy trying to avoid work.'

'You know what this means, don't you?' Dan put in gravely. 'The insurance company won't pay out.'

Josh turned pale. 'Of course they will,' he disagreed. 'What are you talking about?'

'I mean that the shop was left unlocked so they won't meet the claim.'

'They won't know that it wasn't—' began Josh lamely.

'Of course they'll know,' interrupted Billy. 'We'd have to submit a police report with the claim. The report will say that there was no forced entry. These insurance companies are on the ball when it comes to paying out money. If you don't take the correct security precautions, they don't pay up. There won't be any point in us submitting a claim.'

'The coppers might catch the crooks and get the stuff back,' said Josh.

'And Marilyn Monroe might come to live next door,' was Billy's ironic response. 'That pottery will be miles away by now, already sold on.'

'The last thing I said to you was don't forget to lock up,' Molly reminded him.

'If Josh is sure he did the locking up properly, might it be how he said – that the thieves were so clever it just looks as though there was no forced entry?' suggested Hattie, ever the protective mother.

'No, Mum, that isn't how it was.' Billy's manner was kind but firm. 'I know that you don't like to think ill of Josh but there's no point in your making excuses for him this time because the truth is staring us in the face. He forgot to lock up and his carelessness is going to cost us a lot of money.'

'They didn't take everything,' Josh ventured warily. 'They didn't touch the stockroom.'

'They took enough to make a big hole in our stock. This time of the year too,' Billy tutted. 'We're going to have to work every hour God sends to get more stock on the shelves so that we don't lose the whole of the Christmas trade.'

'It was naughty of you, Josh,' said Hattie in the mildest of admonishments.

'Naughty of him?' blasted Billy. 'It was downright bloody criminal. He ought to be sacked.'

'Oh, Billy.' His mother was shocked. 'We wouldn't do that to one of our own.'

'Maybe not, but he deserves it.' Billy turned to his brother. 'I can tell you this, mate. Dan and I won't be the only ones working overtime to make up for what we lost. You will be too. You can't do the throwing but there'll be plenty of other jobs to keep you busy, we'll make sure of that. You'll stay on until every last bit of dust has been swept up and this place is like a new pin. And you leave the place unlocked and you're dead, I can promise you that.'

'You'd better tell those precious mates of yours that you won't be seeing them of an evening,' added Dan.

'Honestly, anyone would think I did it on purpose, the way you lot are carrying on,' Josh objected gloomily. 'Anyone can make a mistake.'

'You make more than most because your mind isn't on the job. Well, one more blunder like this, mate, and you'll be down the labour exchange sharpish,' warned Billy, his voice rising. 'You're a bloomin' liability.'

Deciding that some sort of defusing agent was necessary, Molly said, 'I think I'll make some tea.'

'Good idea,' agreed Hattie.

Billy and Dan spared no effort to make up for what had been stolen, and Josh was made to pull his weight. They weren't able to recoup their

70

losses altogether and had to accept that their Christmas profits would be much less than usual. But their extra work did compensate for some of the stolen pottery. The decision about electric ovens was postponed yet again to avoid any extra expense at this time.

Molly enjoyed the run-up to Christmas enormously this year, and lived the whole thing through the eyes of her daughter. The excitement generated in Rosa through school activities – the Nativity play in which she played an angel, the school party and all the other extracurricular jollies – filled the home. Then there were the carol singers, the cards, the purchasing of presents, everything culminating in a glorious feeling of bonhomie. Not having to watch every penny made a big difference. It was such a treat to buy gifts without agonising. The whole thing seemed to have an added shimmer this year.

Then Brian came home and everything changed . . .

Molly was used to his bad temper, but the foul mood he was in when he arrived home on the afternoon of Christmas Eve really was beyond the pale. She was busy doing her Christmas baking and feeling festive, the flat infused with the Christmassy aroma of mince pies and sausage rolls. Her efforts at a warm welcome fell on stony ground. He moved away when she tried to greet him with a hug and made only the most perfunctory effort at conversation. Having dumped his holdall on the floor by the front door, he went into the living room and sat in the armchair.

'Look at the tree, Daddy,' cried Rosa, far too excited to be deflated by his gloominess. 'Isn't it lovely? Mummy did it and I helped.'

'Very nice,' he said, barely even glancing at Molly's glittering handiwork, which was standing in all its finery in the corner by the window.

That night when he got back from the pub Molly had something to tell him.

'Angie and Dan have invited us round to their place for a Christmas drink tomorrow, before lunch,' she said enthusiastically, putting some extra gifts around the tree while he settled down on the sofa. 'That'll really put us in the mood. We can leave the turkey in the oven cooking as we'll only be out for an hour or so.'

'We're not going,' he announced.

'What . . .?'

'You heard.'

'But, Brian—'

'Don't go on about it,' he interrupted. 'I don't want to go, and that's an end to it.' He observed Molly through a pall of smoke from his cigarette. 'There's no need to look at me as though I've committed a crime. No law I know of says I have to socialise with your mate.'

'But it was nice of them to ask us.'

'Nice, my arse,' he scorned. 'They just wanna show off their house.'

'No. They were just being friendly. It's what people do at Christmas.' He replied with a shrug.

'But I'd like to go, and it'll be nice for Rosa to see Patsy on Christmas morning. The kids are looking forward to it,' she tried to persuade. 'Surely you can make the effort for us.'

'Nope. We're not going.'

She gave the matter some thought and came to a decision. 'All right, if you really don't want to go, I won't press you. But Rosa and I will go.'

His eyes popped. 'Oh, that's a nice homecoming, that is,' he scowled. 'My wife telling me she's buggering off out on Christmas morning.'

'Come with us.'

'No.'

'Look, for some reason you've come home acting as though you're going to die tomorrow,' she told him, 'and you're doing your level best to spoil Christmas for Rosa and me. But I'm not having it, Brian, not this year. My daughter and I are going to Angie's tomorrow whether you like it or not.'

He looked at her, perceiving a change. She'd become more assertive while he'd been away. There was a new vitality about her somehow, which he hoped had nothing to do with the likes of Billy Beckett. The thought gave him a stab of pain. When he was away he was able to cast thoughts of Molly aside; he had too much going on in his own life to worry about what she was doing. But as soon as he saw her, all the old jealousy flared up again.

He hadn't wanted to come home for Christmas but had thought he'd better do his duty, especially as he'd not been coming back at weekends. Being with Molly and Rosa seemed dull in comparison to the life he was leading in Norfolk where he could come and go as he pleased and had a twenty-one-year-old girl who was crazy about him. What man wouldn't be enjoying himself? Roll on the end of the holiday and Norfolk. He couldn't wait to get back there.

Beryl had been none too pleased about his leaving her over the holiday. Naturally, being under the impression that he was single and serious about her, she'd expected him to spend Christmas with her. What she would do if she found out she was just a fling didn't bear thinking about. He'd made up some story about having to spend Christmas with his parents, both of whom had actually been dead for years.

But now he said in reply to Molly, 'There isn't much I can do about it then, is there, if that's the way you feel?'

'Why not come with us? You might enjoy it, you never know,' she suggested.

'I wouldn't.'

'OK. As you wish. We'll only be gone for an hour or so. Mum will be here around midday so I can't be long.' Although she'd tried to persuade him to go with them – in the lingering belief that she should try to make things better – she was relieved that he'd refused. He would have deliberately exaggerated his lack of social graces out of spite to embarrass her, and she'd have been on edge the whole time.

'That's a pretty little Christmas tree you've got,' said Molly's sister, Peggy, a tall, thin, sharp-featured woman with bleached hair cut into a short, feathery style. 'Fits in quite nice in that corner.'

'Yes, it does, doesn't it?' said Molly graciously, as though she hadn't noticed her sister's condescending manner. She usually tried not to rise to the bait.

'You've done wonders with the room,' Peggy went on in the patronising attitude that was second nature to her, 'considering that you have so little space. It can't be easy.'

'We manage.'

'You two can share the pouf,' Peggy instructed her children, Tommy and Maureen. 'Shove up, Reg, and make room for Mum on the sofa next to Rosa. Cor, it's a bit of a squash in here, Moll, with all of us crammed in.'

'I'll get some chairs from the kitchen,' said Brian, and left the room.

'You'll have to come over to us next time,' suggested Peggy. '*We've* got plenty of room.'

It was the afternoon of Boxing Day. Peggy and Reg were visiting Joan, and paying a duty visit to Molly while they were in the area.

'Christmas cake, anyone?' offered Molly.

'Just a sliver for me, dear,' said Peggy.

'I hate Christmas cake,' announced Tommy, a spoiled child of ten.

'It's yucky,' added eight-year-old Maureen, who was equally as overindulged.

'Would you like some chocolate log then?' suggested Molly patiently.

They both said they didn't like that either, or mince pies or fairy cakes or anything else Molly cared to suggest. So she got on and sliced the Christmas cake for the others.

'Peggy and Reg were saying that they've put their Christmas tree in the hall this year,' said Joan as Molly passed the tea and cake around. 'Though they do have plenty of room for it in their big through lounge, of course. They've knocked the wall through, you know, so it's an open-plan lounge-diner now. Very modern and smart.'

'So you said, Mum.'

'You sister's never satisfied, Moll,' said Reg, a big jolly man with none of his wife's pretentiousness. 'As soon as I've paid out for one thing to be done, she wants something else doing. We'll never be rich, not with her expensive tastes.'

'You really must come over to the house, Moll,' suggested Peggy.

'That would be nice.'

'I'll give you a ring sometime soon to fix something up.' She paused thoughtfully. 'But, of course, you're not on the phone, are you?'

'You can always ring me at work.' She thought it most unlikely that Peggy would call her, soon or in the future. They didn't have anything in common.

'Oh yes, you've got this little job now, haven't you?' said Peggy, blatantly supercilious.

'That's right.' Pointless to add that it was more than just a 'little job' because Peggy would find some other way of belittling her.

'Just as well you've got something to occupy you, with Brian working away,' Peggy went on, giving her sister a pitying look. 'It must help ease the loneliness for you. Poor old you, all on your little ownsome.'

If only she knew, thought Molly, but just said, 'Yes, poor little me.'

'She manages, don't you, Moll?' Putting Molly down was Brian's prerogative and he wasn't prepared to let his stuck-up sister-in-law do the same. 'She's made of strong stuff, our Molly.'

'Course she is,' added Reg.

Ignoring the show of support for Molly, Peggy cast her eye around the room. 'You can make these little council places quite cosy, can't you?' she said. 'It's surprising.'

'There's nothing surprising about it.' Brian's hackles were up. 'It's a nice flat. It might not be as posh as your house but it suits us.'

There was an awkward silence. Molly and Brian exchanged a glance in a rare moment of accord.

'We've no complaints,' said Molly sharply. 'We waited long enough for it.'

'I think Peg just meant that you'd got it looking nice,' put in Joan, trying to keep the peace.

'Exactly,' Peggy confirmed.

'Any more tea, anyone?' came Molly's timely intervention.

In the kitchen waiting for the kettle to boil, Molly sighed with relief that the visit was almost over. She doubted if the guests would stay much longer. Still, Rosa had had a good Christmas and that was all that mattered. Christmas Day had passed without incident. She and Rosa had spent a pleasant hour at the Platers' before lunch. Joan had joined them for the meal and stayed until late in the evening. Brian had been quieter than usual but had seemed preoccupied rather than bad-tempered. He'd gone to the pub at lunchtime, but had been forced by the fact that the local was closed in the evening to stay at home. Ensconced in the armchair he'd worked his way through the Christmas booze while Molly and her mother passed the time playing ludo, and snakes and ladders with Rosa.

Now Molly took a tray of tea into the other room.

'We'll make a move when we've had this,' announced Peggy.

Thank God for that, thought Molly, but said politely and with fingers metaphorically crossed, 'You're welcome to stay for the evening. We've plenty of everything. We could have a game of cards if you like.'

'Thanks, but no. If a frost comes down tonight the roads will be icy,' said Peggy, 'and we don't want to risk dangerous driving conditions.'

'I don't wanna stay here, anyway,' piped in Tommy, showing off his bad manners. 'You haven't got a telly and there's a pantomime on tonight.'

If all goes well, we might be able to watch the TV panto on our own set next Christmas, thought Molly, but said, 'Oh, well, you'd better not stay then because you wouldn't want to miss that.'

'No fear,' said his sister.

'I wish we had a telly, Mum,' said Rosa wistfully. 'Everyone else has got them.'

'That "everyone else" you're always talking about is a very lucky person,' teased Molly. 'It seems there's nothing she doesn't have.'

'Oh, Mu-um,' tutted Rosa, blue eyes resting on her mother in friendly admonishment. 'Lots of my friends at school really have got a telly. I'm not making it up.'

'Everything comes to those who wait,' was Molly's answer.

No sooner had things got back to normal after Christmas than everything was sent awry at the pottery by a virulent flu bug, which affected both Rosa, and Peter, who'd never properly recovered from his last attack. Molly wasn't able to go in to work with Rosa sick, but Billy brought the typewriter round to the flat so that Molly was able to do some work from home when Rosa was over the worst. Hattie couldn't leave the office unattended all day so it fell to Josh to fill in for Peter at the shop.

Fortunately Rosa made a speedy recovery and went back to school sooner than Molly had anticipated.

'Molly, thank God you're back,' said Billy when she turned up for work unexpectedly one morning.

'It's been chaos without you,' added Hattie.

'You've saved the day for us because we need Josh here to help us get a special order out,' Billy told her. 'Peter's still off sick so Josh is at the shop. If you could take over from him just for a couple of hours so that he can come back here to give us a hand, it would be a great help.'

'Course I will. But has he already gone to the shop?' asked Molly.

Billy nodded. 'We didn't realise that you'd be coming in so he went straight to Notting Hill from home,' he explained. 'He'll be on his way there now.'

'I'll get over there right away and send him back,' she told them.

'As soon as I think he'll have arrived at the shop I'll get on the phone to tell him that you're on your way so he can be ready to leave as soon as you get there,' suggested Hattie.

'Good idea,' approved Molly.

Had Josh been where he should have been – inside the shop – Hattie

75

would have been able to get through to him on the phone to tell him that Molly was on her way and the subsequent drama would have been avoided. As it was, Molly saw something she wasn't supposed to and all hell broke loose . . .

'You've been rumbled,' was how Molly put it when she appeared from the office after Josh had been back in the shop for a while.

He looked startled. 'What are you doing here?'

'I've come to take over so that you can go back to Hanwell.' She faced him across the counter. 'Good job I did, as it happens, because I saw you in action; saw your little scam.'

'Scam?' He gave her a pitying look. 'What are you waffling on about?'

'Don't act the innocent with me,' she warned. 'I watched you hand one of our vases over to a market trader and put the money in your pocket. No sales receipt; no questions asked. There would have been no comeback on you if I hadn't happened to spot it.'

'You saw no such thing.'

'Don't mess me about, Josh,' she told him. 'I saw the whole transaction. And I know you haven't put the money in the till because I've been watching from the back. If you were going to put it in you'd have done so by now.'

'You're been spying on me . . .'

'I was giving you time, hoping you'd put the money where it belongs.'

'Poking your nose in—'

'I'm only here because you're needed at the pottery,' she cut in. 'Your mother was going to ring you to let you know I was on my way. If you hadn't been outside doing your mucky little deal, you'd have answered the phone and I'd have been none the wiser. As it was I saw the whole thing on my way into the shop.'

'I've done nothing wrong.'

'Oh, for heaven's sake, grow up and accept the fact that you've been found out,' she said irritably. 'There's no point in your denying it because I saw you do it. And don't tell me you were going to put the money in the till later because we both know that isn't true.'

He finally accepted that the game was up but not with good grace. 'Well, why shouldn't I make a bit on the side?' he mumbled, simmering with umbrage. 'I don't get paid nearly enough for what I do.'

'You will, when you've learned the job.'

'My mates who work in factories earn much more than I do,' he complained. 'They can afford all the latest gear. I'm the poorest of the lot yet I'm the only one whose family's in business. That can't be right, can it?'

'Robbing your own though, Josh,' Molly rebuked. 'It's low even for you. After all the extra work the potters had to do after the burglary that

76

you caused, I can't see them forgiving you on this one.'

'You're gonna tell them then?'

Molly gave the matter some thought. Maybe there was another way round this that would be more beneficial. 'That depends on you,' she said.

'What do you mean?'

'You put the money you got for the vase in the till, promise me you'll never do anything like this again and start giving me some respect and co-operation instead of constant aggression, and it need go no further. Otherwise I shall tell them all what you've done, including your mother.'

'You wouldn't . . .'

'Watch me.'

Josh was used to being in trouble with the family because he was rarely out of it with everyone except his mother. But she was a useful source of income to him. Even apart from what he stole from her purse, she could always be relied on for a bit of extra dosh with a little gentle persuasion. If she found out about this, it would be much more difficult to win her round.

'Seems like I don't have much choice.'

'That's right. So, do we have a deal?'

'S'pose so.'

She held out her hand for the money. 'Come on. Stump up.'

He dipped into his pocket and handed her a five-pound note.

'And the rest,' she said.

Looking aggrieved he fished out another couple of notes.

'I won't sink so low as to make you turn your pockets inside out,' she told him.

'You wouldn't find anything if you did,' he said haughtily. 'You've got the lot.'

'I shall keep a close eye on the stock in this shop in future and if I suspect that you've taken so much as an egg cup, I won't hesitate to blow the whistle on you. The same goes for your attitude towards me. The instant you stop treating me with normal human respect, out comes the secret.' She pointed to her head. 'I've got it here, you see, to be used at any time. It isn't going to go away.'

'Bloody con woman.'

'What was that, Josh?'

'I just said, you're quite a woman.'

'Good. You're getting the hang of it already,' she said with a wry grin. 'Now you get back off to Hanwell and leave me to run things here. Be back here by two thirty so that I can get away to collect Rosa, please.'

'Will do.'

As he left, a potential customer came in and Molly prepared to do business with a smile on her face.

Molly was always considering ways to improve the business, and one day in early February she came up with something that excited her.

'I've had an idea,' she told Hattie one day in her office. 'A small thing that will add something to the pottery with hardly any expense and only a minimum amount of extra work for us.'

The other woman looked up from the filing cabinet. 'Let's hear it then.'

'Well, you know we have the occasional party of school children come to look around, to see how pottery is made?' she began.

'Mm.'

'Why don't we build on this and encourage visits from adult groups – Townswomen's Guild, Rotary Clubs, craft classes, youth clubs and so on? Just make it known that visitors are welcome – by appointment only, of course. We could put a notice in the library and in the church halls where groups meet. Word will soon get around. The visits would have to be on Saturdays because people are working during the week. But they would be for only an hour or so, and we wouldn't do them often enough for them to be a nuisance.'

'It's a nice idea. But how will it help the business, apart from creating goodwill?' enquired Hattie. 'I mean, we can hardly charge a fee.'

'Of course not. But we can open a little shop for people to buy from when they've finished watching the demonstration and had the tour.' She pointed through the glass partition to a deep alcove at the office end of the workshop where boxes and sundry items were lying around 'That corner is completely wasted. We could make that into the shop; get some postcards done of the pottery and have the boys make some small souvenir items as well as the bigger stuff. People enjoy buying knick-knacks to take home when they've seen the things actually being made. It'll cost next to nothing to set up. A few shelves, a lick of paint and a counter, that's all. We don't need doors.'

'Do you know, I think you might have hit on something,' said Hattie, interest growing. 'We'll have to see what the boys think about it.'

'I don't imagine they'll object. I mean, it isn't as though we'll have visitors very often. We'll keep the bookings well spaced out. And you and I can run the shop between us. Unless there's a visit we won't have customers, being so out of the way, so it won't interfere with our normal work.'

'Bags I take the visitors round and tell them the history of the place,' Hattie said jokingly. 'I enjoyed doing the last one. I felt as though I was doing it for George.'

'You won't get any competition from me over that job,' Molly assured her.

'So, the next step is telling the others,' said Hattie.

Molly nodded. She knew one of the boys who wouldn't put up any objections to anything she suggested. She'd had no trouble at all with Josh since they'd made their deal.

'It looks lovely,' said Angie, casting her eye over the newly created shop, which contained pottery, craft books, postcards and souvenir items such as jam pots and candle holders. 'It's really smartened up a scruffy corner.'

'We're pleased with it,' said Molly.

'Have you got many parties booked?' enquired Angie with interest.

'Just a few,' Molly told her. 'And they're well spread out. We're not booking too many. It'll become a burden if we do that, having to come in on a Saturday.'

'Mm, there is that.' She grinned, changing the subject. 'Anyway, Moll, come on, if we don't get away soon the day will be gone and it'll be time to collect the kids from school.' It was mid-morning and Molly was taking the rest of the day off to go shopping with her friend in Oxford Street. Dan was taking Angie to a smart and very popular nightspot – The Talk of the Town in Leicester Square – for her birthday treat in a few weeks' time and she wanted something special to wear. Molly had been enlisted as consultant.

'Are you sure you can manage here on your own, Hattie?' Molly was concerned.

'I think I might just muddle through,' smiled Hattie. 'Go and enjoy yourself and forget about this place.'

They got off the tube at Marble Arch and walked along Oxford Street to Tottenham Court Road, going into every dress shop. Angie tried several outfits on but was loath to make the final decision for fear she might see something she liked better elsewhere. They then retraced their steps and went to a ladies' outfitters they'd already visited. Angie was now ready to buy the dress she'd tried on. It was blue with a full skirt, a fitted waist and two wide shoulder straps.

'What did I say when you came in the first time?' said the pushy sales assistant, who'd taken a dim view of Angie leaving without buying the first time around. 'I said you'd be back. Didn't I say you wouldn't find anything better anywhere in London? You look a million dollars in that dress. Even Liz Taylor couldn't outshine you in that.'

The purchase complete, the two friends went to Lyons Corner House for lunch.

'Isn't it heaven having a day out together, Moll?' remarked Angie over braised steak and two veg. 'Just a few hours on our own with no kids; no responsibilities.'

'Smashing,' agreed Molly.

'We used to come up to the West End regularly for our clothes when we were single, didn't we?' she recalled.

'Yeah, and never bought a damned thing until we'd walked from Marble Arch to Tottenham Court Road and back again.'

'Those were the days,' smiled Angie.

'Happy times,' agreed Molly wistfully. 'But nothing stays the same, and in your case I'm sure you would say that your life has changed for the better.'

'Definitely. I'm so lucky. I married the man of my dreams and have the daughter I always wanted. I wouldn't want life any other way.' Angie looked at Molly. 'How are things going with you and Brian these days?'

'Fine.' Molly gave a wry grin. 'Now that he's away and we hardly ever see each other.'

'Oh, Molly, you are awful,' Angie giggled.

'I'm not trying to be funny.' Molly didn't pretend quite so much to Angie about her marriage now, though she still tried not to bad-mouth Brian. 'I'm just saying what's true.'

'It seems such a terrible shame.' Angie's tone became serious.

'It is. But ours never was a love story, was it?' Molly reminded her. 'It was a marriage of convenience that never worked out, as hard as I tried to make it. You can't force something that isn't there and is never going to be. Brian's working away is the best thing that could have happened for both of us. He would never admit it, but he was glad to go back after Christmas, and he doesn't come home at weekends.'

'What would you do if you met someone else?'

'Nothing,' Molly said without a moment's hesitation. 'I'm married to Brian and I'd never be unfaithful to him.'

'But you might get a second chance of happiness,' her friend suggested.

'I'd pass it by. If Brian met someone else and wanted us to split up, I'd let him go without any argument. But as far as I'm concerned, he stepped in when I needed him and I'll always be grateful to him for giving Rosa respectability,' she said. 'So, the chance of happiness with someone else just isn't an option. Not while Brian still wants our marriage to continue, anyway.'

'But you're still young,' Angie reminded her. 'Too young to have to spend the rest of your life with someone who is wrong for you. Who can say what might happen in the future?'

'Nobody can, of course,' agreed Molly. 'But the way I feel now, I've no intention of doing anything other than sticking the marriage out. Now that he's away, it isn't a problem. It's a tragic admission to have to make but it's the way it is. I would have loved a happy marriage but it just wasn't meant to be. I've got Rosa and she's my life.'

'You've got me too, kid,' added Angie. 'I'm always here for you, you know that, don't you?'

'I do and that means a lot.' Molly became grave. 'Your friendship is one of the most important things in my life. It's comforted and sustained me over the years. You've always been there in good times and in bad.'

'The same goes for me,' said Angie, her eyes becoming moist. 'In those dark days when I was ill, you were my lifeline. And now, when something good happens to me, you're always there to share it with me.'

Molly dug into her handbag for a handkerchief and blew her nose. 'Blimey. I don't know what's brought on all this emotion,' she said thickly. 'I think we'd better talk about something else before we both burst into tears.'

'I think we should too.'

'So you're off to The Talk of the Town, then,' said Molly, moving on swiftly. 'That's *some* birthday treat.'

'We've never been but it's supposed to be fantastic.'

'Everybody's talking about it,' said Molly. 'Even I've heard of it and I don't have a social life.'

'That's why Dan decided to push the boat out,' Angie said. 'They get the biggest names in show business appearing there in the cabaret.'

'He's one hell of a man, that husband of yours,' commented Molly. Brian had forgotten her birthday earlier in the year, but Angie had made the day special with a birthday tea at her place and gifts from her and the girls.

'He's the best.'

Seeing the tenderness in her friend's eyes at the mention of her husband, Molly felt an unexpected shiver of fear. The love that Angie and Dan had for each other was so special it made them seem acutely vulnerable, somehow.

Chapter Six

'Are you sure that the diamond solitaire at the back isn't too expensive, Brian?' asked Beryl as they peered at the engagement rings in the jeweller's shop window.

'Is that the one you like best of all?'

'Well . . . yeah, but I don't want to be greedy.'

'If that's the one you want, then that's the one you shall have,' he told her in a tender tone. 'Nothing's too much if it's going to make my girl happy.'

Her huge brown eyes gazed into his, full lips hovering in a smile. 'You're really something else, do you know that, Brian?' she said admiringly. 'I don't know what I've done to deserve someone as lovely as you.'

'Enough of your soft soap,' he teased her, slipping his arm round her and thinking what a little smasher she was with her long hair and peachy skin. 'You'll have the ring you want without any of that.'

'I wasn't just trying to get round you,' she told him earnestly. 'I really mean it.'

He believed her and it felt good. 'Come on then, let's go in so that you can try it on. Let's get ourselves engaged.'

'Ooh, Brian,' she breathed. 'Just hearing you say that brings me out in goose pimples.'

'I should hope so too,' was his light-hearted response. 'It isn't every day you get engaged.'

He hadn't intended to take things this far; he'd just got swept along. When he was with Beryl his marriage seemed almost not to exist. Anyway, the engagement was only a sweetener. To keep Beryl loving him and also to stay in favour with her mother. Flo Brown had made it clear from the outset that he trifled with her daughter's affections at his peril. He had no intention of actually marrying her. Molly was still the only woman for him, even though she never looked at him in the way that Beryl did, as though he was the most wonderful man alive. Putting a ring on her finger was merely a means of keeping his feet well and truly under the Browns' table until he was ready to return home to Molly.

Meanwhile his wife was going to get short pay this week because he

83

had to cover the cost of the ring. He'd send her something. She could whistle for the rest.

The ring fitted Beryl perfectly so they left the shop with it on her finger.

'I can't wait to show my mum,' she said, spreading her hand and gazing at the diamond from different angles. 'She won't half be impressed.'

Flo Brown was, indeed, impressed by Brian's expensive commitment to her daughter. But Brian's pals had the opposite reaction.

'You must be off your head, mate,' said one of them, to a chorus of agreement from the others. 'Having a good time while you're away from home is one thing, putting your head in a noose is quite another.'

'I know exactly what I'm doing,' Brian assured them.

'So your special night out lived up to all expectations then?' said Molly.

'It was wonderful,' replied Angie.

'Did Dan think you looked good in the dress?'

'Oh, yeah,' she said, smiling at the memory. 'He said I looked gorgeous.'

It was the Sunday afternoon after the Platers' night out, and Molly and Angie were out walking by the canal with the children while Dan was busy in the garden at home. The weather was fine, the air sweet with the approach of spring, the straggling hawthorn bushes that edged the towpath showing incipient signs of May blossom, a tangle of wild flowers and stinging nettles flourishing in equal quantities. The children ran on ahead to watch the craft going through the six locks at the Three Bridges.

'Don't go too near the edge, you two,' Molly shouted after them.

'We won't,' they called back.

The commercial traffic on this stretch of the canal had declined to such an extent that most of the narrowboats waiting in the lock, originally working barges, were now converted into pleasure boats on hire for holidays, modernised and painted in bright colours. The two women caught up with their offspring and stood at the side of the lock watching. But as it took a narrowboat one and a half hours to clear the flight, they ambled onwards after a while.

Continuing along the towpath, they passed the old wall surrounding St Bernard's Hospital – known locally as the 'loony bin' – then walked alongside overgrown wasteland and warehouses until they came to a quiet stretch flanked by trees, the children running and skipping ahead.

A sudden scream rent the air.

'Rosa's fallen in,' shrieked Patsy, staring into the water, on the verge of hysteria. 'Heeeeelp, heeeeelp, heeeeelp!'

Molly tore along the towpath to where her child was floundering in the filthy water. Off came her jacket and she was in without a moment's hesitation. Because Rosa was panicking and flapping her arms Molly couldn't get a grip on her and she slipped under. The water here covered Molly's shoulders and was certainly deep enough to drown a small, frightened child.

'It's all right, darling,' she said breathlessly, managing to raise her daughter's face above the water. 'Mummy's here.' But Rosa was so terrified, she fought against her and went under again.

Suddenly someone else was there, lifting Rosa and wading with her to the bank. The rescuer was the last person on earth she would have expected . . .

With Josh carrying the sobbing Rosa, they all hurried to Hattie's house, as it was the nearest, where Rosa's wet clothes were stripped off and she was put into a warm bath. Molly and Josh did the same soon after. There was no real harm done. Rosa was very shaken but uninjured. Molly, however, was very aware that the consequences could have been much more serious had Josh not stepped in. She was effusive in her thanks.

'Nothing to it,' he responded breezily. 'I was taking a short cut home from a mate's house and saw her fall in.'

'It was lucky you did take the short cut,' she told him gravely, relief making her sound rather dramatic.

'It's no big thing, you know.' He looked embarrassed. 'I just happened to be there, that's all.'

'It's a big thing to me,' Molly came back in a serious tone. 'I dread to think what might have happened if you hadn't been there and helped out.'

'I always knew my boy had it in him to be a hero,' praised Hattie, swelling with pride.

'He certainly is a hero in my book,' added Molly. 'I don't know how to thank you, Josh.'

The sound of a motorbike approaching heralded the arrival of Billy. 'Oi, oi, what's all this then?' he asked, coming into the kitchen where they were all gathered, Rosa wearing a dressing gown of Patsy's that was kept at her gran's for when she stayed overnight, Molly wrapped in one of Hattie's. 'You lot having a kinky party or something.'

'Your brother has made us all very proud, that's what,' replied Hattie, smiling.

Billy looked at Josh with a puzzled grin. 'What's he done? Managed to get through half an hour without going into a sulk?' he enquired in a jovial manner.

'Don't be rotten,' admonished Angie, and went on to tell Billy what had happened.'

'Blimey, I didn't know you had it in you,' responded Billy, giving Josh a friendly slap on the back. 'Well done, mate.'

'Well, I couldn't very well look the other way, could I?' Being the 'good boy' wasn't Josh's style and he wasn't comfortable with it. His mates would think he was a proper sissy if they could hear all this slush he was getting from the family. 'Now will you all stop going on about it, please?'

Most of the time Molly was a happy and confident single mum, which was effectively what she was now that Brian was away. But that evening – still shaken by Rosa's accident – she felt desperately alone and in need of company. In this vulnerable frame of mind, she was very pleased to receive a visitor . . .

'Angie thought you might be feeling a bit tense tonight after what happened this afternoon and might welcome some company,' Dan explained.

'That's so thoughtful of her.'

'She couldn't come herself because Patsy's unsettled after what happened and Angie doesn't want to leave her. So she wondered if I would do instead.' He put a bottle of wine on the kitchen table. 'We thought a glass or two of this might help.'

Molly burst into tears.

'Oh Lord, I must have lost my touch with women if all I can do is make you cry.' His levity was deliberate to save her from embarrassment. He handed her a handkerchief. 'That's what being married does to a man. You lose your technique from lack of use.'

'You fool,' she said, blowing her nose and smiling. 'I'm crying because I'm so touched. Angie always seems to hit the right spot with me.'

'She ought to after all the years you've been friends.'

'You're both so good to me.'

'As you are to us,' Dan pointed out. 'Now if you get some glasses I'll open the wine.'

'We don't have a corkscrew,' Molly was forced to admit. 'This isn't a wine-drinking sort of a home.'

'Not many are,' he said, producing a corkscrew from his pocket. 'It's quite a new idea for ordinary people like us so I thought you might not have one. I know Brian is strictly a beer man. I am usually too and wouldn't drink anything else in a pub. But a glass of wine indoors is nice and relaxing. It's getting to be quite the thing since more people started going abroad for holidays, apparently.'

They settled down in Molly's living room and chatted easily. 'It's very good of Angie to lend you to me for the evening,' she remarked.

'Angie and I have each other all the time,' he pointed out. 'A couple of hours apart isn't going to kill us.'

She sipped her wine, feeling more relaxed with every swallow. 'What about Josh this afternoon, then?' she remarked. 'Talk about the hero of the hour.'

'Yes, he certainly turned up trumps.'

'I've always thought there was some good in him somewhere.'

'They say there's good in everyone but it's hard to believe that of Josh, the way he behaves most of the time.'

'Mm, he can be a pain. I get the idea that he feels like the odd one out in that family, though,' she confided. 'I mean, Angie and Billy are so close and he's so much younger. He's always the butt of the jokes.'

'He can be a right heathen, though.' Dan sucked in his breath and shook his head slowly. 'I don't think it helps having his mum give in to him all the time.'

'Hattie certainly has a weak spot when it comes to him,' agreed Molly. 'It must be that her maternal instinct blinds her to his faults because she's so level-headed and fair-minded in every other respect. I'm sure it must have something to do with Angie and Billy being such pals. She thinks he feels left out and tries to make it up to him.'

'I always reckoned that national service would be the making of him,' remarked Dan. 'But he isn't likely to go in because he has a weak chest and probably won't pass the medical. Billy and I were talking about it the other day. Two years in the army would have sorted him out.'

'Well, after today he can't do wrong in my book,' Molly confessed. 'I thought I was going to lose my little girl, and because of him I didn't.'

Dan's warm eyes rested on her face. 'It must have been awful for you,' he said sympathetically.

'I'll say . . .'

'It's times like this you miss Brian, I expect,' he surmised.

'I've got used to him not being around,' was her noncommittal reply.

'Were you able to let him know what happened?'

'No. He can't be contacted by phone and there's no point in worrying him with it in a letter, as there was no real harm done. I'll mention it the next time he comes home for a weekend.'

Inevitably, the subject eventually turned to work.

'I've been thinking again about getting electric ovens installed,' Dan mentioned. 'I really think it's something we should do.'

'It'll have to be done at some point, that's for sure,' Molly agreed. 'It's the times we live in, progress and all that.'

'We'll have to have a meeting sometime soon and take a vote on it,' he suggested.

'Good idea. Meanwhile,' she said, raising her glass with a tiny drop of wine left in it, 'thanks for your company this evening. It's been lovely.'

'I've enjoyed it too.' The warmth of his smile gave her an inner glow. He was such a smashing bloke. Angie was very lucky.

Wanting a few private words with Josh the next day, Molly managed to catch him in the yard during his tea break. He was leaning against the wall, smoking a cigarette.

'I just wanted to say again how much I appreciate what you did yesterday,' she told him. 'You saved my daughter's life and for that I am eternally grateful.'

The sudden hatred in his eyes was chilling. 'Good. I'm glad you're grateful.' His tone startled her in its harshness. 'Because now you can show your gratitude as regards a certain matter.'

She stared at him. 'What are you talking about?'

'I'm sure you won't want to say anything to the family about that little bit of business I did on the side now, will you?' he said with a malicious gleam in his eye. 'I mean, you wouldn't want to shop the man who saved your kid's life.'

He was barely believable. 'You're better than this, Josh.'

'No,' he was quick to deny. 'What you see is what there is.'

'Are you so afraid you might have any redeeming features you eradicate them before they have a chance to show themselves?'

'Nothing as deep as that,' he made plain. 'I'm certainly not the hero you've been making me out to be since yesterday. Anyone would have jumped in and got your kid out of the cut. I just happened to be there at the time and couldn't very well ignore the situation. But since I did do it, I've decided that it will come in very useful.'

'So you're going to renege on our deal?'

'That's right,' he confirmed, apparently without compunction. 'I've finished dancing to your tune, having to be polite and all the rest of it. So you can say goodbye to all that malarkey. You're too much in debt to me for saving your daughter's life to say anything to the family about what happened. So don't talk down to me in future.'

'That's something I've never done,' she denied hotly. 'I would never do that to anyone.'

'Ooh, not much. You should listen to yourself,' he argued. 'You're always having a go at me.'

'Only because you're so damned awkward about every single thing, or you were until we made our little arrangement,' she informed him.

'And I will be again if you try to boss me about in future, and there ain't a damned thing you can do about it.' He drew hard on his cigarette and blew the smoke in her face. 'One good turn deserves another, that's the way you'd see it. There's no way you'd grass me up now, not after what I did yesterday.'

'What makes you so sure?'

'I know what you mothers are like. Your kids are everything to people like you and my mum and Angie. You'd do anything to protect them, and if someone does what I did for Rosa, there's no way you'd drop me in it.'

'You really are evil,' she told him through gritted teeth. 'I've defended you in the past. I've always believed there was some good in you, despite your constant hatefulness. But now I know that my faith was misplaced. You don't have a decent bone in your body. Anyone who would stoop so low as to use the saving of a child's life to their own advantage has got to be rotten to the core.'

'I've never tried to pretend otherwise,' he said with a nonchalant shrug. 'You were the one who started going on about my being some sort of a hero. You didn't hear me agreeing with you. One thing I never do is pretend I'm something I'm not. I am what I am and I'm not ashamed of it.'

'Then you should be.'

'Mind your own flamin' business,' he snapped, 'and keep on minding it. You've no right to tell me what to do, so don't even think about it.'

Without another word, Molly turned and walked back to the office, feeling bitterly disappointed in him. He was right, of course: she wouldn't spill the beans about him; not someone to whom she owed her daughter's life. But she knew he was going to give her a whole lot of aggravation again and make an issue about every little thing. Never in front of his mother, of course; he was far too cunning for that. But trouble ahead didn't bother her nearly as much as the final shattering of hope for him as a human being. She had been so sure he had a better side. But she'd been wrong. He was the bad apple in the Beckett barrel.

Molly and her mother and Rosa sometimes went shopping in West Ealing on a Saturday afternoon. Knowing that her mother enjoyed a wander around the shops when she wasn't working, Molly made herself available as often as possible to go with her. Part of the ritual was calling in to Lyons for a cup of tea and a doughnut for the adults, and a vanilla and strawberry ice cream for Rosa. One particular Saturday in spring the tea-shop was packed and they couldn't find a vacant table so stood hovering with the tray waiting for someone to leave.

'Cooee, over here,' came a familiar voice, and Molly saw Hattie, Angie and Patsy sitting at a table on the other side of the room.

They went over and exchanged greetings.

'If we put some of these bags on the floor, we can make room for you here with us,' suggested Angie 'That's it, Rosa, you sit next to Patsy.' She grinned. 'Just as if you'd want to sit anywhere else but beside your mate.'

They all squeezed in, companionably chatting about their purchases. Angie had brought a spring suit in one of the local dress shops; Hattie had bought a pair of shoes from Dolcis. 'You can strike lucky sometimes and get just what you want around here – another time you have to go to the West End.'

'My Peggy buys all her clothes from the West End,' said Joan proudly.

'Really,' responded Hattie politely.

'Oh, yes, she can afford West End prices,' she went on unabashed. 'She's done very well for herself, has Peg. Very well indeed.'

Molly was mortified at her mother's blatant boastfulness while Angie and Hattie nodded and tried to look interested as she informed them in boring detail of her elder daughter's material acquisitions: the car; the television; the new furniture.

'Well, you and I won't be out shopping anywhere next Saturday, will we, Hattie?' put in Molly in a desperate bid to change the subject.

'We certainly won't,' the other woman replied with a smile. 'With a bit of luck we'll be busy selling pottery this time next week.'

She was referring to the fact that the following Saturday afternoon they had a coach party of visitors from a branch of the Townswomen's Guild coming to the pottery for a demonstration.

'They're gluttons for punishment, these two,' grinned Angie, teasing them. 'They don't have to have the bother of parties of people coming to look around. The business does well enough without that. But what do they do? They land themselves with extra work on a Saturday.'

'It'll only be now and again,' Hattie reminded her. 'Anyway, we're looking forward to it, aren't we, Moll?'

'Yeah, it should be fun.'

'It was all Molly's idea,' explained Hattie in a complimentary manner. 'I'd never have thought of it in a million years. She's the imaginative one.'

'Trust Molly to come up with a daft plan,' said Joan disparagingly. 'She's always been like that. If there's a silly idea, she'll find it.'

'It wasn't a daft idea, Joan,' defended Hattie, becoming heated. 'It was a damned good one, as it happens. Anything we can do to put the pottery more firmly on the map can't be a bad thing. Besides, it's nice for people to be able to come and see how the things are actually made. We don't want the ancient crafts to die out through lack of interest, do we? It doesn't hurt us to put a couple of extra hours in every now and then.'

The atmosphere was fraught with tension. The others – realising that this had gone beyond general conversation and had developed into a spat between Hattie and Joan – kept a diplomatic silence.

'I suppose not,' said Joan indifferently.

'You must be very proud of your daughter, Joan.' Hattie wasn't prepared to let this go.

'Very much so,' said Joan, misunderstanding her. 'As I was saying, our Peg's done very well for herself.'

'Not Peggy.' Hattie was furious now. 'I'm talking about Molly. Aren't you proud of what a fine young woman she's turned out to be?'

'Well, I . . .'

'If you're not, you ought to be.'

'I am, of course,' she said, 'but Peggy's always been the achiever of the family.'

'I'm talking about people, not new things,' rebuked Hattie, while everyone else squirmed with embarrassment. Molly had never seen Hattie so angry. 'Anyway, Molly isn't doing too badly for herself either.'

'Yes, she did have a bit of luck inheriting a share in the pottery,' admitted Joan.

'A bit of luck, you call it,' bellowed Hattie, Angie now urging her to lower her voice. 'There was more to it than luck. My husband, God rest him, left her a part share in the pottery because of what she did for our daughter when she was ill, and also because she put so much into the job when she worked for him. A great deal of thought went into his decision. He wasn't the sort of man to do things lightly.'

'Really?' Joan was beginning to look uncomfortable.

'Yes, really,' confirmed Hattie sharply. 'Did it ever occur to you when she was spending all that time with Angie that it was a kind thing for a young girl to do, to give up her time for a sick friend? Girls of that age want to be out having fun. A lot of her other friends steered clear.'

'Of course I knew she was kind—'

'Yet all you ever do is put Molly down and praise that Peggy of yours,' Hattie cut in.

'Mum, that's enough,' warned Angie. 'Everyone in the place is looking at us.'

'Let 'em look.' Her mother wouldn't be deterred now that she'd got the bit between her teeth. 'I'm going to have my say about this because it needs saying.' She fixed Joan with a stare. 'I'll tell you this much, Joan Rawlings, your daughter is making a real success of her job at the pottery. None of us knows what we would do without her. And she's a good daughter to you as well; she calls in on you regularly, always makes sure you're all right. And all you ever do is go on and on about Peggy. It's Peggy this, Peggy that. What about Molly? Where does she fit into your scheme of things?'

'It's none of your business, Mum,' Angie reminded her, putting her hand on her arm as though to restrain her.

'Thank you, Angela,' said Joan haughtily, then turned back to Hattie. 'You heard what your daughter said, it isn't any of your business so keep your mouth shut.'

'The truth hurts, eh?'

'Oh, I'm not staying here to be insulted.' Joan began to gather her things.

'I think perhaps we'd better go,' Molly told the others. 'Finish your drink, Rosa.'

Molly and Rosa muttered their goodbyes and they left in a painful silence.

'Fine friends you have,' mumbled Joan as soon as they were out of earshot. 'Bloody cheek that woman's got. Fancy telling me how to run my family.'

'I don't know what got into her,' responded Molly, still smarting from the incident. 'She's usually the most easy-going of people.'

'She's no business to say those things.'

'No, you're quite right, she hasn't,' came Molly's dutiful agreement. But she couldn't help feeling touched that Hattie thought highly enough of her to leap to her defence with such vigour.

'You've really done it now, Mum,' admonished Angie after Molly and Joan had departed. 'It isn't like you have to have a go at someone like that.'

'No it isn't, but that woman gets right up my nose,' was her explanation. 'Always going on about that Peggy and never a good word to say to Molly. She's always been the same; she used to do it when you were children. It's a wonder Molly has grown up as well-adjusted as she has.'

'I think she gets hurt by it,' Angie mentioned, 'even though she would never show it.'

'Of course she gets hurt, anyone would,' Hattie opined. 'She's only human.'

'I hope Joan doesn't give Molly a hard time over your outburst,' said Angie worriedly. 'She might blame her for it.'

'Why would she do that?'

'She might think Molly's been talking to you about her.'

'Oh Lord, I didn't think of that. I was too carried away to worry about the consequences. I'd better go round to Joan's later on to smooth things over,' she said. 'I meant every word of what I said but I don't want Molly to suffer for it.'

'It'll be worth keeping the peace for Molly's sake,' suggested Angie. 'You don't have to grovel to Joan or anything. Just a few well-chosen words should do the trick.'

'Me and my big mouth,' tutted Hattie, making a face. 'I'll just have to swallow my pride and apologise to the woman for Molly's sake.'

There was a gathering of motorcycles outside the Acorn café in Hanwell Broadway one evening a few days later. Billy's was among them. He was inside with a group of pals, all genuine motorbike enthusiasts rather than the Hell's Angels types that gave motorcyclists such a bad name. Casually dressed in windcheaters, they were sitting around a table.

'It's about time we gave the bikes some throttle, you know,' suggested one of them. 'We should give them a chance to really open up.'

'We haven't had a long run-out in ages,' agreed another.

'How about a run down to Brighton at Easter?' put in Billy, cradling a mug of tea. 'It'll be a right laugh.'

'Good idea,' approved someone. 'There'll be bags of talent down there over the Bank Holiday too.'

'Exactly,' grinned Billy.

They were still discussing the idea when someone spotted a disturbance outside in the street, through the window. 'Oi, oi, looks like there's a bundle in the making out there. The teddy boys are at it again.'

'Oh, no, it's only my bloomin' brother,' wailed Billy, looking out of the window. 'The silly young sod. He can't stay out of trouble for five minutes.' He took a closer look. 'Even so, three of 'em on to him isn't fair. I'm not having that.'

The café emptied as everyone clattered outside.

'Here, what do you think you're doing?' intervened Billy, dragging a dark-haired youth away from Josh while one of his mates tackled the other, leaving Josh fighting with a ginger-haired lad. 'If you're gonna fight, fight fair with even numbers.'

'I'll teach you to go sniffing round my girl, Beckett,' roared the redhead, ignoring Billy. 'You won't do it again after I've finished with you.'

'Go after your girl,' snorted Josh, managing to hold the other boy back. 'I wouldn't touch her with an extra-long bargepole. And if you had eyes in your head, you'd see why. Where did you say you met her? Battersea Dogs' Home?'

'Hey, hey, that's enough,' reprimanded Billy. 'There's no call for that sort of talk.'

'I'll kill yer,' began the redhead, throwing a punch at Josh and missing.

'You couldn't knock the top off an ice-cream cornet,' responded Josh, waving his fists about.

Suddenly matters were taken out of Josh's hands as his mates and his enemies laid into each other. Billy's friends couldn't stand back and let it happen so there was a real rumpus. The sound of a police whistle sent them scurrying in different directions. Billy told Josh to hop on the pillion and they roared away.

'We'll just have to hope that Mum doesn't get to know we were involved in the scrap,' said Billy when they drew up outside the house. 'She'll go spare if she does find out. You know how she disapproves of fighting.'

'And you never did when you were my age, I suppose,' challenged Josh, swinging off the bike.

'I could always defend myself,' Billy readily admitted. 'A man's got to be able to do that to survive, especially in the army. But I didn't go looking for trouble. Never have done. Never seen the point of violence.'

'Why did you join in tonight then?' wondered Josh.

'I said I don't go looking for trouble, but if it comes my way I don't stand back,' Billy explained. 'You were in bother and needed my help.'

'Why would you help me when you hate the sight of me?' Josh wanted to know.

'I don't hate you.'

'You act as though you do.'

'What do you expect when you behave like a spoiled brat all the time?' Billy told him, still sitting astride the BSA. 'But you're my brother and us Becketts look after our own.'

Josh was silent for a moment, thinking. Then: 'We really gave 'em some, didn't we?' he said.

'Not half.'

The front door opened. 'Is that you, Billy?' Hattie called into the dark.

'Yes, Mum.'

'Who's that with you?'

'It's Josh.'

'You're not usually in this early.' She remarked.

'Nothing much going on,' fibbed Billy. 'So we thought we'd come and keep you company.'

'Aah, that's nice. You're just in time for a play on the telly,' she said.

'We'll be in soon,' called Billy, wheeling his bike round to the back of the house with Josh in hot pursuit.

'I ain't watching no soppy play on the telly like some old geezer,' objected Josh in a low voice. 'I'm going off to find me mates.'

'No, you're not. You're watching the play with Mum,' his brother told him firmly. 'I only lied to her about why we are home early because the truth would upset her. It isn't a good idea to go back to the Broadway now because there'll be coppers about.'

'Staying in watching the telly, though,' said Josh in disgust. 'I'll never be able to hold my head up again. Me mates will think I've gone soft.'

'I've had my evening ruined because of you and your fighting,' Billy told him. 'I was in the middle of planning a trip to Brighton at Easter. So stop complaining and go and make the cocoa.'

'Cocoa?' Josh was appalled.

'That's right,' confirmed Billy, chuckling. 'Mum likes a cup of cocoa of an evening and you know what they say about when in Rome . . .'

'So the coal-fired kiln will disappear from the landscape altogether soon then, will it?' asked one of the visitors as they gathered round the smoking kiln as part of the tour and Hattie had explained their future plans for electric firing.

'I don't expect we will actually demolish it right away. But we are planning to use electric ovens at some time in the future so it won't be in use then.' The decision had been made to go electric but Billy still insisted that there was no hurry. 'I don't know when the changeover will take place. It could be a while before we actually get the new ovens installed.'

'It won't alter the finished product, will it?'

'Not at all,' Hattie was quick to assure them. 'Everything will still be hand-crafted just the same as always. Firing will be a lot easier for us, that's all. We have to move with the times and take advantage of labour-saving devices. Many craft potteries have already made the change.'

'I hope you don't demolish it,' said someone, looking up at the chimney, shading her eyes from the spring sunshine. 'It's such a well-known local landmark.'

'I'm sentimental about it too, especially as my late husband built it,' Hattie told her.

'It won't be the same without it there,' said someone else. 'You can see it for miles.'

'As I've said, I don't know if it will be demolished,' Hattie went on. 'But it won't be smoking for too much longer.' She gave a wry grin. 'I know that our near neighbours will be very relieved to hear that.'

When the tour and pottery demonstration were over the visitors piled into the little shop and made significant spaces on the shelves, buying mostly souvenirs – egg cups, postcards, small pots and so on – though some larger pottery was also purchased.

'I think we can call that an unqualified success, don't you?' said Hattie, after they'd gone.

'Definitely,' agreed Molly.

'I enjoyed it too,' said Angie, who hadn't wanted to miss the visit and had been there throughout. Her role had been to look after Rosa and Patsy, who had been a big hit with the visitors.

'You lot had an easy time compared to us,' chipped in Billy jokingly. 'Us working men did all the graft. Isn't that right, Dan?'

'Dead right.'

'You poor hard-done by things,' laughed Angie. 'The truth is you both enjoyed every minute, showing all those women how clever you are.'

'Yeah, they were getting fancied rotten,' put in Josh. Even he was in a good mood. 'Same age group, you see; not a woman among them under forty.'

'Watch it, you,' warned Billy good-humouredly.

'When we get a party in from the youth club, it'll be your turn, love,' smiled Hattie, starting to count the takings.

'The youth club,' said Josh, looking pained. 'I think I'm a bit past schoolgirls and table tennis fanatics.'

'Dancing girls then,' laughed Billy.

'That's more like it,' said Josh with unusual good humour.

Beryl was full of wedding talk. 'You have to book everything up ever so early, Bri,' she told him.

'Really?' he replied absently, being deeply immersed in the *Daily Mirror*.

'Oh, yeah. At least a year ahead, so I've been told,' she confirmed, her cheeks flushed with excitement. 'Or you risk not being able to have the wedding at the church of your choice.'

'Fancy that.' He was still preoccupied with the newspaper and only half listening.

'So I think we'd better set the date now, and get the church booked . . . and the reception,' she went on happily. 'Once we've done that we can relax, knowing that it's all safely booked up.'

He looked up sharply, paying attention now. This was all getting dangerously out of hand. But even as panic began to rise, he consoled himself with the thought that everything could be cancelled as easily as it was booked and he wouldn't be around to take the flak. A part of him was enjoying it, though, because there had been nothing like this when he'd married Molly. No adoring bride longing to be his wife because she loved him; no church or flowers or party to organise. Just a quick register office do and something that passed as a reception at Molly's mother's place afterwards.

'So when do you have in mind then?' he enquired.

'I thought an Easter wedding would be nice.'

His eyes bulged because Easter was almost upon them. 'What!' he burst out.

'Not this Easter, you idiot,' she giggled. 'I'm talking about Easter of next year.'

'Of course. I should have realised.' He tried not to look too relieved.

'So what do you think about next Easter then?'

'Suits me fine.' It was just a fantasy for him, of course. He'd be long gone from here by then. But sometimes he found himself wanting to make fiction into fact; to make a new start with Beryl who thought more of him than Molly ever could. There was, of course, the little matter of his already being married to be taken into consideration and he had no intention of becoming a bigamist. Or of getting divorced, come to that. Oh no, he could never let Molly go. There was no doubt in his mind about that. His feelings for her were too deeply embedded in his psyche. So, in reality, this thing with Beryl didn't have a long-term future. But it was quite fun pretending.

'I'll start making enquiries then.' She paused thoughtfully. 'And talking of Easter – this coming one – shall we go out for the day on Bank Holiday Monday?'

He had to think on his feet because Molly would probably be expecting him home for the holiday. Still, he could always write and tell her he was working all over Easter. Yes, that was what he would do. He'd much rather be here in Norfolk with a woman who doted on him than at home playing dad to a child who wasn't even his.

'Yeah, let's do that,' he said. 'A bank holiday outing will be smashing.'

Chapter Seven

'I had a letter from Brian this morning to say he won't be coming home at Easter,' Molly told Angie. 'He's working all over the holiday, apparently.'

Working my eye, thought Angie, but said, 'Well, his loss is my gain because I'll be looking for company. Dan's got a date with a paint brush and wallpaper. He's decorating the lounge and it'll be best if Patsy and I keep out of the way as much as possible.'

'There's always the fear that he might put a paint brush in your hand if you stay around,' smiled Molly.

'He wouldn't dare,' she laughed. 'Running the home is my department, maintenance is most definitely his.'

'I'm a dab hand with a paint brush,' said Molly lightly. 'Hobson's choice, in my case, though. If I didn't do the decorating, it'd never get done.'

'Don't offer to teach me,' warned Angie with a wry grin. 'That's something I can live without.'

'Wise girl.' Molly moved on. 'So we can keep each other company over the holiday then?'

'Yeah. Even if we just take the kids over Churchfields, I expect we'll manage a few laughs. Mum will be on her own on Bank Holiday Monday. Maybe she'll fancy some company too.'

'The boys going out?'

'Yeah. Billy's going down to Brighton on his motorbike for the day, and Josh will be off out with his mates as usual.'

'If it's raining we'll play ludo or snap or something with the kids at my place, out of the way of Dan's decorating,' suggested Molly. 'The weather usually manages to do the dirty on us on a Bank Holiday Monday.'

'It'll take more than a drop of rain to stop us having a giggle, won't it, kid?' smiled her friend.

'It sure will,' agreed Molly.

Hattie invited Molly and Rosa to join the family for lunch at The Hawthorns on Easter Sunday. It was a friendly gathering over a delicious meal of roast chicken and all the accompaniments. Billy was full of his trip to Brighton the next day.

97

'Are you taking a girl with you?' enquired Molly, helping herself to another roast potato.

'What, with all that spare bank holiday talent about on Brighton pier?' he grinned. 'Not likely!'

'Honestly, you men,' tutted his sister good-humouredly. 'You've got one-track minds, the lot of you.'

'I hope you're not including me in that,' came Dan's mild objection.

'You were no angel before you started going out with me,' she reminded him.

'Maybe not, but I've been a paragon since you got me in your clutches, you've seen to that,' he teased her. 'I mean, where am I going to be when you lot are all out enjoying yourselves tomorrow? At home slaving away with a wallpaper brush. That must tell you something about me.'

'It tells us plenty,' put in Hattie. 'It tells us that your wife has got you well trained.'

'Under the thumb,' disapproved Josh.

'You're right, mate,' agreed Dan light-heartedly. 'But I'm there willingly.'

'You'll do,' approved Angie.

'He's a good lad,' added Hattie.

'So . . . are there a crowd of you going on this Brighton trip, Billy?' Molly wondered.

'Four of us,' he replied. 'All young, single and ready for anything.' He rolled his eyes, laughing. 'I don't know if there'll be any empty pillions on the way back. Depends how many of us get lucky.'

'It's high time you settled down,' opined his mother. 'You're coming up to twenty-five. You can't run around playing fast and loose for ever.'

'I've a few years left in me yet,' was his swift reply to that. 'I'm in my prime.'

'It's a wonder those mates of yours have stayed single so long,' Angie mentioned.

'Numbers have dropped off lately, I must admit. Several of the lads have got spliced and can't come out to play,' he told her. 'The rest of us enjoy the single life and want to stay that way.'

'They'll all get married eventually,' Angie replied. 'Then you'll have no one to knock around with.'

'I'll cross that bridge when I come to it,' Billy said. 'In the meantime I intend to carry on enjoying myself.'

'Think of me with my wallpaper brush when you've living it up in Brighton,' said Dan.

'Oh, yeah, I shall have you on my mind all the time,' replied Billy. 'I don't think.'

'I wish we were going to the seaside, Mummy,' said Patsy.

'Maybe we'll go at Whitsun,' her mother suggested. 'Daddy will have finished the decorating, and the weather will be more settled by then.'

'I'll bring you back a stick of rock to keep you going, sweetheart,' said Billy.

'Will you bring one for Rosa too?'

'Of course I will,' he promised. 'I wouldn't leave her out.'

This produced whoops of delight from the children and the meal progressed to its end against a background of noisy conversation and banter.

'What's your mum doing today, Molly?' enquired Hattie when everyone had finished eating.

'She's gone to Peggy's.'

'Oh, good, as long as she's not on her own.'

'I wouldn't have come if she had been,' Molly told her. 'I wouldn't leave her on her own on Easter Sunday.'

'She could have come with you,' suggested Hattie warmly. 'The more the merrier.'

Wild horses wouldn't have dragged Molly's mother to Hattie Beckett's house. Joan had told Molly that although she'd accepted Hattie's apology for her outburst in Lyons when she'd called to see her afterwards, she'd only done so to get rid of her, and hadn't forgiven her. She'd said she thought she was a dreadful woman and didn't want to be in her company *ever again*.

But now Molly just said, 'Another time perhaps.'

Hattie nodded, then heaved a sigh. 'Well, I suppose we'd better think about clearing away or we'll still be sitting here talking at teatime,' she said.

'It was a smashing meal, Hattie,' praised Molly. 'Thank you so much.'

'Thank you, Mrs Beckett,' added Rosa politely.

'Thank you both for coming,' said Hattie, warming Molly's heart. 'We love having you.'

Billy and his mates were standing outside a fish bar on Brighton seafront, deciding what to do next, when he saw her: the girl in the red sweater and black pedal pushers, her golden hair blowing in the sharp salty breeze. The ease with which Billy attracted women had given him rather a blasé attitude towards them. But there was nothing casual about his instant reaction to this one. She was so gorgeous he was rather in awe of her but desperate to get to know her. How was he going to do it, though? She was with a crowd of girls walking along the prom, and didn't look the sort who'd want to be picked up. There was only one thing for it. He had to seize the moment.

'Where's Billy rushing off to?' wondered one of his mates.

'Chasing skirt, of course,' came the reply.

'Excuse me,' said Billy, catching up with the girl from behind and tapping her lightly on the shoulder.

'Here, what do you think you're doing?' she demanded, swinging round to face him and throwing him a glare. 'Creeping up behind me and making me jump?'

She was even lovelier close up, he observed. Vivid blue eyes, a pert little mouth and lustrous, shoulder-length hair. 'Sorry. I didn't mean to startle you.' He gave her one of his most melting smiles, hoping he looked sufficiently contrite to win her over. 'Do you have the right time, please? My watch has stopped,' he fibbed.

'You could have asked anyone that,' she admonished. 'There was no need to creep up on a girl.'

'I didn't creep.'

'It seemed like it to me.' She looked at her watch. 'Anyway, it's nearly one o'clock. Happy now?' she said, and turned away ready to catch up with her friends.

'Don't go . . .'

Turning back to him, she said curtly, 'Look, I don't know what sort of girl you think I am but I don't pick up strange blokes.'

'You'll be all right with me then because I'm not the slightest bit strange,' he grinned, deliberately misunderstanding. 'A more ordinary sort of a fella you won't find anywhere.'

'You know what I mean.' She was beginning to soften, a hint of a smile visible now. 'You're not backward in coming forward, I'll say that much for you.'

'Standing back gets you nowhere, I've found,' he replied. 'Anyway, how else could I get to speak to you? I mean, it isn't as though we're likely to get formally introduced.'

'I suppose not . . .'

'Are you down just for the day?' he enquired.

She nodded. 'We came on the train. You?'

'A crowd of us came on motorbikes.' He couldn't take his eyes off her and wanted to know all about her. 'Where are you from?'

'Shepherd's Bush.'

'Oh, that's a coincidence because I live a few miles down the Uxbridge Road at Hanwell.'

'We're both on the same side of London then.'

'Mm.'

Her friends were calling for her to hurry up.

'Do you have to go with them?' he ventured.

'Of course I do. I came with them, so I can't very well desert them, can I?

'You could take a break from them and meet up with them again later on,' Billy suggested.

'I suppose I could. I'm not sure, though . . .'

'Any one of them would do the same if they met someone,' he swiftly suggested. 'Blokes would, anyway.'

100

'And if I come with you, what do you have in mind?' she wanted to know.

'Whatever you fancy.' He looked up at the sky, which was clear and blue with grey-edged clouds scudding across it. 'The wind's a bit chilly but it looks as though it might stay dry so we could take a stroll on the pier, have a drink, something to eat, a look around the amusements. Whatever you like.'

She ran an approving eye over him, noting the dark hair and deep rich eyes, the strong shoulders supporting the black leather jacket. 'I'll just go and tell the girls that I'll see them later,' she finally decided.

'I'll do the same with my mates.' He grinned at her. 'I'm Billy by the way. Billy Beckett.'

'I'm Sally,' she returned. 'Sally Smith.'

'Higher, Mum,' urged Rosa on the swing. 'I want to go higher so can you push me harder?'

'You'll go over the top if I do,' warned Molly. 'You're swinging quite high enough.'

'I want to go higher too,' chipped in Patsy.

'No, this is just right.' Angie was firm. 'Anyway, you'll both have to come off the swings in a minute and let someone else have a go.'

'I'm dying for a cuppa,' said Hattie, from a seat nearby.

'Me too,' added Angie. 'When we can drag these two away from the swings, let's have a walk down to the café in the Bunny Park. You can have an ice cream, kids.'

The magic words had the desired effect. 'Cor, yes, please,' they chorused.

They were in Churchfields and had been there for most of the afternoon. The sunshine was intermittent and there was a cold breeze. But they all had coats on and were on the move so they weren't too uncomfortable. The lovely old trees that were so abundant in this park were in fresh new leaf, and clusters of daffodils splashed the landscape with colour.

The mothers and girls walked to Brent Lodge park and refreshed themselves in the cafeteria. The adults were ready to go home now but the children got distracted in the little zoo and wanted to wait until the peacock fanned out its tail feathers.

'I think I'll go on home and get tea ready for us,' said Hattie, shivering. 'I'm getting a bit cold now. You follow on in your own time and there'll be some food waiting for you when you get back.'

'That'll be nice, Mum,' approved Angie. 'I hope this damned peacock isn't going to keep us waiting too long before putting on a show. I fancy going home myself.'

'See you later then,' said Hattie, striding off.

'We won't be long.'

'You hope,' added Molly with a wry grin. 'It all depends on that ruddy peacock.'

Billy and Sally didn't get round to meeting up with their friends again that day. They became too wrapped up in each other even to think about it. Conversation came easily, as did laughter. He learned that she was twenty-one, was currently without a boyfriend and worked in an office in Shepherd's Bush. They walked around with the crowds, wandered along the pier, spent time in the amusements and visited various cafés. Billy knew somehow that this meeting was significant; that his life was about to change.

'Fancy coming home on the bike with me instead of going by train with the girls?' he suggested as the afternoon drew to a close. 'We can have a fish supper before we leave and I'll deliver you right to your front door.'

'Yes, please,' she said eagerly. 'That sounds like fun.'

It was turned five thirty by the time the peacock finally obliged its audience, and Molly, Angie and the girls finally set off for Hattie's across Churchfields.

'I've enjoyed today, Moll,' remarked Angie as they walked under the viaduct and headed for the Broadway. 'Just a simple outing to the park but it was nice.'

'I've had a good time too. And back to your Mum's for tea to round it off,' said Molly. 'Lunch yesterday, tea today – I'm really being spoiled.'

'You know Mum, she enjoys a houseful.'

'Luckily for me.'

'Dan should be there when we get back too,' Angie went on. 'He said he'd meet us there. He was expecting to finish the decorating this afternoon.'

'Aah, look at the pussycat,' said Patsy as a ginger cat appeared from a front garden, his great green eyes fixing on her as he miaowed pitifully.

'Isn't he sweet?' added Rosa, as the animal rubbed circles around her legs. She bent down and fondled its head. 'He lets you stroke him. He's ever so tame.'

'He might be a she,' Patsy pointed out.

'Let's not split hairs, darling,' suggested her mother.

'I want to stroke him,' said Patsy, bending down.

But the cat had had enough petting, and streaked away. Patsy darted off in pursuit.

'Come back here, Patsy,' shrieked Angie, tearing after her daughter who was heading for the main road at a busy junction. 'Patsy, mind the road!'

Everything happened so fast after that, it was a blur to Molly when she thought back on it. The cat darted across the road, and Patsy went after it, heedless of the fact that she was in the path of an oncoming car. Before anyone could stop her, Angie threw herself forward and pushed her child to safety. There was a screech of brakes and a thud, and Angie was lying in the road. She was very still.

A crowd quickly gathered and one of the shopkeepers called an ambulance. Molly was on her knees beside her friend while some kind person held on to Patsy and Rosa.

'Look after Dan and Patsy and Mum for me, Moll,' Angie uttered weakly, blood running from the corner of her mouth. 'Please promise me you'll do that.'

Struck with terror but trying not to show it, Molly held her hand. 'I don't need to promise you that because you'll be doing it yourself,' she said, biting back the tears. 'The ambulance will be here in a minute. They'll soon get you to hospital.'

'Promise me, Moll.'

'All right, I promise,' Molly said just to please her.

'Thanks, Moll,' Angie said in a whisper, her lids drooping. She had lost consciousness by the time the ambulance arrived.

Molly couldn't go with her to the hospital because the children needed her with them. Patsy was sobbing and Rosa looked very frightened. Through a blur of tears, Molly watched the ambulance race out of sight. She had never prayed harder in her life.

It was late that night and Molly was at The Hawthorns waiting for Billy to come home from Brighton to tell him what had happened. The rest of the family were at the hospital. Molly had put the children to bed and was in the kitchen on her own, trying to sit but mostly pacing up and down. Hattie had telephoned from the hospital about half an hour ago to say that there was no change. Angie was still unconscious.

Telling Hattie and Dan about the accident had been the hardest thing Molly had ever had to do. Hattie had been happily humming a tune in the kitchen when Molly and the children had arrived; she was putting the finishing touches to the table, which was laden with sandwiches, apple tart and home-made cakes. Dan had been looking pleased with himself too because he'd finished the decorating. Then Molly had shattered their mood with just a few words. They'd dashed off to the hospital and she'd waited here for Josh to come home to tell him the awful news.

Soon she was going to have to go through the whole thing again with Billy.

Billy was talking to Sally outside her house. It had been the most wonderful day of his life and he didn't want it to end.

'I've had a smashing time, Billy,' she told him. 'Thanks ever so much. And thank you for bringing me home.'

She was thanking *him*. 'No need to thank me,' he said. 'I've had a belter of a time too.'

'I'm glad.'

'Can I see you again?' came his inevitable enquiry.

'Course you can.' They got on so well, tactics were unnecessary. They both knew their meeting was important.

'Are you free on Saturday night?' he asked.

She nodded.

'Fancy going up the Palais?' he asked. 'It's good on a Saturday night.'

'I'd like that.'

'I'll come over on the bike but have my suit on under my jacket. About seven thirty. OK?'

'I'll look forward to it.'

Billy, who never had any qualms about kissing a girl good night, felt shy about kissing Sally. She was so special he didn't want to put a foot wrong. But she might think he didn't fancy her if he didn't, so he gave her a smacker on the lips, to which she heartily responded. He said he'd see her on Saturday, got on the bike and roared away into the night.

His heart was singing as he raced down the Uxbridge Road. This was what people meant when they talked about there being a right one for everybody. He'd always thought it was rubbish until now. He'd had plenty of girlfriends; fancied himself in love once or twice. But he'd never met anyone who'd made him feel like Sally had made him feel today: happy, excited, full of hope for the future. He couldn't wait to see her again.

That's funny, someone's still up at this late hour, he thought, seeing the lights on as he drew up outside the house. He took the bike round the back and went in at the kitchen door.

'Molly,' he said in surprise, 'what are you doing here?' He walked into the empty kitchen, looking around. 'Here on your own? Where is everybody?'

'They're at the hospital.' Her mouth was so dry she was hardly able to utter the words.

His smile faded. 'Hospital?' he echoed.

'I'm afraid there's some bad news, Billy.'

'What's happened?' he said in a fast breathless tone. 'Is it Mum? Has something happened to Mum?'

'No, no. Your mum's all right.'

'Oh, thank God. Who is in hospital then?'

'There . . . there's been an accident,' she forced the words out, feeling sick. 'Angela was knocked down by a car.'

His face turned grey. 'Is she . . . how bad is she?'

'They've just phoned from the hospital.' She couldn't do this; she couldn't tell him but knew that she must. Her words sounded distant. She didn't even feel herself saying them. 'She . . . she died ten minutes ago.'

104

She caught him as his legs buckled and held him until he steadied himself. Whey-faced and shaking he said he must go and join the others at the hospital right away and tore out of the door. Seconds later she heard him roar away on the bike. She rushed to the bathroom to be sick.

They all came back an hour or so later and everyone sat around drinking tea, talking and weeping. Molly couldn't go home anyway because Rosa was asleep in bed here but she felt they needed her here with them even though she wasn't family. Angie had been such an important part of her life, her blow almost equalled theirs. It was the most painful thing she had ever experienced.

'Thanks for everything, Molly,' said Hattie. 'For waiting here and telling the boys.'

'The least I could do.'

'I can't believe it,' said Billy, holding his head. 'It just isn't fair. The bloke who knocked her down should be hanged. I'll kill him if I get hold of him.'

'That sort of talk won't bring her back,' said Hattie thickly, her eyes red and swollen.

'It wasn't the driver's fault,' Molly told them sadly. 'Patsy ran out right in front of him and Angie dashed into the road after her. He didn't stand a chance.'

'She was too young to die,' Billy went on, too distracted to be rational. 'Twenty-six. It isn't right.'

'No, son, it isn't right or fair,' wept Hattie, her voice distorted by grief. 'My lovely daughter, taken so young. They say everything happens for a reason but I'm buggered if I know what possible reason there could be for this.'

Dan was saying nothing, Molly noticed. He had a deathly pallor, and looked strange around the eyes; as though there was no life in them.

No one even considered the idea of going to bed. They just talked themselves out and dozed in the chairs. The next morning Hattie said she would look after Patsy as Dan, being the next of kin, would have lots to attend to. There was no school because it was the Easter holidays and Molly wasn't due to go in to work. But Hattie asked if she would mind going in for a few hours, and she would look after Rosa. Someone ought to be there to answer the phone, and Hattie didn't feel up to going herself.

It was when Molly left The Hawthorns and went home to get changed that the full force of Angie's death began to register. Her best friend and soulmate had gone. No more chats, no more laughs, problems thrashed out or exchange of daily minutiae. She'd been closer to Angie than her own sister, her mother; everyone. Now there was no one to turn to. The pain was deep and aching. Like many ordinary blessings, her friendship with Angie had been not exactly taken for granted but relied upon always to be there.

Sitting at the kitchen table, her coffee went cold as she was lost in thought. There was a wailing inside her she couldn't release. She remembered Angie's dying wish and realised that the family's grief must be worse than her own. It didn't help. She still felt wretched. Deciding she must pull herself together, she washed her face and combed her hair, went to the post office to send a telegram to Brian – since there was no phone at his lodgings and she thought he should be notified of news of this magnitude – then she went to see her mother.

'Angie dead?' breathed Joan, turning pale and sinking down on to a chair. 'I can't believe it.'

'Me neither,' said Molly.

'Poor Angie. Her poor mother,' Joan went on, her voice barely a whisper. 'How do you cope with a thing like that? I mean you're not meant to outlive your children.'

'And Dan and Patsy,' mentioned Molly. 'What's it going to be like for them?'

'Put the kettle on, will you?' requested Joan, sounding winded. 'My legs are like jelly.'

Molly made the tea and poured them each a cup. 'I don't know what I'm going to do without her either, Mum.' Suddenly she needed physical comfort from her mother. She wanted to feel her arms round her and hear her soothing words. In that fleeting selfish second, she wanted someone to acknowledge *her* loss, to realise that *she* as well as Angie's family had had the heart torn out of her.

'You'll miss her, of course; you've been friends a long time,' said Joan in her restrained way. 'But it isn't as though you're family. It isn't like losing a sister or anything.'

It felt worse, but Molly just said, 'No, of course not.'

'I'll pop round to Hattie's to offer my condolences later on,' Joan said.

'That's nice.'

'I can't stand the woman,' Joan was quick to point out, 'but this is no time for bad feeling.' She paused, looking at Molly. 'If you need me to look after Rosa, I'll do what I can when I'm not out at work myself. I know that Angie used to help you out in the holidays if you were stuck.'

'Thanks, Mum. I appreciate that.'

Molly knew that the offer of help with Rosa was the nearest thing to solace she would get from her mother, but she was making an effort and that meant a lot.

When she left her mother's Molly went into work, glad to have something to do.

Billy was there working at his wheel.

'Need to keep busy,' he explained when she went over to him. 'Josh has stayed home with Mum. You know him, any excuse to skive off.'

She guessed that the jibe was his way of trying to keep some sense of normality at this most abnormal of times. 'Still, at least this time he has a genuine reason,' she pointed out.

'Mm, there is that.' He sighed, shaking his head. 'Honestly, Moll, I don't know how Mum's going to get through this. It was bad enough for her losing Dad, but Angie too . . .'

'I'm worried about her too,' she confided. 'We'll all have to make sure we give her plenty of support.'

'I can't get over how everything can change so suddenly,' he went on. 'I was on top of the world coming back from Brighton because I met this terrific girl. Rolling along on the bike back from her place I was so happy and excited about the thought of seeing her again. Not a care in the world. Then wallop, I lose my sister and everything falls apart.'

Something deep inside Molly grew and rose up into the back of her throat and she could hold back the tears no longer. 'I know I'm not family,' she sobbed, 'but Angie was such a dear friend. We were closer than sisters and I don't know what I'm going to do without her.'

'Come here, you.' He got up from his wheel and hugged her, both of them weeping. 'You're bound to miss her as much as we do. I don't know what any of us are going to do without her, especially Dan and Patsy. We'll all have to help each other.' They held each other for a long time in an embrace of pure friendship. Eventually – when they were both calmer – he moved back.

'Now look at you, you've gone and got clay all over your clean clothes.'

'That's the least of my worries.' She felt slightly better; the tears had released some of the tension. Billy had given her the comfort she'd so much wanted from her mother.

'Ooh, my Gawd, the telegram boy is coming here,' gasped Flo Brown, her hand flying to her throat as she stared out of the window. 'Lord Almighty, someone must have died.'

'Don't panic, Mum,' Beryl tried to calm her. 'It doesn't have to be bad news.'

'Well, we wouldn't have won the pools, would we, 'cause we don't do them? So what else can it be but bad news?'

She opened the door and took the telegram with a shaky hand. 'Oh. It's for you, Brian,' she said, flushing with relief and sinking into an armchair. 'Ooh, that's given me quite a turn. Thank Gawd you two decided to come home for your dinner today and I wasn't on my own. I thought I was gonna pass out cold.'

Beryl and her mother watched Brian anxiously as he opened the telegram.

'What is it, Bri?' asked Beryl, biting her lip. 'Who's it from?'

The news of Angie's death shook him rigid and he was reeling from it. He had to think quickly, though, because questions were going to be asked.

'It's from my sister, Molly,' he lied. 'Her best friend has been killed in an accident.'

'Oh dear. How terrible,' sympathised Beryl.

'What a shocking thing,' added her mother. 'She couldn't have been very old.'

'Twenty-six.'

'That's awful,' said Flo.

'Did you know her well?' asked Beryl.

'Yeah. I knew her.' He'd never liked Angie but her death was a blow because she was of his generation and expected to be around for many years ahead. 'I'll have to go back to London for the funeral,' he told them, guessing that Molly would be devastated, and feeling duty-bound to go with her to the funeral. 'To give my sister a bit of support, you know.'

'Would you like me to come with you for company?' offered Beryl.

'No, no, I'll be all right on my own,' he swiftly assured her.

'I think I should come,' she persisted. 'We're going to be married soon and I want to be there for you in bad times as well as good.'

'It's sweet of you to offer but I'd better go on my own,' he tried to dissuade her. 'My sister will be upset and might want me to herself.'

'Oh, yeah, there is that,' said Beryl in an understanding manner. 'Just as long as you know that I'm always there for you when you need me.'

She really was the most warm-hearted girl. 'That's nice to know,' he said.

'I didn't even know you had a sister,' Beryl remarked.

'Haven't I mentioned her?' he said innocently.

'No.'

He shrugged. 'I don't know why. Just didn't get round to it, I suppose.'

'Oh, well, give her our heartfelt condolences when you see her,' said Beryl.

'Will do.'

Phew, that was a close one. Thank God he'd had his wits about him and come up with a sister, or things could have become very tricky. He didn't want to upset the applecart here. It was far too comfortable.

Because The Hawthorns was bigger than Dan's house and was where Angie had grown up, they had the funeral from there. It was what Hattie wanted and Dan respected that. There were a great many mourners and practically the whole town had turned out as the funeral cortège passed slowly along the Broadway. The cemetery had been packed too.

'It's a good do they've put on, I'll say that much for them,' Brian

108

remarked to Molly back at The Hawthorns for the wake. 'Plenty to eat and lots of booze. It was worth coming back to London for.'

'You heartless bugger,' she admonished. 'Is that all you care about, your creature comforts?'

'Course not,' he denied. 'But as they've put on such a good spread we might as well make the most of it.'

He didn't understand how utterly bereft she felt. He'd never had a good word to say for Angie so Molly had been amazed that he'd bothered to come home for the funeral. But he'd made the effort and had been sympathetic in his own clumsy way when he'd first arrived, so she supposed that was something in his favour.

She left him talking to a relative of the Becketts and went over to Dan.

'It was a lovely service,' she said.

'Yeah, I suppose so.'

'Patsy seems to be holding out quite well.' Dan had decided that Patsy would not attend the funeral so she'd stayed with a neighbour and had only joined them for the social gathering afterwards. Rosa was being looked after by Molly's mother.

'She's too young to understand the full impact,' he said dully.

'Yes, of course.'

'If there's anything I can do at any time, you only have to let me know,' she told. 'I can collect Patsy from school and look after her until you finish work, for instance.'

'Thanks. It's nice of you.' He seemed frozen; he even looked different. His normally healthy complexion was mushroom colour and his eyes were lifeless. 'Can I get you a drink?' he offered politely. 'Or something to eat?'

'I'm all right for the moment, thanks,' she said. 'And I'll help myself to some food when I'm ready. Just remember I'm always there for you. We've always been good friends, Dan. I'm sure Angie would want that to continue.'

'Of course,' Dan said woodenly.

'I'll go and have a word with Hattie now,' she told him, sensing that he wanted to be left alone. 'I see that Patsy's with her.'

'See you later then.'

Watching her walk across the room towards Hattie and Patsy, Dan felt the anger inside him rise and fester as the thought that had haunted him ever since the accident came unwanted into his mind; a fact that had been mentioned by no one. If Patsy hadn't run into the road that day, his wife would still be alive now. The torturous truth filled him with resentment towards his beloved daughter, as well as loathing for himself for harbouring such feelings. He knew he was being unfair and must never articulate his thoughts to anyone. The blame for his wife's death must not be put on the shoulders of a seven-year-old child.

★ ★ ★

'How are you getting on, Hattie?' asked Molly.

'Surviving, just about,' she sighed, moist-eyed and pale. 'It's been the most terrible day of my life, though. George's funeral was bad enough, but this . . .'

'Can I play with Rosa later on, Auntie Molly?' interrupted Patsy, sounding subdued.

'Yes, of course you can, love,' said Molly. 'As long as it's all right with your dad.'

'You don't want to stay with your gran then?' Hattie said, teasing her.

'I think she just wants some company of her own age,' Molly suggested.

'Yeah, course she does,' nodded Hattie.

'Dan's taken it hard, hasn't he?' mentioned Molly as Patsy wandered off.

'He's withdrawn right into himself,' replied Hattie, shaking her head. 'You can't get him to talk about it at all. He's hardly said a word since it happened.'

'I've noticed how quiet he is.'

'And how about you, love?' enquired Hattie. 'How are you bearing up?'

'I . . .' Molly couldn't speak.

'Come here.' Hattie hugged her, tears running down her cheeks. 'We'll help each other, you and me.'

Josh sauntered up. 'Are you all right, Mum?' he asked with obvious concern. Even Josh had rallied round his mother at this awful time.

'I'll never be all right again, son,' she told him sadly. 'But I'm coping. Molly and I are just shedding a few tears together.'

'Anything I can get you?' he asked.

'No, but go and make sure all the guests are all right, will you, son?'

'Sure.'

'I'm lucky to have such sons,' Hattie confided to Molly. 'I know Josh can be a bit of a scallywag but he's being a good boy now. Poor Billy's so cut up, I don't think he knows what day of the week it is. He and Angie were so close. He's been good to me though; no one could have done more.'

'I'll go and have a few words with him,' Molly said, and went to find him.

'Hi, kid.' Billy looked pale and drawn. 'How's it going?'

'I'm managing. You?'

'The same as you,' he said. 'We just have to get on with it, don't we?'

'That's about it.'

'Poor old Dan,' he went on to say. 'He's in a right state. God knows how he's going to manage. Those two were so devoted.'

'Your mum and I were just talking about him.'

Billy glanced across the room. 'Someone's having a good time, anyway,' he said, looking at Brian, who was in conversation with someone and swigging whisky as though they were about to run out. 'I reckon one of us will have to carry him home the way he's knocking it back.'

'Oh, no,' Molly groaned. 'I turn my back for five minutes and he shows me up. He just has to overdo it every time.'

'Funerals have that effect on some people,' Billy pointed out, to spare her embarrassment. 'I've had a good few to drink myself, and more than one of our relatives are already three sheets to the wind.'

In the event, Dan gave Molly and Brian a lift home in his car because Brian was in no fit state to walk.

'Thanks for helping me out with him,' she said to Dan after they had dragged Brian into the bedroom and left him sleeping it off on the bed.

'That's all right.'

'I feel bad about Patsy. I said she could come and play,' she told him. 'But a small flat with a drunken man in it is no place for a child to be.'

'No.'

'The children will be back at school next week and Brian will have gone back to Norfolk so she can come and have tea with Rosa after school and I'll look after her until you've finished work, if you like,' she suggested. 'I expect Hattie will be back at work soon and she works longer hours than I do so it'll be easier for me to look after Patsy.'

'Thanks,' he said stiffly. 'I know I should have but I haven't got around to thinking about practicalities yet. I just can't seem to think straight.'

'It's only natural,' Molly consoled. 'Thanks again for helping me with Brian.'

'No problem.' He headed for the front door and opened it. 'See you then,' he said.

'See you.'

All ready for her date with Billy, Sally Smith gave herself the once-over in the wardrobe mirror and was pleased with what she saw. She was wearing a white low-necked blouse, a black pencil-slim skirt with a red bolero jacket and black stilettos. She didn't usually wear a huge amount of make-up but she'd made a special effort tonight and her hair was worn in its usual natural style.

She was just in time. He would be here at any minute. It was just coming up to half-past seven. She went downstairs to the living room to wait for him.

'You look lovely, dear,' said her mother, giving her an approving look. Her parents were watching the television. They were an ordinary middle-aged couple and Sally was their only child. 'Are you going out with a boy?'

'That's right.'

'I thought you might be.'

'Anyone special?' her father enquired.

'Very special.'

Neither enquired further, knowing how irritable girls of that age got if quizzed about details. They would find out in their own good time.

'What time is he coming for you?' asked her mother.

'He'll be here any minute,' she said, going to the window.

Half-past seven came and went. Eight o'clock. Eight thirty. Sally was fuming. All that chat he'd given her in Brighton – she'd really believed it. She'd honestly felt that there was some special chemistry between them. And none of it was true because he'd humiliated her by standing her up. Bloody cheek! As well as angry she was bitterly disappointed because she'd liked him so much. She had no address or phone number for him. Not that she would have used them if she had. She wasn't grovelling to the likes of him.

'Perhaps you could go out with your girlfriends,' suggested her father helpfully. 'Seems a shame to stay at home when you've taken so much trouble to get ready.'

'They'll all have gone out by now,' she snapped.

'I suppose they would have,' agreed Mrs Smith warily.

'Anyway, I wouldn't want them to know I'd been stood up. I'd be a laughing stock,' she burst out, hot tears burning her eyes.

'Oh, love,' said her mother kindly, 'try not to upset yourself too much.'

'I'm not upset, not in the least,' Sally denied, and thundered upstairs to her bedroom, slamming the door behind her.

'They've all gone at last,' sighed Hattie, sinking into an armchair. 'I can't say I'm sorry. I'm absolutely worn out.'

'Put your feet up, Mum, and I'll get you a nightcap,' offered Billy. 'Would you like a brandy?'

'No more alcohol for me today, son,' she said, stifling a yawn. 'But I'd love a cup of cocoa.'

'I'll make you one then,' he offered.

'I thought we were never gonna get rid of them,' put in Josh. 'It's turned eleven o'clock now and they've all been here since this morning.'

'People get talking at a time like this, don't they?' she said wearily.

'You can say that again,' agreed Billy.

'It's understandable. Relatives who haven't seen each other for years meet up and have a lot of catching up to do. They mean well and they think they're being supportive by staying on for a long time.' She paused, remembering something. 'I thought that Brian Hawkins really let Molly down by getting himself plastered.'

'He's a waster, that bloke,' was Billy's scathing response. 'She's too good for him.'

'That's common knowledge,' agreed Hattie. 'He's nothing but a liability to her.'

'Can I have something stronger to drink than cocoa, Mum?' asked Josh. 'There's plenty of booze left over.'

'Help yourself, son.'

They settled down in the armchairs, Hattie with her cocoa, the boys with a glass of beer each.

'The day has got a peculiar feel to it, don't you think?' remarked Josh.

'All the days have felt queer to me since the . . .' Hattie swallowed hard, 'since the accident.'

'It doesn't feel like a Saturday night at all, does it?' added Josh.

Saturday night! Alarm bells rang in Billy's head. It was Saturday night. He'd had a date with Sally tonight at half-past seven. In the shock of his sister's death and the build-up to the funeral he'd forgotten what day of the week it was. She'd think he'd stood her up. Oh God, he hoped he didn't lose her over this. Not that on top of everything else.

His first instinct was to jump on his motorbike and go over to Shepherd's Bush now, despite the late hour. But his mother needed him here and he wouldn't leave her. Not tonight.

'Would you like a biscuit with your cocoa, Mum?' he asked kindly.

'I think I might be able to manage a custard cream, please, dear,' she replied. 'I've hardly eaten a thing all day, even though there's been enough to feed an army.'

'I'll go and get the biscuits for you then,' he said, going to the kitchen.

Chapter Eight

It was almost noon the next day before Brian emerged in his dressing gown, looking like death, a hand clamped to his brow. 'Ooh, my head. It feels as though the Cup Final is going on inside it,' he groaned, sitting down at the kitchen table. 'Get us some Alka-Seltzer, will you, Moll?'

Without comment she did as he asked, putting the tumbler of fizzing liquid down on the table in front of him rather forcefully, causing him to wince.

'Hey, steady on.' He swallowed the contents of the glass and made a face. 'I'm feeling very delicate this morning.'

'Don't expect any sympathy from me.'

He looked at her, his eyes narrowed as though he was in pain. 'Ooh, you're a bit narky this morning,' he remarked.

'Can you blame me?'

'All I did was have a few drinks.'

'No, what you did was use a sacred occasion, the funeral of my dearest friend, as an excuse to get paralytic,' she corrected. 'I was disgusted with you.'

'So that's all the thanks I get for coming all the way from Norfolk to give you moral support.'

'Moral support? From you?' Her manner was sharp and questioning. 'Don't make me laugh. All you ever give me is aggravation and embarrassment.'

'After all I've done for you.' He still had his hand to his head and was peering at her through half-closed eyes. 'You've got a very short memory when it suits you.'

'Oh, change the record, for goodness' sake,' she urged him. 'How much longer are you going to keep ramming that down my throat? You married me because you wanted to. It was all your idea, as I remember. You were dead keen and I've never stopped being grateful to you. But don't talk to me about moral support because I haven't had any of that from you for years.'

'I wish I hadn't wasted my money on the fare home,' he grumbled. 'All I get from you is earache.'

She also wished he hadn't come home. She was out of the habit of being treated like a slave; of tending to his hangovers, and putting up with his moods. She didn't want him in her bed either. The only saving grace of his getting drunk was that he was incapable of making any demands on her.

'What time is your train?'

'You can't wait to get rid of me, can you?' he accused.

It was hardly surprising that she was eager to see the back of him but she said, 'The reason I asked is because I wondered if you'd want your Sunday dinner a bit earlier.'

'Just wondered about my Sunday dinner, my arse.' His voice rose to a shout. 'You want me out of the way. You've probably got some bloke lined up. He'll be in here before I get to the end of the street, I bet.'

'Don't be so childish.'

'You have, haven't you?'

His unfounded accusations finally got her so rattled she wanted to slap him, and her hand rose in an involuntary movement. But before she had time to strike, there was an interruption from the doorway.

'Stoppit, stoppit,' sobbed Rosa. 'I don't like it when you're here Daddy because you're always horrid to Mum. You shout all the time. Why don't you go away?'

Her words echoed into an agonising silence. Molly hadn't realised Rosa was in the flat. She'd been playing outside in the street and the door was left on the latch for her. Instinctively protective, Molly went to her and put a comforting arm around her.

'Out of the mouths of babes, eh?' Brian snarled. 'I know when I'm not wanted.'

'She's just a child, Brian, she didn't mean it.'

'I did mean it, I did.' Rosa struggled from her mother's arms and fled from the room.

Molly went after her and found her sitting on the edge of her bed weeping.

'Grown-ups can't agree all the time, love,' she tried to explain, smoothing Rosa's hair from her damp young brow and wiping her tears. 'Everyone has rows. The same as you sometimes quarrel with Patsy.'

'I hate it when he's here. He's always nasty to you. I hate him, I hate him.'

'I probably raised my voice to him too.' Molly wanted to be fair to Brian, even though she knew that Rosa didn't love him and was happier when he wasn't around. Although she had never told her daughter that Brian wasn't her father, she sometimes wondered if Rosa instinctively knew. She had never shown any affection towards Brian, even as a toddler, and never seemed to expect any from him. 'It wasn't all his fault.'

The conversation was halted by the appearance of Brian. 'It's all right, you can both relax,' he said coldly, his pale face darkened by overnight shadow. 'I'll get washed and dressed, pack my things and shove off. I'll be gone in half an hour.'

With immaculate timing, one of the neighbourhood children knocked at the door to ask Rosa to go out to play, leaving Molly and Brian alone.

'There's no need for you to go off in a huff,' Molly told him. 'Rosa's just a kid. She isn't old enough to control her feelings or choose her words.'

He shrugged. 'I might as well go anyway. I'm too hungover to want anything to eat so I'll push off and get an earlier train.'

'Look, you can't blame me for being angry with you.' No matter that he was the transgressor, he still managed to make her feel that she was somehow in the wrong and should justify herself. 'Losing Angie has hit me harder than anything I've had to deal with before. The last thing I could handle yesterday was you needing to be carried home.'

'Yeah, I suppose I was out of order,' he agreed in the sudden realisation that it suited him to get away as soon as possible. 'Sorry about that, babe. But I think I'll get off back to Norfolk a bit sharpish. It's a long journey. I don't want to get back too late because of work tomorrow.'

'I can see your point.'

Less than half an hour later she saw him off. As she closed the door behind him she felt weak with relief, and sensed that he felt the same. How on earth were they going to adjust to being together all the time when the job in Norfolk was finished? It didn't bear thinking about. She felt terribly alone suddenly. She was used to a bad marriage, but she would never get used to not having Angie to turn to. The dark, aching grief touched every aspect of her life.

What a waste of time that had turned out to be, thought Brian, as he walked to the bus stop. He'd have been better off staying in Norfolk and going to the pub with Beryl as usual. She didn't care how drunk he got. She was usually in a worse state than he was on a Saturday night, anyway.

All he'd got in return for his trip to London was a raging hangover and a load of grief from the wife. All right, so she had lost her best friend and was feeling a bit low, but there was no need to take it out on him. He'd always reckoned she'd thought more of Angie than her own husband, anyway.

Never mind, he'd done his duty and come home for the funeral. It had served another purpose too, because he wouldn't be expected to return for a good while now. So he was free to enjoy his bachelor life – uninterrupted – with the doting Beryl.

'Is Sally in, please?' asked Billy when a woman he assumed to be her mother answered the door to him.

117

'No, she isn't,' she said coolly, having been primed by Sally when they'd seen him approaching the house through the window.

'Can you tell me when she'll be back, please?' he persisted. 'I need to see her urgently.'

'You've got a nerve showing your face around here,' said a thick-built man with a mop of greying hair, appearing by the woman's side. 'After letting our girl down last night. She doesn't want to see you again, so bugger off.'

The door was slammed in his face.

He knocked again.

'Clear off,' came her father's booming voice from the hall.

Billy shouted through the letter box, 'I know you're in there, Sally. I must see you. I'm really sorry about last night. Please just let me explain.'

The door opened and her father stormed out. 'If you're not off this doorstep in five seconds I shall call the coppers,' he threatened. 'Five . . . four . . . three . . .'

'My sister was knocked down by a car and killed,' interrupted Billy in desperation. 'The funeral was yesterday. I've been in such a state all week, I forgot what day it was. That's why I didn't turn up.'

'I've heard some excuses in my time but that just about takes the biscuit,' reproved her father. 'You ought to be ashamed of yourself, coming out with a thing like that.'

'I wouldn't make up something like that,' Billy told him in a subdued tone and the pain in his eyes was obvious. 'I thought the world of my sister. She was the best. Anyway, as you're not prepared to listen, will you just tell Sally that I'm sorry about last night, please? That's all I ask.'

He marched off and was about to get on his motorbike when Sally came rushing out of the house.

'Oh, Billy, Dad's just told me,' she said breathlessly. 'I'm so sorry about your sister.'

'Oh, thanks.'

'When did it happen?'

'She died ten minutes before I got home on Monday night after leaving you,' he explained. 'I've been in a hell of a state ever since. I've hardly known what I've been doing, let alone what day of the week it was. When I realised it was Saturday late last night I wanted to get on the bike and come over right away but I didn't want to leave Mum. She needs me right now, as you can imagine.'

'Come inside,' Sally invited gently. 'We can talk properly indoors.'

After such a bad start, Billy got along famously with Sally's parents. Her father was an electrician, her mother a housewife. Billy told them something of his family background. They were very sad to hear about Angie.

118

'It's only six months since my dad died so it's a shocking blow. We're all breaking our hearts, but God knows how Mum must feel,' he told them, puffing out his lips and shaking his head. 'My brother and I can give her plenty of support. But we can't ease her pain.'

'Knowing that you're there for her will help, though,' suggested Mrs Smith.

'Keep that in mind, son,' added her husband.

'I think she'll feel better when she gets back to work,' Billy told them, and went on to explain about the pottery. 'There's nothing like being busy to take your mind off things.'

They nodded in agreement.

'My sister's husband's taken it very hard, the poor bloke,' Billy went on to say. 'It's going to take more than work to put him right, I reckon.'

'Any children?' asked Mrs Smith.

'A little girl,' replied Billy. 'The poor mite's bewildered at the moment.'

'Aah,' came a sympathetic cry from Mrs Smith.

They chatted for a while longer, then Billy said he had to get back because he didn't want to be out for too long. Sally went with him to the gate.

'I'll understand if you can't get away or if you don't feel like going out much at the moment,' she told him. 'People go into mourning, don't they?'

'Angie wouldn't want us to mope about,' he said. 'We're not that sort of family, anyway. But obviously I shall need to be at home more often than usual for a while to give Mum some company in these early days. Perhaps you and I could just go for a quiet drink together at the weekend. I wouldn't stay out too long, though.'

'Whatever's best for you, Billy.'

He dug into his pocket for his wallet from which he extracted a Beckett Pottery business card. He wrote his home number on the back and handed it to her. 'I think you'd better have one of these so that you can contact me if you need to at any time. We don't want a repeat performance of last night.'

'I'll say we don't.' She glanced at the card. 'Thanks for this.'

He felt pierced with joy just at being with her, and was immediately ashamed. He shouldn't be feeling happy about anything with poor Angie dead and buried. But he couldn't stem the jubilation that Sally's very existence evoked in him. He hardly knew her, and it was far too early to tell if they had a future together, but he felt as though he could get through anything with seeing her again to look forward to.

Although Angie had never actually worked at the pottery, she was very much a part of the place, and the fact that she would never again call in for a chat hung over them all to such an extent the air of gloom was tangible. No one seemed to have anything to say; even the workshop radio was switched off.

After a week or so of this dreadful morbidity, Hattie asked Molly to go with her into the workshop.

'Listen up, everyone,' Hattie said loudly and purposefully, 'I've got something to say.'

The men stopped what they were doing and waited for her to continue.

'This place is like a ruddy morgue and Angie wouldn't want that, being the person she was, full of life and laughter. Obviously none of us is in the mood to split our sides laughing but I think we ought to make a bit more of an effort to cheer up, with respect to her and our own sanity. We have to come to work every day so let's try and have a bit of normality about the place.'

There was a murmur of agreement although Dan stayed silent, looking grim. Billy turned the radio on. He didn't join in as he usually did but at least the sound of Lonnie Donegan's 'Rock Island Line' made the atmosphere a little better.

'Well done, Hattie,' said Molly, going over to her, only to see that she was crying.

'They're young. It isn't right for them to go about like the living dead,' she said thickly. 'We've had enough death and misery in this family just lately.'

'Come here,' Molly said, giving her a hug, then leading her back to the office, her own eyes wet with tears. 'We'll get through this somehow, I promise.'

'I'm so glad I've got you, Moll,' the older woman confided. 'The boys are a couple of gems but sometimes another woman is what you need. I miss my Angie so much.'

'Me too, Hattie,' said Molly sadly. 'Me too.'

'When will Daddy be coming for me?' Patsy enquired.

'Any minute now, I should think, love,' replied Molly.

'Will I have time to finish this picture?' Patsy asked. Both the children were busy with the crayons at the kitchen table.

'If not you can finish it tomorrow,' suggested Molly, who collected Patsy from school every day and looked after her until Dan had finished work.

'It's almost done anyway,' the child announced proudly. 'What do you think, Auntie Moll?'

It was a picture of a house under a bright yellow, spiky sun and three people with huge red grins. 'It's Mummy and Daddy and me,' she explained.

'It's lovely,' complimented Molly. 'Well done.'

'Do you think Dad'll like it?' It seemed of great importance to her. 'I've done it specially for him, to cheer him up.'

120

'I'm sure it will.' There was a knock at the front door. 'Here he is now. You can find out for yourself.'

With childish zeal, she followed Molly to the door and rushed up to her father. 'Hi, Dad,' she greeted.

'Hello, Patsy,' he said wearily, absently patting her head.

'Do you like my picture?' she asked, handing it to him. 'It's us. You and me and Mummy.'

He looked at it but didn't say anything.

'When we look at it we'll think of her,' the little girl added hopefully.

Molly's heart broke to see his cold attitude towards his daughter. He'd been distant with her ever since Angie's death, and it tore Molly apart. For a moment she thought he was going to rip the picture up. It had obviously upset him; his dark frown made that abundantly clear. He looked at it again, then at Patsy and handed it back to her.

'It's very nice,' he said dully. 'Now get your things together quickly so that we can go home. It's been a long day.'

His rejection of her hung palpably in the air. Molly felt it as if it was her own.

'Rosa, will you go with Patsy to get her things and play in your bedroom while Uncle Dan and I have a chat?' she requested. 'I'll call you in a few minutes.'

'What's all this about?' he demanded as Molly closed the living-room door behind the children. 'I don't have time for a chat. I want to get away.'

'You're breaking her heart, Dan,' she said worriedly.

'I don't know what you mean.'

'Yes, you do. Patsy is seven years old and has just lost her mother. She needs her father like never before. You must grieve, of course, but don't shut yourself off, especially not from Patsy.' She looked at him, her blue eyes steady and full of determination. 'From what I've seen, all you ever do is push her away. I haven't seen you show her any love since Angie died and she's hurting dreadfully, the poor little thing.'

'It's none of your business.'

'It's everyone's business when a child is suffering,' she pointed out.

'I don't make her suffer,' he denied, horrified at the suggestion. 'I've never laid a finger on her.'

'There are more ways of harming a child than with physical violence. Indifference from a loved one is a painful thing,' she told him. 'I can hardly believe how much you've changed. Patsy spends her whole time trying to please you, and all you do is turn your back o her.'

'What do you expect?' he retaliated. 'If it wasn't for her Angie would be alive today.'

'Oh, so that's it.' Molly was shocked. 'You blame her for the accident.'

'She ran into the road, didn't she?' he reminded her bitterly. 'If she hadn't done that her mother wouldn't have needed to throw herself in front of the car to save her life and lose her own. The child's been told not to go in the road often enough.'

It was as though he'd driven a fist into Molly's chest. 'She's a little girl, Dan. Her enthusiasm for the cat pushed all thoughts of road safety out of her head,' she told him gravely. 'Even though she hasn't said anything, she might already be feeling responsible for her mother's death. It's up to us to make sure that any such thoughts don't take root by not mentioning the details of what happened. If she finds out that you're blaming her, she'll be scarred for life.'

'I don't intend to tell her.'

'She'll guess as she gets older if you carry on as you have been,' Molly stated categorically. 'Angie's death was an accident. Passing blame isn't going to bring her back. You can't burden a seven-year-old child with a thing like that. It could cause serious psychological problems.'

'If you say so,' he said with weary indifference. 'Though I really don't see what business it is of yours.'

'We've been friends a long time, Dan,' she said in a softer tone. 'I know you're hurting and you want to hit out. But please don't do it to Patsy. She's been through enough.'

'Look, I really appreciate your helping me out with her, collecting her from school and so on.' His face was grim and twisted. 'But I don't appreciate your telling me how to behave towards my own daughter. Now I'm going home. I have to get Patsy to bed.' He gave her a hard look. 'Contrary to what you believe, I do actually look after her properly.'

'I'll see you tomorrow then,' Molly said sadly.

Driving home, Dan wondered why he'd said those things to Molly. He'd vowed that he would never make his feelings known to anyone about Patsy's part in the accident. It must have occurred to the others but everyone had kept a diplomatic silence. With the best will in the world he couldn't stop the thoughts and feelings coming. There was this burning rage inside him that made him feel as though he hated Patsy. It was as though losing his wife had killed his love for his daughter.

But he knew he must make an effort with her. 'What did you do at school today?' he asked dutifully.

'Nothing much,' she replied, still smarting from his attitude towards the picture.

'You must have done something.'

'Sums and spelling and stuff,' she said miserably.

'It was a very good picture you drew for me,' he said to ease his conscience. 'We'll put it up on the wall, if you like.'

With a child's capacity for instant forgiveness, she said, 'Oh, can we really, Daddy?' She was pitifully grateful for the smallest crumb of affection.

'Yeah, course we can.'

'Cor, thanks, Dad.'

'That's all right.'

He pulled up outside the house and a familiar feeling of dread consumed him. He loathed going inside, knowing that Angie wouldn't be there. He loathed himself for his self-pity but was powerless against it.

Until recently, Molly wouldn't have believed anything could hurt so much. All the pain of her life – deserted and pregnant at nineteen, an unhappy marriage, a lifetime of being second best to her sister – paled into insignificance against the agony of losing Angie. Everything Molly did, everywhere she went, reminded her. Walking by the canal in her break, memories flooded in. They'd played here as children; climbed, jumped, skipped, giggled. The dreams and longings of adolescence had been shared here. Later they'd walked here with children of their own, watching them play, seeing them grow. In Churchfields Angie's spirit was in every fresh-scented breeze that rustled through the trees.

Even shopping in the Broadway prodded at the relentless ache of missing her. All the shop assistants knew they were friends because where there was one, there was usually the other. People were sad but felt awkward and didn't know what to say to Molly.

She confided in Hattie one day at work when they both happened to be at the filing cabinet. As time had passed she'd realised that Hattie needed to talk about her daughter. Angie had been a friend as well as a daughter to Hattie, who now seemed to need Molly's friendship. Molly certainly welcomed hers. They drew strength from one another.

'I want to weep because the memories of her are all around me but I'm glad too that I'm in the places where we were together,' said Molly. 'It makes her feel closer somehow.'

'I know, love,' sighed Hattie. 'I can feel her in the very air I breathe.'

'I don't think I'll ever get used to her not being around.'

'Nor me.' Hattie paused, thinking. 'Look, why don't you and Rosa come round to our place for tea on Saturday?' Hattie had always spent Saturday afternoons with Angie, and Molly suspected that she found that time of the week particularly hard to bear. 'I'll have Patsy round. She and Rosa can play in the garden if the weather's nice. I'll invite Dan but I doubt if he'll come. He's a miserable bugger these days – withdrawn right into himself. He doesn't seem able to cope at all. Probably be glad to get shot of Patsy. Never seems to have time for the poor love.'

'I think he's too traumatised to know what he's doing,' said Molly, needing to defend him suddenly. 'He adores her really.'

'Oh, yeah, I know that,' Hattie was quick to agree. 'He's always been a good father. But he's in a world of his own now that Angie's gone, and Patsy, she needs him so much, the poor little duck.'

'Anyway, Rosa and I would love to come on Saturday but I'll have to check with Mum first,' Molly told her. 'She sometimes likes me to look round the shops with her if she's not doing anything.'

'Bring her with you,' suggested Hattie warmly. 'She'll be very welcome.'

'That's very kind of you, Hattie,' Molly said. 'I'll speak to her about it and let you know.'

Predictably, Joan didn't welcome Hattie's invitation but agreed to go along with Molly out of courtesy and to offer support to the grieving woman. It was a fine spring afternoon on Saturday, and Patsy and Rosa had a whale of a time in the garden.

'It's good to see them enjoying themselves,' remarked Molly, as the adults sat on some rather ancient wooden garden chairs on the lawn watching them. 'They have to play in the street when they're at my place.'

'They're probably just as happy with that,' said Hattie.

'They like the fact that there are a lot of other kids about, certainly,' mentioned Molly. 'More people to join in the games.'

'A garden's better for them, though, isn't it?' put in Joan. 'Peggy's got a nice big . . .' Her voice tailed off. The least said the better about Peggy to Hattie, who was obviously jealous of how well she had done for herself.

They were interrupted anyway by Billy ambling out into the garden, followed by Josh, who sat down on a wooden bench near his mother.

'It's a pity you two girls aren't boys,' said Billy to the children, who were playing leapfrog on the grass.

'Why?' wondered Patsy.

'I could play football or cricket with you if you were.'

'We can play those,' said Rosa gamely.

'Yeah, we can,' added Patsy. 'But we like other games better. Rounders or feet-off-ground are our favourites.'

'What about a game of hide and seek?' suggested Billy.

'Cor, yeah,' chorused the girls.

'Come on, Josh, you too.'

'Not me, mate. I'm well past that sort of thing.'

'This afternoon you're having a second childhood,' his brother informed him. 'So get off your arse and help me out here. And you women aren't going to sit about doing nothing either. On your feet. You too, Joan.'

'Not me.'

'We'll provide the refreshments. You men can provide the entertainment,' instructed Hattie. 'That's a fair trade. Go on Josh, get moving.'

Complaining bitterly, he went to join Billy and the girls.

'You can't be outwardly miserable when there are children around, can you?' Hattie remarked. 'No matter how much your heart is breaking you've got to keep cheerful for them.'

'That's very true,' agreed Joan.

'I don't expect Billy wants to play hide and seek any more than I do, but he's making the effort to keep them entertained,' Hattie went on.

'He's very good with the children, isn't he?' Molly mentioned.

Hattie nodded. 'He'll make a wonderful dad.' She gave a wry grin. 'If he ever settles down and has any kids.'

'I heard that,' said Billy, who happened to be passing on his way to find the children. 'And I might surprise you on that front before very long.'

'Really?' said his mother. 'Another new girlfriend?'

'That's right.'

'Where's the surprise in that?'

'She isn't that new. I've been seeing her for a while, as it happens. Anyway, she's different,' he told her, becoming serious. 'As a matter of fact I'm thinking of bringing her home for Sunday tea sometime soon.'

'Blimey. It must be serious.'

'It is.'

Dan appeared unexpectedly through the back gate.

'You decided to come after all then,' greeted Hattie. 'I'm glad about that.'

'I thought I'd drop in.'

'Hi, Dad,' said Patsy, running to meet him.

'Hello, Patsy,' he said, ruffling her hair when what the child so obviously wanted was a great big hug.

'You're just in time for a game of hide and seek,' Molly told him.

'Bad timing on my part then,' he replied.

'Don't be such a spoilsport,' admonished Hattie. 'You're as bad as Josh.'

'All right then,' he said with a noticeable lack of enthusiasm, his face gaunt, his eyes sad. 'What do you want me to do?'

The game progressed, the men eventually tiring of it and leaving the children to play on the swing. The women went inside to get the tea: salmon and cucumber sandwiches, toasted teacakes, home-made seed cake and other traditional favourites.

'I suppose you two are off out tonight,' said Hattie to her two sons when they were all seated around the dining-room table.

'Can't stay in on a Saturday night, can you?' said Josh. 'Well, you can't when you're young and single, anyway. That would be the height of social failure.'

'Well, I'm meeting my special girl.' Billy was still very considerate of

125

his mother's feelings even though some time had now elapsed since Angela's death. 'That is, as long as you'll be all right here on your own, Mum.'

'How many more times must I tell you, I don't need a nurse,' she admonished good-humouredly.

'Mum and I will be here for a while, anyway,' mentioned Molly.

'Can I stay the night, Gran, and keep you company?' asked Patsy.

'Course you can, pet,' agreed Hattie. 'As long as it's all right with your dad.'

'No, it isn't all right with me,' he said with electrifying effect. 'She's coming home.'

'But, Dad—'

'No buts about it,' he snapped. 'You're not staying the night here and that's that.'

'But why not?' Hattie wanted to know. 'She's stayed here lots of times before; when you and Angie used to go out. There's a bedroom ready for her.'

'She is not sleeping here tonight because I've said so.' Dan's voice rose angrily. 'She's got to learn that she can't have her own way all the time.'

The silence was so abrasive, it made Molly smart. Rosa looked worried while Patsy's eyes were brimming with tears.

'That's a bit hard on her, isn't it, mate?' ventured Billy.

'What do you know about it?' Dan growled. 'You haven't got any kids.'

'No, but—'

'So stop telling me how to bring up mine.'

'I was only saying.'

'Well, don't bother because I can do without your advice.'

'Look here, Dan,' intervened Hattie. 'You're not the only one hurting, you know. We're all in pain too. But life goes on. We all have to make an effort.'

'Oh, I've had enough of this,' he declared, standing up purposefully. 'Come on, Patsy. We're going home.'

'But she hasn't finished her tea,' Hattie pointed out.

'I'll give her something at home,' he informed her briskly. 'I'm quite capable of feeding my own child, you know. Come on now, Patsy. Get whatever you brought with you and go out to the car.'

Pale with fright, and with tears rolling down her cheeks, she slipped off her chair and left the room.

'This is all wrong, you know, Dan,' admonished Hattie, 'the way you're carrying on.'

'None of your business.'

'She's my grandchild, which makes it my business.'

'Grandparents have no legal rights,' he reminded her. 'So I want no more criticism. Do you hear? And he marched from the room, leaving a troubled silence behind him.

'That is one screwed-up man,' said Billy at last. 'He's been my best mate for years but he's turned into a stranger. I don't know him at all now.'

'I don't think any of us does,' sighed his mother sadly. 'Well, let's finish our tea. Any more seed cake, anyone?'

But they all seemed to have lost their appetites.

When they left Hattie's, Molly asked her mother if she would take Rosa home and look after her for a short time because there was something she had to do.

'Oh, no. Not you,' was Dan's greeting when he opened the door to her.

'I'm afraid so.'

'I suppose you've come to give me an ear-bashing, even though I've made it clear that I don't want any lectures or advice.'

'Can I come in, please?'

'I'd rather you didn't . . .'

'Please. Just for a few minutes.'

With a sigh of seething irritation, he stood aside and she went through to the lounge, a smart room with an overall effect of pale green and cream shades, and sleek contemporary furniture. With icy politeness, Dan invited her to sit down.

'Patsy's in bed,' he explained as though to pre-empt her enquiry, 'and yes, I have pacified her and read her a story and done everything a father should.'

'I'm not here to check up on you.'

'Oh, really? What are you here for then?'

'To see if I can help in any way, actually,' Molly informed him.

'Have you developed a way of raising people from the dead then?' was his sarcastic response.

She didn't rise to it; just lowered her eyes. 'I miss her too, you know, so do Hattie and Patsy and Billy and Josh,' she reminded him. 'But we don't take our grief out on other people.'

'What Angie and I had was something so special you couldn't possibly understand.'

'Obviously I haven't had first-hand experience of it because I haven't been lucky in love,' she readily admitted. 'But Angie was a very dear friend and I feel as though my world has fallen apart now that she's gone. And how do you think poor Hattie must be feeling, losing her daughter? She didn't deserve what you gave her earlier – not allowing Patsy to stay, just to prove that you're in charge when it comes to your daughter. You're glad enough of Hattie to look after her when it suits you.'

Perched stiffly on the edge of the armchair, he stared at the floor. 'Yes, you're quite right,' he admitted, looking up with a weary sigh of acceptance, his torment visible in his eyes. 'I suppose I'd better go and see her tomorrow and apologise.'

'She'll appreciate that.' Molly was thoughtful for a moment. 'Would you let Patsy come to the park with Rosa and me tomorrow afternoon?' she asked. 'Patsy seems to get comfort from being with Rosa. Friends are so important at that age.'

'She gets a damned sight more pleasure from being with Rosa than with me, that's for sure,' he said miserably.

'Children need other children,' she pointed out, deciding not to add that he wasn't fit company for anyone at the moment, let alone a seven-year-old child.

'I suppose so.'

'I'll pick her up about two o'clock then, if that's all right, and have her back here by teatime.'

Dan's head was bowed and his body began to shake as he tried to stifle his sobs. As she instinctively went to comfort him, he shrunk away. 'Please go, Molly,' he said, covering his face with his hands. 'I want to be on my own.'

Molly knew she must respect his wishes but she left the house feeling extremely anxious about him. He was normally such a caring man and a devoted father. It was shocking what terrible things grief did to people.

Molly was even more worried about Dan the following week when he ruined a batch of pottery through firing the kiln at the wrong temperature. It was too high and everything was warped.

'He's getting to be a liability,' Billy confided to her worriedly one day in the workshop when Dan had gone outside for some fresh air. He'd taken to doing this; he usually stood by the canal staring at nothing. 'I mean, I know the bloke's grieving for his wife, and I'm really sorry for him, but he's beginning to cost the firm money now. He really will have to get a grip.'

'He will in time, I'm sure.'

'He needs to, for Patsy's sake more than anything,' Billy went on. 'We can make up for the loss of stock – these things happen in craft work like ours for all sorts of reasons – but a little girl's feelings are more difficult to mend.'

'I'm as worried as you are about it,' she confessed. 'Patsy seems to want to spend all her time at my place with Rosa, rather than at home with her dad. You can see her tense up when he comes to collect her.'

'I wish there was something we could do to help, but he won't let anyone near,' Billy continued. 'I've tried but he just won't have it.'

'I know. I've tried too.'

'I think the world of the man,' Billy went on. 'We've been mates since we were schoolboys, but he's hell to be around at the moment.'

'You can say that again.'

'This latest fiasco of a firing has made me think it's time we stopped using the coal-fired kiln and got electric ovens installed,' he said, changing the subject slightly. 'We've already decided to do it so I think the sooner the better now. Mistakes are made and accidents happen whichever method you use in a delicate operation like ours. But I think the time has come for the firm to spend some money on modernisation. It will get rid of all the filthy hard work involved in firing the oven and make life easier all round.'

'There won't be any argument from the others about that so we'd better start getting it organised,' Molly said.

'Wotcha, Molly,' greeted Syd – who ran the antiques stall outside the pottery shop – when she arrived one fine summer's morning. He was one of the rogue traders who disregarded the council's rules and traded here on other days of the week besides Saturdays. 'How's it going, luv?'

'Not so bad, Syd. Yourself?'

'Earning a crust, you know,' he replied cheerfully. 'How are things in the pottery trade?'

'Pretty good, thanks.'

'How's Hattie now?' All the traders around here knew the Beckett family because they'd had the shop for such a long time. 'Still cut up about young Angie, I expect.' He shook his head. 'A shocking thing to happen.'

'She's coping, I think. She's a tough old bird.'

'How about Angie's husband?'

Molly's brow furrowed. 'Not good,' she told him gravely. 'Not good at all.'

'Poor bloke. My heart goes out to 'im. It doesn't make sense, does it? A thing like that.'

She shook her head.

'How are the brothers?'

'They're all right. Missing their sister, of course, but they're learning to live with it.'

'I've always liked Billy. He's a smashing fella, straight as a die and always ready for a laugh and a joke. But the younger one's a shifty young weasel.' Syd was a plain-speaking man and didn't hold back for fear of causing offence. 'I wouldn't trust him further than I could throw him. When I saw him hanging around the market last Saturday, I kept my eyes well fixed on my stock. I always do when he's around.'

There was nothing odd about Josh coming to Portobello market in his spare time. Thousands of people did. Molly had been here herself many times, long before she'd had to come every week for business. On Saturdays it was a seething mass of people with everything from carrots and cucumbers to solid silver trays on display. But she felt uneasy knowing that Josh had been hanging around near the shop at a weekend. Had he been setting up some dodgy deal?

'Anyway, I must get on, Syd,' she said, careful not to make any comment. 'See you later.'

'Cheers, luv.'

Peter was busy setting out some new stock when Molly went into the shop.

'I love the new range,' he commented after they'd exchanged greetings. 'Very modern. The colours are fabulous.'

'A joint effort between Billy and Dan, Billy's design, Dan's the expert on colour.' Although Dan's work had deteriorated, he'd done a good job with the shades of colour on this range.

Peter stood back, putting his head at an angle as he studied his display. The pottery had a series of circles intermingled with squares in the most glorious shades of pinks and blues. 'Mm, that's just about right, I reckon.'

'You've done a good job,' she praised. 'It looks lovely.'

'Thanks.'

'Been busy?' she enquired.

'Yeah, business has been quite brisk,' he replied. 'The sunshine brings the punters out in droves.'

'As long as they don't stay out there enjoying the sun instead of coming in here,' she laughed.

'I'll set up shop outside if I find that's happening,' he said jokingly.

'I don't know what the market inspector would have to say about that,' was her light response.

'Anyway, how are things over at Hanwell?' he asked. 'Are the boys used to the electric ovens yet?'

'They're like kids with a new toy,' Molly said with a smile.

'I bet.'

'Mind you, they do have cause to be pleased because the new ovens are brilliant and save a whole lot of work. They should have done it years ago.'

'George didn't fancy the idea, did he?'

'No, he wasn't one for changes.'

'I know. He used to chat to me about the changing times and how bewildering it all was,' Peter remarked. 'He often used to come to the shop.'

'I think even George would approve if he could see how efficient the new system is now that it's up and running.'

'I'm glad it all went well. Will you be having the bottle kiln knocked down?' he enquired chattily.

'We've no immediate plans for demolition,' Molly informed him. 'There's so much sentimental value attached to it, no one seems in a hurry to get rid of it, though it'll have to go eventually. It's fine for the moment, though, standing there idle.'

'I'm sure the neighbours aren't missing it being operational,' he said, 'because of the smoke.'

'I'm sure they're delighted.'

'The local residents near the Fulham pottery are pleased they've gone electric, so I've heard,' he told her. 'They were always making complaints.'

'Progress, eh, Peter?'

'Indeed. They'll be sending the stock by road instead of by barge next,' he went on. 'Canal transport is another thing that's out of fashion.'

'Funny you should mention that, as it happens,' she said. 'There is talk at the pottery about getting a van. You won't know us soon, we'll be so up to date.'

'It'll be tuppence to talk to you soon, then,' he grinned.

'That'll be the day.'

'Just kidding.'

They went into the office and Molly gave him his wages and he gave her the weekly sales sheet and a cup of tea. 'You *have* had a good week then,' she mentioned, looking at the figures.

'Yeah, pretty good, as I said. The market is getting more popular every week and the more punters who come to that, the more people pop in here to have a look. Not many leave without buying something even if they only came in to have a nose.'

'Did Josh come in to the shop last Saturday?' she enquired.

'No. Why, should he have done?'

'No, I just thought he might have called in to see you as he was in the area, that's all,' she said, feigning a casual air. 'But it isn't important.' She looked across at him and swiftly changed the subject. 'Any problems?'

'Not problems. Just a few things I need to tell you,' he said. 'I'm low on lampshade bases in the aqua range and I need various items in the floral.'

She wrote down his queries, stayed for a brief chat and left. She felt uneasy all the way home on the tube about the fact that Josh had been hanging around the market without calling in at the shop. He was up to something; setting up some deal or other at the expense of the pottery stock, she was sure of it. There was nothing she could do. She could hardly demand to know why he'd been in the market since he had every right to be there. All she could do was keep an eye on things without him realising that she was suspicious. If she gave him enough rope . . .

Looking at her watch, she felt tension knotting tight in her stomach because she was later than she'd planned and she needed to get back for Rosa, who was being looked after by Molly's mother. The school summer holidays were a headache for Molly now that she was working and Angie wasn't around to help out, Hattie being tied up at the pottery. Molly cut her hours and took time off to be with her daughter but, logically, she couldn't take six weeks off. She had a responsibility to the job. She couldn't expect to be paid if she didn't do the work.

She got by with the occasional help of her mother, who looked after both girls when she wasn't working herself. Hattie's cleaning lady, Vi – a kind and capable mother of grown-up children – came to the rescue when she and Dan were stuck. She looked after the girls at Hattie's house so that they could benefit from the garden and having a parent within shouting distance.

In pursuit of a happy home life for her daughter, Molly was very well organised domestically, especially on working days. Nourishing meals were planned in advance and she was up early attending to chores while Rosa was still asleep, something she wasn't allowed to do when Brian was home.

But for all her careful organisation, the unexpected was a constant hazard. Just when things were running smoothly Rosa would go down with some minor illness or have some other problem that needed attention. So Molly found herself permanently torn between work and parental responsibility. It was an emotional thing as much as practical; a sense that she must be failing at one or the other even though she tried to give her all to both.

There was no easy answer because now that she received very little support from Brian – nothing for weeks on end sometimes – she was more reliant on the money than ever. It was just her and Rosa now.

Chapter Nine

'What do you think of this dress, Bri?' asked Beryl, waving a glossy bridal magazine under his nose.

They were cosied up together on the sofa in the Browns' living room, but Brian was far more interested in the sports page of the newspaper than wedding clothes.

'Very nice,' he said absently with barely a cursory glance at the picture.

'You don't like it, do you?' she said, sounding peeved. 'I can tell by your voice.'

One wedding dress was much the same as another to him, especially as he was never actually going to see her wearing it. 'Of course I like it, but you'll look lovely whatever dress you wear,' he said craftily.

'Flattery won't get you anywhere,' she told him curtly. 'Not if you're not going to take an interest in the wedding, anyway.'

'I will when it gets nearer the time, but it's miles too early to be talking about wedding frocks.'

'It isn't that far off,' she disagreed. 'It's only a matter of months. It's summer now; the wedding is next Easter. It'll soon come round.'

A bolt of panic shot through him. He was getting in over his head here. If he didn't call a halt to it soon, he'd end up in prison for bigamy. Calm down, he admonished himself. There's still plenty of time. You've got months before you need to disappear. Enjoy it while you can.

'Let's have another look then,' he said to appease her, putting down his newspaper and studying the magazine properly. 'Yeah, something like that would look a treat on you, with your gorgeous figure.'

His feigned interest brightened her. 'You really think so?' she said, squinting at the picture from different angles.

'I wouldn't say so if I didn't.' Something slipped into his mind that would make him appear to be really entering into the wedding spirit. 'But I thought you weren't supposed to let me see the dress before the day. Isn't it reckoned to be unlucky?'

'I won't show you the one I finally decide on,' she told him girlishly, softened by his change of attitude. 'I'm just playing around with ideas at the moment.'

'I see. Anyway,' he began, taking the magazine from her and putting it down, 'I can think of better things to do than look at magazines when your mum's out and we've got the house to ourselves, can't you?'

'Ooh, not half,' she giggled, sinking into his arms.

Rosa and Patsy were in the middle of a game of ludo when Dan came to collect his daughter after work one evening.

'Can I stay another five minutes, Dad?' she asked. 'I'm winning.'

'No, not tonight, Patsy,' he replied, appearing not to give the matter any thought.

'Oh, Da-ad . . .'

'Don't give me a hard time,' he warned. 'I said no and I meant it.'

'I'll walk her home when they've finished the game if you're in a hurry,' suggested Molly. 'They've been playing so well it seems a pity to break it up.'

'Good as gold,' added Joan, who just happened to be visiting her daughter. 'They have their squabbles like all kids, but I've rarely seen two children get on so well. Reminds me of Molly and Angie at that age. They were exactly the same. It can't do any harm for her to stay on for a few extra minutes, surely.'

Dan threw Joan a stormy look but didn't make any comment. He turned to his daughter. 'Come along, Patsy,' he insisted.

'But, Dad—'

'Don't argue,' he said with sudden ferocity. 'Just do as you're told and get your things together.'

Patsy turned pale, huge tears meandering down her cheeks. Without another word, she slipped off her chair and went to get her school bag from the hall. 'Thank you for having me, Auntie Molly,' she said politely, reappearing and standing hesitantly in the doorway.

'A pleasure, love,' was Molly's warm response. 'See you tomorrow.'

'Thanks for having her,' added Dan in the brisk tone that had become second nature to him recently. 'Bye for now, Mrs Rawlings.'

'Ta-ta,' she said coolly.

When Molly came back from seeing him out, Joan said, 'That bloke wants putting right about a few things. It's nothing short of cruelty the way he treats that child.'

'Now you're exaggerating, Mum,' admonished Molly, on the defensive. 'He's just a bit firm with her, that's all.'

'He's more than just a bit firm,' Joan opined. 'Is it any wonder she doesn't want to go home?'

Molly gave a worried sigh. 'He's a changed man since Angie died, that's for sure,' she admitted.

'I don't know him as well as you do but he always seemed a nice sort of chap to me,' Joan went on. 'But he's a real cold fish to that little girl.'

'It's terrible what grief does to people,' Molly observed. 'The man we are seeing now isn't Dan.'

'Well, he should make more of an effort, even if only when he's with his child,' Joan said hotly. 'He's lost his wife and we're all very sorry for him but his daughter is still around and she needs him.'

'These things aren't quite as simple as that, though, are they?' questioned Molly. 'Presumably if he could have snapped out of it he would have done so.'

'He should go and see the doctor if it's beyond his control.' Joan was getting angrier with every word. 'You can get pills for that sort of thing these days. Hattie must be worried sick. I know I would be if it was one of my grandchildren being upset like that.'

Molly wanted to get off the subject. She was already in a state of anxiety about Dan and Patsy, and her mother pontificating about it only exacerbated her concern. Fortunately she knew of a sure-fire diversion.

'Have you spoken to Peggy lately?' she enquired.

It worked like a dream. 'Yeah, I rang her from a call box the other day,' Joan said excitedly, all thoughts of Patsy pushed aside, 'and you'll never guess what.'

'They're having a new carpet?' tried Molly.

'They don't need it,' Joan informed her with an air of hauteur. 'They've not long had fitted carpet put in. I told you.'

'Did you? Sorry. It must have slipped my mind.' Molly couldn't keep track of Peggy's acquisitions and had no intention of trying. She had the more important matter of the Platers on her mind. 'So what is it that I'll never guess?'

'They're having a holiday abroad,' Joan burst out gleefully. 'They've got it all booked up and everything.'

'How lovely. Where are they going?'

'Spain.'

'I bet they're excited.'

'I'll say.'

Molly couldn't help thinking how nice it would have been if Peggy had invited her mother along. She and Reg had so much and they did so little for Mum. Still, at least the foreign holiday served its purpose, as far as Molly was concerned. It would keep Mum going for ages, and allow Molly to drift off into her own thoughts. Dan and Patsy were on her mind rather a lot lately, and her thoughts were always of a worrying or unhappy nature.

Dan drove home in silence, the beauty of the apricot-tinted evening sky serving only to heighten his melancholy. Such things as this, which used to fill him with joy, now had the opposite effect.

When they got in, he sent Patsy upstairs to get ready for bed and put some milk on the stove to heat for her Ovaltine. Hunger pangs reminded him that his own constitution needed attention. He'd get some beans on toast or something later on when he'd settled Patsy down for the night.

He didn't bother much for himself during the week, Patsy having already eaten at Molly's.

He was staring absently into the saucepan waiting for the milk to get hot enough when his daughter came downstairs in her pyjamas. She stood behind him and made a request that shook him to the core.

'Can I go and live with Rosa, please, Dad?' she asked him politely, almost as though she was asking for a biscuit to go with her drink.

Flinching, he swung round to face her. 'Don't be so silly, Patsy,' he burst out, trying to sound authoritative whilst winded from the blow.

Her dark eyes were like moons in her sad little face. Her genetic inheritance was poignantly striking to him at that moment. She was the living image of her mother. 'I'm not being silly,' she told him with a nervous quiver in her voice. 'I think it's a very good idea.'

'You'd rather live there than here with me?'

She didn't reply; just stared up at him, biting her lip.

'You think you'll get all your own way if you live there, I suppose.'

'No. Auntie Moll doesn't take any nonsense.' Her voice was high and tight. 'She tells us off if we're naughty. She doesn't let us do just what we like.'

'So, it's just because you'd rather not live with me then, is it?' he asked, dreading her reply.

'Well . . . er, yes,' she replied nervously, her cheeks brightly suffused. 'I thought you'd be pleased.'

Although he was speaking in an even tone, panic was rising to almost unbearable proportions. It seemed vital that he stay in control so he struggled not to show it. 'And what brings you to that conclusion?'

'All I do is make you miserable, and that makes me feel all sort of sick inside,' she told him solemnly. 'So it would be better if I wasn't here. If Auntie Moll says no because she hasn't got enough room, then perhaps I could go to Gran's. She's got plenty of space.'

Humbled by her logic, Dan was lost for words. He poured the milk into the cup and stirred her drink with a trembling hand. 'There you are,' he said, handing it to her. 'Would you like a biscuit with it?'

'No, thanks.'

'Are you going to drink it watching the telly?' This was a request she made every night.

'No, I'll go straight to bed.' She gave him a questioning look. 'So can I go and live with Rosa or not?'

Hardly able to utter any words at all, he heard himself say, 'I'll think about it.'

'OK,' she said, and left the room with a quiet dignity that belied her tender years.

He sat at the kitchen table with his head propped on his fists. What a brute he was and what a mess he'd made of being a widower. He'd driven his little daughter away with his own inability to cope with

Angie's death and his selfish need to blame someone for it. His shame was all-consuming, a great surge of hot pain creeping all over him.

His eyes burned with tears as the truth hammered into his brain over and over again. In rejecting him, Patsy was actually reaching out to him. She was hurting and needed him to make it better; to be there for her as he'd always been in the past. She was a little girl who wanted things to be as they were when her mother was alive. She was too young to understand that they never could be again.

But it was up to him to make them as good as they could be for her. They didn't have Angie but they did have each other, and Patsy was so very precious to him. He must somehow find the courage to walk in the light with her and suffer the darkness of his own personal hell in private.

Mopping his tears and managing to compose himself, he headed for the stairs. He could hear Patsy sobbing in her room. How could he have done this to her? Hadn't she had enough pain without him adding to it? He knocked on her door, feeling more nervous than a schoolboy in trouble. She told him to come in in a muffled tone and he found her lying face down on the bed with her head buried in the pillow.

'I've come to ask you to forgive me and give me another chance,' he said softly, sitting on the edge of the bed.

No reply.

'I know I've been really bad and I don't deserve it, but please help me out, Patsy.'

She lay very still for what seemed ages, then turned over slowly and looked at him warily, her face wet and blotchy, eyes red and sore.

'I don't want you to go and live somewhere else,' he told her gently.

'Don't you?' Her voice was hoarse from crying.

Tenderly he wiped her tears with his handkerchief. 'No, I most certainly do not,' he confirmed thickly. 'I want you with me. You're my special girl and I love you very much.'

'Oh, I thought—'

'I know I haven't shown it much lately,' he cut in, smoothing her hair back from her brow with a tender touch, 'but everything will be different from now on, I promise.'

With only a brief hesitation she threw her arms round him and he hugged her, sobbing.

'Everything will be better now, sweetheart,' he said, blowing his nose. 'We don't have Mummy but we do have each other. From now on you are going to be my first priority. I'm sorry I've been so horrid.'

'It's all right, Dad.'

'You're everything to me and I've hurt you badly,' he said. 'But from this moment on I'll be here for you – always. And we'll have fun again, like we used to.'

'It won't be the same without Mum.'

'No, it won't. But wherever she is she'll be wanting us to make our life together, you and me,' he said. 'I'll try and stop being such a grumps.'

'You haven't been that bad.'

'I have.'

She made a face. 'Well, maybe a bit,' she admitted with a half-smile.

'But not any more.'

'I didn't really want to go and live with Rosa,' she confessed. 'But I do like being there, though, because Rosa's my best friend, and Auntie Molly's such good fun.'

'Well, I can't promise to be as much fun as she is but I'm certainly going to try to do better,' he promised. 'You come first from now on.'

She slipped her arms around his neck and held him tight. Feeling her thin little body against his, his love for her hurt in its intensity.

'Would you like me to read you a story before you go to sleep?' he asked.

'Yes, please,' Patsy said, and there was a serenity about her he hadn't seen in a long time.

'Pick out which story you want then,' he said, kissing her brow.

She slipped out of bed and got her book of fairy tales from the shelf.

'Once upon a time . . .' he began.

Before he'd got to the end of the first page she was fast asleep. It must be the first time she'd fallen asleep feeling secure in a long time, he thought.

Dan got Hattie and Molly together in the office for a chat the next morning.

'I've been a pig, I know. I've been hateful to everyone, especially my daughter,' he told them. 'And I'm so ashamed.' He went on to tell them about Patsy's shocking request. 'It shook me rigid, I can tell you.'

'It's enough to shake anyone,' said Hattie.

'It brought me to my senses, though. And it's all going to change,' he announced resolutely. 'Patsy's going to be my life from now on.'

'About time too.' Hattie gave him a hug. 'We've all been so worried about you – about both of you.'

'Thanks. I don't deserve your support.' He looked ruefully from one to the other.

'You'll get it whether you deserve it or not,' said Molly with a wry grin.

He managed a smile, the first one they'd seen in a long time. 'From now on I'll do whatever it takes to give Patsy a good life,' he declared. 'Now that Angie isn't here the responsibility is all mine and I'm going to make damned sure she gets the best possible chance in life.'

'Good for you,' approved Hattie, 'and you've got all of us behind you.'

'I know.' He looked at Molly. 'As a start to my new resolve, perhaps Rosa would like to come and play with Patsy at my place at the weekend,' he suggested. 'Patsy spends enough time at yours. It's about time I did something in return.'

'I'm sure Rosa would love that,' Molly smiled.

'Saturday afternoon perhaps.'

'That'll be fine.' She winked at Hattie, then looked back at Dan. 'As you'll be child-minding, Hattie and I can go off and have a nice leisurely walk round the shops.'

'Sure,' he said. 'I can give them their tea. So you needn't hurry back.'

'I think we'll take him up on that offer, eh, Moll?' Hattie smiled.

'Definitely,' she agreed.

'The improvement in Dan is a load off my mind, I can tell you,' confessed Hattie one Saturday afternoon a few weeks later when she and Molly were having tea and a bun in Lyons at West Ealing. Joan was doing an extra shift at work so wasn't with them. 'He's much more like his old self.'

'He's still racked with grief – you can see it in his eyes – but he's making a real effort now with Patsy,' said Molly, spreading butter on her bun. 'This will be the third Saturday afternoon he's had Rosa round to play, and she has a lovely time from what I can hear of it. Probably spoils them rotten.'

'I think he's firm when he has to be, though. And at least he's pulling his weight now,' Hattie pointed out. 'I mean, you do look after Patsy every weekday after school and as often as you can at other times. I think he was too deeply entrenched in his own grief before to realise that he wasn't giving anything back.'

'I'm sure it wasn't intentional,' she said. 'Anyway, having Patsy after school is no trouble to me. In fact it makes things easier because Rosa is never happier than when her pal is around.'

'You and Angie were just the same,' she said wistfully. 'She used to go around with a face like a broom handle when you weren't with her.'

A tense moment passed between them which needed to be acknowledged. 'It was the same for me,' said Molly sadly. 'Still is, actually.'

'I know how hard it must be for you, love,' responded Hattie, sipping her tea. 'You and me will just have to make do with each other. Having you as a friend has helped me, I know that much.'

'Likewise.'

Hattie cleared her throat. 'Billy was saying that Dan's work has reverted to normal too,' she mentioned. 'So that's another worry off our minds.'

Molly nodded. 'Thank goodness for that,' she said. 'The firm can't afford too many mistakes.'

They fell into a comfortable silence as they finished their snack. 'So, where else do we want to go?' asked Hattie after a while.

'I wouldn't mind a look round Rowse's.' Molly was referring to a local department store. 'And I need to pop into Marks and Spencers to get Rosa some new underwear. How about you? Have you anything else to get?'

'Nothing special but I'd like to have a look in The Hole-in-the-Wall.' This was a gap in the shopping parade containing a few market stalls. 'The fish and meat stalls sell off anything they've got left on a Saturday really cheap.' Hattie's love of a bargain stemmed from earlier hard times and was a habit that had lingered even though she didn't need to watch the pennies so much now.

'Come on then, let's go,' said Molly, gathering her bags.

The girls were being overly exuberant when Molly arrived at Dan's house to collect Rosa. They were running through the house and into the garden, shrieking and laughing.

'Oh dear,' said Molly. 'Sounds as though you've been having a fraught time. I hope they haven't been playing you up too much.'

'They've only just started going mad,' Dan assured her. 'Been angels all afternoon. Out in the garden most of the time.' He paused for a moment then issued a stern command that resonated throughout the house. 'Oi, you two, that's enough of that noise. Pack it in *now*.'

Instant silence.

'Someone's got the magic touch,' smiled Molly. 'I wish they took that much notice of me.'

'Just a fluke,' he confessed. 'It doesn't work every time.'

'I'm impressed, though,' she told him lightly. 'But seriously, has Rosa behaved herself?'

'No trouble at all.'

'Good, that saves me having to read the riot act,' she grinned. 'So I'll collect her and be on my way.'

'Oh,' he looked disappointed, 'I was hoping you'd have time for a cup of tea.'

Well, well. This really was progress. He'd been making an effort lately, yes, but it didn't normally run to this kind of sociability. 'Thanks. I'd love to,' she accepted graciously.

He made the tea and they drank it at the kitchen table. 'So, did you buy anything nice?' Dan asked conversationally.

'Not really. It was more of a wander then serious shopping,' she said. 'Hattie misses her Saturday afternoons with Angie, and my being around helps to fill a void.' She gave him a cheeky grin. 'And, of course, now that we've got a regular baby-sitter we're free to go without dragging the kids around the shops, bored stiff and whinging.'

'I enjoy having them.' He paused, looking at her. 'I'm sorry I took everything you did for Patsy for granted for so long,' he told her. 'I don't know how I could have been so thoughtless.'

140

'You just got a bit caught up in your own feelings for a while, that's all.'

'Self-pity, in other words.'

'Well, whatever it was, thank goodness you've seen your way out of it.'

He nodded, pensive for a moment. 'I want the best of everything for Patsy, you know.'

'Don't we all for our children?' she responded. 'I'm the same about Rosa.'

'But the feeling is ultra strong with me now that my head's clearer,' he explained, 'I suppose because it's finally come home to me that her wellbeing and future depends entirely on me. There's no Angie to help make the decisions.'

'It is a huge responsibility, bringing up a child alone,' Molly said in an understanding manner, 'and I can speak from experience.'

'But you have a husband,' he pointed out, looking at her quizzically.

'He's never there. When he was he never used to take any part in her upbringing.' It was an explanation, not a complaint. 'So as it's been that way ever since Rosa was born I'm used to feeling entirely responsible for her. I wasn't suddenly plunged in at the deep end like you've been.'

'I see.' Dan sipped his tea, pondering. 'I still get dark times and plenty of them. I suppose I always will because I'll never stop missing Angie,' he told her, 'but I do seem more able to hide my despair from Patsy now. I don't get the horrors so much when I'm with her, anyway. She cheers me up now that I've stopped blaming her.'

Molly nodded, finishing her tea. 'Well, I really must be off,' she said. 'Thanks for having Rosa.'

'A pleasure,' he said. 'And thanks for staying for a cuppa. It was nice to have a chat.'

'I enjoyed it too.'

She collected her daughter and they walked home in the late summer evening, already an early hint of autumn in the air. Molly reflected on how much she'd enjoyed Dan's company. It was so good to see him behaving normally again. Bringing a child up alone was a solitary business and Dan was realising that now that his wits had returned. Her own loneliest time of the day was after Rosa had gone to bed at night. Sometimes then she felt the need for someone to share it all with. Still, she managed well enough on her own and she'd rather that than be fielding criticism from Brian.

'What are those pictures of, Dad?' enquired Patsy over breakfast one morning when her father opened a letter and a wad of photographs fell out.

'They're photos of your uncle and auntie and cousins in Australia,' he replied, glancing through them.

'Can I have a look?'

'Have you finished your breakfast?'

She nodded.

'Have a quick look then,' he said, handing them to her, 'but don't make yourself late for school. You can study them properly when you get home.'

'OK.'

While she perused the pictures he read the letter from his brother, Derek. Disillusioned with life in Britain during the period of post-war austerity, and attracted by the opportunities offered elsewhere, Derek had emigrated to Australia and never looked back. He'd met and married an Australian woman and now had two little daughters. He loved the way of life out there and had no intention of returning to England. He was obviously doing well at the moment, Dan observed. The photographs of his house and the big car standing in the drive illustrated that. Derek had gone to Australia as a motor mechanic but had moved into car sales and was now a sales manager.

'It looks nice there, doesn't it, Dad?' remarked Patsy.

'Yes, it looks lovely.'

'How old are my cousins?'

'One of them is about your age, the other is a little older than you.'

'Have I ever seen them?'

'No, they were born after your uncle went away to live,' he explained. 'They're Australian born and bred. I've never seen them either.'

'Will we ever see them?'

'It isn't very likely.' He wanted to be realistic. 'Australia is a very long way off. It costs a lot of money for the fare.'

She handed the photographs back to him. They were of Derek and his family standing outside his house, a great big detached place surrounded by lawns, everything drenched in sunshine. Derek certainly wouldn't have had a home and a car like that if he'd stayed here.

According to the letter, his brother had just had some sort of a promotion. 'It's a great life here, mate,' he wrote. 'A terrific place to raise kids. You should give it a try. A new start is just what you and Patsy need right now.'

Dan put the letter back into the envelope. 'Right, princess, it's time to go to school,' he reminded her. 'Go and brush your teeth and get your things together and we'll be off.'

'OK, Dad.'

As she hurried upstairs, he began clearing the dishes. An idea was beginning to form . . .

Billy and Sally were smooching around the dance floor at Hammersmith Palais. It was the last waltz, the lights were low and she had her head on his shoulder.

142

'I've had a smashing time,' she said dreamily as the music ended and they left the floor, joining the surge of people heading for the queue to collect their coats.

'I always do when I'm with you,' he said.

'I bet you say that to all the girls.'

'I might have done once upon a time,' he admitted because he wanted to be honest with her, 'but not any more. You're the only girl in my life now.'

'Aah, that's sweet.'

'I don't usually get serious with a girl. I've always been a confirmed bachelor,' he confided in a loving mood. 'But it's different with you.'

'Oh, Billy.'

'One thing I never do is take a girl home to meet the family because Mum immediately starts planning her outfit for the wedding,' he went on. 'But you and I have been seeing each other for a while now, and I'd love you to meet them . . . if you'd like to, that is.'

'Oh yes!'

'I'll arrange it with Mum then.'

'I hope she likes me,' Sally frowned.

'Of course she'll like you. Who wouldn't?' he assured her. 'And you'll love her. Everyone does.' He paused. 'Anyway, having settled that we'd better get in the queue for the coats.' He was inwardly glowing. He'd never felt like this about anyone before. Sally was the only girl for him; he had absolutely no doubts about that.

Patsy had some exciting news to tell Molly one day a few weeks later. 'Guess what,' she said excitedly as she sat at the table with Patsy to fish fingers and baked beans. 'Dad and I are going to see my cousins in Australia.'

'Oh, Patsy, that'll be lovely for you,' enthused Molly.

'We're going on a big ship,' she announced proudly.

'How exciting,' responded Molly.

'Patsy said they have lots of sunshine there, Mum,' put in Rosa, entering into the spirit.

'Yes, I believe the weather is sunnier than ours.' Molly was wondering how long they would be away because it took so long to get there. It wouldn't suit Billy if Dan was away from work too long. 'I'm sure you'll have a brilliant time, Patsy.'

'Yeah,' she breathed. 'I wish Rosa could come too.'

'You'll have to tell her all about it when you come back,' suggested Molly.

'I will . . . and I'll bring her a nice present.' She paused before adding, 'I'll bring one for you too.'

'That will be lovely,' smiled Molly. 'We'll look forward to it.'

The children finished their tea and were playing snap in the living

room when Dan arrived to collect Patsy. Molly made him a cup of tea –
a habit she'd got into since he'd thawed out and become more friendly –
and they sat down at the kitchen table to drink it.

'I hear from Patsy that you've got an exciting trip planned,' she
mentioned.

He tutted, grinning. 'I told her not to say anything just yet,' he said. 'I
might have known she'd spill the beans.'

'That's kids for you. Keeping secrets isn't their strong point.' She
offered him a biscuit. 'So, when are you thinking of going?'

'I'm not sure yet. Before Christmas I expect,' he replied.

'It'll be nice to see your brother again and meet his family, won't it?'
Dan nodded, nibbling a digestive biscuit.

'How long are you going for?' Molly enquired chattily.

He gave her a strange look. 'Well, we're not going all that way just for
a holiday,' he replied. 'It's on the other side of the world.'

She stared at him blankly. 'You don't mean . . . you can't mean that
you're going for good.'

'Of course I do,' he confirmed, as though there could be no other
possible explanation. 'We're going to Australia to live. We're emigrating.'

Molly was so shocked she spilled her tea on the table. 'Oh, Dan,' she
said, getting up to fetch a cloth, 'I thought you were talking about a
holiday.'

'Hardly,' was his response. 'Provided everything's in order with my
application, we'll be living there. But I'm not expecting any trouble
because I'm a skilled craftsman so I have something to offer. They're
crying out for people like me.' He looked at her. 'So, what do you think?'

'I think it's the worst thing you could do at this time,' she blurted out.

'Oh? Why's that?'

'Because it'll be so traumatic for Patsy so soon after losing her
mother. She needs stability in her life now. She's obviously still feeling
insecure.'

'It's for Patsy I'm doing it, and I wouldn't go ahead if I thought it
would be upsetting for her in any way,' he said on the defensive. 'I'm not
a cruel man and Patsy is my priority. Anyway, she wants to go; she's
thrilled to bits about the whole thing.'

'She thinks it's a holiday, that's why,' Molly told him. 'A trip to see
her cousins.'

'I've told her we're going to live there.'

'It obviously hasn't registered. Children of that age don't have any
sense of distance and the practicalities of life. She doesn't realise that
she'll never see her gran or her uncles or Rosa again. She's talking about
bringing Rosa and me a present back.'

'In that case I'll make sure that she does understand what's going to
happen, and I can assure you she'll still want to go,' Dan insisted.

144

'She might want to go but what about when she's actually there and we're all here?'

'Now look here, Molly,' he cut in, prickly now. 'It's up to me to give her the best chance life can offer and this will be a wonderful opportunity for her. The standard of living is high out there. There are chances for people there that don't exist here. My brother and his family have a great life. It'll be a brand-new start for us both, and exactly what we need.'

'Please don't do this, Dan.' She'd never been more certain of anything than that this was the wrong thing for Patsy. 'She's recently lost her mum – don't make her lose all the other people who love her too.'

'She'll have relatives out there who'll love her. One of Derek's daughters is about the same age so she'll have a friend right away,' he explained. 'Derek is as keen as mustard for us to go. He's going to put us up at his place until we find a house of our own. And we'll stay in the same neighbourhood as them when we do move so we won't be on our own.'

'Patsy still has to start a new school, get used to a new culture, and make new friends,' Molly pointed out. 'She can't rely entirely on her cousins for company of her own age.'

'Thousands of people emigrate to Australia from this country every year,' he reminded her. 'They soon adapt, and so will she.'

'She's still trying to adapt to life without her mother,' Molly reminded him. 'I think that's enough for any little girl to cope with for the moment. Dragging her halfway across the world isn't going to help her one little bit.'

'You're entitled to your opinion, of course, Molly.' His tone was increasingly sharp. 'But that's as far as it goes. You've no right to tell me what I should and shouldn't do for my daughter.'

'Just before Angie died she made me promise to look out for you and Patsy,' she told him. 'I wouldn't be keeping that promise if I didn't try to talk you out of something that is so very wrong for the child.'

'That's only your opinion.'

'Yes, and I know I have no right to interfere but I feel so strongly about this. It might be the right thing for you, Dan, running away because you think the pain of losing Angie will disappear in Australia, but it isn't right for Patsy.' Molly was very heated now. 'My heart breaks at the thought of her out there, when the novelty wears off and she realises that she isn't going to see any of us ever again.'

'Anyone would think I was going to take her out there and abandon her, to hear you talk.' His eyes were bright with defiance. 'I shall be there for her, looking after her, loving her and making sure she's happy.'

'I know that, Dan, and I know that you're planning all this with the very best intentions,' she said in a softer tone, 'but I still think you've made the wrong decision.'

'Only time will tell.'

'And have you thought what this is going to do to Hattie? She's already lost her husband and her daughter in less than a year. Now you're going to take her only grandchild away.'

'Yes, I have thought about it and Patsy must be my priority,' he told her, 'I have to do what's best for her. I don't want to hurt Hattie, of course, but Patsy has to come first.'

'I don't think you're doing this for Patsy at all,' she burst out through dry lips.

'No?'

'No. You're doing it for yourself. You're looking for a new challenge to take your mind off your wife's death, which you still haven't come to terms with properly. You think it will hurt less somewhere else. You think you'll forget in all the hustle and bustle of getting used to a new country, away from the place so full of memories. But it'll be there wherever you are. You have to face up to it and get on with your life.'

'Which is exactly what going to Australia is all about, for goodness' sake,' he said. 'I'm moving on.'

'You're running away.'

'You've got a cheek, accusing me of that,' he objected. 'You've no right.'

'I know I haven't,' she was forced to admit in a subdued manner. 'I'm sorry.'

'I should think so too. Anyway, my decision is irreversible so let's drop the subject before we have a serious falling-out.' He was unshakable in his judgment.

'Look, I'm not saying that emigration isn't a good idea.' She couldn't let it go even though it was none of her business, and she knew that she was pushing her luck. Patsy was far too important to her, and so was her own promise to Angie. 'As you say, thousands of people have done it since the war with great success. I'm just saying that now isn't the right time for you to do it. Leave it for a year or two. At least give Patsy a chance to heal after losing her mum. She'll become less vulnerable as time goes by.'

'Now is exactly the right time for us to do it,' Dan argued, his voice rising. 'The younger she is the easier it will be for her to adapt.'

Molly was distraught; she felt sick at the thought of Patsy among strangers. But what could she do? 'So your mind is made up then?' she said dismally.

'Yes, I've just finished telling you, for God's sake.' He left his tea and stood up purposefully, as if to go.

'When will you tell Hattie and the boys?'

'Sometime soon,' he replied. 'When the right opportunity arises.'

'Let's hope Patsy doesn't blurt it out to them like she did to me, before then.' She shook her head slowly. 'Hattie will be even more hurt if the news reaches her that way. The poor woman will be in despair.'

'Mm . . .' Dan thought about this for a moment. 'I'll make Patsy promise not to say anything. And I'll make sure she knows how important it is this time.'

'Oh well, Dan,' Molly gave a miserable sigh of resignation, 'as you've just said, it's your business, your decision.'

'At last, the penny's finally dropped,' came his hard response.

Molly's heart felt like lead as she saw Dan and Patsy walk away that evening.

Chapter Ten

It was a big day at The Hawthorns. Sally had come for Sunday tea to meet the family for the first time. Everyone was spick and span, the boys in suits, Hattie wearing her best twinset and pearls. She'd even been for a shampoo and set yesterday in honour of the occasion.

'You sit there, next to Billy, Sally dear,' she said, giving the girl a warm Beckett welcome. 'I know the two of you won't want to be parted.'

'Thank you, Mrs Beckett.' Sally was very polite.

'Do call me Hattie, please,' she requested sociably. 'We're all friends here.'

Sally smiled nervously. She wasn't timid by nature but loving Billy as she did made her vulnerable. His family meant a lot to him and she *so* wanted them to like her.

'Would you like anything else brought in from the kitchen, Hattie?' This was Molly from the doorway. She was invited to most Beckett family occasions since they'd lost Angie. Hattie seemed to want her there as friend and helper, and Rosa was good company for Patsy.

'No, not at the moment, Moll. We'll bring some more sweet stuff in later. You come and sit down. As soon as Molly was seated, Hattie invited everyone to help themselves.

'So you live at Shepherd's Bush then, Sally,' said Molly to get the conversation going as they all began to tuck into savoury sandwiches and rolls. She could see that Sally was on edge. It must be daunting, meeting this crowd for the first time, she thought.

'That's right,' nodded Sally.

'She's a proper little Bush Babe,' teased Billy, smiling at her affectionately.

'You've got a smashing market,' remarked Molly to put Sally on home ground and help her to relax. 'I used to go there every Saturday afternoon before I got married. Angie and I never missed it.'

'It's always crowded on a Saturday afternoon.' Sally still didn't sound quite at ease.

'There are a lot of trendy shoe shops around the Green too,' added Molly, having noticed how hip Sally was.

'Some of the highest stilettos in London can be bought round our way,' Sally informed them proudly, visibly loosening now that Molly had guided the conversation towards a passion of hers – the latest fashions.

'She'll break an ankle one of these days, walking in those things,' said Billy lightly.

'You sound like somebody's father,' admonished Molly, tactfully taking Sally's side. 'Most fashionable women would willingly risk a broken ankle to wear pretty shoes.'

Sally gave Molly a grateful smile.

'Your dad's an electrician, I gather,' contributed Dan to keep the dialogue flowing.

'That's right.'

'We know who to call when we get problems with our new electric ovens then,' he joked.

'That's right,' she said with a half-smile. 'I'm sure he'd be happy to help.'

Molly thought how pretty she was, with her blonde hair cut into a feathery style. 'I like your hair, Sally,' she complimented. 'It's a lovely style.'

'Thank you. I'm glad you like it. I only had it cut recently. I usually have it longer than this,' she said, flushing with pleasure at the compliment.

'Did you have it done in the West End?'

'At their prices. Not likely,' she replied with a wry grin. 'I had it done locally. An Italian hairdresser has opened a shop in the Bush, and he's brilliant at cutting the new styles. All my friends had their hair restyled there so I decided to take the plunge. People come from all over London to have Antonio cut their hair.'

'A bloke doing your hair,' disapproved Billy. 'I don't like the sound of that. It's a bit too intimate.'

'Women love him,' Sally chuckled, teasing him. 'Antonio's very popular. You have to book up weeks in advance to get an appointment with him.' She paused, a gleam in her eye. 'And you can stop worrying, Billy, because he isn't interested in women – except to do their hair.'

There was an awkward silence. Hattie cleared her throat.

Then Josh blurted out, 'I'm not surprised with a name like Antonio.'

'I bet his real name is Syd and he's from Acton or Willesden or somewhere like that,' Billy put in. 'These male hairdressers pretend to be continental to bring in the punters. It makes them seem more glamorous.'

'People wouldn't go twice if they weren't good at the job, though, no matter how glamorous they seem,' Molly pointed out. 'Sally's Antonio obviously knows what he's doing.'

'Does your "hairdresser" have a flash name, Josh?' asked his brother, looking at Josh's DA.

'He's a barber,' objected Josh.

'I thought you'd have a *hairdresser* for a fancy style like that,' teased Billy.

'You're only taking the mick 'cause you're jealous,' retorted Josh.

'Now, now, boys, that's enough of that.' Hattie thought it was time to move on. 'Does your mother have a job, Sally?' she enquired chattily.

'She's a housewife.'

'I used to be one of those until I got roped in to work at the pottery.' She gave a sigh of mock sadness. 'Oh, happy days. I remember them well.'

'Come off it, Mum,' admonished Billy jokingly. 'You love your job at the pottery.'

'Just kidding,' she grinned.

'Billy's told me all about the pottery,' mentioned Sally. 'Perhaps I could have a look around later on?'

'Course you can, love.' Hattie was warmed by her interest. 'Billy can take you over there after tea.'

'It's very unusual, having your own working pottery in your garden,' said Sally. 'It must be fun.'

'It's handy,' Hattie told her.

The conversation flowed naturally after that. Now that the ice was broken everyone felt more at ease.

'Chocolate cake, anyone?' Hattie invited.

There was an affirmative chorus.

'Right, let's get you kids fixed up first,' she said, turning to the girls, who had been subdued so far, listening to the adult chatter. She cut them each a slice and proceeded to do the same for the others.

It was at that moment of supreme goodwill and harmony that a chance remark from Patsy led to a dramatic change in the atmosphere.

'Do they have chocolate cake in Australia, Gran?' she enquired.

'I should think so, love,' replied her grandmother. 'But what on earth has put a thing like that into your mind?'

Dan threw his daughter a warning look. Molly held her breath and prayed the child would get the message in her father's eyes and drop the subject. But it wasn't to be.

'I just wondered if we'd be having it when we go there,' said Patsy.

'We're not going to Australia, love,' said Hattie, misunderstanding her.

'Daddy and me are,' she informed her knowingly. 'We're going there to live.'

'Don't be daft, love,' said Hattie absently, concentrating on the job in hand. 'Going to Australia to live? I dunno, you kids don't half get some funny ideas.'

'We really are going, Gran,' Patsy persisted. 'Ask Dad if you don't believe me.'

A troubled silence crept over the room. A scarlet flush spread from Hattie's neck to her face. She stared at Dan with the cake slice poised in mid-air. 'What . . . what's she talking about?' she asked eventually.

151

He looked extremely sheepish. 'I was going to tell you . . . soon,' he explained. 'Patsy promised not to say anything.'

'So it's true?'

He nodded.

'When?' Her voice was almost a whisper.

'This side of Christmas, I hope.'

'Oh.' Her flushed cheeks were now paper white.

She was obviously very shaken but said no more on the subject – out of respect for their visitor, Molly guessed. The boys took the hint and kept quiet about it too. The conversation became general, anything from the latest Marilyn Monroe film to the weather. But the mood was fraught with tension and Sally must have felt it.

As soon as tea was over, they all made themselves scarce, guessing that Hattie wanted to be alone with Dan. Billy took Sally over to the pottery to show her around, Josh went to his room, the children went to play in the garden and Molly started on the dishes with the kitchen door firmly closed.

'I know you're upset, Hattie,' said Dan when they were alone in the living room.

'You're damned right I am. I don't know how you can even think of taking Patsy away at this time,' she said. 'Buggering off across the world on some sort of a whim . . .'

'It isn't a whim.'

'It's pretty darned sudden.'

'That doesn't mean I haven't thought about it long and hard because I have,' he assured her. 'And I've decided it's the best thing I can do for her.'

'Don't you think she's suffered enough disruption lately, what with losing her mother and you going cold on her for months?' she questioned. 'For pity's sake, Dan, give the child a break.'

'Which is exactly what I'm planning to do,' he returned. 'I can't bring her mother back but I can do everything in my power to give my daughter the best possible chance in life.'

'But you'll be taking her away from all the people she loves and needs,' Hattie pointed out. 'Her family, Molly and Rosa.'

'She'll have family out there,' he informed her and went on to tell her about his brother and his wife and daughters.

'But they'll all be strangers to her,' she reminded him, her voice shrill with emotion. 'She needs people and things that are familiar to her at the moment.'

He sighed. 'Look, Hattie, I realise that it will be hard for you, losing your grandchild so soon after losing Angie, and really I do hate to hurt you like this,' he said with genuine contrition, 'but I must do what is best for Patsy in the long term.'

152

'Don't you think I want what's best for Patsy too, Dan?' she pleaded with him. 'Of course my own heart will break to have her taken out of my life, but it will break even more for her. I would never stand in the way of my family doing anything to better themselves, you know that. But I really think this is the wrong time to disrupt that little girl. Later on perhaps, but not now.'

'She wants to go.'

'Only because she sees it as an adventure; she's too young to understand how she'll feel not to have people around her that she loves; that she'll probably never see any of us again.' She looked at him gravely. 'I think the world of you, Dan. You were a wonderful husband to my daughter and you've been good to me over the years. But I really think you're making a big mistake over this.'

'We'll have to agree to differ on this one then,' he said, 'because we're definitely going. Everything has been set in motion and I'm not going to change my mind.'

'On your head be it then,' she said coolly. 'I hope you can live with yourself.'

'Oh, for heaven's sake,' he snapped, 'I'm taking her to a young country full of opportunity, not a concentration camp.'

'You're taking her away from all she knows at a time when she's especially vulnerable,' Hattie stated categorically.

'I'm not going to change my mind, Hattie.'

'In that case there's nothing more to be said on the subject. You know how I feel and I won't change my mind either.' She gave him a hard look. 'Now I'm going to help Molly with the dishes.'

Dan stayed where he was in the armchair, deep in thought. Was he really doing something so terrible in taking Patsy away? Molly thought so and now Hattie. And the rest of the family would probably turn against him over it too.

But how could it be wrong if Patsy was going to grow up in a healthy environment with a nice home and good opportunities for the future? It was his duty to give her the best life could offer. He wanted her to have chances he'd never had; special chances to make up for losing her mother. He had doubts about it, naturally. It was a huge step to take. It was going to be a wrench for him personally, leaving people he was fond of and the place where he had grown up; where he had courted and married Angie. As uncertainties crept in, he crushed them before they had a chance to settle, banished them by reminding himself that it would be a relief to escape from the ghosts of his wife that were everywhere in Hanwell and its environs. Every time he walked down the street, he expected to see her round the next corner; every tree and paving stone had a memory, and he still couldn't get used to the house without her.

There were times when you had to trust in your own judgement at the expense of popularity, he told himself. A fresh start was definitely what was needed for Patsy and himself, with the emphasis on Patsy. He would make it good for her. She was his whole life now that Angie had gone, and he'd do everything in his power to make her happy.

Sally was most impressed with Beckettware. 'It must be fun to have such a creative job,' she remarked, admiring the stock for sale in the shop.

'I wouldn't go so far as to call it fun.' Billy gave a wry grin. 'It's bloomin' hard graft.'

'Yeah, but to make beautiful things is a damned sight more interesting than copy-typing all day, which is what I do.'

'There is a lot of job satisfaction in being a potter, I must admit – when it's going well, anyway, and that isn't all the time by any means.'

'Was it what you always wanted to do?' she asked conversationally.

'Yeah. I never even thought of doing anything else,' he replied. 'Just followed my dad into the business, having watched him work all my life.'

'Your mum seems very nice.'

'Yeah, she's one of the best,' Billy agreed. 'I knew you'd like her.'

'She's very upset about your brother-in-law going to Australia, isn't she?'

'Phew, I'll say she is. I'm gutted too. I hope you weren't too embarrassed when you could suddenly cut the air with a knife, back there.'

'Not at all. I feel sorry for your mum, though. She carried on as though nothing had happened but you could see how shaken she was.'

'I bet she's having a right go at Dan now that she's got him on his own.' Billy made a face. 'I shall have a few words to say to him about it too, later on. I mean, fancy dragging the poor little mite off to a strange country so soon after losing her mum. What is he thinking about?'

'I suppose he thinks he's doing the right thing,' Sally suggested. 'I mean, he seems a decent sort of a bloke, the sort who would want the best for his child.'

'He is a good bloke but he's got it wrong on this one.'

'You can't be sure of that, Billy,' she pointed out. 'Lots of people emigrate.'

'And I'm sure they do very well for themselves but it isn't right for my niece at this particular time,' he told her. 'She's still not over losing her mum. She needs us around her.'

'It's lovely that you care so much.' Sally squeezed his arm. 'But try not to get too upset about it because there's nothing you can do to stop him if he's determined to go. She is *his* child, after all.'

'I know that. But as Patsy's uncle I'm entitled to give him my opinion,' he said, his voice rising with emotion. 'And I shall do that in no uncertain terms.'

'All right, Billy, calm down.'

He turned to her. 'Sorry. The last thing I intended was to burden you with family problems on your first visit,' he said, looking contrite. 'If Patsy hadn't let the cat out of the bag, Dan would have told us at a more convenient time, certainly not in the middle of a family tea with you as the guest of honour. It wrecked the whole thing.'

'No, it didn't.'

'It wasn't how I planned it.'

'It doesn't matter, honestly.'

'Let me give you a tour of the workshop and we'll come back in here and you can choose something to take home.' He was anxious to get off the emotive subject because it upset him dreadfully and he didn't want to spoil the day – any more than it had been already – for Sally.

'Are you sure?' she said, her eyes sparkling. 'I don't want to take your profits.'

'Don't worry, I'll cover it.'

He showed her the work benches, the potter's wheels and rows of part-finished items on the shelves, and answered her many questions. The electric ovens – which were in a room off the main workshop – were duly shown off. The soft earthy smell of clay and paint permeated everything.

In the shop Sally chose a small bowl in deep blue with paler shades of blue interwoven into it.

'I shall keep it on my dressing table and think of you every time I look at it.'

'You're so sweet,' he said, kissing her.

'Not only sweet, I hope,' she smiled.

'Sexy too,' he added.

'That's better.'

They stayed a while longer, talking and looking around. Then Billy said, 'I think it's probably safe to go back to the house now. I should think Mum's finished reading the riot act to Dan.'

'Let's give it a try then,' she said. 'I want to get to know everyone better.'

It had been a warm and mellow autumn day. Now the sun had gone down and it was cold and misty as they walked across the garden. She paused by the bottle kiln. 'You don't use this any more, you say?'

'No, not now.'

'Will you have it knocked down?'

'Eventually, yes, unless we decide to keep it for sentimental reasons.'

'Might you do that?'

Billy thought about it. 'I don't think so because it would have to be regularly maintained to keep it safe,' he explained. 'We can't just leave it to rot because it would be dangerous. And I don't think any of us are prepared to do the work that involves, not in the long term anyway.'

'Shame really when you think of how hard your dad worked to build it.'

'Mm, I know. Some people see it as a historical treasure; others as an eyesore they'll be glad to see the back of,' he told her. 'I suppose it will come down in the end. But there's no immediate rush.'

'There's something sad about it, somehow,' she remarked, looking up at the top, shrouded in mist. 'It's as though it's been abandoned.'

'It has,' Billy grinned, his arm placed firmly around her shoulders. 'It's had its day, a victim of progress. We all have to move with the times.'

'I know but there's just something about it.' She looked up again and shivered. 'Ooh, it's kind of scary too. It sort of frowns down on you.'

'You daft thing,' he laughed. 'It's just a pile of bricks and mortar. It won't fall down on you.'

'I know that,' she assured him. 'It just seems sinister standing there in the mist.'

'Come on, let's go indoors before you go completely loopy,' he said tenderly.

'I thought Billy's young lady was very nice, didn't you, Hattie?' said Molly the next day at work.

'Lovely. And they seem so right for each other. I hope they stay together.'

'Me too.'

The other woman sighed. 'It was a pity the occasion was completely ruined by the news from Dan.'

'It wasn't ruined,' corrected Molly.

'It put a damper on things, though, didn't it?'

'Well, just a bit,' Molly was forced to admit. 'But Sally and Billy are too wrapped up in each other to bother too much about anything else. Anyway, after you'd had a talk to Dan, things cheered up.'

'It was all an act,' she confessed. 'I wanted to shut myself away and weep, if the truth be told.'

'I'm sad about it too,' admitted Molly. 'But he's made up his mind and we have to respect that, though I shall have another go at him if I get the chance.'

'You might as well talk to the wall,' sighed Hattie, 'for all the notice he takes.'

'Unfortunately, I think you're right,' agreed Molly.

There was a great deal of excitement in the Hawkins household at the beginning of December. Due to a special bonus from the pottery profits, they were able to join the legions of people who now had the magical wooden box standing in the corner. Keeping it as a surprise for Rosa, Molly had it delivered while she was at school.

156

'A television,' was her breathless reaction when she and Patsy went into the living room after school and saw it standing there, the walnut-veneered double doors closed across the screen. 'We've got a telly. Oh, Mum, I can't believe it.' She hugged her mother. 'You didn't tell me we were getting one.'

'I wanted it to be a surprise.'

'Oh, wow!' She opened the doors. 'How do you turn it on?'

'You do it like this,' said the experienced Patsy, turning a knob. 'You have to wait for it to warm up before the picture comes on. There won't be anything on yet. Children's programmes don't start until later.'

'I know that,' announced Rosa with a touch of indignance. 'I've seen the telly at your house, remember.'

'We'll be able to watch *Crackerjack* on Friday,' realised Patsy with enthusiasm.

'I can't wait,' enthused Rosa, adding excitedly, 'Ooh, look, the picture's coming.'

Leaving the girls staring at the test card, Molly went to the kitchen to get their tea. It had given her a great deal of personal satisfaction to be able to buy this addition to the home. It was fortunate that she had a regular wage to cover the normal household expenses too because she couldn't rely on Brian. He rarely sent anything now.

While she was slicing a loaf on the breadboard, the children's conversation drifted out to the kitchen from the open door of the living room.

'It's great that you've got a telly,' Patsy was saying. 'We'll be able to watch it here when we get in from school from now on, and talk about programmes we've seen in our own houses as well when we're not together.'

'Yeah, it'll be smashing,' agreed Rosa.

Molly felt sick. They wouldn't be doing anything together come Christmas because Dan and Patsy were leaving for Australia the week before. All the emigration paperwork had been completed. His house was in the process of being sold and would be left in the hands of the agent if it wasn't finalised before he left. He was keeping his share of the business to hand down to Patsy in the future, and would be a sleeping partner until then.

Most worryingly for Molly, she had noticed that Patsy spoke as though she was still going to be seeing Rosa in the same way as she did now, as though Australia was just a holiday, though she had been told that they were going for good, and spoke about living there. She obviously didn't fully appreciate the situation. She certainly had no idea of the enormity of the impending change.

Emptying a tin of spaghetti into the saucepan, Molly saw it through a blur of tears.

★ ★ ★

When the subject of Christmas came up, Brian found himself with a serious dilemma.

'If you go off and leave me for Christmas again this year, we're finished,' Beryl declared emphatically.

'Oh, come on, love . . .'

'I mean it, Brian. You either stay here or you take me with you to your parents, or it's over between us.'

'But it's difficult—'

'We're engaged now,' she cut in. 'So I don't expect to spend Christmas on my own.'

'You'll have your mum.'

'That isn't the same and you know it,' she rebuked. 'You know perfectly well what I mean.'

'Yeah, I suppose so.'

'Anyway, isn't it about time I met your parents?'

'You wouldn't go and leave your mum on her own at Christmas, surely.'

She thought about this. 'No, I don't suppose I would,' she admitted.

'There you are then.'

'But even apart from Christmas, I ought to meet your folks sometime as we're getting married soon.'

'Of course you should, and you will,' he said feebly.

'When though?' she persisted. 'I shall begin to think you're ashamed of me if you don't soon take me to meet them.'

'Of course I'm not ashamed of you and I will take you to meet them some time soon,' he lied, digging himself even deeper into a hole. 'It's just that it's such a long way and when I've been working hard all week, I don't feel like doing a lot of travelling at the weekend.'

'Mm, I can understand that,' Beryl said reasonably. 'But getting back to Christmas – as I wouldn't want to leave Mum on her own over the holiday, you'll have to stay here because I'm not prepared to spend Christmas without you.'

'They'll be upset if I don't go,' he said lamely.

'And I'll be upset if you do,' she spelled out, 'so you'll just have to write to them and tell them you won't be seeing them this year. Make some excuse.'

'But, Beryl—'

'I mean it, Brian. If you do go away you can take your ring with you and find new lodgings when you come back.'

'That's a bit harsh . . .'

'But necessary.' She doted on him, but she could be very assertive when she wanted her own way. She knew just how far she could push him and was confident that she wouldn't have to carry out her threat. 'I'm your fiancée and as such have the right to some consideration.'

Brian's thoughts were racing. Molly would be expecting him to go home for Christmas. But he didn't want to go and neither did he want to lose Beryl – not until he absolutely had to. He'd got far more emotionally involved with her than he'd intended. He'd never expected to feel anything for her beyond lust.

His feelings for Molly had always been painful in their intensity, heightened by the fact that they weren't reciprocated. With Beryl he felt comfortable and content. She would take no nonsense from him – as she was currently displaying – but he never doubted her feelings for him and that made him feel good about himself. Life here in Norfolk suited him – being with a woman who adored him, and having no responsibilities. He'd have to scarper soon because this wedding was getting frighteningly close. But not just yet. He wasn't ready to give Beryl up for the time being.

'OK, you win,' he said. 'I'll stay here and spend Christmas with you.'

She threw her arms around his neck. 'I knew you'd see things my way in the end, babe,' she said, kissing him. 'You're great and I love you to bits.'

God knows what he was going to tell Molly, he thought, but he'd come up with something. There was plenty of time – still a few weeks to go until the holiday.

'Rosa's hoping for a bike for Christmas, Dad,' Patsy informed him when he was putting her to bed one night. He'd just finished reading her a story and she was lying back, her dark hair loose on the pillow. She looked so much like Angie at that moment, he could hardly bear it. 'She's not sure if she'll get one because her mum might not be able to afford it but it'll be the best fun if she does 'cause we can go out on our bikes together. She has to have turns on mine at the moment.'

Dan frowned. His daughter seemed to have forgotten something. 'But we won't be here, sweetheart,' he reminded her gently. 'We'll be on the way to Australia at Christmas.'

'Oh yeah. I'll have to wait until I get back to see if she got the bike.'

Tension drew tight. He'd made the situation perfectly clear to her on several occasions and she'd seemed to understand. 'But we're not coming back, darling,' he pointed out. 'We're going there to live. I explained it all to you – you remember. You said you wanted to go.'

'I do. I want to go on the boat and everything and see my cousins . . .'

'That's all right then.'

'But when will I see Rosa again?'

His mouth dried, his heart pounded. He mustn't fudge the issue because she deserved the truth. 'Not for a very long time,' he explained, feeling terrible. 'If things go really well for me we might be able to afford to come back for a holiday at some time in the future but maybe not until you're grown up. As I've told you, Australia is a very long way away and it costs a lot of money to get there and back.'

'We . . . we might not ever come back then?'

He winced. 'We might not.' It hurt him to utter the words.

'So I won't see Gran or Uncle Billy or Uncle Josh or Auntie Molly again either.'

'It is possible that you won't.'

'What . . . never?'

'Nothing is definite, but yes, that could happen.'

'Oh.' The brutal truth was finally beginning to dawn. 'Can't they come with us?'

He bit his lip. 'No, love,' he said dully. 'That isn't possible.'

'I don't want not to ever see them, Dad.' Her voice wobbled horribly. 'I love them all.'

'You'll be fine when we get there,' he assured her, managing to sound positive. 'You'll have a new uncle and auntie and two cousins. You'll soon make new friends too.'

'But Rosa's my friend.'

'You'll probably find someone you like even better than Rosa,' he suggested hopefully, his heart like lead. The last thing he needed this close to departure was trouble from his daughter. He was anxious enough himself about the whole thing. 'We'll have a smashing life there, I promise.'

'But I don't want to leave everybody,' she said, her eyes filling with tears.

'You can write to them.'

'It won't be the same.'

'I did tell you that we were going there to live, Patsy,' he pointed out.

'I know but I thought we were coming back.' She looked utterly crestfallen.

'Look, I shall miss them all too,' Dan told her, 'but we'll soon get used to it. Anyway, you'll have me. I'll look after you the same as I do here.'

'I won't be able to watch Rosa's new telly with her,' she complained, 'or see what she has for Christmas or go there after school or anything.'

'You'll have plenty of things to look forward to in Australia,' he told her. 'You'll have just the best time ever with your cousins. All sorts of treats.'

'Will I?' She sounded extremely doubtful.

'Yes, you will,' he promised. 'They're all so looking forward to seeing you. I had a letter from your uncle just the other day. They're all really excited about us going.'

'But I want to come back.'

'You'll have to trust me on this one, darling,' he said on a firmer note.

'But, Dad—'

'You're too young to know what's best for your future so it's up to me to decide,' he told her. 'I really do believe it'll be a good thing. I

160

wouldn't have gone ahead with the arrangements otherwise. You know I wouldn't want you to be miserable.'

'I'll never come back . . .' She was becoming more disconsolate by the second.

He scratched his head, his eyes clouded with concern. 'Well, we're going and that's all there is to it.' He was stern now. 'So there's no point in making a fuss about it. We'll be together, that's the main thing.'

'I might forget about Mummy when we're not in this house,' she said, her dark eyes resting on him soulfully. 'I remember her here, in the kitchen, in the lounge, putting me to bed . . . everything.'

He was close to tears himself. But he couldn't let a seven-year-old child influence him on an issue as important as this. 'You'll never forget her, sweetheart, wherever we are,' he assured her. 'And neither will I. She'll always be in our hearts.'

'Will she?'

'Of course she will, all the time.' He smoothed her brow tenderly, then brushed it with a kiss. 'Off to sleep now or you'll be tired at school tomorrow.'

She turned over. ''Night, Dad,' she said thickly.

''Night, Patsy.'

Pausing outside her door, he heard her crying softly and it tore at his heart. Sometimes you had to be cruel to be kind, he told himself. One day she'd thank him for taking her to Australia; when she was grown up and enjoying the advantages. There was a dreadful ache nagging in the pit of his stomach though, as he went downstairs.

When Dan came to Molly's to collect Patsy after work on the day of the school Christmas party, the girls gave him a full account of the riotous celebrations; everything from pink blancmange to pass-the-parcel. When they'd finished their excited report, and the adults went into the kitchen for their usual cup of tea, Molly carefully closed the door.

'I know you're going to say I've to mind my own business but I feel I must tell you that Patsy is breaking her heart over this Australia thing,' she said, pouring the tea. 'She really doesn't want to go now that she realises it's for good.'

He heaved an eloquent sigh. 'I don't suppose Rosa wants to go to bed at night but you still make her go, don't you?' he said. 'She doesn't like going to the dentist either but you take her because it's for her own good.'

'That isn't the same thing at all.'

'Where would we be if we let children have their own way about everything?' He was snappy because she'd touched a raw nerve. 'Patsy isn't old enough to know what's right for her. It's my duty to give her the best chance in life I possibly can. There are opportunities out there for a good life.'

'I'm not doubting the greatness of Australia or the advantages of emigration,' she told him. 'An old schoolfriend of mine went to Sydney a few years ago with her husband and kids and they all love it, according to her mother.'

'Exactly my point.'

'It's the timing, Dan,' Molly went on determinedly. 'This isn't about a place and an improved standard of living. It's about a little girl who lost her mother and is now about to lose everyone else she loves.'

He looked grim. 'I do actually think she has feelings for me too, you know,' he pointed out gruffly.

'You've deliberately misunderstood me.' She was sharp now. 'Of course she loves you. You know very well what I meant.'

'I ought to,' he sighed. 'I've had Hattie on my back trying to talk me out of it ever since she's known about my plans. I'll be glad when we've gone and are away from all the negative influences. It's no wonder the child doesn't want to go, with you lot on at her the whole time.'

'Oh, come on, that really isn't fair,' she objected hotly. 'We've done everything we can to convince her that it'll be good in Australia and she'll love it. We've all been positive about it in front of her, regardless of our own opinions.'

'All right, all right, you've convinced me,' he said in a sharp but conciliatory manner. 'There's no need to break a blood vessel over it.'

'She's unhappy, Dan . . .'

'She'll get over it once we get there.'

'Won't you please reconsider?' She was begging now, such was her concern for Patsy.

'No. And I don't want to hear another word about it. At the weekend we'll be gone,' he declared. 'So get used to it and get off my back.'

'But—'

He got up and headed for the door, his tea barely touched. He opened the door and turned to her. 'Look, Molly, I know you mean well and you really do care for Patsy but how and where I bring her up is my business, no one else's.' His manner was sad but determined.

'I'd be failing Angie if I didn't try to persuade you to change your mind,' came her spirited response. 'I know in my heart that it's the last thing she would want for Patsy.'

He was very pale, his mouth tight and drawn. 'The decision has been made and is going to stand,' he announced.

She shrugged.

'I'll collect my daughter and be off then,' he said. 'Thanks for having her.'

'A pleasure.'

After they'd gone Molly sat on the sofa with her arm round Rosa, needing to feel her close. She stared unseeingly at the television screen, which was showing a current affairs programme. Rosa had her head in an

Enid Blyton Famous Five book and was reading aloud slowly and falteringly in a soft voice.

The room was adorned with paper chains, and a Christmas tree stood in the window, its coloured lights shining out into the street. Everything was in place for the festive season the same as every other year. But Christmas seemed bleak indeed this year. Not only would it be the Becketts' first Christmas without Angie but Dan and Patsy would be gone too. Poor Hattie. It was going to be hellish for her.

It was bitterly cold on Saturday morning, the heatless winter sunshine gleaming on the frost-covered walls and privet hedges of Darley Avenue. They were all gathered outside the Platers' house to see Dan and Patsy off in a taxi: Molly and Rosa, Hattie and the boys.

Hattie hugged Patsy and smothered her face with kisses. Billy picked her up and gave her one last cuddle. Even Josh seemed moved by the parting, and embraced her briefly. When Molly put her arms round Patsy she thought the child would never let her go. Rosa was pale and subdued. The little girls didn't hug; they just promised to write to each other in oddly formal voices. Eventually – sniffing and wiping her eyes – Patsy got into the taxi.

Billy and Josh shook hands with Dan and wished him good luck. Hattie hugged him. 'All the best, son,' she said, biting back the tears so as not to upset Patsy even more. 'I don't want you to go but since you're determined to do it, I hope it all goes well for you. Good luck and don't forget to write regular.'

He held her tightly for a moment. 'I won't,' he said, drawing back.

Molly gave him a peck on the cheek. 'I know I've given you a hard time lately but I do wish you well, Dan,' she said, swallowing hard on the lump in her throat. 'Make sure you look after yourself as well as Patsy.'

'Will do,' he said thickly.

And suddenly the taxi was rolling away down the street and turned the corner out of sight.

'Let's go home for a cuppa,' said Hattie, tears flowing freely now that they'd gone.

'Yeah, let's do that, Mum,' said Billy, putting a comforting arm round her.

She turned to Molly and Rosa who were looking bewildered. 'Come home with us, you two?' she invited warmly. 'You need company at a time like this.'

'Thanks, Hattie. I think you're right,' agreed Molly, taking Rosa's hand.

The dejected little gathering headed in the direction of the canal. No one seemed to notice the cold.

163

Chapter Eleven

Feeling like Satan himself, Dan sat next to his daughter in the taxi. Dry-eyed now, she was sitting well back in the seat, looking small and vulnerable. She'd pulled away when he'd tried to comfort her.

'Excited about going on the big ship?' he asked hopefully.

'S'pose so.'

'It's something new for us both,' he tried. 'Won't it be fun?'

She nodded miserably.

'I bet your cousins are really excited about seeing you now that we're actually on our way,' he ventured.

'Mm.'

His own enthusiasm had been punctured by her gloom and he was struggling to revive it. 'They'll all be waiting at the dock to meet us when we get off the boat,' he reminded her.

But she seemed more interested in her relatives this side of the ocean. 'I hope Gran isn't too sad,' she muttered, almost to herself. 'I don't like it when she cries. It makes my tummy go all wobbly.'

'Your gran will be fine,' Dan assured her. 'She's got your uncles and Auntie Moll and Rosa. They'll keep her cheerful.'

'Will they?'

'Course they will. Anyway, she's a very strong lady, your gran. She'll be all right.'

As all further attempts at conversation fell on deaf ears, he drifted into thought as the taxi headed for the station along the Uxbridge Road. He felt emotionally bruised. Partings were never easy but he hadn't expected this one to be quite so difficult. He should have been prepared, of course, since the Becketts were more like blood relatives than in-laws. His own parents had both died young; within a year or two of his marriage to Angie.

Seeing Hattie struggling not to weep as she'd said goodbye to her only grandchild, and the desperate way Patsy had clung to her, had all but wrecked his self-control. Then there had been the agonisingly restrained parting of the two little girls. But this was no time for negative thoughts. He must cast them out and stay positive. This was a very special chance for Patsy and there was no point in emigrating if all you could think about was what you had left behind. He had to look to the future, not dwell on the past. They were moving on to better things and their life in England would be finished the instant they boarded the ship.

He tried to concentrate his mind on such practicalities as finding a house and settling Patsy into an Australian school. But all that came were images of himself collecting his daughter from Molly's place after work and taking her home to the house he had grown to hate but which now seemed very dear to him, for some reason.

Angie came into his mind so vividly. It was as though she was there in the taxi with him. He could feel her; smell her soft feminine fragrance; hear her voice. He focused on the future to blank her out and realised with a shock that he'd been doing that ever since he'd come up with the emigration plan. He hadn't dared to consider how she might have felt about it because he knew in his heart that she wouldn't approve. In fact, she'd be horrified to know that he was taking Patsy away from everything that was familiar to her. But Angie was dead and it was up to him to decide what was best for Patsy.

Now his wife felt so close her presence was a tangible thing. She was accusing him of being a quitter, of trying to escape from his own grief and using Patsy as an excuse. Angie's voice beat into his brain, saying that the special thing he wanted for Patsy wasn't on the other side of an ocean. It was here with people she loved. But it wasn't Angie speaking. It was a voice within himself.

'Oh God,' he cried despairingly, not realising he'd uttered the words aloud. 'What have I done?'

A small hand curled into his. 'Sorry I've upset you, Dad,' said Patsy, drawing the wrong conclusion. 'I'll try to be good in Australia, I promise.'

He couldn't speak for the rising swell of tears. 'Oh, Patsy,' he managed at last, holding her close to him, 'you haven't upset me, sweetheart.'

'What's the matter then?'

'You mean so very much to me,' was all he could say.

'Well, I suppose I'd better be going,' said Molly after about her fourth cup of tea at The Hawthorns. 'I've got some shopping to do in the Broadway, and I need to call in on Mum to see if she wants to go to West Ealing this afternoon.'

'Yeah, I must get on too.' Hattie's voice was leaden. 'No point in sitting about feeling sorry for ourselves, is there? They've gone and that's all there is to it. Anyway, you boys will be wanting some food.'

'I'll go and get some fish and chips to save you cooking, if you like, Mum,' suggested Billy helpfully. 'You've had a rotten morning. You could do with a break from the stove.'

'Billy's right, Mum,' agreed Josh, who could be compassionate when he really put his mind to it. 'You take it easy.'

166

Exhausted with emotion Hattie said, 'Thanks, boys, that would be nice. I've no heart to do anything at the moment. Them going away has sapped all my energy.'

'Why not come round the shops with me and Mum this afternoon?' suggested Molly. 'It might take your mind off things for an hour or two.'

'I don't feel like it, love.'

'Do you good, Mum, to get out,' said Billy.

'I'll call in on my way just in case you change your mind,' said Molly, worried about her friend. The departure had been a cruel blow and she'd already been through so much. 'If you don't fancy it, it doesn't matter.' Molly turned to her daughter who'd hardly said a word since the taxi turned the corner. 'Let's get our coats on then, love.'

As Rosa trotted off ahead of Molly to the hall, Hattie remarked, 'The poor little mite is broken-hearted.'

'It'll take time for her to get used to it but kids adapt quicker than we do,' said Molly.

Rosa came tearing back into the room. 'There's a taxi outside,' she cried excitedly. 'I saw it through the hall window. I think Patsy and Uncle Dan are in it.'

'They must have forgotten something,' muttered Hattie as they all trooped to the door. 'He's cutting it a bit fine, isn't he? They'll miss the boat.'

Dan was getting out of the taxi when they opened the front door.

'What have you left behind?' enquired Hattie.

'You lot.' He was smiling in a way he hadn't done in a long time as he helped Patsy out of the taxi and paid the driver, who was unloading the luggage. 'And as you're not emigrating to Australia there's not much point in us going, is there?'

They all just stood there staring at him, not quite able to believe it.

'While you're gawping, can I use the phone to call the shipping company?' asked Dan. 'I need to let them know we won't be on board.'

Now they knew it was true.

'Not before I've given you a smacker,' said Hattie, rushing up and hugging him, tears running down her cheeks.

Molly and Hattie whooped for joy as Dan dashed indoors. They hugged Patsy while Rosa stood aside, looking bewildered.

'Want to come to my house to play this afternoon?' Patsy asked her somewhat bemused friend.

'Yeah, that'll be smashing,' smiled Rosa, and the two little girls went inside together, almost as though nothing had happened. The status quo had resumed and the disruption was already history.

'You'd better make that fish and chips for seven, Billy,' instructed Hattie, and Molly hadn't seen her look this happy since before her daughter died.

★ ★ ★

167

That afternoon Rosa went to Darley Avenue to play with Patsy while Molly went to West Ealing with her mother. Hattie decided to stay at home and hug the good news.

'Well, how does it feel to be on dry land instead of at sea?' Molly asked Dan later. She'd come to collect Rosa and was having a companionable cup of tea with him in the kitchen.

'Good – very good.' He offered her a biscuit. The girls were playing with their dolls in Patsy's room. 'I can't believe how stupid I've been. We both nearly lost everything we care about.'

'You certainly know how to wind people up,' she told him in friendly admonishment. 'I feel as though my emotions have been put through the wringer.'

He raised his eyes in a gesture of self-deprecation. 'Sorry about that. I've given you all a bad time, I know.' He was very contrite. 'You were right all along. It was *so* wrong for Patsy. It's a pity it took me until the last minute to realise it.'

'Better late than never.'

Dan seemed to need to talk so Molly asked, 'What happened in that taxi to make you change your mind?'

'Angie.'

'Angie?'

'I know it sounds ridiculous but she felt close to me suddenly, as though she was actually there.' He paused, thinking back. 'It was really weird but it made me face up to what I'd known all along but wouldn't accept: that all I was doing was running away.' His eyes became moist. 'When I think of what I almost did to my daughter because of my own selfishness . . .'

'You were misguided rather than selfish,' Molly said. 'You'd convinced yourself you were doing it all for her, hadn't you?'

'Yes, I had,' he admitted, thinking about it as he spoke. 'Right up until the truth dawned in the taxi, I really did believe I was doing it for her. I'd had doubts all along, naturally. Anyone making such a life-changing decision would, I should imagine. I banished them by telling myself it was the right thing for Patsy. But suddenly everything you said came home to me. I was looking for a new challenge to assuage my grief. But that'll be with me where I am, I know that now. You can't run away from yourself. I was desperate to escape from all the memories of Angie around here. But then it all sort of fell into place and I realised that I didn't want to lose them, not a single one. I want to be where she was. The more reminders of her the better.'

Molly gave an understanding nod.

'The truth began to dawn when I thought about Patsy in a new school and all I could see in my mind was myself collecting her from your place after work and her and Rosa meeting me at the door. I thought of her having to go through the ordeal of making new friends and not having you lot around her. Then there was Hattie's obvious heartbreak when she said goodbye to her – the memory of that was tormenting me. I just couldn't go through with it.'

'Thank goodness you couldn't.'

He drank his tea and rested his head on his fists. 'I can't tell you how relieved I am to be here. If I hadn't seen sense at the eleventh hour, we'd have been on that boat now. And once I'd gone I'd have felt I had to stick it out.'

'It's lucky you had trouble selling your house, as it turned out, isn't it?' she mentioned.

'Not half. I'll get on to the agent first thing Monday morning to tell them to take it off the market.

'It was a good job you left it furnished too, with instructions to the agent for everything to be auctioned when the house was finally sold.'

'I did that because I wanted everything to stay the same for Patsy until we'd gone,' he told her. 'I didn't want her to be uncomfortable in the run-up, with nowhere to sit and no carpet on the floor. I wanted it to be her home right up until the end.'

'That was thoughtful of you.'

'I'm not all bad, you know.' He gave her a wry grin. 'Even though you and Hattie have thought I was a brute this past few months.'

She gave him a knowing smile but didn't deny it.

'Anyway, that's all in the past.' Dan looked around the streamlined kitchen. 'Do you know, Moll, for the first time since Angie died. I actually feel as though this is home.'

'Because you came so close to losing it, I expect,' she suggested.

'Or maybe I've finally accepted that she's never coming back and I have to get on with life as it is and let the pain take its course.'

'Whatever the reason, I'm very pleased for you and Patsy, Dan.' She gave him a sheepish look. 'I'm also very pleased for myself. My life would have been hell until Rosa got used to being without Patsy. She'd have been moping about like a little lost soul.'

He shook his head. 'I can't believe how thoughtless I've been. Causing everyone such grief.'

'I think we might all manage to forgive you, as long as you don't get more mad ideas like that.' Molly stood up. 'But now I must collect my daughter and go home.'

'So soon?'

'Yes, I have to make supper.'

He thought about this, raking his thick chestnut hair back with his fingers. 'Look I haven't got anything special in because I didn't expect to be here,' he explained, 'but I did dash down the shops earlier for some essentials. I could knock up something simple for the four of us. I could do with some company after such a traumatic day, and the kids would love it.'

'I'd like that too, Dan,' she smiled.

'Good. All we need to do now is decide what's on the menu. I expect Patsy will want her beloved burgers with whatever we have. She's mad on them.'

'So's Rosa, and every other kid in London since they appeared in the shops.'

It was past ten o'clock when Molly got Rosa home. Dan hadn't been able to give them a lift because his car had been sold in the expectation of emigration. But Molly didn't mind the walk, even though it was cold; she rather enjoyed it and was feeling oddly happy and relaxed. She and Dan had got talking and the time had flown by. Naturally the children were too cute to remind them and had played quietly in Patsy's bedroom.

'I'm glad Patsy didn't go away, Mum,' confessed Rosa when Molly tucked her into bed.

'Me too, love,' she said. 'Very glad.'

It hardly seemed possible that a day with such a dire beginning could have taken such a dramatic turn for the better, she thought. She had really enjoyed the evening too, and was glad to be on good terms with Dan again. The atmosphere between them had been intermittently fraught with hostility ever since he'd said he was going away. But this evening they'd reverted to normal. They'd talked about Angie most of the time, as usual, but they had touched on other subjects too; ordinary everyday things. Having known each other for so long they never lacked for conversation. He was a nice bloke; she hoped he'd find love again one day.

Rosa's hopes were rather more immediate. 'I wish Christmas would hurry up and come,' she said sleepily. 'It's taking such a long time.'

'The sooner it comes, the sooner it will be over,' Molly said, kissing her brow. 'And you'll have to wait a very long time for the next one.'

'I still want it to come quickly.'

'It'll come,' said Molly. ''Night, love.'

''Night, Mum.'

On the morning of the day before Christmas Eve Molly answered the telephone in the office to be informed by the operator that there was a long-distance call for her from Norfolk. Having told her to put it through, Molly found herself listening to the voice of a stranger.

'Is that Mrs Hawkins?' asked the man.

'Yes.'

'I'm a mate of your husband's,' he explained. 'He asked me to give you a bell.'

Molly's hand flew to her throat. Something must be wrong or Brian would have called her himself. 'What's happened to him?' she asked, panicking.

170

'Nothing serious,' he replied. 'But he is laid up. He's got flu and it's gone to his chest.'

'Oh Lord. Is he very bad?'

'Not too good.'

'I'll come to Norfolk,' she said at once. 'Tell him I'll get there as soon as I can. I'll find out the times of the trains.'

'No, no,' the man said swiftly. 'He said to tell you that there's no need for anything like that.'

'But I must—'

'It's a very contagious strain of flu, apparently,' he cut in. 'Everybody around here is going down with it and he doesn't want to risk passing it on to you. Says he doesn't want to spoil Christmas for your little girl.'

'Oh . . .'

'The only thing is – he isn't well enough to travel home. So he won't be back for the holiday.'

'I'll come there then,' Molly suggested again.

'No, there's no need really.'

'But he's my husband,' she persisted, imbued with a sense of duty. She didn't love Brian but she hated to think of him ill and alone. 'I can't just leave him there on his own when he's ill – especially at Christmas.'

'He's being well looked after,' the man assured her speedily. 'The doctor has given him some medicine and his landlady is taking good care of him.'

'Oh, that's good of her. Not all landladies would want to bother with a sick lodger.'

'This one's a real gem; just like a mother to him, running around after him and spoiling him rotten.'

'I bet he loves that.'

'That's what I told him.'

'So, are you sure I don't need to come?'

'Certain,' he confirmed in a definite tone. 'He told me to tell you not to think of travelling all this way. Says that he'll get home for a weekend as soon as he's back on his feet again.'

'So I'll see him then, if he's sure he doesn't want me to come.'

'He's positive, honestly.'

'Give him my love then.'

'Will do . . .'

The money must have run out because the pips cut him off.

Molly replaced the receiver, feeling deeply ashamed of her intense relief that Brian wouldn't be home for the holiday. How awful for a wife to feel that way about her husband. But he'd put such a damper on things last year she'd been dreading his being around. And his mate did seem very certain that there was nothing seriously wrong with him.

★ ★ ★

In Boxham High Street a man came out of a telephone box and joined another who had been listening outside.

'Well, did she seem convinced?' asked Brian.

'Yeah, she sounded quite concerned about you, an' all,' said his pal. 'You don't deserve her.'

'Are you absolutely sure that there's no chance of her coming here?' He needed further assurance. If Molly turned up and found out what he was really up to over Christmas, the fat really would be in the fire.

'You were listening,' he reminded him. 'You heard every word I said. You heard me make it clear that it wouldn't be necessary and she realised it.'

'What did she actually say?'

'That she wouldn't come as you're being looked after,' he said. 'Anyway, she wouldn't want to ruin the kid's Christmas, would she? Coming all this way and staying in some lodgings in a strange town.'

'No, that's true.'

'It's a dangerous game you're playing, though, mate,' warned the man. 'You won't get away with it for ever. I'm surprised you have for this long. Even if your wife doesn't twig – sooner or later – Beryl will.'

'I'll make the most of it while I can then,' was Brian's chirpy response.

The man held out his hand. 'That's a quid you owe me for doing your dirty work,' he declared.

Brian handed over the money. 'Thanks, mate. I'm grateful to you.'

'Any time. I think you're a fool and I didn't enjoy lying for you to someone who sounded so nice but the dosh will come in handy.'

'I'll treat you to a pint as a bonus,' Brian told him. 'You've got me out of a jam.'

'I'll have a whisky as you're feeling grateful,' said his mate.

'Don't push your luck,' joked Brian.

'You're the one who's doing that,' warned the man as the two of them walked along the High Street to the nearest pub.

'Problems?' enquired Hattie, who had heard the conversation because both women were in Molly's office looking through the post.

'Nothing serious,' replied Molly. 'It was a friend of Brian's to tell me that he's gone down with flu and won't be coming home for Christmas.'

'Aah, what a shame,' Hattie sympathised.

'I thought I ought to go to Norfolk but he insisted that there's no need. His landlady is looking after him very well apparently.'

'That's just as well. You don't want to be miles away at Christmas, especially for Rosa. And neither do you want to catch the flu.'

'Exactly,' agreed Molly.

Hattie lapsed into thought. 'Why not come to us for Christmas Day?' she suggested. 'It won't be as jolly as usual – our first without Angie – but Dan and Patsy are coming so the kids will have each other for company.' She paused. 'Bring your mum with you, if you like.'

'She's going to Peggy's this year,' said Molly, 'arriving there on Christmas Eve and staying over.'

'All the more reason to come to us then,' Hattie urged her. 'You'll be more than welcome. In fact I'd love it if you came. We'll all be feeling a bit emotional because of Angie so we can cheer each other up. We'll have to make an effort for the children, anyway.'

'Thanks, Hattie,' Molly said gratefully. 'I'd love to, and I know Rosa will be thrilled.'

'Good. That's settled then.' Turning her attention to a letter she was holding, Hattie asked, 'Now what do you think about this request we've had for a visit in the spring from the Acton branch of the WI . . .'

Joan was very cynical about Brian staying in Norfolk over Christmas. 'Seems a bit fishy to me,' she said that evening when she called at Molly's. They were sitting at the kitchen table and Rosa was watching the television in the other room so they could speak freely. 'I mean, you want to be in your own home when you're ill, don't you? It's only natural.'

'He's not well enough to make the journey, apparently,' Molly explained.

'He'd have got here if he'd really wanted to, with it being Christmas.'

'Bringing the flu with him too,' Molly reminded her mother, 'so that Rosa and I would probably have gone down with it over Christmas.'

'There is that, I suppose. But he hardly ever comes home now, does he?'

'No.' Molly could hardly deny it.

'Don't you ever wonder why?'

'He's told me why,' replied Molly. 'It's a long way to travel and he doesn't fancy the journey after working all week. I think it's perfectly understandable.'

'You wouldn't catch Reg staying away from Peggy for so long.'

Here we go again, thought Molly, but said, 'Well, they have a perfect marriage, don't they? Brian and I have never come anywhere near that.'

'You've got a lot to thank Brian for.'

'Have you ever heard me deny it?'

'It'll be your own fault if he's got another woman,' she went on, as though Molly hadn't spoken.

'Ah, so that's your theory, is it?' responded Molly. 'You think that's the reason he doesn't come home – because he's busy with someone else.'

'Don't tell me it hasn't crossed your mind,' was Joan's swift reply. 'Any woman would be suspicious if her husband was away all the time and showed no sign of wanting to come home. I mean, he's a young man.'

Molly had wondered about that from time to time but it was such a relief not to have Brian at home, she didn't really mind what the reason was. It was a dire state for any marriage to be in but she couldn't help her feelings. 'Of course I've thought about it,' she admitted.

'Why haven't you got on a train to Norfolk to sort it out then?' Joan wanted to know.

'Because I have responsibilities here,' Molly reminded her. 'I have a living to earn and a young child to raise. Anyway, if he's fallen in love with another woman there isn't much I can do about it, is there?'

'Fallen in love,' Joan snorted as though Molly had just told her that Brian was about to take up holy orders. 'Don't talk wet. It'll just be the old how's-your-father he's interested in. It's in a man's make-up. They've no self-control when it comes to that sort of thing.'

'Well, I'm certainly not going to Norfolk to catch him at it,' Molly told her.

'You should fight for your man.'

If she was in love with him she would do whatever it took to keep him. But she just said, 'Leave it, Mum . . .'

No chance of that now that Joan had the bit between her teeth. 'You've only yourself to blame if he's looked elsewhere,' she accused. 'You've driven him away, going out to work against his wishes.'

'It's just as well I am able to earn a living,' Molly informed her, 'because I get no support from him.'

'Well, I hope you're not going to bring scandal on the family with a divorce,' Joan went on. 'We were only spared disgrace before because Brian stepped in.'

With you shoving me into his arms, Molly thought, but said, 'Yeah, yeah, I know. Anyway, all this about Brian and another woman is pure supposition so let's change the subject, shall we? Are you looking forward to going to Peggy's tomorrow?'

'Oh, yes,' Joan replied, with an instant change of mood. 'They always look after me very well when I go there.'

The implication being that Molly didn't – at least it felt that way to her. 'Is Reg coming to collect you in the car?' she wondered.

'Oh, no, the shop will be busy on a Christmas Eve. I shall go by bus but I expect he'll run me home in the car on Boxing Day or the day after.'

'But how will you manage with your case and all the presents to carry?' Molly was concerned.

'I'll be all right. I'm only taking a small overnight bag for my clothes, and the presents aren't heavy,' she explained with a note of assertion, as though pre-empting any criticism of Peggy that Molly might make.

'I'll give you a hand with your luggage to the bus stop,' Molly offered.

'There's no need.' Joan threw Molly a look. 'They're very good to me, you know. Nothing's too much trouble for them when I'm there.'

From what Molly had heard, her mother spent most of the time doing Peggy's domestic chores, but she deemed it wise not to mention it. 'Rosa and I are going to the Becketts as we'll be on our own,' she told her.

'Oh, I see.' At least she had the grace to look a little sheepish, as she hadn't even asked Molly if she might need company over Christmas. 'I'm sure you and Rosa would be very welcome at Peggy's, you know. Why not give her a ring?'

'I'd rather be here on Christmas morning for Rosa to open her presents at home.' She and her mother had already exchanged gifts, and hers and Rosa's were hidden away. 'We'll walk round to Hattie's in time for lunch. It'll be nice for Rosa because she'll have Patsy for company.'

'Yeah, there is that.'

'Anyway, Mum, let's have a Christmas drink together, shall we?' invited Molly to lift the atmosphere. 'Sherry?'

'Please.'

Each with her sherry, and a glass of lemonade for Rosa, they went into the living room.

'So, I don't suppose you're excited then, Rosa?' said Joan, teasing her in a rare moment of humour.

'Ooh, not much,' laughed Molly. 'If she gets any more wound up she'll explode.'

'I feel as though it'll never come,' said the child, sighing impatiently.

'It'll be here and gone before you know it,' said Joan dismissively. 'This time next week you'll have forgotten all about it and be bored stiff with all the presents.'

Her mother was quite right, of course, but to spell it out so bluntly to an excited child seemed rather tactless to Molly.

However, Rosa wasn't put off that easily. 'I won't,' she said cheerfully.

Molly raised her glass. 'Well, here's to a happy Christmas, Mum,' she put in swiftly, for fear her mother would destroy the festive spirit completely. 'Raise your glass to your gran, Rosa. You won't see her tomorrow.'

'Happy Christmas, Gran,' she said dutifully.

Christmas Day passed pleasantly after an early start. Rosa was delighted with her new bike, which Molly let her ride to the Becketts', with her walking behind.

Naturally everyone was painfully aware of the latest empty place at the Christmas dinner table and it was a poignant moment when they raised their glasses to Angie and George. But an effort to be cheery was made by all because of the children, though they were too taken with their new bikes – Patsy's swiftly purchased by Dan after the emigration was cancelled – to bother unduly about the mood of the adults.

The house was decorated as usual with paper chains and all sorts of glittering paraphernalia. A huge Christmas tree stood in the hall and there were bowls of sweets, nuts and fruit liberally spread around the house. Hattie wanted everything to be as near to normal as possible for the sake of the children.

No one was in the mood for the party games they usually played on Christmas afternoon but the girls were happy amusing themselves so everyone else just sat around talking and eating sweets. Billy went over to Sally's on the bike and brought her back for tea, after which they gathered around the television to watch a pantomime.

Molly stayed later than she intended and Rosa was so tired, Dan drove them home in the second-hand car he'd purchased to replace the one he'd sold, thinking he wouldn't need it. Patsy was half asleep too. They left the bikes at Hattie's because they couldn't get them both in the car.

'I'm glad today is over,' Dan confessed to Molly as the children chatted in the back of the car.

'I can imagine,' she said. 'I don't suppose Hattie is sorry to see the back of it either. Christmas always intensifies sadness. Angie hasn't been far from my thoughts today either, but then she rarely is.'

From the back seat came a request. 'Can I play with Rosa tomorrow, Dad?' asked Patsy.

'You'd better ask her mother,' he replied. 'They might already be doing something.'

'We've nothing on,' Molly told him.

'So, which house is it to be, mine or yours?' he asked.

She thought about this. 'If it's dry in the afternoon why don't we take them to Churchfields on their new bikes?' Molly suggested. 'It'll be a nice walk for us too.'

Cries of approval came from behind.

'It seems the decision has been made for us,' Dan smiled.

'I'll see you tomorrow then,' Molly said as they drew up outside the flats.

'About two o'clock at Hattie's to collect the bikes, and we'll go from there,' he suggested, getting out of the car and opening the door for her.

'We'll be there.' Molly slid out. 'Thanks for the lift.'

'Thanks, Uncle Dan,' echoed Rosa sleepily as he helped her out.

'A pleasure,' he said.

That same evening Billy and Sally drew up on the motorbike outside her house.

'Well, did you enjoy yourself?' he asked as they walked towards the gate.

'It was sh . . . ma . . . sh . . . ma . . . shing,' she said, her voice noticeably slurred. She was swaying slightly and sucking on a sweet. She always had boiled sweets with her, though Billy teased her about ruining her teeth. 'Reeelly good. Tha . . . nks.'

She walked right into the gate.

176

'Hey, you're supposed to open it first,' he reminded her affectionately, opening it for her, whereupon she walked unsteadily to the house with one foot on the path and the other in the flower border.

'Whoops,' she laughed as he took her arm and guided her on to firmer footing.

'Someone must have been spiking your lemonade, I reckon,' Billy suggested lightly.

'Yeah,' she giggled drunkenly.

When they reached the front door she seemed to sober up a little. 'I'm ever so tired, Billy,' she explained slowly, 'so would you mind not coming in?'

He was disappointed because he and Sally usually got down to some serious snogging after her parents had gone to bed. But he said, 'No, of course I don't mind.' She was fumbling with her key in the lock. 'Here, let me do that for you.'

He saw her safely inside, kissed her good night and left, feeling puzzled. She was obviously tiddly but she never drank alcohol. In all the time he'd known her he'd never seen her touch a drop. She said she didn't like the taste, so she stuck to soft drinks. Someone had been having fun at her expense and Billy had a pretty good idea who that someone was . . .

'I never touched her drinks,' Josh denied hotly when Billy confronted him after their mother had gone to bed. 'What would be the point? She isn't my girlfriend. I've no reason to get her drunk so that I can have my way with her.'

'Meaning that it was me.' Billy was offended. 'I wouldn't do that to Sally.'

'Well, no one else that was here would have a motive, would they?' Josh pointed out.

'Some immature people think that sort of thing is funny,' Billy said meaningfully. 'They do it for a bit of a lark.'

'It wasn't me, Billy, I swear,' Josh denied again. 'She probably had a few crafty ones when you were looking the other way. There was plenty of booze about and everyone was helping themselves to what they wanted.'

'Why would she do a thing like that?'

'Dunno,' shrugged Josh. 'You can't expect me to know what makes women tick. You're the expert.'

Billy stroked his chin. 'I can't see what purpose she would have—'

'Perhaps she wants you to think she doesn't have any vices,' cut in Josh. 'Wants you to think she's whiter than she actually is.'

That didn't make sense to Billy because Sally knew he didn't disapprove of alcohol. But there didn't seem to be any other explanation. The whole thing was best forgotten. He certainly wasn't going to embarrass Sally by mentioning it. 'It was probably just my imagination,' he said to protect her.

'Children are resilient little creatures, aren't they?' Dan remarked to Molly the next day as they walked through Churchfields, the children cycling on ahead on the path, well wrapped up in warm coats, scarves and red bobble hats knitted by Hattie. The weather was invigorating: cold and breezy, the sun very occasionally breaking through the grey-tinged clouds that were rolling swiftly across the sky. The park that was so lush in summer was bleak now, the viaduct etched against the sky through the skeletal trees, the church spire seeming to touch the clouds.

'They certainly are, but what brings you to that conclusion at this particular moment?'

'Well, I know that Patsy misses her mum; she still cries for her at times. But she can also manage to enjoy life. Look at her now. She's having a whale of a time.'

'And you can't enjoy life?'

'No. Everything is merely endured for me. I don't enjoy anything; I just get through the days, thankful when each one is over,' he said.

'Still, you're able to put up a front now, though,' Molly observed. 'So that's an improvement.'

'Patsy shocked me into that by asking if she could go and live with you,' he reminded her. 'But I never feel normal like I used to. I don't think I ever will now that Angie's gone.'

'That's a bit bleak, Dan.'

'It is. But I don't see how anything can be normal for me without her.'

'It will be eventually, I should think,' was Molly's opinion. 'It isn't even a year yet since she died.'

'There's this sick pain that won't go away,' he confided. 'I get pleasure from Patsy; just being with her and watching her grow. But even that is tinged with sadness because I'm not sharing it with Angie. I think about her all the time and I don't want to forget her for a second. I'm scared if I let go for a moment she'll fade into the past.'

'You'll never forget her,' Molly said, 'but you're a young man with a long way to go. It's bound to get better for you.'

'Maybe.'

'I must admit that not a day goes by when I don't miss Angie,' Molly confided. 'Ordinary little everyday things that I would have told her, I can't now. I miss the laughs, the chats, just the fact that she was always around. We go back such a long way, you see.'

'Yes, you do. It must be hard for you, losing such a close friend,' he sympathised.

'It is.'

'I've been too wrapped up in myself to worry much about how other people might be feeling, though I have been concerned about Hattie, of course.'

'She's had a rough time, the poor love – losing George, then Angie.' Molly turned and smiled at him. 'Still, you gave her the best Christmas present *ever* when you changed your mind about Australia. I'll never ever forget the look on her face when you arrived back and told us.'

'I don't think I will either,' he said. 'She didn't know whether to laugh or cry so did a bit of both.'

'It was one of those moments that get imprinted in your memory.'

'Mm. It didn't make up for all the grief I caused her before that though, did it?'

'I wouldn't be so sure about that. Emigration wasn't one of your most brilliant ideas, I admit,' Molly told him. 'But that's all in the past now and your coming back in the taxi gave Hattie such joy. There's no pleasure without pain, remember.'

'Hattie's had a bit too much on the pain side of things just lately.'

'It hasn't seemed too well balanced for her this past year, I must admit,' she agreed. 'Let's hope she doesn't have any more upsets.'

'I really hope she's had her share – for a good few years, anyway.'

They walked on in silence for a while; then Dan returned to the subject that was so much on his mind. 'I think I'd feel guilty if I felt happy,' he told her. 'It would seem as though I was betraying Angie.'

'You wouldn't be, though.'

'It feels that way.'

'Well, I'm enjoying this walk, anyway,' Molly said in an effort to prevent him from sinking into despair. Her cheeks were flushed from the cold, the wind blowing her blonde hair. 'It's a bit on the chilly side but it clears the head after all that overindulgence yesterday.'

'It certainly does.'

She turned to look at him; his thick hair was ruffled by the wind, his tawny eyes a little less sad than they had been lately. 'Be careful,' she joked. 'You might have to admit to enjoying it too.'

'Yeah, I'll have to watch that,' he said, taking the joke in good part.

'I think Angie would forgive you for finding pleasure in a walk in the park with your daughter, you know.' She paused, looking ahead. 'And talking of your daughter, she's just taken a tumble off her bike.'

They ran towards Patsy, who was already scrambling up when they reached her, with no real damage done to herself or the bike. Her father gave her a quick cuddle and she was soon back in the saddle.

'I told you children were resilient, didn't I?' he grinned at Molly as the children rode on ahead.

'Ooh, Dan,' she said in mock admonishment, 'you really will have to be careful.'

He looked at her, puzzled. 'Why?'

'You were smiling again and meaning it too,' she explained with a saucy grin. 'If you don't watch yourself you might start laughing.'

'And it'll all be your fault,' he came back at her, and they walked on together in the winter sunshine.

Chapter Twelve

Although business was slow in the shop in the new year, things were buzzing on the production side as the potters laboured to restock the shelves depleted in the Christmas rush. They were also exhibiting Beckettware at a craft fair in London quite soon. And there was never any shortage of work in the office.

A busy lifestyle suited Molly. A high activity level energised her, kept her buoyant throughout the day. Keeping up to date with her work in the office was a constant battle with her part-time hours, but she wasn't defeated by the challenge. Occasionally she had to come in for a few hours at the weekend to catch up, in which case either Hattie or Dan would look after Rosa.

Molly saw quite a lot of Dan outside working hours, which was inevitable given the closeness of their offsprings' friendship. She continued to mind Patsy after school, and Rosa usually went to play with her friend at Dan's at some point over the weekend. Molly and Dan got on well. Their mutual love of Angie was their main connection but the fact that they had children of the same age meant they had plenty of other things in common.

But the pleasant rhythm of Molly's life was interrupted towards the end of January when Brian came home for the weekend . . .

'You look well,' she observed when he arrived Friday night after Rosa had gone to bed, having not bothered to inform Molly that he was coming. 'Your flu attack doesn't seem to have had any lingering effects.'

A brief hiatus, then, 'I had flu, not double pneumonia,' he snapped, his highly developed instinct for self-preservation making him edgy.

'No need to bite my head off,' she responded. 'Even flu can leave you feeling very run down.'

'I was lucky, I suppose,' he said, hoping he sounded convincing, and adding quickly, 'I was feeling really rough over Christmas, though.'

'Mm. That must have been awful for you.' She paused, casting a thoughtful eye over him, noticing a considerable expansion to his person. 'That landlady of yours must be feeding you well.'

'I have put on a bit of weight,' he said as though rather proud of it. 'She's such a terrific cook and she isn't mean with the portions either.'

Treble helpings of suet pudding every mealtime by the look of his

181

extra chins and corpulent middle, she thought, but moved on without comment. 'You should have let me know you were coming then I could have—'

She was cut short. 'I'm your husband and this is my home; I can come and go as I please without giving notice,' he interrupted irritably.

'Of course, but—'

'I thought you'd be pleased to see me.'

She avoided having to lie by saying, 'I only meant that if you'd let me know, I'd have got in the food you like.'

'The shops are open tomorrow so where's the problem?'

'There isn't one.'

'Exactly.'

Absence hadn't made the heart grow fonder, she was sad to perceive. There was such friction between them she was relieved when he said he was going out to the pub. When he got back, half-cut and aggressive, he commented on the television set.

'You've obviously got more money than I have,' he observed. 'So perhaps I should stop sending you any.'

'That's a good one, since you haven't sent any for ages,' she retaliated.

'You don't need it, by the look of things,' he stated moodily. 'If you can afford to go out shopping for a television set, and a bike for Rosa for Christmas, perhaps it's you who should be sending money to me.'

'It's up to you and your conscience what you do about financial support for Rosa and me,' she said wearily. 'I've no intention of trying to force you to do anything.'

'I'm glad to hear it,' he declared with an air of rebellion. He leaned back in the chair, staring into space, then his lids drooped, his mouth fell open and his snoring was enough to wake the entire neighbourhood.

Not a pretty sight, she thought, as she left the room and headed for bed.

The following afternoon a row erupted over a prior arrangement of Molly's.

Not knowing that Brian would be at home, she and Dan had arranged to take the girls to the park. When Dan called at the flat – unaware that things had changed – she explained the situation and he took Rosa with him and Patsy. But not before Brian had embarrassed Molly to a toe-curling degree by being hostile towards Dan. He blatantly ignored him and turned the volume on the television up to make it obvious that he wasn't welcome.

'You're very matey with him, aren't you?' Brian said accusingly, as soon as she shut the door behind Dan and the children.

'Yes, we are good friends,' she admitted without hesitation. 'It's because of the girls. There was no need for you to be so rude to him.'

He narrowed his eyes at her suspiciously, ignoring her comment. 'Oh, so that's it; that's what's been going on behind my back.'

'Don't be so ridiculous,' Molly rebuked. 'We're bound to see a lot of each other as our daughters are best friends. Now that Angie isn't around and he's bringing Patsy up, we can't really avoid each other.'

'But you were going out with him this afternoon,' he said with a burning stare.

'Only to the park with the children,' she reminded him, her voice rising with irritation. 'What could be more innocent than that?'

'God knows what happens when the kids have gone to bed at night.'

'How can anything happen when he's in his house and I'm here?'

'Are you trying to tell me that you're never together without the children?'

'Only at work,' she said, 'and there are plenty of people around then.'

In that Brian had demanded nothing of her in bed last night – much to her relief because she couldn't bear him to touch her now – she was certain that her mother was right and he had found someone else because he was a man with a large sexual appetite. So this was clearly a case of double standards but she knew he would deny it if questioned, and things would get even nastier.

'I don't believe you,' he stated. 'I think you're carrying on with him.'

'Oh, Brian, give me a break.'

'It didn't take you long to climb into your best friend's husband's bed, did it?'

That was one accusation too many. Molly swung her hand across his face so hard her palm stung. 'How dare you?' she rasped. 'How dare you accuse me of such a thing?'

He stood there holding his face and looking at her in astonishment. She had never dared to do such a thing before. 'You spiteful cow,' he said through clenched teeth.

'You drove me to it.' She was trembling and hardly able to believe she'd done that, since violence wasn't normally in her nature. She needed to distance herself from him for fear she might lose control again if he continued to goad her. 'I'm going to do some ironing in the kitchen. I know how that annoys you, and had I known you were coming I would have made sure it was all done and out of the way. But if you turn up unexpectedly, you'll have to take us as you find us.'

'You speak as though I'm some distant relative.'

'Not at all. You've been away a long time,' she reminded him. 'It's only natural that Rosa and I would get used to your not being around. In the same way as you're accustomed to your life in Norfolk without us, I should imagine.'

'I suppose so,' he agreed quickly, because he didn't want to linger on the subject of his life in Boxham. Questions might be asked.

'There's usually horseracing on the telly on a Saturday afternoon, or sport of some kind,' she informed him. 'So why don't you watch that while I get on with the ironing?'

He shrugged and sat down in the armchair while she went to the kitchen. His presence here depressed her terribly. She was also extremely disappointed to have missed her outing to the park with Dan and the girls. It was good fun when the four of them were together. Still, Brian's going back tomorrow, she thought with relief. This line of thought reminded her again of how abysmal it would be when he came back permanently; he'd be complaining about every single thing and expecting her to account for her every move. But he was her husband so she would just have to try harder. She put the ironing board up and set to work while Brian snoozed in front of the television.

The evening of the same day Beryl and her mother were sitting at a table in the local pub where Beryl usually went with Brian on a Saturday night. She was furious with Brian for going off for the weekend without her – his mother was ill, apparently – and she was blowed if she was going to sit at home moping. That wasn't her style. So she'd put on her tightest sweater, clingiest skirt, highest stilettos, and dragged her mother down to the pub so that she didn't have to go on her own. A few gins and some harmless flirting was just what she needed to cheer her up.

'He's only gone to see his mother,' said Flo. 'Surely that should go in his favour. A man who looks after his mum is a man you can trust.'

'Why wouldn't he take me with him if he thinks so much of me?' pouted Beryl.

'Because his mother's ill,' her mother replied. 'Would you want to see a complete stranger if you'd had to take to your bed?'

'No, I suppose not,' she said, softening a little, mostly from the effects of the gin. 'But he doesn't seem at all keen for me to meet his people.'

'All in good time,' comforted Flo.

''Ello, darlin',' said Mick, one of Brian's mates from the building site. 'Where's lover boy tonight?'

'Gone to see his sick mother,' she told him.

'Oh, really.' All the boys knew about Brian's double life. 'Well, will you let me buy you a drink?' He turned to Flo. 'Something for you, an' all?'

'That's very civil of you,' smiled Flo. 'I'll have a gin and orange, please.'

'Beryl?'

'The same please.'

Mick – a dark-haired hunk who'd seriously fancied Beryl for ages – sat down at their table. 'You don't mind if I join you, do you?'

'Course not.' Beryl glanced across the room at a crowd of men from the building site who were standing near the bar. 'We're flattered that you'd rather be with us than your mates. You men usually like to stand together at the bar.'

'Not when there's such a good-looking alternative,' he said, his dark, heavy-lidded eyes resting on Beryl suggestively.

Still angry with Brian and with several gins inside her, Beryl responded with one of her sexiest looks. 'Flattery will get you everywhere,' she said invitingly.

'Behave yourself now, Beryl,' put in her mother. 'You're spoken for, remember.'

'Mu-um,' objected Beryl, glaring at Flo, 'I'm not some little kid. I know how to behave.'

Just then there was an interruption. 'Well, well, if it isn't Flo Brown,' said a middle-aged man, appearing at the table. 'The wife said she thought it was you over here. Haven't seen you for a while, love. How are you?'

'Not so bad. Yourself?'

'Mustn't grumble,' said the man who'd moved to Boxham from London at about the same time as the Browns, and lived nearby. 'Come and have a drink with me and the wife.' He glanced towards Beryl and Mick. 'Leave the young 'uns on their own for a while. We're sitting at a table over in the corner.'

'Go on, Mum,' urged Beryl, who was enjoying Mick's attention and didn't want her mother cramping her style. 'Go and have a drink with your friends.'

Flo looked doubtful, guessing what was on her daughter's mind.

'I'm not going anywhere,' Beryl assured her. 'I'll still be here when you come back.'

'OK then,' said Flo, rising. 'Shan't be long.'

'That's a shame,' said Mick when Flo was out of earshot. 'You staying here, I mean. I was hoping that you and me could make a night of it; go on somewhere else; have a few drinks and . . . well, get to know each other better without your mum's beady eyes on us.'

'I'd better not.'

'I've had my eye on you ever since I first saw you, do you know that?' he told her.

'I thought you were supposed to be a mate of Brian's,' she said in girlish admonishment. 'And here you are trying to get off with his fiancée.'

'I work with Brian but he isn't actually a mate of mine,' Mick made clear.

'But you know I'm engaged to him, don't you?' she pointed out. 'I thought there was a code among you blokes about that sort of thing.'

'Among mates there is, but – like I said – Brian isn't a mate, as such.'

'Be that as it may,' she said, enjoying the power of her sexuality, especially as the ring on her finger gave her the security of not having to impress Mick; she was only doing so for fun, 'I'm engaged so not available.'

'Let me get you another drink.'

'Thanks,' she said, getting tipsier by the minute.

After she'd consumed another couple of gins, he said, 'You're looking a bit flushed, Beryl. Would you like to go outside for some fresh air?'

She might be three sheets to the wind but she wasn't too far gone to know what he had in mind. 'Look,' she began in a slow, laboured voice, 'it's nothing personal. You're a really good-looking bloke and everything, but I'm not the sort of girl to cheat on my fella.'

'Why did you come in here looking like that then?' he asked, fixing his eyes on her tight sweater.

'Didn't fancy staying in,' she replied in a matter-of-fact tone. 'Why should I when Brian's gone swanning off for the weekend without me?' She leaned forward in a confiding manner. 'I'm livid with him, to tell you the truth.'

'I don't blame you,' he sympathised artfully. 'He must be off his head to go away and leave a lovely young girl like you on her own at a weekend.'

She could criticise Brian as much as she liked but she wouldn't allow anyone else to do the same. 'He couldn't help it,' she defended. 'His mother's ill so he had to go.'

'While the cat's away . . .' he said with a licentious smile. 'Come on, let's go off on our own.'

'How many more times must I tell you . . . *no.*'

Fuelled by alcohol, Mick's temper rose. 'Come on, Beryl. You know you fancy me rotten.'

'Whether I do or not doesn't come into it,' she declared. 'I love Brian and I won't betray him.'

'Like he doesn't betray you, you mean,' he blurted out meaningfully.

'What are you talking about?' she asked woozily. 'Brian doesn't betray me.'

'Oh, not much,' came his cynical reply.

'There's no need to get nasty just because you can't get your own way.'

'Gone to see his sick mother, my arse,' scorned Mick. 'He'd have a job as she's been dead for years.'

'What! But why would he tell me—'

'Wake up, you dozy cow,' Mick cut in. 'He's gone home to his wife for the weekend.'

'That's a wicked thing to say.' She was outraged.

'It's true though, babe,' he told her. 'He's got a wife and daughter at home in London.'

'He can't have,' she protested. 'He's marrying me in a couple of months' time.'

186

'If he does he'll get done for bigamy,' Mick informed her. 'But he'll have scarpered long before then.'

'This is just a pack of lies to get me to go off with you,' she accused him.

'Ask any of the boys, if you don't believe me,' he suggested, looking over at his mates. 'They'll soon confirm it. Everyone knows what he's been up to.'

'I will, don't worry.' Even though her senses were dulled by alcohol, and it was inconceivable to her anyway that what Mick said might be true, a knot of fear was beginning to creep in. She followed him over to the men.

'The lady's got something to ask you, lads,' Mick told them.

They stopped talking, looking at her and waiting.

'He's trying to get me to believe that Brian's married,' she explained. 'He's making it up, isn't he?'

There was an awkward silence.

'He's telling me these lies because he's after me himself,' she went on. 'I know it isn't true.'

One of the men said to Mick, 'You bloody stirrer. You should have kept your mouth shut.'

She stared at them. 'Are you saying it's true?'

Nobody said anything.

'It is, isn't it?' Her voice was almost a whisper.

'Sorry, love,' said one of the men at last. 'Brian's been stringing you along.'

As she turned and walked away, her legs like jelly, she heard one of them say, 'You've dropped Brian right in it now, Mick. He'll give you a right roasting when he gets back.'

The awful truth had a sobering effect and Beryl's head cleared a little. She was still fuddled but the whole thing began to make sense now; the fact that she hadn't met his people, his eagerness to go home at Christmas. Everything he'd said since the day she'd met him had been lies. It had all been just a game to him. With tears scalding her eyes, she went to find her mother.

'Can we go home, Mum?' she requested.

'Course we can, love,' Flo said without asking any questions since her daughter was obviously distressed about something. Now wasn't the moment to find out what it was; not in a pub full of people.

The two women left the pub, Flo's comforting arm round her devastated daughter.

Brian was feeling pleased with himself on Sunday evening as he walked down the street towards his lodgings with his overnight bag. He was glad to be back. Going home had been a pain and he'd only made the effort out of duty because he didn't go at Christmas. Now he was back where he belonged; where he got his own way about everything; well, almost everything. Beryl could be a bit of a spitfire when she was riled but she never stayed angry with him for long, and her mother couldn't do enough for him: meals on time, washing and ironing done to perfection. It was great.

He walked up the path and nearly tripped over something in the dark outside the front door. What the hell . . .? It was his big suitcase. What was that doing there?

He turned his key in the lock and went straight through to the living room where Beryl and her mother were sitting on the sofa looking like thunder.

'If we'd had time to get the locks changed you wouldn't have got in,' announced Flo. 'But as you are in, you can give me your key and sling your hook. Don't come back. *Not ever.* Do you understand?'

'What are you talking about?' He looked at Beryl. 'What's she going on about, love? What's happened?'

Beryl leaped up and lunged at him, pummelling her fists against his chest. 'You liar, you rotten stinking liar!' she shrieked, beside herself with rage and pain. 'It's all been lies, every bit of it. Every single thing you've ever said to me. *Lies, lies, lies.*'

'I haven't got a clue what you're on about,' he said, holding her by the arms to field her blows, seeing black rivers of mascara trickling down her face.

'You're married,' she screamed, her voice distorted with emotion. 'You've got a wife and daughter in London and you've no intention of marrying me, you never did have.'

'Who's been telling you daft stories like that?' He spoke as though she was a child.

'Don't patronise me—'

'Don't make it worse by denying it,' came Flo's authoritative intervention. 'We know that you're married, so now you've been found out, at least be man enough to admit it.'

Brian's shoulders slumped. He let go of Beryl and she stood back, looking at him with contempt. 'All right, as somebody has obviously put the boot in, I admit it,' he said, adding without any prior intention, 'But I'll leave my wife. I'll get a divorce and you and me will get married, Beryl. We'll have to wait longer than you thought but I'll do it. It's you I want to be with.'

'Liar.'

'How many times have I been home since I've been here in Norfolk?' he asked.

'Not many.'

'Exactly. If I wanted to be with my wife, I would have gone home to her but I stayed here with you. Surely that must tell you something.'

'It tells me that you like a good time, that's all,' she said thickly, wiping her eyes with a handkerchief. 'But you had no intention of marrying when we planned, did you? Come on, let's hear you say it.'

He lowered his eyes shamefully. 'Well, no, I didn't. I couldn't, could I, as I'm already married?'

'You pig, you lousy rotten pig,' she choked out, fresh tears falling.

'I was going to tell you, honest I was,' he told her. 'I kept trying to but it's been so good between us I didn't want to spoil it. I was going to tell you—'

'You were gonna scarper, more like,' interrupted Flo. 'You were going to leave my daughter waiting at the altar.'

'No, I wouldn't have done that. I would never do a thing like that to you, Beryl.'

'I can't believe anything you say now,' said Beryl.

'Look . . . my marriage is over,' he announced.

'They all say that,' responded Flo. 'I suppose you're going to tell us now that your wife doesn't understand you.'

'Ours is a marriage in name only,' he tried to explain. 'I'll leave her.'

'You'd walk out on your daughter,' disapproved Beryl.

'She isn't my child,' he informed them. 'I only married Molly because she was in trouble and I felt sorry for her; to save her kid being branded a bastard.'

'If you think we're gonna believe that old codswallop—' began Flo.

'This is between Beryl and me,' Brian said, throwing Flo a furious look. 'It's got nothing to do with you. So why don't you clear off and leave us to sort it out?'

'Don't go, Mum,' requested Beryl. 'I don't want to listen to any more of his rotten lies anyway.' She stared coldly at Brian. 'Get out, go on.'

'And where am I supposed to sleep tonight?'

'In the gutter, for all we care,' said Flo.

'But I've paid my rent – in advance.'

'What's owing to you is in an envelope on the hall table,' Flo informed him. 'So go on, give us your key and bugger off out of it, and don't show your face around here again.'

He looked persuasively at Beryl. 'You can't really want this,' he begged her.

'I do,' she declared, sounding breathless and shaky. 'You've hurt and humiliated me, and betrayed your wife. I never want to see you again.'

'Out,' ordered Flo, walking to the living-room door and standing by it meaningfully, holding her hand out for the key.

'All right, I'm going,' he conceded gloomily, handing it to her.

On his way to the front door, he picked up the envelope from the hall table, grabbed his overnight bag and left.

When Flo went back into the living room, her daughter was sitting on the sofa, sobbing her heart out.

'I really did love him, Mum,' she said. 'I really did.'

'I know,' said her mother, sitting down and putting her arm round her. 'Have a good cry, love, then you'll have to try and forget him. I know you can't imagine it now, but it will stop hurting after a while. You're a pretty girl; you'll soon find someone else.'

Brian walked down the street, wondering where he was going to sleep tonight. It was too late to find new lodgings now so he'd have to doss down with a mate and find something more permanent tomorrow. He had no intention of going back to London because of this setback. The freedom of living away from home was too good to lose. He'd stay for as long as there was work. Besides, he wasn't going to let Beryl go that easily. He'd soon talk her round once he got her on her own, without her mother interfering.

Giving the matter thought, he decided it was probably all for the best that the truth had come out. He would never have had the courage to tell her himself so would have had just to disappear before the wedding and lose Beryl altogether. Now all he had to do was persuade her that he would leave Molly and they could get back to normal.

He was surprised by how much he wanted Beryl in his life. It was only ever meant to be a fling but it was more serious than that now. Losing her had proved it to him. Whether or not he would actually ever leave Molly for her, he wasn't sure. But he needn't worry about that for the moment. Getting Beryl back was the important thing.

The next day at work Molly had the chance of a few quiet words with Dan in the workshop. Hattie and the boys had gone over to the house for lunch. Dan was particularly busy so was just having a sandwich at his workbench and Molly never took a proper lunch hour as she didn't work a full day.

'I just wanted to say sorry about Brian's rudeness to you on Saturday,' she said.

'There's no need to apologise,' he assured her. 'It's water off a duck's back to me.' He sipped a mug of tea Molly had made for them. 'Did you have a good weekend?'

'Awful,' she blurted out.

His brow furrowed. 'Oh. Why? What went wrong?'

She didn't normally confide in people about her marriage but she found herself doing so now. 'Things are really bad between Brian and me,' she told him. 'We just don't get on. I've got used to him being away, I suppose. We seem to spend the whole time sniping at each other when he's home.'

'I'm sorry.'

Dan was one of the few people who knew that Rosa wasn't Brian's child. Molly had given Angie permission to tell him because she hated having secrets from her husband. 'We should never have got married.

190

But when you make a mistake you have to live with the consequences, don't you?'

'Up to a point, yes,' agreed Dan. 'But when it comes to marriage, if you've given it a chance and done everything you possibly can to make it work – as I'm sure you have – and neither of you is happy, I see no point in staying together.'

'People do though, don't they?' she pointed out. 'Even when they've grown to loathe each other. Marriage vows are powerful things.'

'Divorce is still a dirty word, I grant you, even in these modern times. Marriage is still sacrosanct.'

'I think couples often stick it out because it's easier, especially for women if they're reliant on their husband for financial support.'

'But you're not, are you?' he reminded her. 'You're a working woman.'

'Even so, I still feel I owe it to Brian to stay with the marriage. I mean, not many men would have done what he did for me,' she said. 'I've made my bed, as my mother would say.' She paused, fiddling with her nails. 'Anyway, he's gone back now and he doesn't often come home so it isn't too bad.'

'It shouldn't be like that for either of you,' Dan opined.

'People have worse things to put up with.'

'Yes, they do but that doesn't make your situation right,' he said. 'You deserve better than him.'

'Brian isn't a bad man,' Molly defended. 'He's changed over the years, become bitter because I've never been able to love him as he wants me to. It's altered him. So you could say that I've made him what he is today.'

'I think you're piling too much guilt on yourself with that theory,' was Dan's opinion. 'Brian is what he is. I've known him for years and he's always been a difficult bloke to get on with. Things could have turned out as they have even if you'd got married under more normal circumstances. You don't know a person until you live with them.'

'That's true. Anyway,' she began, embarrassed that she'd spoken so openly to him, 'I shouldn't be burdening you with my problems, making you spend your lunch break being a marriage guidance counsellor.'

'I don't mind in the least,' he assured her. 'But I shouldn't be advising you. I have no right.'

'It was me who brought the subject up and now I'm going to change it,' she said. 'Did you have a good weekend?'

'Yeah, it was all right,' he said with a lack of enthusiasm. 'We missed you in the park on Saturday, though.'

His words warmed her. 'Sorry about that. Brian would have had a fit if I'd gone out and left him on his weekend home. After he went on Sunday, I had to go to my mother's for tea, otherwise I would have popped round so that the girls could see each other. Rosa was deeply fed up because she had to survive the whole day without seeing her pal.'

'Likewise Patsy.'

'Thanks for taking Rosa with you on Saturday.'

'You thanked me at the time.'

'Oh.'

'You'll be able to come yourself this weekend, won't you?' Dan said.

'Try stopping me. This weekend I'll be back to normal.'

'Good.'

Back at her desk she reflected on what she'd just said about being back to normal. Back to normal should be when Brian was at home, not when he was away. When he was back for good there would be no more outings with Dan and the children because Brian didn't believe it was possible for a man and a woman to have a platonic friendship, and would immediately forbid it. She'd have to cross that bridge when she came to it because it didn't bear thinking about.

Brian didn't attempt to see Beryl for a few days; he thought it best to give her a chance to cool down; give her time to miss him. But on Friday evening he was waiting for her outside the grocery store in Boxham High Street where she worked, at closing time. He was standing in the shop doorway out of the rain.

'Beryl,' he said, approaching her as soon as she appeared.

'Get lost.' She didn't even look at him; just concentrated on putting her umbrella up.

'We need to talk.'

'You might. I don't.'

'Just give me a chance to explain.'

'There's nothing to explain,' she said, marching towards the bus stop, her high heels clicking against the ground. 'The facts speak for themselves.'

'Not necessarily.' He was walking beside her.

'You're a married man and I'm not a home wrecker – those are the only facts I'm interested in,' she spelled out for him. 'I'd never have got involved with you if I'd known the truth.'

'Just ten minutes,' he persisted. 'We could go for a coffee somewhere. There is a place just round the corner . . .'

She walked on in silence.

'Please.' He was begging now.

'No.' She was adamant. 'It's pouring with rain and I want to go home, so shove off.'

He took her arm. 'Don't touch me,' she ordered, shrugging him off.

'All I'm asking for is a few minutes of your time,' he said, the rain soaking his hair and running down his raincoat. 'I won't touch you, honest. At least just give me that.'

192

She slowed her step and he could sense her weakening. 'All right,' she agreed without looking at him. 'But ten minutes, that's all.'

They went to a nearby coffee bar where the air was warm and fragrant with the aroma of coffee, the windows clouded with steam from the hissing espresso machine.

'Get on with it then,' Beryl said, spooning sugar into her coffee and staring into the cup. 'Say what you have to say so that I can go home.'

Brian stirred his espresso, then looked up at her, his eyes full of contrition. 'Look, I'll admit that all I had in mind at first was a fling,' he told her with a grave expression. 'I didn't intend to get serious about you. But it just happened. I fell deeper and deeper in love with you and I just couldn't give you up.'

'But why get engaged to me when you knew you couldn't marry me?' she demanded.

'I got carried away,' he explained. 'I knew it was what you wanted and I began to want it too – a lot, as it happens. So I just went ahead and did it.'

'Knowing you wouldn't go through with it?'

He lowered his eyes, hoping he looked sufficiently ashamed. He was desperate to get his feet back under the Browns' table. He'd found new digs on the other side of town but they weren't a patch on Flo's. The meals were edible but not up to her standard, and there was none of the special treatment he'd become accustomed to. Anyway, he wanted to be close to Beryl, he really did. They were good together and he wanted their relationship to continue. 'Yeah, knowing that.' He couldn't very well deny it. 'It was make-believe but it felt real – I suppose because I wanted it so much.'

'You've really hurt me, Brian,' she told him.

'I know.' He tried to take her hand across the table as she put her cup down but she pulled it away. 'And I'm *so, so* sorry. But it can all still happen for us. I meant it when I said I'd leave my wife. I'm never there anyway, so she won't notice the difference. But I'll end the marriage properly – get a divorce.'

'They take years to come through, and you have to have grounds,' she reminded him. 'It's all very messy and complicated. I don't want to be involved in anything like that.'

'I'll let her divorce me,' he suggested eagerly. 'She'll want to when she finds out about us anyway. And she'll have grounds, won't she?'

'I'd have to be the co-respondent, you mean?'

'Not if you don't want to be,' he assured her quickly, sensing her reluctance. 'There are other ways around these things.'

'You'd deprive your little girl of her father for me?' It was an accusation.

'Rosa isn't my daughter,' he explained. 'What I said on Sunday is true. Molly and I were good mates – we'd known each other since we were kids. Some bloke got her in the family way and scarpered. She was left in trouble and I stepped in to save her reputation.'

'Did you love her?'

'Yeah, I was nuts about her then. I wouldn't have done it otherwise.' For some reason he couldn't bring himself to lie about that. 'But she didn't love me then and doesn't now. She'll be glad to get shot of me.'

'Do you still love her?'

'Give over. If I did I would go home to her at the weekends, wouldn't I? But I hardly ever do because I'd rather stay here with you.'

Beryl mulled this over. 'Mm, I suppose there is that,' she said, only partially convinced.

'So, how about it, Beryl?' he asked, confident that he'd talked her round. 'How about us giving it another try now that it's all out in the open? I'll move back into your place and we'll make a new start.'

Finishing her coffee, she thought about it. Then, 'No, thanks,' she said, shocking him.

'Oh. Beryl, why?' he entreated. 'I've been straight with you now. Honest.'

'Maybe you have now, but I could never believe a word you said after the lies you've told me in the past.' She gave him an icy stare. 'Anyway, I know that you're married now. I didn't before so there was an excuse. I couldn't live with myself knowing that I was with someone else's husband.'

'But, Beryl, I'll leave her, I swear . . .'

'I'm not interested, Brian,' she asserted, picking up her handbag and rising with a purposeful air.

He stood up. 'Please, just give me another chance.' He was grovelling now. 'I promise I won't let you down.'

'No.'

'Beryl—'

'If you follow me out of here,' she cut him short, her expressive brown eyes cold and determined, 'I shall ask the manager to call the police.'

'You wouldn't . . .'

'Try me.' She looked at him long and hard. 'I mean it, Brian. And if you come anywhere near me again at any time in the future, I'll have you done for harassment.'

With that she swung across to the door, leaving him standing there speechless and in a state of shock. He ordered another coffee and sat down at the table staring gloomily into space, his damp clothes sticking to him. In making herself unattainable Beryl had sharpened his appetite for her even more. But, of course, that was obviously what she had in mind with this show of strength. She was punishing him; playing hard to get to keep him keen. He'd get her back. Oh yes, he wasn't going to let this hitch put him off. He didn't give up that easily.

★ ★ ★

At the bus stop Beryl was standing in the queue, the rain dripping off her umbrella and tears running down her face. She was far too distressed to hide them. So much for the feisty modern woman who'd just put Brian in his place, she thought miserably. If he could see her now . . .

Chapter Thirteen

Peter had some rather worrying news for Molly when she went to the shop one day the following week.

'Shoplifting!' she exclaimed. 'Oh no!'

'Afraid so.' A customer had just left, and Peter and Molly were talking in the shop where the stock was now fully replenished. 'It must be happening when I'm busy in the office. But I have to spend a certain amount of time out there to keep the paperwork up to date.'

'Of course you do. Anyway, you'd hear the shop bell if anyone came in, wouldn't you?' she pointed out. 'And you'd be out here like a shot to serve them so they wouldn't have much time to grab their spoils.'

'Mm . . . that's what's been puzzling me,' he confessed. 'The only other time it could possibly happen is when the shop is very busy. Someone could slip something under their coat then without my noticing, I suppose, though we don't get Woolworths-size crowds in here; it's too specialised.'

Molly nodded; her thoughts were racing.

'Anyway, I thought I ought to let you know because it'll show up in the books eventually and I don't want you to think that I've been on the take,' he explained.

'That's the last thing I would ever think of you,' she assured him. 'We all trust you implicitly.'

'Just covering my back.'

'I understand.' She tapped her chin with her thumbnail, looking at him. 'So how long do you think it's been going on?'

'It's hard to say,' Peter replied. 'Obviously I don't check the stock every day. It seems to be intermittent, though. As long ago as last summer, I noticed more stuff seemed to be missing than I'd sold but then it stopped so I didn't worry you with it, especially as every retailer has a certain amount of theft. But it's happening regularly now. Someone's getting greedy.'

Molly knew exactly who that someone was, but she wouldn't put a slur on the Beckett family by telling Peter. Not until she had proof anyway. He was no fool, though. She guessed he had his suspicions but was wise enough not to cast aspersions on a member of the family who employed him. She'd suspected last summer that Josh was up to something and now she knew she'd been right.

'Well, keep an eye on things and I'll try and think of a way to get to the bottom of it,' she told Peter. 'In the meantime you can rest easy that no one would ever suspect you.'

'I'm glad about that.'

They went into the office and she gave him his wage packet and collected the paperwork. After a discussion concerning the business, she got up to leave.

'See you next week then,' she said.

He clapped his hand to his brow as though remembering something. 'I knew there was something I had to ask you,' he said quickly. 'Can you arrange cover for me next Thursday morning? I've got to go to the dentist to have a tooth out. All being well, I'll be here in the afternoon, though.'

Perfect, she thought, a plan having already formed. 'Certainly, I will, Peter,' she assured him. 'I'll make sure that somebody's here to open the shop on Thursday morning.'

Leaving the premises, she stopped to have a few words with Syd at his stall.

'You off back to Hanwell, Molly?' he asked, smiling at her as she approached him, a thick scarf wound around his neck, his cap pulled down against the bitter weather, grey woollen mittens on his hands.

'Yeah, back to the grind,' she laughed, shivering and hugging herself. 'But before I go I want to ask if you might be willing to help me out with a little job I have to do, strictly between you and me.'

'It depends what it is, o' course,' he said cheerfully, 'but if I can I will.'

'This is the plan . . .'

When Molly got back to the pottery, she went straight over to the potters. Dan was busy at his wheel, Billy was at the work bench painting a vase and Josh was attaching handles to jugs.

'Peter needs someone to fill in for him at the shop on Thursday morning. I can't do it because I have to go to the school for Rosa's medical,' she fibbed. 'So I was wondering if Josh could do it.' She looked from Josh to the other two. 'If you can spare him, that is.'

'I'll do it,' said Josh helpfully.

'Yeah, we can spare him,' said Billy, adding jokingly, 'We'll be glad to get rid of him for a few hours.'

'No more than I'll be glad of a break from you lot of slave-drivers,' retorted Josh.

Only Molly knew why he was being so co-operative about a stint at the shop. In the office she informed Hattie that she herself would be out for a while on Thursday morning for Rosa's medical.

198

'All right, dear,' Hattie said affably.

So far so good, thought Molly.

Syd watched Josh arrive at the shop on Thursday morning, later than Peter usually got there. The other shops in the parade had been open for business for a while. A couple of people were waiting outside, stamping their feet against the cold. They followed Josh in. Syd waited until they came out clutching their purchases, then asked one of the other traders to look after his stall for ten minutes or so. He strolled over to the shop and went in.

'Wotcha, mate,' he said to Josh, who was behind the counter doing something at the till.

'Morning, Syd,' replied Josh, looking up. 'What can I do for you?'

Syd leaned towards him in a confidential manner. 'Wondered if I could have a quiet word,' he said.

Josh looked slightly wary. 'Oh, yeah? What about?' he asked in a low voice.

'A little bird told me that you're not averse to doing a bit of business on the side.' He tapped his nose. 'No names, no pack drill. Know what I mean?'

Josh's eyes lit up. He was too greedy and too much of a small-time crook to be overly cautious. 'That depends,' he said. 'To certain people I can trust, yeah, I might be interested in something like that.'

'You know me, son. I mind my own business and turn a blind eye to what people around here get up to as long as it doesn't interfere with me.'

'Is that right?' Josh gave him a studied look. He'd never had much to do with Syd beyond the odd greeting as he passed his stall, but he seemed genuine enough.

'Anyway,' continued Syd, getting to the point, 'my missus is very partial to fine pottery and I'd like to get her something a bit special for her birthday. But I'm not prepared to pay your marked prices.'

'I'm sure we can work something out,' said Josh. 'You choose what you want and then we'll talk dosh.'

Syd browsed among the colourful articles so beautifully displayed in their various ranges. 'This is nice,' he said, picking up a chunky, multicoloured vase. He looked at the price sticker on the bottom. 'It's fifteen quid so how much would you let me have it for?'

'A tenner.'

'Half price or I'm not interested,' bargained Syd.

Josh considered it for a moment. He didn't have time for long-drawn-out negotiations; he needed to close the deal quickly before a customer came in. 'You're a hard man but, all right – half price.'

Syd picked up the vase and took it over to the counter, reaching into his pocket for the cash while Josh wrapped it in tissue paper and put it into a carrier bag. Syd put the money on the counter and picked up his purchase. 'Thanks, mate,' he said, turning to leave.

'A pleasure doing business with you,' was Josh's cheerful response. 'Any time you want anything in this line at a special price, I'm your man.'

When Syd had left the shop, Josh fingered the money lovingly, then stuffed it into his pocket with a triumphant gleam in his eye.

'I'll take that,' said Molly, appearing beside him.

'You,' he gasped, swinging round to face her.

'I saw and heard the whole thing,' she informed him briskly. 'For the second time, Josh Beckett, you've been nicked.'

'You've been spying on me.'

'That's right,' she freely admitted. 'I came here straight after taking Rosa to school, knowing that you wouldn't be here in time to open the shop at nine o'clock as you should be. I got a key cut the other day from the set we keep at the pottery – as you would be using that one – and let myself in. I've been waiting in the stockroom at the back until Syd came in, as we'd previously arranged.'

'I've been set up.'

She nodded.

'He was in on it.' Josh was disgusted. 'The sly old git.'

'That title suits you better,' she told him. 'Syd's an honest man who takes a dim view of someone robbing their own family. I knew if I gave you enough rope you'd hang yourself.'

'What are you rambling on about, woman?' he asked scornfully.

'I suspected you were up to your old tricks again as far back as last summer.'

'Dunno what made you think that,' was his sulky response.

'I heard you were hanging around the market at weekends and guessed that you weren't out shopping; you were touting for business among the traders, putting the word about that you can let them have expensive hand-crafted pottery cheap through the back door. You've been lining your own pockets while filling in for Peter here, as well as coming into the shop after hours to take stuff out. You'd have no trouble getting in since you have access to a set of keys.'

Josh was admitting nothing; just staring at her with contempt.

'You made a big mistake when you got too greedy,' she went on. 'A little now and again you could get away with – for a while. But you've stolen enough for Peter to think he's got shoplifters. When he told me that I knew it was time to get the proof to get you nailed.'

'You bitch.'

'Never mind about all of that. Just give me the money Syd gave you,' she said briskly. 'Then I'll go and get the vase and put it back on display.'

'You're devious.'

'I've had to be to catch up with a slimy weasel like you,' Molly said. 'Come on, give me the cash.'

Scowling at her he handed it over. 'If they paid me a decent wage for the job I do, I wouldn't be driven to this sort of thing,' he complained.

'That was your excuse last time I caught you at it,' she reminded him. 'And it's no more valid now than it was then. You'd do this sort of thing however much you were earning because you're greedy.' She paused thoughtfully, looking at him. 'You also do it because it gives you satisfaction to know that you're outwitting Billy and Dan.'

'Why would I wanna do that?'

'Because they're pals and they make you feel like an outsider.'

'Oh, I see. So you fancy yourself as a shrink now, do you?' he sneered.

'Not at all. Just an observer from outside of the family.'

'Glad you realise that you are actually *outside* of the family. The way the others carry on anyone would think you are a part of it.'

'A close family friend is what I am and that's how they treat me,' Molly corrected. 'And as a friend they trust me to look after their interests.' She fixed him with a steady look. 'You remember the terms of our deal and what I said I'd do if I caught you stealing again?'

'Of course I remember. But the deal's off now because you owe me for saving your daughter from drowning. I thought I made that clear.'

'And I thought I made it clear when I said that if I caught you stealing from the business again, I would tell the others.'

'You'd grass on someone who saved your daughter's life?' he said accusingly.

'I've kept quiet until now but that's no longer possible because the business can't afford to have chunks removed from the profits on a regular basis. Anyway, what you're doing is wrong.'

'You owe me . . .'

'Yes. But I'm not going to pay you back by letting you get away with stealing a second time,' Molly asserted. 'I dealt with it myself last time in the hope that you would mend your ways. It hasn't worked so now I have no choice but to hand the matter over to people with a larger share in the business than I have.'

His eyes narrowed on her with hatred. 'I wish I'd left your kid to drown now,' he ground out.

She scrutinised him. 'I don't believe you,' she said frankly. 'But anyway, that's beside the point.' She put the money in her purse.

His eyes widened. 'Here, put that where it belongs – in the till,' he accused.

'It belongs in my purse because that's where it came from,' she explained. 'I gave it to Syd to give to you. Now I shall go and get the vase back from him.'

'You scheming cow.'

'It's what you've made me,' she came back at him. 'But I haven't got all day to stand here arguing with you. I must get the vase and replace it and then get back to the pottery. You'll hang on here until Peter comes in this afternoon, won't you?'

'Aren't you afraid I'll do more business on the side?' he said scornfully.

'Not really, because if you do it will be the last time,' she told him. 'The problem is out of my hands now.'

'You won't tell 'em,' he taunted. 'You wouldn't have the bottle.'

Without replying she left the shop and went to see Syd at his stall.

'Thanks for your help, Syd.'

'A pleasure, love,' he said, handing her the vase. 'I'm glad we pulled it off.'

'How much do I owe you for your part in it,' she enquired.

'Leave it out,' he replied. 'I don't want paying for helping a pal to catch a thief.'

'I owe you one, Syd.'

Having taken the vase back to the shop, Molly hurried to the station. She felt no sense of triumph as she sat on the tube to Ealing Broadway, only profound disappointment in Josh. It was true he'd used an act of decency to his own advantage but he had actually saved Rosa's life. She still couldn't quite rid herself of the idea that behind that evil exterior there was a morsel of good. Even if she was right, it would never show itself if his dishonesty was allowed to continue unpunished.

But telling the family was going to mean treading through an emotional minefield. The more she thought about it the more worried she became. One member of the family in particular was going to be devastated . . .

When Dan came to collect Patsy after work, Molly told him the whole story over a cup of tea in the kitchen while the girls were playing in the living room.

'Why, the wicked young bugger,' was his furious reaction. 'Fancy stealing from his own family.'

'It is pretty low.'

'Why have you kept it to yourself for so long?'

'I needed proof.'

'But he was doing it before and you caught him, you said, so you had proof then.'

'At that time I thought it best to deal with it in the way I've just told you about,' she explained. 'And it worked for a while. I warned him that if he did it again I would tell the family.'

'Why didn't you say anything when you got back from the shop today?'

'I intended to, but then . . .' She bit her lip. 'I didn't exactly get cold fect but I did decide that it would be sensible to talk to you about it first, you being only related to the family by marriage,' she explained. 'Because now that it's actually come to the crunch, I'm wondering if I'm doing the right thing in telling them. It's going to cause such anger and pain.'

'I don't see that you have a choice,' Dan said without hesitation. 'He's robbing us all blind. You and me as well as his brother and mother. They have a right to know what's been going on.'

'It's his mother I'm worried about,' Molly confessed. 'Hattie dotes on him. It'll break her heart and she's had enough heartache recently.'

'Mm, there is that,' Dan agreed worriedly.

'I'm wondering if there's any way we can protect her from this.'

'I'd like to but I don't see how we can. We'll have to put it to the vote, of course, but personally I think Josh should be dismissed from the firm and I'm fairly sure Billy will feel the same. We can't hide that from Hattie, can we? Anyway, she's allowed a vote as a part-owner of the business.'

'Do you really think that sacking him is the only answer?'

'I honestly don't see how he can stay with the firm,' Dan replied. 'I mean, he's a liability. Not only is he stealing from us, he doesn't pull his weight either. He'll bankrupt the lot of us the way he's carrying on.'

'But what will it do to Hattie to discover that her son's a thief?' Molly reminded him. 'She knows he's bad-tempered and difficult, but a thief . . .'

'She will be very upset, and I'm as worried about her as you are. But she'll have to know. The boy could get into worse trouble outside the family and end up in bother with the police if he's allowed to get away with this. I know this might sound hard, and I hate to have to say it, but it's time Hattie faced up to the truth about him anyway, instead of always making excuses for him.'

'Poor Hattie,' sighed Molly. 'Let's hope she doesn't want to shoot the messenger.'

'She wouldn't do that. Not Hattie.'

'She might turn on me for keeping it from her and being so devious. I lied about having to go to the school this morning so that I could be at the shop and catch him in the act. But I had to be absolutely sure. I didn't want to say anything to anyone until I was.'

'Hattie's a sensible woman,' Dan pointed out. 'She'll realise that you acted with the very best of intentions. She'll defend him, naturally. It's what parents do, especially mothers. You'd stand by Rosa whatever she'd done, wouldn't you?'

'Of course.'

'Frankly I think you've been brilliant, coping with this on your own,' he praised her. 'It takes courage to take someone like Josh on. He's a nasty piece of work.'

'Oh, come on, he's only a petty thief, not a gangster,' Molly pointed out. 'He's no Al Capone.'

'Even so, taking him on all on your own takes some bottle,' he insisted. 'I bet he's given you some choice lip.'

'He's called me a few things,' she admitted. 'But there was nothing else I could do but deal with it myself because I had to be sure.' She made a face. 'Now comes the worst bit: telling the others.'

'Would you like me to do it for you?'

'No, no, of course not.'

'Sure?'

'Positive. I must see the job through to the bitter end.' She was adamant. 'I'll do it first thing in the morning. We'll have a meeting in the office.'

'Surely we don't have to go so far as sacking him,' said a fully informed and very shocked Hattie. 'We can't do that to one of our own.'

Unaware of the storm about to break, Josh had been sent to the Broadway to get postage stamps while this meeting was taking place. As he could be relied upon to take three times as long as the errand actually warranted, they knew they were safe for a while.

'One of our own who's been stealing from us,' Billy reminded her. 'I know it seems hard, Mum – and I'm as gutted about it as you are – but we can't keep him on. He's too expensive. Besides, he needs to learn a lesson. He can't be allowed to get away with this sort of thing.'

'Maybe if we kept him away from the shop . . .' suggested Molly, hoping to soften the blow for Hattie. 'He wouldn't have the opportunity to steal then.'

'He'd find a way of nicking the stuff from here then – between the pottery being finished and packed. If he gets away with it he'll keep on doing it,' was Billy's opinion. 'Anyway, it's a question of trust. I don't want to work with someone who's been stabbing us in the back.'

'Me neither,' added Dan.

'He's always been a pain in the arse around the place, forever whingeing and skiving off,' Billy went on. 'It's a pity he didn't have to do his national service. That might have given him some backbone.'

'He *is* your brother, Billy,' admonished his mother.

'Which makes it even harder to take. To think that my own flesh and blood would do something like that to his family.'

'What about if you were to give him a good talking to, Billy?' suggested Hattie hopefully. 'I know he doesn't show it but he admires you a lot. If you give him a thorough trouncing it might just do the trick.'

'That's a good idea,' added Molly supportively. 'Once he knows you all know what he's been up to, he probably won't dare to do it again. We could make him pay back the cost of what he's stolen out of his wages.'

'You women are far too soft,' declared Billy. 'He's done wrong and he must be punished.'

'Hear, hear,' agreed Dan.

'He'll be getting off light with just a sacking,' Billy pointed out. 'If this wasn't a family firm, the police would be involved. Then he'd be in real trouble.'

There was a murmur of agreement.

'If we're too easy on him, he could end up becoming a hardened criminal,' Billy continued. 'And I'm sure you don't want that, Mum.'

Poor Hattie was whey-faced and had nervous red blotches suffusing her neck and face. 'Of course I don't. I just feel so bad about sacking my own son from his family firm.'

'If he's forced to get a job somewhere else, he really will have to work for his money,' Billy pointed out. 'It might make him appreciate what he had here.'

'It's all been such a shock,' sighed Hattie, trembling slightly. 'He's always been the most difficult of my children but I never dreamed he would do anything like this.'

Billy – who was sitting next to his mother at the desk they were all seated around – put his hand on her arm. 'I know this is really hard for you, Mum. It's hurting me too. I mean, I am his brother and I do care about him despite the grief he gives us all. Because of that I say we have to take firm action, for his own good as much as anything else. There's no other way.'

'I suppose not,' she agreed miserably.

'So let's put it to the vote – all those in favour of dismissal for Josh.'

The two men raised their hands immediately. Slowly Molly lifted hers, and Hattie finally followed suit with extreme reluctance.

'Right. He should be back in a minute,' said Billy. 'We'll have him in and tell him.'

'He's going to have one hell of a shock,' said Molly, her stomach churning. This whole thing had made mincemeat of her nervous system. 'He didn't believe I would actually go through with it and tell you.'

'Thank God you did,' said Billy.

Josh was indeed shocked; and furious. 'You can't throw me out,' he protested when Billy had broken the news. 'I'm a Beckett and this is a family firm.'

'All the more reason to sack you, you thieving git,' roared his brother.

'You can't keep me out for good,' he was simmering with umbrage, 'because when I'm twenty-one I get a partnership. It was written in Dad's will.'

'With the provision that the existing partners consider you to be making a contribution to the firm,' Billy reminded him. 'You certainly aren't doing that. Even apart from the nicking you've been doing, you've never taken the slightest interest in being a potter.'

'Only because you treat me like the errand boy.'

'It's all part of the learning process,' Billy reminded him. 'We all had to go through it. Anyway, we've given you plenty of chances to gain practical experience but you'd sooner skive off than learn how to throw a pot.'

Josh looked at his mother. 'Mum, surely you're not going to stand back and let them do this to me,' he said in a whining tone.

'You've done wrong, son.' She forced herself to be firm. 'You've let me down; you've let us all down. Now you have to pay the price.'

Josh turned on Molly. 'It's her, isn't it?' he snarled with a burning stare. 'She's turning you all against me.'

'You've done that without any help from anyone,' corrected Billy. 'Molly just happened to be the one with the savvy to catch you at it, that's all.'

'Cow,' he spat at Molly.

'Hey, hey, that's enough of that,' reproached Dan, fiercely defensive. 'If I catch you saying anything like that to her again, you'll get more than the sack, I tell you.'

'That goes for me too,' supported Billy.

'You mustn't blame Molly, son,' said Hattie wearily. 'She had to tell us. It was her duty as a family friend and a partner in the firm.'

'You're all in it together,' Josh accused, his voice shaking with anger. 'It's a conspiracy to get rid of me.'

'Oh, grow up, for God's sake,' snapped Billy. 'You've been thieving and you've been caught. At least be man enough to take your punishment and stop trying to blame everyone else. Now pack up your stuff and get out.'

Josh looked at each one in turn with contempt – excluding his mother. 'I'll get you all for this,' he ground out. 'You'll regret this one day.'

'Just go,' sighed Billy.

Josh turned and left, the door almost coming off its hinges with the force of the slam he gave it.

There was a grating silence in the aftermath.

'I'll put the kettle on,' said Molly.

When the men had gone back to the workshop, after a post-mortem and a cup of tea, Molly went over to Hattie, who was sitting at her desk, head on fists, staring into space. She was very pale.

'I'm so sorry, Hattie,' Molly tried to console her. 'I would give anything to have spared you this. But I couldn't turn a blind eye any longer.'

'You did what you had to do,' she assured her sadly. 'I'm just so deeply disappointed in Josh.' She sighed. 'I don't know; you do your best to bring your kids up right, and this is how they repay you.'

Molly put her arm round Hattie's shoulder. 'It's only Josh,' she reminded her gently. 'The others haven't let you down.'

'I know,' she admitted. 'I'm that upset I hardly know what I'm saying.'

'If it's any comfort to you,' said Molly, 'I've always thought Josh had some good in him somewhere, and I still do, even after all this.'

'They say we're all a mixture of good and evil, don't they?' Hattie paused, mulling it over. 'It's a pity Josh seems more prone to the latter.' She looked at Molly and managed a half-smile. 'Still, it's nice to know that I'm not the only one with faith in him.'

'Heaven knows why I still have it since he's given me nothing but trouble since I've been at the firm, but it won't go away,' Molly told her.

'I've an excuse, being his mum.' Hattie took a trembling breath. 'You don't stop loving them or believing in them because they do wrong.'

'Of course not.'

'Motherhood isn't always a bed of roses, is it?' Hattie said, almost to herself. 'But I don't regret a moment of it.'

'Me neither.' Molly looked at her. 'Would you like me to get you another cup of tea?'

'Thanks for offering, but I think I'll go across to the house for a while. All the upset has made me feel a bit queasy.'

'I'll get your coat for you,' Molly said, her heart aching for this woman who had endured so much.

Josh was upstairs in his bedroom when Hattie got home. Her queasiness forgotten in her concern for him, she knocked on the door and he told her to go in. He was lying on the bed, staring at the ceiling.

'I suppose you've come to tell me to pack my things and get out,' he said bitterly, putting his hands under his head and turning to look at her.

'Of course I haven't,' she replied, sitting down on a chair by the bed. 'You know me better than that. I would never do a thing like that to one of my children.'

'No, I suppose not,' he conceded. 'But why didn't you stand up for me against them, Mum? Why didn't you stop them giving me the sack?'

'Because you deserved it, Josh.' She dragged the words out, every one piercing her with pain. 'What you've been doing is wrong. Stealing from anyone is bad enough, but robbing your own flesh and blood is the lowest of the low. You can't expect to get away with something like that.'

'But you're the one person I can always rely on to take my side.'

'I've never had to defend you against anything as bad as stealing before,' she said gravely. 'Anyway, perhaps I've done too much of that in the past. Maybe if I'd been a bit firmer with you when you were growing up, we wouldn't be having this conversation now.'

'So even you're turning against me.'

'Of course I'm not. I'll always be here for you, and this will be your home for as long as you want it,' Hattie assured him.

'That's something, I suppose.'

'But I'm desperately disappointed in you, Josh,' she continued. 'You've let yourself down as well as me. I never thought a son of mine would stoop so low as to steal from his own. And not so much as a word of apology.'

'I'm not saying sorry to that bunch of bigheads.' Contrition didn't come easy to him but he was fond of his mother, even though he used her dreadfully and pilfered from her on a regular basis. 'I'm sorry I've upset you, though, Mum.'

'I should think so too,' she acknowledged firmly. 'I hope you mean it.'

He looked away. 'Course I do,' he said, his voice gruff with embarrassment.

'I want you to make me proud of you, son,' she went on. 'I don't want to spend my life making excuses for you. I don't want to feel ashamed.'

'Huh! And what exactly am I supposed to do to make you proud?' he asked, looking at her.

'Nothing special,' she told him. 'If you were to stop being hateful, stop thieving and go out and get yourself an honest job, that would be a start.'

'Get a job!' He was shocked at the suggestion.

'That's what I said.'

'I can't do that, Mum.'

'How else are you going to get the money to pay your way?' she enquired, struggling to stop her voice from quivering. 'You can't expect to live here and not pay me anything at all for your keep.'

'But I thought—'

'You thought I would let you sit around the house all day, making no contribution, and give you money to go out with your mates at night,' she finished for him. 'Well, that wouldn't be good for you or fair to me.'

'You can afford it,' he reminded her. 'Dad left you well provided for.'

'That isn't the point,' she emphasised. 'As responsible adults we all have to pay our way in the world. You pay for your keep now – even though what you give me is only a fraction of what it costs to keep you – and you must do so again once you've found another job. Billy pays his way and so will you. If you make no contribution things will be even worse between you and your brother. Anyway, you like to have the latest clothes and to go out of an evening, and you'll need money for that.'

'Where will I get a job?' Josh wailed. 'I mean, I don't have enough experience to apply for a job at the Fulham pottery. They've probably got school-leavers who are more advanced than I am.'

'You've never shown any interest in the job, that's why.'

'They've not been willing to teach me, more like.'

208

'That just isn't true, Josh,' Hattie corrected. 'I work at the pottery, I've seen what goes on there.' She paused, mulling it over. 'As you're not particularly interested in becoming a potter, why not try something completely different? There are plenty of jobs about at the moment.'

'Doing what exactly?' he asked sulkily.

'That's for you to find out. But I want to see you making an effort.'

'Dunno where to start.'

'Go down the labour exchange. If they don't have anything you fancy, look in the local paper.'

'Give me a chance,' he objected. 'I'm still in shock and need time to recover.'

'All right. But don't leave it too long. The longer you leave it the harder it'll be because you'll lose all your confidence, hanging about the house.' She got up and walked to the door, then turned and looked at him. 'You don't have to do anything grand to make me proud of you, you know, son. Honesty and effort are all I ask of you. If you were to sweep the streets and make a good job of it, I'd be proud.'

'I shouldn't have to go out looking for work,' Josh grumbled. 'My place is at the pottery. I've got rights.'

'You forfeited your rights the day you started stealing,' she reminded him.

He didn't reply; just stared at the ceiling, looking sorry for himself.

Downstairs in the living room, Hattie stirred the fire with the poker then sat in an armchair, quietly sobbing. Being hard on Josh had probably hurt her far more than it had him, she thought, because she loved him and was also beset by a feeling of pity for him. Despite her constant struggle to create family harmony, he'd never fitted in with the others; never got on with anyone except her. Even George had said he was lazy and not to be trusted. Sadly, George had been proved right. This was the reason he had included those special conditions in his will as regards Josh's inheritance.

Was she to blame for the way he was, Hattie agonised. We are all the product of our upbringing, it was true, and she'd always been a soft touch as far as he was concerned; always defended him against what she'd seen as bullying by his older siblings. But as far as she could remember – and she really was trying to be honest with herself – she'd always done her best to bring him up to be a decent human being; given him the same moral guidance as the others. The standards she'd set for them all had been high.

Whether or not she was to blame, she couldn't be sure but she did know one thing for certain: she was going to have to be a whole lot firmer with him in the future if he was to make anything of himself at all.

It wouldn't be easy. Even though he'd done wrong, her heart ached for him. Anyone who behaved the way he did couldn't be happy. He had an even more miserable time ahead of him too, because a new employer would expect him to work hard for his money and Josh wasn't used to that. But, however much pain it caused her, Hattie was determined to remain strong and not give in to him about finding work. He must stand on his own two feet and show some mettle at this time of personal crisis if he was ever to be a responsible and worthwhile adult.

Chapter Fourteen

The winter dragged on with the usual crop of coughs, colds and flu. Rosa went down with a nasty attack of the latter so Molly took time off work to look after her. When she was better but still recuperating, Hattie's trusted cleaner Vi came to sit with her for an hour or so during the day so that Molly could go into the office, feeling torn as she always did in these situations. Even a part-time job as flexible as hers didn't protect her from the misery of conflicting loyalties. With a living to earn she simply had to steel herself.

They employed a replacement for Josh, a serious-minded sixteen-year-old called Frankie, who was passionate about pottery and keen to learn. In total contrast to Josh, he was quiet, polite and well behaved to the point where he just seemed to blend into the background.

Absurdly, Molly found that she missed having Josh around the place. As awful as he was, he'd been a personality, an integral part of the pottery and it seemed odd not having to do battle with him every day. He'd got a job at a local cardboard carton factory and – judging by his surliness whenever Molly saw him at Hattie's – it wasn't a success.

'They make him work for his money, that's why he's going around with a face like yesterday's leg o' mutton,' was Billy's opinion, expressed to Molly and Dan only out of his mother's hearing because, even now and despite what Josh had done, it hurt her to hear ill of her younger son. 'And he's having to manage on his wages since there's no chance of going on the fiddle when you work at a place like that. The demand on the street for cardboard boxes with some soup or tinned fruit manufacturer's name printed all over it is nil, I should imagine.'

'Having to work hard for his living must be instilling some sort of discipline in him,' suggested Dan. 'Which can only be to the good.'

'Up to a point,' agreed Billy. 'But I still say national service would have been the making of him.'

'The army isn't the answer to everything, you know, Billy,' Molly pointed out. From what she'd heard of national service it sounded brutal in the extreme. 'Anyway, it wasn't his fault he didn't pass the medical.'

'I'm not saying it was. But if ever a lad was in need of some really hard character-building stuff, it's my brother. Even Elvis didn't get out of doing his service,' he said, referring to reports from across the Atlantic that the King had just started a two-year stint in the army, much to the disgust of his fans.

'We'll just have to hope he improves with time,' said Molly. 'For Hattie's sake.'

The days began to lengthen and harsh winter winds softened into spring breezes, fragrant with the scent of a fresh new season. Brian came home for a weekend in March and was moodier than ever. When Molly enquired as to the reason, she was told that his new lodgings weren't as comfortable as the other place. When asked why he'd changed his digs he said the original landlady had decided to give up taking lodgers.

While the papers were full of a CND march from London to Aldermaston, due to take place at Easter, Molly had something else on her mind: the anniversary of Angie's death, which fell not at Easter but on an ordinary working day. In some ways it seemed longer than a year since Molly had last seen her friend, yet the accident was as vivid as if it had happened yesterday: the shock, the grinding pain in the aftermath. Angie's absence didn't seem to get any easier. Sometimes – just for an instant – Molly would forget and find herself planning to share some piece of trivia with her.

On the morning of the anniversary, an air of gloom hung over the pottery as tangible as a physical presence. Molly held the fort while Hattie, Billy and Dan went to put flowers on the grave. Molly went along later, alone; she finished work a bit early and called at the cemetery before collecting the children from school.

'Oh, kid, I don't half miss you,' she said at the graveside, unembarrassed to be speaking aloud. She bent down and added a spray of spring flowers to the others that had been put on the grave today. 'I miss all the laughs and the chats . . . and the moans if one of us had the hump about something.' She arranged the daffodils into a vase she kept at the grave. 'I'm keeping an eye on Dan and Patsy and your mum, like you asked. They're all soldiering on but missing you like mad. Billy's got a steady girlfriend called Sally and seems quite settled, at last. We all like her a lot and I think you'd approve of her too. Billy's good to your mum; he says he'll stay home to keep her company tonight, seeing what day it is.' She stood up. 'I see quite a lot of Dan because the girls are still practically joined at the hip. He's still lost without you. He always will be, I think.'

She stayed a while longer, remembering and thinking, then she walked to the school to collect the girls, calling at her mother's on the way to ask her a favour . . .

'Molly,' said Dan in surprise, answering the door to her that evening.

'You can tell me to go away if you like and I won't be in the least offended,' she made clear. 'I'm here because I thought you might need

212

some company, this being the anniversary. Thought you might get a bit morbid here on your own.'

'Come on in.' He looked pleased as he ushered her inside. 'Who's sitting with Rosa?' he asked, taking her coat and hanging it on the hallstand.

'My mum.' She followed him into the lounge. 'I arranged it with her this afternoon after I'd been to the cemetery. It was there I got the idea.'

'Why didn't you tell me you were coming when I collected Patsy?' he asked. 'I'd have laid on some food.'

'That's why I didn't tell you,' she explained. 'I wanted to keep it casual. I thought after Patsy went to bed you might start looking back and feel low so I decided to just turn up. You know me well enough to realise that you can tell me to push off if you'd rather be alone.'

'I'm really glad you came, as it happens,' Dan said with a half-smile. 'It was thoughtful of you. Sit down and make yourself comfortable.'

'I've done this for myself too, you know,' she informed him, sitting down in an armchair. 'Today has been difficult for me as well. I got to thinking that Hattie and the boys have each other to talk to at a time like this, whereas you and I are outsiders in a way. You're not blood-related, and although I was very close to Angie and I love Hattie to bits, I am just a friend. Obviously you talk to Patsy about her mother but there's a limit to how much you can say to a child.'

'I think you've probably saved me from sinking into a sea of despair,' he confessed. 'The black dogs have been hovering all day and began to take a hold after Patsy went to bed.' He paused. 'Actually, I was just going to have a glass of whisky to ease the pain. Will you join me?'

'Whisky isn't really my tipple.'

'Sherry?'

'Lovely.'

'I keep a little booze in the house now that I can't go down the pub for a pint,' he mentioned, taking some bottles and glasses from the sideboard.

'Being a single parent does put paid to your social life,' she remarked, as he handed her a glass of sherry. 'But I'm sure Hattie would baby-sit for you if you wanted to go out for a drink one evening. I'd offer to do it myself but I can't leave Rosa – though you could always leave Patsy at my place.'

'Hattie's always offering, and I have been down the pub with Billy on the odd occasion,' he told her. 'But I don't often go. I didn't when Angie was alive. Just sometimes I used to fancy an hour or so down the local of an evening, talking to the blokes down there. I don't think it's fair to ask Hattie to baby-sit while I go out enjoying myself, no matter how willing she is. She's got quite enough to do, and I'm not really bothered about going out at the moment.'

He poured himself a whisky and they stood up and chinked their glasses. 'To Angie,' they said simultaneously.

Ensconced in armchairs opposite each other, they sat in quiet contemplation for a while before lapsing into reminiscence about the time when Angie had been around and the things that had happened when they'd all been together, recalling many happy times.

'I talk to her in my mind, you know,' Molly said.

'Me too. All the time.'

'Not only in my mind either.' She made a face. 'I found myself talking to her out loud at the grave today. Anyone who happened to be around must have thought I was dotty.'

'People do that at graves,' Dan said. 'It's perfectly permissible. I don't think anyone who saw you would have thought of carting you off down the road to St Bernard's.'

'I'll just have to take your word for that,' she said with a wry grin.

They moved on to talk of other things: life, the pottery and, inevitably, the children.

'On the subject of the kids, why don't we take them somewhere further afield one of these weekends?' Dan suggested. 'Patsy asked me to take her to Chessington Zoo the other day and it'll be more fun with company.'

'I'm sure Rosa would be all in favour of that.'

'How about Sunday afternoon then, if the weather's nice?' He seemed enthusiastic.

'Suits me.'

Relaxed by the alcohol, Molly stayed longer than intended until a glance at her watch had her leaping up. 'Mum will give me a right wigging if I don't get back soon,' she said. 'I didn't realise it was so late.'

He got her coat and held it while she slipped into it. 'It's my fault. I kept you talking,' he said.

'Not at all,' she smiled. 'I did my share of nattering.'

At the front door, he said, 'Thanks for coming, Moll. It's really helped. I never thought I would laugh today but somehow we both managed it.'

'Yes . . . we did.'

There was a silence and Molly guessed they were having similar thoughts.

'Angie would be pleased we've managed to cheer each other up, I should think,' she said.

'Do you?'

'I do.'

Another odd silence.

'See you tomorrow at work then,' she said.

'Will you be all right walking home on your own, only I can't leave Patsy?'

'I'll be fine.'

''Night then, Moll.'

''Night, Dan.'

Walking down the street, aware of an inner glow, she finally admitted to herself that her feelings for Dan were changing. The platonic friendship based on mutual grief and their children's close bond had become tinged with something else for her. It was more than just a physical thing, though that was a strong element. It was warmth, empathy, emotion, a feeling of excitement and joy in his company. She realised that she was falling in love with him.

It couldn't come to anything, of course. Even apart from the fact that she was married, the scandal it would cause if they got together this soon after Angie's demise didn't bear thinking about. Anyway, the situation wouldn't arise because he didn't feel for her in that way. As far as he was concerned they were just mates. She doubted if he was capable of seeing any woman but Angie in romantic terms. You couldn't manufacture that sort of thing if the spark wasn't there. So all she could do was continue to enjoy his company and keep her feelings to herself.

Hattie arranged with Dan to have Patsy at The Hawthorns for the afternoon on Saturday. Her granddaughter asked if her best friend could go along too, and when Molly went to collect Rosa, Hattie invited her to stay for tea. She did the same thing to Dan when he came to collect Patsy so there was quite a gathering around the tea-table. Everyone was in good spirits after the emotion of the anniversary, except for Josh, who sat in stony silence.

'How's the job going, Josh?' enquired Molly sociably.

'All right,' was his abrupt response.

'I suppose you're well settled in now,' she persisted, trying to draw him out.

'Mm.'

'Have you made any friends there?'

'What's it to you?' he snapped, cheeks flaming, eyes bright with temper.

'I was only making conversation.'

'Well, don't bother,' he told her aggressively. 'I'm out of your hair at the pottery so you got your own way about that. Don't expect me to be civil to you as well.'

'Hey, you watch your tongue,' admonished Billy.

'Yeah,' added Dan, frowning at him.

'Don't be rude, son,' was Hattie's weary contribution.

'That's it, all gang up on me like you usually do.'

'We're not—' began his mother.

'Yes, you are. You always do.' He piled some sandwiches on to his plate and stood up purposefully. 'I'll eat my tea in my bedroom in peace.'

With that he stomped from the room.

Flushed, Hattie tutted, shaking her head. 'He's still very bitter,' she said. 'Just doesn't seem able to accept that what he did deserves the punishment he was given. Thinks we're all against him.'

'He knows full well the seriousness of what he did,' was Billy's opinion. 'It's easier to make excuses and blame everyone else than face up to it, that's all.'

There was an uncomfortable silence. To ease an awkward moment, Molly said, 'On a more cheerful note, Dan and I are taking the girls to Chessington Zoo tomorrow afternoon . . . weather permitting, of course.'

'Yeah, won't it be fun?' said Patsy excitedly.

'I like the funfair best,' added Rosa. 'The animals are a bit too smelly.'

Molly turned to Hattie. 'Why don't you come with us, Hat? It'll be a nice afternoon out.'

'That's a good idea,' enthused Dan. 'There'll be plenty of room for you in the car. The girls are only little.'

'Yeah, come with us, Gran,' urged Patsy.

'You go with 'em, Mum,' added Billy. 'You'll only be here on your own otherwise. I expect I'll be out with Sally and Josh is bound to go off somewhere with his mates.'

'It's nice of you to ask,' Hattie began, looking from Molly to Dan, 'but I think I'd like a quiet afternoon. Put my feet up and read the Sunday paper.'

'Aah.' Patsy was disappointed. 'Go on, Gran, come with us. It'll be the best fun.'

'You can tell me all about it afterwards. I'll look forward to that,' said Hattie.

'Oh, please come—'

'Leave it, Patsy,' came Dan's firm intervention. 'Your gran works hard all week. She's entitled to some peace and quiet on a Sunday afternoon.'

Patsy finally accepted it and tucked into a slice of her grandmother's home-made chocolate cake.

Dan's comments set Molly thinking about the older woman's abundant energy. Well into her fifties, she did a full-time job at the pottery, ran the home like clockwork, pandered to her sons' every need and still managed to find time to do all her own baking. A shop-bought cake or pie was unheard of in the Beckett house. It was no wonder she fancied a quiet Sunday afternoon now and again.

Reflecting on the conversation, Molly realised how keen she'd been to inform everyone about the Chessington trip. It was common knowledge that she and Dan spent time together because of the children but now that they were having a proper outing further away, it seemed vital that no one got the wrong impression. Her growing feelings for him were so strong, it was almost as though they were visible to other people. That's what comes of having a guilty conscience, she admonished herself.

'You ready for some of this chocolate cake, Molly?' asked Hattie, cake knife poised.

'Yes, please. I couldn't miss out on one of your cakes.'

Smiling, Hattie cut her a slice.

Although the atmosphere had been soured by Josh, it became more relaxed and jolly now. But his presence in the house cast a dark shadow over everything. Molly's heart went out to Hattie, and guessed that coping with his difficult behaviour hurt and exhausted her.

The following afternoon Billy walked up the path to Sally's front door, whistling a tune in happy anticipation of seeing her. He rang the bell. No reply. That was odd; she was usually looking out for him and opened the door before he reached it. He rang again and when there was still no sign of life, he banged hard with the knocker. Her parents sometimes went out visiting relatives on a Sunday afternoon, he recalled. But Sally was expecting him so she wouldn't have gone out. They'd planned to go to the West End to see a film and have a bite to eat afterwards in the Wimpy in Leicester Square.

He rang again and again; kept his finger on the bell. Still nothing. He shouted through the letter box. No response at all. Puzzled, he walked across the small front garden, pressed his face against the window and peered through the net curtains into the front room. It was empty. Remembering that it was the sitting room and the family mostly used the living room at the back, he walked around the block to the back alley and made his way up the back garden.

He was beginning to get really anxious now. Why hadn't she given him a bell if something had come up and she couldn't make their date? Admittedly, the Smiths didn't have a telephone in the house but they did have an obliging next-door neighbour who let them use theirs to save them going to the call box at the end of the street. If the neighbours weren't at home, Sally could have called him from there. Surely she wouldn't stand him up. Not Sally; not at this stage in their relationship. They hadn't had a row or anything like that.

He tried the back door and to his amazement it was open. So there must be somebody in because they wouldn't leave the house empty with the door unlocked.

'Sally,' he called.

All was silent. There wasn't a sound in the house – not a creak or a rustle. How strange. Baffled and uneasy, he went through to the living room.

'Christ Almighty,' he gasped, eyes bulging. 'What the hell's going on here?'

Sally was lying on the floor with her eyes closed. Breathless with fear, he went down on his knees beside her and was relieved to see the faint rise and fall of her chest.

'Sally,' he said, gently nudging her shoulder. 'Sally, can you hear me?'

No reaction. She was motionless. He called her name again; begged her to speak to him in a desperate attempt to reach some level of consciousness. There was no response.

'Bloody hell,' he muttered to himself, raking his fingers through his hair distractedly. 'You need a doctor, girl – and right away.'

'Can I use your phone, please?' he asked Sally's next-door neighbour.

'Oh, I dunno about that,' said the middle-aged woman, eyeing him coolly through her spectacles. 'It isn't a public service, you know.'

'It's an emergency,' he explained, voice gruff with worry. 'I need to call an ambulance.'

'Who's ill?'

'Sally from next door. She's out for the count on the floor in there. I've just found her. Her mum and dad are out and I'm afraid to move her.'

Instantly the woman's attitude changed. She shouted into the house, 'Charlie, ring for an ambulance will you – and sharpish. Young Sally next door has gone into a coma. I'm going in there.'

'Righto, love,' came the reply. 'I'll do it straight away.'

'A coma,' gasped Billy. 'Oh my God!'

'It's her diabetes, son,' the neighbour said as they hurried to the Smiths' house. 'She must have gone too long without food. Something to do with the insulin causes it.'

'*Diabetes?*'

'That's right.'

'What, Sally . . .?'

'Surely you knew she was a diabetic,' said the woman. 'You've been going out with her long enough to know that.'

'She's never said a word about it.'

'That's typical of Sally. She doesn't let it cramp her style, you see,' she informed him as they hurried up the Smiths' back garden path. 'Never makes any fuss about it. Just injects herself with insulin every day and gets on with her life.'

'Injects herself.' He was horrified. 'The poor thing.'

'Ooh, don't let her hear you say that,' she advised him strongly. 'She doesn't make heavy weather of it and doesn't allow anyone else to either. You'd never know she had it except for when something like this happens, and it isn't very often.'

'I can't believe it.' Billy was still trying to take it in.

'The silly girl should have told you so you'd be prepared if she had a turn when she was with you. As far as I know it happens if she goes without food for too long but I don't know the details. It could be caused by other things too.' They reached Sally, who was still unconscious. 'Help me to get her on to her side, will yer, son, to stop her swallowing

218

her tongue?' urged the neighbour. 'With one leg over the other. That's right.'

'Will she be OK?' asked Billy, on his knees beside her. 'I mean, she won't die, will she?' He'd never been so frightened in his life. His lovely Sally in a coma – it seemed unreal.

'We don't know how long she's been like it, do we?' The woman looked grave. 'I'm no expert but I think it could be dangerous if she's been in this state for too long.'

'Oh God!' He turned even paler with fright.

'Don't panic now. If we get her to hospital quickly she should be all right,' encouraged the woman. 'They'll inject glucose into her and it'll bring her round. Usually leaves her with a stinking headache, though.'

'There must be something we can do while we're waiting for the ambulance.'

The woman thought about this. 'I think I remember her mum saying something about trying to get sugar into her but it's difficult to get her to take it apparently.' The sound of an ambulance bell could be heard distantly, growing louder by the second. 'Thank God for that,' she said, going to the window. 'They're here.'

'Help's at hand, Sally,' said Billy tenderly, on his knees beside his motionless loved one, his eyes hot with tears. 'You'll be all right. I'll be with you. I'll go with you in the ambulance.'

Billy sat by Sally's hospital bed. She'd regained consciousness some time ago but refused to see him initially, even though he'd been granted permission to go on the ward outside of official visiting hours. The nurse told him that she'd been instructed to thank him on Sally's behalf for getting her into hospital but she didn't want to see him. Billy wasn't the type to give up that easily so – putting his natural charm to good use – he managed to enlist the help of the nurse, who finally persuaded Sally to let him see her.

'Thanks ever so much for . . . er . . . dealing with the situation,' Sally said, her face almost as white as the pillows, blue eyes dull and lacklustre. 'I'm sorry you got lumbered with it.'

'Don't be daft . . .'

'We had Sunday dinner early because Mum and Dad were going out and I didn't eat much because I wasn't hungry at that time,' she was eager to explain. 'I intended to have a snack while I was waiting for you. I remember sitting down and thinking I'll get a biscuit or something in a minute. Only I must have left it too late because the next thing I knew I woke up in here.' She bit her lip. 'I really am sorry.'

'Don't apologise, for goodness' sake,' Billy said, holding her hand. 'Just tell me why you didn't tell me you were diabetic and why you didn't want to see me when you came round.'

'I should have thought that was obvious.'

219

'No. Not to me it isn't.'

'For goodness' sake, Billy, it's very embarrassing for me to know that you've seen me . . . well, like that,' she explained, avoiding his eyes.

'Embarrassing? I don't see why.'

'Don't pretend to be thick,' she accused.

'I'm not,' he protested. 'I can't see what's embarrassing about being ill.'

'You know very well what I'm on about,' she said, giving him a shrewd look, then pausing and seeming a little less certain. 'Surely you must do.'

'I think you'd better tell me, don't you?'

'Well, it's hardly the most glamorous state to see your girlfriend in, is it?'

'Oh, Sally. Glamour was the last thing on my mind when I saw you lying there,' he assured her. 'All I could think of was getting you to hospital.'

'Really?'

'Of course. What do you think I am? Some sort of unfeeling monster?'

'Sorry.'

'Don't start that again.'

'Well . . . thanks for looking after me, anyway,' she said in a softer tone.

'Don't keep thanking me,' he tutted. 'Just tell me why you didn't tell me you were diabetic.'

'When we met that first time at Brighton, should I have warned you that if I don't eat at regular times I could go into a coma or have a funny turn and act as though I'm drunk?' She met his eyes in a challenge. 'You'd have been off like a shot if I had done, I can tell you that much.'

'You're wrong. I wouldn't.'

'I bet you would.'

'It would have taken more than that to put me off and that's definite.'

'You can't be sure of that.'

'I can, you know. But all right, Sally, I can understand why you wouldn't want to tell a complete stranger,' he conceded. 'But we've been seeing each other for a year now. Surely there must have come a point when you trusted me enough to tell me. You scared me half to death back there because I didn't know what was the matter.'

'It was bad, I know. I should have told you, and Mum and Dad have been threatening to do it if I didn't. They wanted me to tell you at the very beginning – just in case anything happened – so that you would know what to do,' she told him. 'I made them promise not to. I kept meaning to mention it to you but things were going so well between us, I didn't want to spoil it. Anyway, as these funny turns only happen very occasionally and only if I'm careless about eating . . . well, I just couldn't bring myself to do it.'

'Hiding it from me for all this time must have taken some doing. Wouldn't it have been easier to just tell me?'

'It wasn't that difficult to keep it from you as I'm only ever with you for a few hours at a time,' she explained. 'I've only had one queer turn before this one while I've actually been with you. Usually I get a warning and I suck a sweet and it brings me out of it. This time there was no warning.'

'That's why you always keep boiled sweets on you?'

She nodded.

'And that's why you acted as though you'd been having a secret tipple last Christmas? I accused Josh of spiking your drinks.'

'Exactly. So you'd best apologise to your brother.'

'Oh, Sally,' he said, putting her hand to his lips. 'Fancy going through all this and not telling me.'

'It's no big thing to me now, Billy, because I'm used to it,' she told him. 'I admit I was a bit scared when I was first diagnosed five years ago, and it took me a little while to get used to doing the injections but I'm fine with it now, honestly.' She was very much on the defensive. 'Once upon a time it was a killer. The wasting disease, they called it. These days with insulin, proper care and regular check-ups, you can lead a normal life – depending on the degree to which you have it, of course. I'm lucky I am able to and it's what I aim for. OK, so I had a bit of an upset today but people have far worse things than that to contend with in life. They'll probably keep me in hospital overnight for observation but I'll be home tomorrow and back to normal.'

'You're so matter-of-fact about it.'

'There are two ways of dealing with it. I can either sit about worrying about it and feeling sorry for myself or I can get on with my life,' she told him. 'The first isn't even an option for me. I'm young and I want to enjoy myself. There are limitations, of course – I have to inject myself every day and take more care of myself than perhaps other people of my age – but it isn't a problem for me, really.'

Billy stared at her, full of admiration.

'I can understand that it might be a problem for you, though,' Sally went on, misunderstanding his silence. 'And I'll quite understand if you want to finish with me. It isn't much fun having a girlfriend with health complications.'

'The last thing I want to do is finish with you.' He was astonished at the suggestion. 'I want to be with you and look after you.'

Unintentionally he'd said the wrong thing. 'I don't want looking after,' she objected, her eyes filling with angry tears. 'I'm perfectly capable of looking after myself. I'm not an invalid and I don't want to be treated like one.'

'I respect your position and I would never do that.'

She removed her hand from his. 'Why don't you go and find a girl who's got nothing wrong with her? There are plenty of them about.'

'I don't want any other girl,' he said, and without any prior intention added, 'It's you I want. I love you and I want to marry you.'

Looking up sharply, she said, 'Don't be ridiculous, Billy. There's no need to go to those lengths just because you feel sorry for me.'

'How could I feel sorry for someone who's got everything?' he asked, spreading his hands in a gesture of sincerity. 'You're beautiful, intelligent, funny, brave and the sexiest girl this side of the river.'

'And I have diabetes, which means that I have to watch what I eat, am prone to funny turns if I'm not careful, and sometimes get more tired than other girls of my age,' she reminded him.

'So what? As you've just said, people have far worse things than that to put up with,' he pointed out with brutal candour because it was obvious that any hint of sympathy would drive her away. 'You've just finished telling me how the condition can be controlled these days.'

She wasn't convinced. 'You wouldn't have proposed to me if the coma hadn't happened, would you?' she asked, eyeing him warily.

'I would have – eventually.' He was absolutely convinced. 'I knew the day I met you that you were the only girl for me. OK, so the drama of today prompted me to do it, but it's something I should have done ages ago.' He got down on his knees. 'I know this isn't the most romantic place but, Sally, I love you so much. Please will you marry me?'

Her face melted into a smile. 'How can I refuse?' she said softly.

'Oh, Sally . . .' He went to get up off his knees, lost his balance and landed on the floor.

'What's going on here?' demanded the nurse, bustling on the scene while the other patients enjoyed the entertainment. 'Have you two been having a fight?'

'Quite the opposite,' said Sally dreamily. 'We've just got engaged.'

'Oh, well, congratulations then,' beamed the nurse as Billy scrambled to his feet. 'But engagement or not you've got to go now. The sister'll have my guts for garters if she finds out you're still here.'

'I'm on my way.'

'With force, if necessary,' added the nurse.

He kissed Sally and as he turned to leave she called after him, 'Could you tell Mum and Dad what happened? Not about the engagement – I want to tell them that myself – just let them know where I am.'

'Will do,' he agreed, and walked down the ward with a broad grin on his face. In the corridor he leaped sideways in the air and threw his hands up in triumph.

'Hey, watch yourself,' laughed the nurse. 'You'll do yourself an injury and end up in here with her.'

'Yes, please.'

'You are a fool,' she smiled. 'Get out of here before you turn the place into a complete bear garden.'

He made a gesture of mock surrender. 'I'm going, I'm going,' he said, and swaggered down the corridor, leaving her shaking her head and smiling.

'Can we have an ice cream, please, Dad?' requested Patsy. 'There's a van over there.'

'Let's all have one, shall we?' He turned to Molly. 'Do you fancy one?'

'Please.'

Dan looked around the funfair, which was heaving with people, families out for the afternoon and children everywhere, the swell of youthful voices rising above the noisy fairground music. 'There's an empty bench over there,' he said to Molly. 'You go and grab it while we go and get the ices. What would you like?'

'A strawberry cornet, please.'

He strode off through the crowds with the children trotting beside him, a tall, impressive figure casually dressed in a Fair Isle sweater and light trousers.

The kids were having a whale of a time; Molly was enjoying herself too. They'd done a tour of the animals but the funfair was by far the more popular attraction with the children, who were fearless and wanted to go on everything. Molly and Dan had to accompany them on the scarier rides but it had been good fun and Molly hadn't laughed so much in ages.

Now the others were back.

'One strawberry cornet,' Dan said to Molly, handing it to her, then sitting beside her; the children perched next to him, licking their cornets and chatting between themselves.

'You enjoying yourself, Molly?'

'I'll say. You?'

Dan turned to her thoughtfully. 'I'm surprised at how much, actually.'

'Didn't you fancy an afternoon with the animals then?'

'You really shouldn't describe our daughters that way,' he laughed.

'Honestly,' Molly tutted, but she couldn't hide a smile.

'Sorry, I couldn't resist it.'

'Making jokes, Dan, whatever next,' she teased him.

'You're a bad influence. Or a good one, depending how you look at it.'

'I'll go for the second.'

'Seriously, though,' he went on, 'what I meant was – well, you remember you told me once that I would feel normal again, eventually? Well, I'm beginning to have the odd glimpse of normality lately. It comes and goes but it's a start.'

'And you've had a bit more than just a glimpse this afternoon,' Molly surmised.

'Exactly.'

'Good.'

'Only thing is, I feel guilty about it,' he said, biting into his ice cream. 'I feel as though I'm letting Angie down.'

'She wouldn't want you to spend the rest of your life being miserable,' she told him, adding to make him feel better, 'And if you feel guilty then so should I because I've had fun this afternoon and she was my best friend, remember.'

'Don't you feel as though she should be here enjoying it with us?' he asked.

'I do, of course, and I'm really sad that she isn't, but I know she would want us to make Patsy happy, and Patsy's never happier than when she's with Rosa.'

'There is that.'

'Kids keep you going,' she remarked, moving on swiftly so that he wouldn't have a chance to dwell on his feeling of compunction, 'even if they do wear you out.'

'Phew, they do that all right.'

'You can understand why Hattie wanted to stay at home and have a quiet afternoon, can't you?' Molly mentioned casually. 'I realised yesterday just how much she has to do. She's always on the go.'

'That's why I don't ask her to look after Patsy very often,' Dan told her. 'She's got more than enough to do, without having a boisterous eight-year-old to cope with in her spare time, no matter how willing she is.'

'Josh must wear her out on top of everything else,' said Molly, 'with that bad temper of his filling the house with tension. I don't know how she puts up with it.'

'With great difficulty, I should think,' he suggested, frowning darkly. 'Mind you, she's a lot firmer with him than she used to be, and that takes some doing after giving in to him for so long.'

'It must have broken her heart when she found out what he'd been up to.'

'I'm sure.'

'She's such a lovely woman too,' Molly went on. 'I've become very close to her since Angie died. We're great friends. I think the world of her.'

'Me too.'

Molly finished her ice cream and wiped her hands with her handkerchief. 'If you would like to go out somewhere at any time and you don't want to bother Hattie with the baby-sitting, you can always bring Patsy round to my place, you know,' she suggested. 'She can stay the night to save you hurrying back. The girls would love it.'

'Thanks,' he acknowledged. 'I've nothing planned at the moment but I'll certainly bear it in mind if anything does come up.'

The conversation was brought to a close by Patsy's dulcet tones. 'Can we go on the carousel horses again, Dad, please?' she asked.

'Can we, Mum, please?' echoed Rosa.

Both adults nodded and got up with an air of pleasurable resignation. As they walked towards the carousel Molly said, 'Let me pay for this, Dan.' She had made it absolutely clear at the outset of the trip that she wanted the expenses shared. To her mind, allowing him to pay for her had connotations she wanted to avoid. But he wouldn't hear of it. He'd said this was his chance to repay her for minding Patsy after school every day.

'Absolutely not,' he insisted now.

'Thank you very much then,' she conceded graciously, for fear of offending him.

Standing next to him, waving madly to the children each time they came around on the carousel horses, Molly was imbued with a deep sense of joy. Being with him felt so right, so natural; as though they were a family, something she had never experienced with Brian. She felt so relaxed and close to him, she almost took his arm.

Reminding herself that she must keep a tight rein on her feelings, she found herself in something of a dilemma. As being with him only served to increase her feelings for him, the sensible thing would be not to see him outside of work. But that wouldn't be possible without breaking the hearts of two little girls who wanted to be together.

Just think of him in the same way as he sees you, she told herself; as a friend, another single parent with the same sort of problems. It sounded easy. But matters of the heart were never that simple.

Her reverie was interrupted when she realised that he was speaking to her: 'Shall we let them have one more go on something of their choice after this, then call it a day?'

'What a good idea,' Molly agreed. 'I think they've had enough now.'

'We have, you mean,' Dan corrected. 'I doubt if the terrible twosome will agree.'

'You're right,' she laughed. 'They can never have their fill of this sort of thing. They're sure to give us a hard time. Still, united we'll be stronger.'

'We will indeed.' His gaze lingered on her face. 'I've been so glad of your company this afternoon, Molly,' he said warmly.

'Likewise.'

'These sort of places are so much more fun for us parents when there is another adult around for moral support, don't you think?'

'Definitely.' She wondered if he would be so quick to enlist her company if he knew how she really felt about him. She doubted it; he would probably want to run a mile from such complications.

The ride ended and the children bounded towards them, and were told that the next ride would be the last for today to cries of objection. Dan and Molly exchanged knowing looks and they both burst out laughing.

★ ★ ★

Getting into bed that night Dan was surprised to realise that the black depression that had reached unbearable proportions every night at this time since he'd lost Angie was less intense. In fact, when he thought back on the afternoon, he found himself smiling. Making Patsy happy was obviously good for him. Having Molly and Rosa to do things with helped a lot too. Molly was great. She was strong but fragile somehow; funny but sensitive. She'd turned out to be a real pal and he valued that.

He took his book from his bedside table and stared unseeingly at the print. Memories of the afternoon and the fun they'd had interfered with his concentration. Finally giving up on his book, he closed it and turned out the light. As always he thought of Angie as he settled down to go to sleep, and the usual feeling of grief swept over him. It had become almost a ritual and he expected it. Braced himself almost. But tonight it wasn't the hopeless despair he'd become so accustomed to. It was different somehow: more bittersweet memories of his beloved wife.

On the heels of this realisation came guilt. Angie had lost her life saving their child's. He had no right to so much as a morsel of happiness. But despite his nagging conscience, the all-consuming blackness didn't come.

Chapter Fifteen

Josh stood at the bar of a pub in Hanwell Broadway drinking a pint of beer and feeling sorry for himself. It was Saturday night and he was alone. His mates were all doing their national service, and as none of them was around tonight, he assumed that nobody had managed to get a weekend pass. Some of them had been posted abroad anyway, to Germany, Cyprus or Singapore. The lucky beggars. He wouldn't mind seeing foreign places at the government's expense.

Still, maybe he was better off on his own. The lads weren't the same when they came home on leave; they were full of themselves and boastful, as though being soldiers made them men of the world. They'd been to new places, done new things and they didn't let him forget that he hadn't, relentlessly taking the mick because he'd not had to do his two years. They reckoned there was nothing wrong with him and he'd worked a flanker at the medical, which wasn't true at all. He'd gone through the same procedure as everyone else. In fact, he'd rather have gone in and taken his chances with the psychopathic sergeants he'd heard so much about than be stuck around here on his own.

He felt very much an outsider now; was set apart from his friends by his lack of barrack-room tales to tell. He'd even had a short back and sides haircut in the hope of gaining favour because the others had lost their DAs to the army barber. No one had taken much notice. They'd grown out of the teddy boy thing. The old crowd had broken up anyway now that most of them were around only occasionally.

What a life! No mates, no luck with girls and his family hated him. The way things were at home at the moment, he'd be better off living rough on the streets. Billy had been the golden boy with Mum all week because he got engaged last weekend, the two of them fussing around Sally when he'd brought her home the other night. Anyone would think she was royalty or something, the way they'd carried on. She was coming to Sunday tea tomorrow so Mum would be all over her and Billy. Ugh, it made him sick.

Sally was a right little cracker, though, he had to admit that. But Billy always attracted beautiful women because he had the looks and the chat. As for Josh, he never even got a girl to dance with him a second time, let alone go out with him.

Surely if he was that repulsive they wouldn't even dance with him. He was under no illusions. He knew he was no Marlon Brando but there were uglier blokes around and they managed to have girls on their arms. Perhaps he had some defect he wasn't aware of and that put them off.

And as for the one woman in his life he'd always been able to rely on for support and affection – his mother – she'd completely turned against him since that cow Molly had grassed him up. Until then he'd had Mum in the palm of his hand. But now she'd gone all hard on him and there was no getting around her. It was only because she made him pay his way at home that he was forced to work at a machine all day in a dismal factory where you had to account for every second of your time; you couldn't even have a smoke until the official tea break. And while he was slaving away there, the others were having an easy time at the pottery, a part of which was his by rights as a member of the Beckett family. The fact that Dan and Molly – who weren't even blood-related – had a share in it made him incandescent with rage.

If he'd known it was going to cause this much grief, he wouldn't have bothered with the scam, though he had enjoyed it. It hadn't just been the extra dosh that had been his inspiration – though that had been handy – but the satisfaction of knowing that he was putting one over on the others to pay them back for treating him like England's biggest idiot. He'd felt like the family fool for as long as he could remember, and he'd had enough.

Anger and bitterness simmered and festered. Tightening his grip on his pint glass, he struggled with the urge to kick or punch something. One of these days he'd get even with them, he vowed, the thought of sweet revenge cheering him up a little. More immediately was the problem of what to do with the rest of the evening. Should he go to a jazz club or a dance hall? Jazz clubs had a lively atmosphere and a fair amount of talent but they also attracted a large element of student types who went just because they enjoyed the music. Whereas a dance hall like the Hammersmith Palais was fertile hunting ground and no one pretended otherwise.

Finishing his drink he left the pub and joined the bus queue to wait for the bus to Ealing Broadway where he would get the train to Hammersmith. The Palais offered more opportunity to meet someone. Maybe tonight he'd get lucky, he thought, as he got on the bus.

The following afternoon Molly was walking in Churchfields on her own. Rosa was at a birthday party at a neighbour's flat so Molly had hurried through the chores and decided to make the most of the fine weather before calling in to see her mother. The abundant trees were in fresh green leaf, the sun was shining and the air was sweet and mild.

Being a Sunday afternoon, there were plenty of people about. But that didn't detract from the sense of tranquillity that was ever present in this lush expanse of parkland, despite its close proximity to the Uxbridge Road and its heavy traffic that was more or less constant. The only sounds here were the shouts of children playing, the church clock striking on the hour and the twitter and rustle of birds in the trees, the overall peacefulness occasionally shattered by the Paddington Express thundering over the viaduct.

Dressed in black tapered trousers and a loose blue sweater, Molly strode on in the direction of the church, intending to continue on into Brent Lodge park and then head back, which would mean she had walked a good healthy distance.

Her attention was attracted by someone sitting on a bench under a tree. She stared hard. Josh? It couldn't be. He was more likely to be with a crowd of mates at the cinema or hanging around some coffee bar on a Sunday afternoon than in a park. But on closer inspection she could see that it was him. Undeterred by almost certain hostility, she went over.

'Well, well, Josh. You're the last person I expected to see here,' she remarked, sitting down beside him and bracing herself for a rebuff.

'Really?' he said absently, glancing at her, then staring morosely ahead.

'I thought the cinema or the coffee bar was more to the taste of you and your mates.'

'My mates are all away in the army.'

'Oh, yeah, I suppose they would be,' she realised. 'They go in at eighteen, don't they?'

'Mm.'

'The government will be phasing national service out soon, according to the papers.'

'Not soon enough,' was his querulous response.

'Still, at least you didn't have to go in.'

'I'd rather have gone in than be left with no mates,' he told her.

'It must be a bit lonely for you,' she said understandingly.

'You're not kidding. I went to a dance on my own last night. I mean, how low can you sink? And what a waste of time that was, an' all.'

'You didn't find a girl then?'

'Nah, none of 'em wanna know,' he admitted, driven to confide in her by the depth of his loneliness. 'I reckon I must have BO or bad breath or something.'

'Perhaps you try too hard,' she suggested, amazed at having got this far with him, having tried so many times before to draw him out and received only abuse.

He gave her a pitying look. 'I know how to chat a girl up, thanks very much.' He was indignant. 'I'm not a complete idiot. I can play it cool with the best of 'em.'

'Maybe if you smiled occasionally, it might help.' She was really pushing her luck.

'Huh, what have I got to smile about?'

Her patience was beginning to wear thin. 'A bloomin' sight more than a lot of people,' she replied with emphasis. 'You're eighteen years old, for goodness' sake, with your whole life ahead of you and you're living in an age of affluence and opportunity. The world could be yours if you'd let it.'

'Oh, yeah, with no mates, no girlfriend and a family who hate the sight of me.'

'They don't hate you—'

'They do, you know.'

'Josh, you really are imagining things—'

'Do you know why I'm sitting here on a park bench on my own like some sad old geezer?' he interrupted, glaring at her.

'I don't suppose it's because of the fresh air.'

'Too right it isn't,' he confirmed. 'I couldn't stand to be at home. I was driven out.'

'What did they do to upset you this time?' She suppressed a sigh.

'Billy's girlfriend has come for tea and they're all going on and on about them getting married,' he complained. 'Dan and Patsy are there and they're all making such a big fuss about it, especially Mum. She's all over this Sally woman.'

'It's only natural for your mum to be pleased that Billy has found someone he wants to marry,' Molly pointed out. 'I was delighted when I heard about it. It's about time he settled down.'

'Anyone would think he'd won the war single-handed the way they're carrying on, when all he's done is found a girl who's daft enough to say she'll marry him.'

'I'm sure you're exaggerating about all this.'

'I'm not,' he protested. 'You should hear 'em.'

'The engagement's new, that's why they're going a bit overboard. The novelty will soon wear off,' she suggested. 'Anyway, I thought you'd be pleased about Billy getting married because with him leaving home you'll have your mum to yourself; you'll get all the attention then.'

'Mm, there is that, I suppose,' he agreed half-heartedly, 'though she's gone all narky on me.'

Deeming it wise to steer the conversation away from the delicate subject of a mother-and-son relationship, she remarked, 'Sally seems to be a very nice girl.'

'She's all right, I suppose. Everyone's nice in their eyes except me,' Josh grumbled. 'They shut me out of everything.'

Molly chose her words carefully because Josh had a very short fuse and at any moment was going to realise that he'd let his guard slip and turn on her. 'Don't you think you might have got it the wrong way around?' she dared to suggest. 'From what I've seen you've shut them out. I've been there enough times; I've seen what goes on. They try to include you and you either seem uninterested or fly into a temper.'

'Trust you to take their side.' His tone was ice-hard.

'It isn't a question of taking sides. It's about you taking a good honest look at yourself. I've always been convinced that somewhere inside you there's a different boy from the one we see – a happier and better person altogether.'

'That's why you grassed me up, is it?' he said bitterly. 'Because you thought it would make me a better person.'

'You can never leave that alone, can you?' Molly retaliated. 'As I've told you before, I had to tell them what you'd been up to. I didn't have a choice because they had a right to know. And yes, I did hope that you might show some remorse and make more of an effort when you realised that you couldn't get away with it for ever. Obviously I was wrong.'

'Oh, clear off and leave me alone,' he mumbled, staring at his feet.

'I'm going, don't worry,' she said, her mood sharpening. 'I don't know why I even bothered to try to talk to you because you're just a whingeing young toerag who thinks of no one but himself. You're a taker, do you know that? You never give anything but misery and aggravation to everyone around you. It's about time you gave your mother some consideration, spoiling every family occasion with your wretched moods. It broke her heart to know that you were a thief. Why don't you try to make it up to her instead of making the poor woman's life a misery? And if you're so fed up with living at home, move out. Get a place of your own, a bedsit or something.' She paused, eyeing him shrewdly. 'But of course, you wouldn't do that, would you? Because you'd have to fend for yourself then; you wouldn't have your mother cooking for you and doing your washing. It would cost you a damned sight more to live than it does at home too.'

'Have you quite finished?' Josh blasted, raising his eyes to her with contempt.

'No, not quite,' she replied, standing her ground. 'If you were to start considering other people, they would be a whole lot nicer to you. It isn't bad breath that stops you getting a girl but a bad attitude. You're looking inward at yourself all the time instead of them. You'd be surprised how much more you would get out of life if you were to stop focusing entirely on yourself and take an interest in other people; wonder how they are feeling, instead of you. You only get back what you put into life, and your contribution so far has been nil. Unless you do something about your attitude, you've a lonely future ahead of you.'

Without waiting for a reply, she swung off and continued on her walk, inwardly trembling and feeling oddly on the verge of tears. Josh was the most selfish and obnoxious person she had ever met; he was also the saddest. He had such potential and was wasting his life in anger and resentment, alienating himself from everyone. He wouldn't have a friend left in the world if he didn't change his ways. And as he obviously had no intention of doing that, the outlook appeared bleak for him.

She hated to see anyone ruining their life. When it was a child of her closest friend, who was also suffering because of it, it was even harder to take. What made it even worse was being powerless to help. Josh was full of self-loathing, which made him jealous of everyone around him. Unless he learned to like himself, he couldn't expect other people to warm to him.

He worried her, and was on her mind for the rest of the day.

On Wednesday afternoon, Molly hadn't long been in from collecting the girls from school when Peggy and her mother arrived. Peggy was in the area visiting her mother so Molly was given the honour of a visit too.

'It's half-day at the shop and Reg will be at home to see to the kids when they get in from school,' Peggy explained. 'So I thought I might as well come over, as Mum doesn't work Wednesday afternoons either.'

'Good idea.' They were in the kitchen where Molly was filling the kettle for tea. The children were in the living room. 'The girls will probably go out to play in a minute so we can talk in peace.'

'You still have Angie's little girl every day after school then?' observed Peggy.

Molly nodded, sensing a criticism in her tone. 'Just for a couple of hours until her dad finishes work,' she explained.

'That's a bit of a nuisance, isn't it?' suggested Peggy.

'Not at all,' Molly was quick to deny. 'While I'm collecting Rosa from school I might as well collect Patsy. It's no trouble to me at all.'

'It isn't just collecting her, though, is it?' Peggy went on. 'You have to look after her as well.'

'She's no bother,' bristled Molly. 'It isn't as though she's a baby needing constant attention.'

'Even so, I wouldn't fancy it,' disapproved Peggy, 'and knowing you, you're doing it for free too.'

'Of course I am. It's a favour for a friend. He's offered to pay me several times but I don't want that,' Molly informed her briskly. 'He returns the favour by having Rosa at his place to play at weekends.' She didn't add that he covered all the expenses when they took the girls on outings because she knew that Peggy would cheapen with insinuations something that Molly valued.

Her sister shrugged. 'Don't let yourself be put on, that's all,' she warned.

'That's what I keep telling her,' added Joan, who would say anything to stay popular with Peggy. 'I'm always saying—'

'Yes, all right, Mum,' Peggy cut her short. 'There's no need to go on about it.'

'I was only saying . . .'

'You're always only saying, but you never know when to stop,' tutted

Peggy, with seething irritation. 'You go on and on.'

Joan winced and Molly felt a stab of pity for her, even though her mother brought it on herself with her obsequiousness towards Peggy.

'Sorry,' said Joan in a tone of humility that was never present in her dealings with anyone else.

'Forget it,' Peggy said dismissively, her eyes darting around the room and lingering on something in the corner. 'Ooh, I say, a spin-dryer. We are coming up in the world, Molly. You've moved on from the mangle at last.'

'I'm managing to get a few things now,' Molly told her, refusing to be provoked by her patronising attitude. 'I had a good bonus a few months ago.'

'What you really want, though,' said Peggy with an air of authority, 'is a twin-tub washing machine. Then you can get the clothes washed as well.'

'All in good time,' Molly told her.

'They're very good,' Peggy went on. 'I've had one for ages.'

What a surprise, was Molly's ironic reaction, but she said, 'I've heard they're very good. But I'm managing with what I've got for the moment.'

The kettle whistled and Molly poured some boiling water into the teapot and swilled it around to warm it.

'So what's happening with that husband of yours?' Peggy enquired as Molly made the tea. 'Is he staying away for the duration or what?'

'He'll be back eventually.'

'He's in no hurry to get back, obviously.'

'Not while there's work in Norfolk, which there is for a long time ahead, apparently,' Molly told her in an even tone; she wouldn't allow herself to be goaded. 'There's so much building to be done in these new towns.'

'He's having the time of his life, I bet,' opined Peggy. 'Living a bachelor life while you're stuck here on your own.'

'I've told her he's got another woman,' put in Joan, 'but she won't do anything about it.'

'Perhaps it suits her to let him get on with it,' suggested Peggy, looking at her sister with an inquisitive grin.

'That's for me to know and you to wonder.' Molly forced a grin to make light of it.

'It isn't right the way things are—' began Joan.

Peggy turned on her. 'Oh, do shut up, for goodness' sake, Mum,' she snapped viciously. 'You've made your point on the subject a million times before so give us all a break and give it a rest, why don't you?'

Joan looked wounded, as though she'd been physically assaulted.

'Do us a favour, would you, Mum?' requested Molly kindly. 'Could you pop into the other room and clear the coffee table for me, ready for when I bring the tray in?'

'Yeah, all right.'

As soon as Joan was out of earshot, Molly went for Peggy. 'Take it easy on her, will you? There's no need to keep biting her head off. She's done nothing to deserve it.'

'She's getting on my nerves—'

'And you're getting on mine, the way you treat her,' Molly asserted. 'Don't you realise that you're really hurting her feelings with that sharp tongue of yours? The poor woman is wounded. You can see it on her face.'

'I was a bit short with her, that's all,' Peggy defended. 'Don't tell me she doesn't drive you nuts occasionally.'

'Of course she does, and I expect I do the same thing to her at times. We can all rub each other up the wrong way sometimes; it's only natural,' said Molly.

'Why are you having a go at me about it then?'

'Because you don't even try to hide it,' Molly told her. 'You've no patience with Mum at all. She dotes on you and all you do in return is belittle her.'

'I was doing it in defence of you, so don't go all holier-than-thou on me.'

'I don't need defending, thanks, especially not at the expense of my mother's feelings.'

'Oh, for God's sake . . .'

'Look, Peggy,' came Molly's firm interruption, 'you've always been the favourite. Mum would do anything for you and you don't appreciate it one little bit. I would give a lot for just a fraction of the affection you get from her. For some reason, she never has had much time for me and that still hurts, even now that I'm a mother myself. She can be really cold towards me at times but she's still my mum and she brought me up. I won't stand by and see her bullied. So lay off.'

'All right, keep your hair on,' snapped Peggy.

'You really will have to try to be more patient with her,' said Molly. 'I want you to promise me.'

'Good God, what a fuss over nothing,' complained Peggy with an impatient sigh. 'But yeah, yeah, if you say so.'

'You won't do it again in my hearing because you'll have me on your back if you do.' Molly wasn't ready to let it go. It was too important. 'But don't do it when I'm not there either. I mean it, Peg. You're not being fair to her and if you think about it you'll know I'm right.'

'OK, OK, don't go on about it,' was Peggy's bad-tempered response. 'I promise to try to be more patient. I can't say more than that. Sometimes I'll fail – I'm only human – but I will bite my tongue a bit more.'

'Fair enough.' Molly picked up the tray. 'Let's go and have this tea then, shall we?' she said, leading the way.

Peggy was miles out in her prediction of Brian's life in Norfolk. Far from having the time of his life, he was lonely and miserable. In fact, on the evening of that same day, he was in a local pub drowning his sorrows. He'd had to give up trying to get back with Beryl – for the time being, anyway – since she'd threatened to have him done for harassment if he approached her again.

He lived on the other side of town to the Browns now so never even saw her around. The lads who lodged over that way said they hadn't seen her out and about either. She was never in the pub or the dancehall, which was surprising since she wasn't the stay-at-home type. She seemed to have gone to ground altogether. Someone said they thought she must have gone away.

Mulling the situation over, Brian wondered if he should pack up here and go home to Molly. Now that he didn't have Beryl or decent digs, living at home would be easier, especially now that she had an income. But there were big disadvantages. When he was with Molly, he got all green-eyed and possessive. Beryl had never affected him in that way because he was so sure of her feelings for him. Anyway, Molly had changed; he could no longer control her. Just thinking about that made him angry, and he didn't want all that emotional aggravation.

At least if he stayed in this area he could have another crack at winning Beryl back at some time soon. He wasn't sure if it was actually just Beryl he wanted or the trappings that came with her as well. What man wouldn't want comfortable lodgings, delicious food, freedom to come and go as he pleased, and a girl who doted on him, which she would do again once he'd persuaded her to give him another chance?

Meanwhile he wasn't comfortable with the absence of a woman in his life so it was time he fixed himself up – just temporarily. Come to think of it, the barmaid in here was quite tasty. She looked to be older than he – must be heading towards forty – but she was quite attractive and had what he considered to be the perfect barmaid's figure – plenty up top and a low-necked sweater to make sure it didn't go unnoticed. This wasn't a pub he normally used – he'd come here tonight for a change – so he wasn't on friendly terms with her yet, something he was about to rectify. He checked for a wedding ring and there was none so he shouldn't have too much trouble. His chat-up technique usually got results.

He called her over. 'A pint of best, please, when you're ready.'

'Coming up right away,' she said, pulling a perfect pint with not too much head on it. 'There you go.'

'Thanks, love.' He put the money on the counter, giving her the once-over as she turned to the till.

'That'll soon chase your troubles away,' she said, handing him his change. 'You've been looking a bit down in the dumps, I couldn't help noticing.'

'I was feeling a bit browned off, to tell you the truth,' he confessed matily. 'But I'm all right now.'

'That's the spirit,' she said cheerily. 'It always upsets me to see a man crying into his beer.'

'Talking to you would cheer any man up.' He gave her his most persuasive smile.

'You've plenty of chat when you do start talking then,' she observed, giving him a grin. It was her job to be nice to the customers.

'Only when I meet a good-looking woman like you.'

'I bet you say that to every barmaid you meet.'

'Not every one. I only say it if it's true.' He leered at her. 'So, when's your night off?'

'Thursdays, usually.'

'Fancy coming out somewhere?'

'Sorry, love. I can't.'

'Oh?' Such was his vanity he was shocked. 'Why not?'

'I'm already doing something.'

'Come on,' he coaxed. 'Don't play hard to get. I'll see that you have a good time.'

'I'm sure you will,' she told him. 'But I still can't come because I'm busy.'

'Another night then,' he persisted. 'Or even one night when you've finished work here. I'm sure we can find somewhere that stays open late.'

'Look, I'm flattered to be asked but the answer is still no.' Her tone was noticeably firmer.

'Oh, give a bloke a break,' he kept on.

There was an unexpected intervention. 'Is he bothering you, Doreen?' asked a gruff voice beside Brian, and turning, he saw a man of at least six foot two, with cropped hair, and piercing blue eyes focused threateningly on Brian's face.

'I can handle it, Frank.' She turned to Brian. 'This is Frank, my date for Thursday and all the rest of my spare time.'

'So, push off,' ordered Frank.

'I haven't finished my drink,' Brian protested.

'Too bad about that,' said the man. 'I want you out of here. You're not welcome on my patch.'

'I've as much right to drink here as you,' objected Brian, though he did actually feel very intimidated by the sheer size of the other man.

The man grabbed Brian by his lapels and pulled him closer. 'I don't think so,' he corrected.

'Oh yeah,' bluffed the now terrified Brian, 'and why is that exactly?'

'Because I'm the landlord of this pub and Doreen is my girlfriend,' he explained. 'So sling your hook and if I ever see you in here again you'll only be able to look back on the days when you could walk along the street – from your wheelchair. Out! Now!'

'I'm going, I'm going,' conceded Brian, and scurried over to the door.

There were plenty of other pubs, and willing barmaids were ten a penny, he thought angrily, as he walked along the road to the next hostelry.

Chapter Sixteen

The next day, Molly and Hattie were having a chat at Hattie's desk, Molly perched on the edge.

They were interrupted by Dan. 'Cor, I dunno. Skiving again?' he joshed, coming in and helping himself to a biscuit from the packet on Hattie's desk. 'It's a grand life, eh, when you work in the office.'

'Hey, not so much of your sauce,' admonished Hattie with a flash of humour in her eyes.

'If you've got any vacancies in here, let me know and I'll put in an application right away.'

'Did you come in here just to annoy us or do you have a more productive purpose?' enquired Hattie, in tune with the general mood of banter.

'As much as I enjoy annoying you,' Dan replied, 'I do have another purpose.'

'Get on with it then,' she urged, taking another digestive biscuit.

He turned to Molly. 'Are you doing anything on Sunday afternoon?' he asked.

'Nothing special, as far as I know. Why?'

'I was wondering if it might be a nice idea to take the kids out somewhere in the car.'

'Oh.' This was so difficult. She wanted to say *yes – yes please*. But being with him would only make her even hungrier for something she couldn't have.

'Well, don't overdo the enthusiasm,' he said with irony. 'I just thought it might be fun for the girls.'

And so it would. How could she think of denying the children an outing just because of an adult complication? 'Sorry, Dan. I was just making sure there was nothing else I had to do. But yes, that would be lovely. Do you have anywhere in particular in mind?'

'I wondered about Hampton Court.'

She looked doubtful. 'I'm not sure the girls are old enough to appreciate anything historical yet,' she pointed out. 'They might get bored looking around the palace.'

'They'd love the maze, though,' he reminded her. 'I had great fun in there as a kid.'

'Oh, yeah, so did I,' she said, remembering. 'I'd forgotten about that.'

'So we'd have that as a backup when the sights begin to pall.'

'With that in mind, yeah, it's a smashing idea.'

'Anyway, maybe it's time we introduced a little culture into their lives, and I haven't been to Hampton Court since I was a boy so I'd enjoy seeing it again,' he went on to say. 'As soon as they get bored inside the palace, we'll head for the maze. Have tea by the river if the weather's nice.'

'Lovely.' Molly felt awkward suddenly, realising that Hattie wasn't involved in the conversation. 'Will you come with us, Hattie?' she asked quickly, turning to her. 'We'd both love that and I know the girls would.'

'Yeah, that would be great,' added Dan, taking the hint. 'I didn't include you in the invitation because I know you like to put your feet up on a Sunday afternoon if you get half the chance. It goes without saying that you'd be welcome to join us.'

There was a brief hesitation. 'I do like to relax when I've cleared up after Sunday dinner, but thanks for asking,' she said in a controlled tone. 'I think Sally's coming over for tea, anyway.'

'Well, if you change your mind, we'd love to have you,' Molly made clear.

'You two go with the girls and enjoy yourselves,' Hattie told them, finishing her tea. 'Meanwhile, Dan, any chance of your going back to work and leaving us to get on with ours?'

'Work? You two? Don't make me laugh.'

'Out.' Hattie picked up a file and raised it as though to aim it at him. 'Now!'

He saluted her, clicking his heels together. 'Yes, ma'am,' he said, appropriating a biscuit from the packet and marching from the room in military style, leaving them smiling.

'He's cheered up lately,' observed Hattie.

'Yeah, thank goodness,' agreed Molly. 'I think a lot of it's front, though.'

'The old saying about time being a great healer has finally worked for him,' said Hattie. 'Though it doesn't seem to have done the trick for me.'

'I don't know so much about that,' was Molly's thoughtful response. 'You can laugh and joke now, the same as Dan does. Just because he's brightened up doesn't mean he doesn't still feel terrible inside. He's grieving but he's trying to live now as well. He has to for Patsy's sake.'

'I suppose so.'

Molly got up and went to Hattie, putting a friendly arm around her shoulders. 'I still miss her too, you know,' she said gently. 'Every single day.'

Hattie reached up and put her hand on Molly's. 'I know you do, dear, I know,' she said sadly.

★ ★ ★

The weather was kind to them on Sunday. The mild sunshine of early summer bathed the sixty glorious acres of riverside gardens in which stood Hampton Court Palace, the grandest of all houses built in Britain in the sixteenth century. Molly looked pretty dressed in a blue and white spotted dress with a full skirt, and a white cardigan around her shoulders because there was a light breeze. Dan too was smart, in an open-necked shirt and sports jacket.

'It doesn't seem possible for any house anywhere to have a thousand rooms, does it?' remarked Molly.

'Is that how many rooms there are here?'

'That's right.'

'You're very knowledgeable,' Dan said in a complimentary manner. 'Don't tell me you remembered that from your school trip to Hampton Court.'

'Fat chance,' she laughed. 'I got a book out of the library about royal palaces when I took some books back yesterday, knowing we were coming here.'

'I *am* impressed,' Dan said.

Strolling through the gardens, past the formal flowerbeds, manicured trees, fountains and statues, they eventually made their way inside the palace building. Because the children were quite young, Molly and Dan didn't opt for a guided tour but took the recommended shorter tour through Henry VIII's state apartments and the Tudor kitchens. Despite Molly's doubts, the girls seemed fascinated as they wandered through the largest room in the palace, the Great Hall with its hammer-beam roof lavishly decorated with carved pendants and royal arms and badges. Even more fascinating for Molly were the Tudor kitchens, which were set up as they would have been while in the process of preparing a midsummer feast in 1542.

'A master cook, twelve other cooks and twelve assistants worked in these kitchens,' she informed Dan, reading from an information sheet. 'Imagine that.'

'The King and his household certainly lived in style,' he remarked.

'And how!'

Although they were well-behaved, there was a limit to the children's threshold for history and sightseeing, especially as the sun was shining outside. So they all left the palace and headed for the maze, which was much more to the eight-year-olds' taste. They thought it was terrific fun. Until, that is, it began to seem likely that they would never see the outside world again . . .

'Don't worry, I'll soon get us out of here,' stated Molly in a buoyant mood. 'It's this way. Come on, follow me.'

'Well, so much for your sense of direction,' said Dan a few minutes later when they were still outwitted by the impeccable hedges, and passing other visitors they'd seen before who were similarly baffled. 'This time I'll take the lead.'

'I thought you said you knew the way out, Daddy,' said Patsy after a while, her voice hushed and hinting at desperation.

'I do.'

'Why are we still lost then?'

'These things take time.'

'We'll never get out,' said the child worriedly. 'What are we going to do?'

'Leave it to me, love, I'll find the way out in a minute, trust me,' her father assured her. 'Everyone finds their way out in the end, I remember that from when I came here as a lad.'

For some reason Molly found the whole thing hilarious, which infected Dan, and the pair of them howled with laughter.

'It isn't funny, Mum,' admonished Rosa, blue eyes huge in her small face, lip trembling slightly.

'I know, love.' Molly gave her daughter a reassuring hug.

'There's nothing to laugh about, Dad,' said Patsy, her big dreamy eyes full of worry. 'We could be trapped in here for ever.'

'Don't be daft, of course we won't,' he assured them, trying to be serious.

'What happens to people who can't find the way out?' Patsy wondered gravely.

'They shout for help and the attendant comes and shows them the way,' replied Molly, this becoming a strong possibility for them as they covered the same ground repeatedly and got absolutely nowhere, 'but we'll get out. As your dad says, everyone does in the end.'

It took a while longer but somehow – more by luck than good judgement – they eventually found the exit.

'Phew, I'm glad to get out of here,' said Patsy, laughing shakily with relief. 'I thought we'd never do it.'

'So much for your trust in your father,' said Dan, exchanging a look with Molly.

'I'm never going in there again,' proclaimed Rosa.

'You'll probably want to when you're older,' suggested Molly. 'It's only a bit of fun.'

'Who wants some tea?' asked Dan.

'We do,' the girls chorused.

'Let's go and find the tea-rooms then.'

'It's odd how serious things sometimes strike you as funny, isn't it?' said Molly to Dan.

'Being lost in the maze, you mean?'

'Not being lost as such, though that was a genuine hoot, but the fact that the girls were so worried.' The children had finished their tea and were playing nearby on the grass in the sunshine. The adults were still at the table on the terrace of the Tiltyard Tea-Room. 'The look of sheer horror on the girls' faces. I thought Rosa's eyes were going to pop out of her head. I'm sure a responsible mother like me shouldn't have found it funny but I just couldn't stop laughing.'

He chuckled, remembering. 'Mind you, the possibility of getting out without assistance did begin to seem remote, didn't it?'

She nodded, giggling. 'And that made it even funnier somehow. Inappropriate laughter, I think they call it. People get it at funerals.'

'Must be some sort of a nervous thing.'

'Or I've got a warped sense of humour.' The atmosphere was very relaxed. 'Shall we polish off those two scones as they're going begging?' she suggested. 'The kids have said they don't want them.'

'Yes, let's.' They had already worked their way through cucumber sandwiches and an assortment of fancy pastries.

'It won't do much for our figures but they'll only go to waste otherwise,' Molly said.

'I suspect the girls are saving themselves for a visit to the ice-cream kiosk.'

'I think you're right.' She spread butter on her scone. 'It was a good idea of yours to come here.'

'You reckon?'

She nodded. 'I had my doubts when you first suggested Hampton Court but it's been fun; the kids seem to be enjoying themselves.' She paused, grinning. 'Except for the dreaded maze, of course.'

'It's been fun for me too. These outings of ours work really well.' He looked up from spreading strawberry jam on his scone and their eyes met. For a few heart-stopping moments neither seemed able to look away. Then Dan lowered his eyes and said quickly, 'It's so good for the children, us teaming up to go out. It makes it better for us too, having another adult for company and moral support.'

Molly felt odd; infused with a sort of nervous excitement. Fleetingly she had sensed in him something of what she was feeling. But if it was there, he obviously didn't want to pursue it. So she said, 'I agree. It's lovely for them and easier for us.'

They fell into a silence that seemed somewhat strained now to Molly.

After a while Dan said, 'Billy's trying to rope me in to play in a darts match with him on Friday night at the pub. One of the team has dropped out, apparently.'

'I hope you said yes,' was her instinctive reaction, but realising that she might have seemed presumptuous, she added, 'It's none of my business, of course, but I think a night out with the lads will do you good.'

'I said I'll think about it,' he told her, the change of subject clearing the air. 'I haven't played for ages but I have been known to score the odd bull's-eye in my time.'

'Do you enjoy the game?'

'I used to, yeah.'

'What's there to think about then?'

'Patsy,' he reminded her. 'As I've said before, it doesn't seem right to leave her with someone while I go out enjoying myself. It's different for work or emergencies.'

'I can understand how you feel, Dan, but a spot of time on your own for pleasure needn't be prohibited altogether, surely. I mean, it isn't as if you're down the pub every night of the week, and you're entitled to some relaxation,' she opined. 'You said that Hattie's always offering to baby-sit.'

'I also said that she has enough to do and I don't want to add to it.'

'As I've told you before, you're welcome to bring Patsy round to my place any time you want to go out,' she reminded him. 'She can stay the night, as you'll be late back. The girls will be in their element.'

'You already do more than enough, Molly,' he pointed out. 'I don't want to take advantage.'

'I can't imagine you doing that to anyone. But, honestly, it would be no trouble to me, and Rosa would be thrilled to bits. You know how children of that age love staying the night at each other's houses. They see it as some sort of adventure. Anyway, the offer is there if you want it. I can't say more.'

'Can I, Dad?' burst out Patsy, who'd been hovering nearby and overheard some of the conversation. 'I'd rather stay with Rosa than Gran.' She bit her lip, looking worried. 'I mean, I love Gran and everything, but it'll more fun at Rosa's.'

'Because the two of you will be talking and giggling half the night, that's why,' he suggested.

'No, we won't.' She was very earnest.

'Honest we won't,' added Rosa supportively.

'I can vouch for that,' put in Molly. 'They won't get the chance with me around.'

Dan sighed. 'I haven't even decided whether I'm going yet,' he reminded them.

'Go on, Dad,' said Patsy, with her own agenda in mind. 'You never go out to have fun without me.'

He looked from his daughter to Molly with a half-smile. 'Honestly, my life isn't my own. Forced out of my own home, I dunno . . .'

'Do say you'll go, and that I can stay the night with Rosa,' his daughter persisted.

He looked from one child to the other, then focused his gaze on his daughter, sighing. 'Oh, all right.' He gave her a stern look. 'But you'd better behave yourself.'

'I will, I promise.'

'She won't be any trouble,' Molly assured him.

'I'm not so sure,' he said, giving his daughter a warning grin. 'She can be a right little madam when she's in the mood.'

'And I can be a right old tartar when I need to be,' Molly countered.

'You have my full permission to do whatever it takes to shut them up if they muck about half the night.'

'Thanks, Dad,' said Patsy, and the two little girls went off, talking excitedly about the forthcoming treat.

Dan tutted and rolled his eyes. 'Oh well, I'll have to play darts now whether I like it or not,' he said.

'Not necessarily. But if you do decide against it we shall still have to let Patsy spend Friday night with Rosa,' she said with a wry grin. 'We can't go back on that now that they're looking forward to it. It wouldn't be fair.'

'Mm, you're right. But I will go,' he decided. 'I might as well – being that my daughter has organised her own baby-sitting and can't wait to see the back of me.'

Molly smiled. 'I bet you'll enjoy yourself, especially after a couple of pints.'

'Maybe.' He looked at her in such a way that she experienced another of those intensely intimate moments: a definite fusion of chemistry. Again Dan moved on swiftly.

'Meanwhile, shall we take a look at the rest of the gardens?' he suggested. 'Isn't there a vine here somewhere?'

'Yes.' She studied the guidebook. 'It's the oldest known vine in the world. It's called the Great Vine.'

'There you go again,' he grinned, 'dazzling me with your knowledge.'

'I've just read that in the guidebook, you fool,' she laughed. She raised her hand and pointed, shading her eyes from the sun with her other hand. 'According to this it's thataway.'

'Let's go then.'

They collected the girls and strolled through the magnificent gardens. Just two friends who had teamed up for the sake of their children, Molly reminded herself for the umpteenth time.

The following afternoon, in the office, Hattie said to Molly, 'Billy was saying that he's managed to persuade Dan to play darts with him on Friday night. Billy was talking about it over at the house at lunchtime.'

'Yeah, Dan was telling me about it yesterday when we were out.'

'I'm pleased he's agreed to go,' approved Hattie. 'It's time he had some adult relaxation.'

'Mm. He never goes out anywhere without Patsy, except to work.'

'Which reminds me, I must make sure I get the room ready for Patsy,'

Hattie went on with a slight frown. 'It'll be late when he gets back so she'll need to stay over.' She tutted and brushed her brow with her hand. 'Since I've been working over here, I'm not nearly as well organised at home as I used to be. I just don't have the time now. But I like everything to be just right for Patsy when she comes to stay.'

'Actually, you've been saved a job,' Molly was pleased to inform her, and went on to tell her what had been arranged between herself and Dan yesterday as regards baby-sitting for the darts match.

Hattie seemed a little flustered. Then: 'Oh, I see.'

'Of course, the girls are all for it; they see it as a bit of a lark, I think,' remarked Molly.

Another odd pause. 'Yes, they would do . . . of course,' Hattie agreed at last, adding with a wry grin, 'They'll probably drive you mad, mucking about until all hours.'

'They'll try but I won't put up with any nonsense from them,' she said. 'I've assured Dan of that.'

The door opened and he walked in. 'Talk of the devil,' said Molly.

'Nothing bad, I hope.'

'Not this time,' joshed Molly. 'We were talking about you hitting the highspots on Friday night.'

'If a darts match in the local is a highspot, it doesn't say much for the state of my social life, does it?'

'Mine's even worse,' grinned Molly. 'I don't even get to go to a darts match.'

'You can go in my place if you like,' he kidded.

'Oh yeah,' she riposted. 'I'd be about as welcome as a man in the labour ward.'

'Molly's just been telling me about your baby-sitting arrangements for Friday,' Hattie mentioned. 'I understand the girls have got it all organised.'

'That's what I've come to see you about, actually, Hattie,' he told her. 'To tell you that I won't need to bother you with it.'

'It wouldn't have been a bother. Patsy is never that,' she made clear. 'Still, as long as you're fixed up, that's the main thing. I'm there if you need me another time.'

'Thanks, Hat,' he said, going over and giving her a friendly hug. 'You're a good sort. I don't know what I'd do without you.'

'Enough of your old toffee,' she admonished lightly. 'Don't you be picking up all the chat from Billy.'

'I meant what I said,' he told her, more seriously.

'That goes for me too,' added Molly. 'You're a comfort to us all.'

'Are the pair of you after borrowing money or something?' She was obviously touched and a little embarrassed.

'You're too cynical,' smiled Dan, knowing that was the very last thing she could ever be.

'Go on with you, Dan,' said Hattie, her cheeks slightly flushed. 'Go back to work and leave us to get on.'

Suddenly Molly had an idea for something that was coming up later in the summer; a way of making Hattie realise just how very much she was appreciated . . .

Watching Hattie blow out the candles on her birthday cake after a rousing rendition of 'Happy Birthday' from all around the table, Molly could have wept with joy at the pleasure this surprise gathering had obviously given the older woman. It had been worth every minute of the planning, the work and the subterfuge to see her face when she'd walked into her own dining room this afternoon to find the table laid with a party spread, the room festooned with balloons and presents by her place.

A cheer went up as she extinguished the candles in one go.

'I might be fifty-six but I've still got plenty of puff.'

'More than the rest of us put together,' said Dan.

'I don't know about that, but I'm not in bad shape for an old 'un.' She turned to Molly. 'As you made the cake, perhaps you'd like to do the honours and slice it.'

'Course I will.'

It was late afternoon on a summer Sunday, the weather warm and stormy. Looking back on the preparations for the festivities, Molly thought the most difficult part of all – even more worrying than getting the children to keep the secret – was getting Hattie out of the house this afternoon so that Molly could bring in the food she had prepared in her own kitchen. Dan had collected it in the car and put it in the pottery office before spinning Hattie a yarn about wanting advice on some decorating he was planning at home and needing her to go with him to his house.

As soon as she was safely out of the way, Molly, Billy and Josh had got the food into the house, and while Molly set it out on the table, the men had blown up the balloons and placed them in bunches around the room. The birthday cake had been kept out of sight in Billy's bedroom until the appropriate moment as an extra surprise.

Billy and Dan had been instantly enthusiastic towards Molly's idea for a surprise birthday tea for Hattie. They guessed that, being a woman of simple tastes, she would prefer an afternoon do rather than a more sophisticated celebration in the evening, so that the children could be part of it. Josh hadn't exactly entered into the preparations with gusto – lethargy was more his speciality – but he'd done what was asked of him with reasonably good grace.

'I wondered why those sons of mine didn't give me their presents this morning,' Hattie was saying now. 'I fell for it when they told me they'd rather leave it until Dan and Patsy came round later on with theirs. Thank you, everybody, for the lovely gifts. I really am being spoiled.'

Molly put the first slice of cake on a plate and handed it to Hattie. 'There you are, birthday girl,' she said. 'I hope it meets with your approval.'

Hattie took the first bite. 'Delicious,' was the verdict. 'As light as a feather. Thank you ever so much for making it, dear.' She waved her hand towards the table at the remains of the party fare. 'And for all the rest, everything homemade too. It must have taken you hours to do a spread like this.'

'It took a while,' Molly admitted, 'but I enjoyed every minute. Let's face it, Hattie, apart from the bread, I daren't bring anything shop-bought into this house.'

'Am I that much of a tyrant?' she smiled.

'No, just a very good cook,' replied Molly.

'I helped Mummy to do it,' announced Rosa, looking sweet in a pink party frock, eyes shining like sapphires, blonde hair loose.

'And me,' added Patsy, also dressed for the occasion in a frilly dress.

'I helped more than you,' boasted Rosa.

'No you didn't.'

'Did.'

'Didn't.'

'Oi, you two,' warned Molly.

'Don't fall out today,' said Hattie, more in the manner of a request than an admonishment.

'Yes, pack it in the pair of you,' supported Dan. 'You'll spoil the party.'

Molly continued slicing the cake as the squabbling subsided. She turned to Sally, who had come over on the bus to save Billy having to collect her as he was helping Molly here. 'How about you, are you allowed to have any?' she asked.

'Just a small piece, please.' Catching Billy's worried look she added. 'A little piece won't do me any harm.'

'Good because we don't want you missing out.' Molly turned to Josh. 'A large piece or small?'

'As it comes,' he said in his usual disinterested way.

When everybody had their cake and Molly was sitting down again, Hattie said, 'Thanks, everybody, for all of this.'

'Molly organised it,' said Billy.

'It was a team effort,' Molly corrected.

'I must be getting dim-witted in my old age not to spot that there was a conspiracy going on under my nose.' Hattie was flushed with pleasure.

'Our biggest worry was the kids,' Dan told her. 'They were threatened with all sorts of torture if they so much as breathed a word.'

'And they didn't let you down. Well done, girls,' praised Hattie, dabbing her eyes with a handkerchief. 'Honestly, I wasn't expecting anything like this.'

The moment became fraught with emotion suddenly. Molly's eyes were burning painfully and she was acutely aware of the empty place at the table. Billy made a timely intervention by starting a chorus of 'For She's a Jolly Good Fellow,' and everyone joined in.

Listening to the singing, Hattie was overwhelmed by the love for her that was so tangible in this room. Times like this, when the people she cared about most were gathered around her table, were her happiest. Today was perfect. Well, as good as it could be with the two missing family members, especially her darling daughter. Losing George had been crippling; the loss of Angie was hardly bearable, even now. No mother expects to outlive her child, and Hattie knew that – although life would go on and she would move along with it – she would never really get over it.

What a blessing it was that she had Molly in her life. She'd turned out to be a true friend. No one could ever replace Angie, of course, but Molly was the nearest thing she had to a daughter now.

Another shadow clouded Hattie's joy: her youngest child. Josh seemed to be at war with the world most of the time, and there was no end to his bad temper that flared up over nothing. She'd tried talking to him, reasoning with him and explaining why she'd had to take a firm line with him over the stealing. She told him repeatedly how much he had going for him if only he would change his attitude to life. But he was so full of rage he was simply unreachable. What made it even worse was knowing that he was angry with himself as well as everyone around him. As a mother, she found it excruciating to watch a child waste his life in misery and be unable to do anything about it. He had such a capacity to hurt her too. Many a time he reduced her to tears but not a soul knew about that. She wouldn't give him the satisfaction of realising his power over her, or the others another stick to beat him with. There were times when motherhood seemed like an open wound.

Recalled to the present now that the singing had ended and they were all shouting, 'Hip, hip, hooray', Hattie counted her blessings and smiled graciously.

The air was even heavier and more oppressive that evening. The thunder that had been rumbling distantly all afternoon grew louder, and lightning crackled across the sky and lit up the house. But still the rain didn't come.

Everyone was now assembled in the sitting room where alcohol and savoury nibbles were available for those who wanted them. The children were doing a jigsaw puzzle on the floor, the women were sitting together chatting and Billy and Dan were seated next to each other, discussing work.

Josh was the only one not engaged in conversation. Sitting near the other two men, he looked on in silence. He might as well not have been there, it seemed to him, since no one was taking any notice of him. The sense of isolation that hovered constantly grew as he dwelled on the question of his status in the family and his incongruity in this company. There was no one here he could talk to; no one with whom he had anything in common. He was well past jigsaw puzzles, he could hardly join in women's talk and now that he was no longer a part of the pottery, the men's conversation did not include him.

The loss of his birthright rankled more than anything. The resentment was almost a physical pain – a frustration that made him want to scream. It reached such a pitch he could no longer bear to sit here.

'Just going up to my room for a while,' he said to his mother in a controlled voice as he headed for the door.

'All right, son,' she replied rather absently, since Josh spent so much time alone in his room she was used to him disappearing during family occasions.

Closing the door behind him, Josh headed for the stairs, then stopped, charged with a sudden impulse, and made for the kitchen instead. Removing the pottery keys from the key board, he left the house and hurried across the garden, skirting around the edges to avoid being seen from the window. The sky was black and angry and the thunder and lightning growing in intensity, though it was still dry. Josh was in such a temper he wouldn't have noticed if he'd been drenched to the skin.

'I've got a new design in mind,' Billy was saying to Dan. 'Something really contemporary. A sleek and slimline look for the pottery and a busy pattern to go on it. Not flowers for this one . . . more interwoven shapes of some sort.'

'Sounds interesting.'

'Mm. But I can't quite get a picture of the finished article in my mind.'

'Have you done any sketches?' Dan enquired.

Billy nodded. 'I've been playing around with ideas on paper in my spare time for a while.'

'Let's have a look then.'

'Yeah. OK.' He paused, frowning. 'I've got a feeling I left them in the workshop . . . yeah, I know I did. We'll have to leave it until tomorrow.'

'You could pop across and get them now or, better still, we could both go and have a look over there, to save bringing work into the house at your mum's birthday do,' suggested Dan, his interest aroused. 'We'll only be gone a few minutes.'

'In this storm?'

'It isn't actually raining,' observed Dan, glancing towards the window. 'Thunder won't hurt us. You've got me so curious, I can't wait until tomorrow.'

'All right then,' agreed Billy, as eager to show Dan his ideas as he was to see them.

Billy turned to his mother. 'We're just popping across to the workshop, Mum,' he told her. 'You don't mind us leaving the party for a few minutes, do you?'

'Course not,' she assured him.

'Talk about dedication to the job,' joshed Molly.

'We won't be long,' said Billy, and turning to Sally added with a tender look, 'See you soon, babe.'

'Sure.' She was quite happy chatting to his mother and Molly.

In the kitchen Billy went to the board from which a row of keys hung, looking for the bunch belonging to the pottery. 'That's funny, they're not here,' he muttered.

'Someone must have forgotten to put them back where they belong,' Dan suggested.

'I locked up myself when we'd finished getting the food from there this afternoon and I'm sure I hung them up. It's an automatic thing with me.'

'You must have put them down somewhere in all the excitement.'

'I must have done, since they're not here,' agreed Billy, walking around the room, running his hand along the worktops and looking on the floor. 'They'll be around here somewhere.'

'Don't worry about finding them now because mine are on the sideboard in the other room,' suggested Dan. 'I'll go and get them and we'll look for the others when we get back. I won't be a minute.'

'Let's go in case it does start raining,' said Billy when Dan came back with the keys. 'It's probably waiting for us to step out of the door.'

He was right in his light-hearted prediction. The first huge spots started falling just seconds after they left the house, then the heavens opened with such force, they were soaked through in seconds.

'Bloody hell,' gasped Billy as the sky lit up and thunder cracked overhead, the rain beating on their heads and pouring down their faces as they ran towards the workshop.

'Let's shelter in here until it eases off a bit,' suggested Dan, as they reached the abandoned bottle kiln. 'I can't see a thing with the water running into my eyes.'

'Good idea, mate,' said Billy, and they darted inside out of the rain, glad that they'd never got round to boarding up the doorway.

It was dim and shadowy in the workshop because of the storm and the advancing evening. But Josh didn't switch on the light for fear of attraction attention and being disturbed before his mission was accomplished. He prowled around, looking at the rows of part-finished items on the shelves, representing many hours of fastidious work. There was

251

quite a lot of finished pottery ready for packing on the table at the end: finely crafted pieces that would fetch a good price. When Josh had finished there would be no earthenware pots left at all; just innumerable broken pieces. He smiled in anticipation. This would teach them to deprive him of what was rightly his.

From the finished work, he picked up a large vase in one of the Beckett traditional designs and took it closer to the window to see if he could spot any flaws. The fact that it seemed faultless and would soon be just smithereens made his plan all the more satisfying. Such was his fury he didn't care about the consequences: that this would certainly result in his eviction from the house and the family for good. Sod the lot of them; the sooner he saw the back of them the better, he thought, moving away from the window.

There was a sudden noise that he didn't instantly identify but soon realised that it was rain drumming on the roof and beating against the windows. Blimey, that was some downpour. He turned his attention back to the vase, lifting it ready to smash on the concrete floor. He was about to let it go, when something at the side of his eye made him turn back to the window.

Christ Almighty, it was Billy and Dan on their way over here. Trust them to scupper his plans. Putting the vase down he went back to the window to see if he had time to get out of the other door before they got here. They wouldn't stay long – not in the middle of Mum's party – so he would come back later and make a thorough job of it. Now that the idea was fixed in his mind, he had to do it; to hurt them like this was the only way to ease his own pain.

That's a bit of luck, he thought, seeing the two men disappear inside the bottle kiln. That would give him time to get clear. Even so, he'd have to look sharp because they'd obviously only gone in there to shelter and would come out as soon as the cloudburst lessened.

Locking the front door from the inside, he slipped out of the back, heading across the garden at a run towards the rear of the kiln in case he was seen by the men through the doorway at the front. The rain was still heavy and the thunder awesomely loud. The storm must be directly overhead, he guessed. A flash of lightning lit the garden, a white zigzag across the sky, seeming to split it in two.

He stopped dead in his tracks, watching in horror as one side of the kiln collapsed and he realised it had been struck by lightning. It crumbled to the ground, its solid construction as nothing against the force of the storm. The famous Beckett kiln was now just a pile of rubble with only a small part of the brickwork left standing, and Billy and Dan somewhere in the ruins.

Chapter Seventeen

'This is one heck of a storm,' observed Hattie as the thunder shook the house and the rain lashed against the windows, white electric flashes filling the room.

'At least it'll clear the air,' remarked Molly. 'It's been threatening all afternoon.'

'I hope the boys got to the workshop before the downpour started.'

'Mm, that's a point.'

'I don't like the thunder when it's this loud, Mum,' said Rosa nervously, abandoning the jigsaw for the comfort of her mother's lap.

'It won't hurt you, love, and it'll soon pass over now that it's overhead,' reassured Molly, giving her a hug. She paused, listening. 'What was that?'

'Rain . . . thunder?' suggested Hattie.

'No . . . something else,' Molly explained. 'It sounded like someone shouting.'

'I can't hear a thing above the racket the weather's making,' said Hattie.

'Nor me,' added Sally.

Molly got up and went over to the window. 'I wasn't imagining things,' she told them, lifting the net curtain for a better view. 'Things have been happening out there. In fact, Mother Nature has saved us a job.'

'Oh? How's that?' asked Hattie.

'We won't need to have the old kiln demolished now because it's come down in the storm. Must have been struck by lightning.' She pressed her face to the window, peering out. 'It looks like Josh out there. Must have been him I heard shouting.'

'I thought he was in his bedroom,' frowned Hattie, rising quickly. 'That's where he said he was going.'

'He's not in there now because it's definitely him out there in the garden,' Molly confirmed. 'But there's no sign of the others. They must be in the workshop.'

'Yeah, they would be.' Hattie joined Molly at the window. 'Why doesn't Josh just come inside instead of shouting and carrying on out there in the rain?' she queried. 'We can't hear a word he's saying, and it

253

isn't as though it was a working kiln full of pottery. The damage can be dealt with tomorrow, or after the storm. I know the kiln had sentimental value for us but it had to come down eventually anyway so there's no real harm done.' She fixed her eyes on her son who turned away from the house and dropped to his knees. 'Looks as though he's trying to clear the rubble in this weather. Whatever's got into him?'

'I'm going out there,' said Molly with a strong sense of foreboding. 'Rosa, will you stay in here with Hattie and Sally, please?'

'I'm coming with you,' announced Hattie, realising now that something must be amiss. 'Keep the kids indoors, will you, Sally, please, love?'

'Sure.'

Having seen his mother and Molly at the window of the house and assumed they'd heard him asking for someone to call the emergency services, Josh was on his hands and knees clearing the bricks one by one with his bare hands, the rain running down his neck and soaking every inch of him. 'Billy, Dan,' he shrieked as the current burst of thunder died away, 'I'm coming in. I'm on my way.' All was silent. 'Answer me, please, please answer me.' His voice was distorted by fear for their lives. 'Give us a break, lads. Let me know if you're alive?'

The only voice he heard was his mother's, appearing behind him with Molly. 'What's going on? What on earth are you doing, Josh?'

'Trying to get in there to get Billy and Dan out. They were inside the kiln when it came down,' he explained, breathless with exertion. 'They went in to shelter from the rain.'

'Oh my God,' Hattie gasped.

Frozen with terror Molly clutched her head, her hair and clothes already saturated. In their haste to leave the house they'd not given a thought to their own protection.

'They'll be all right; they're a couple of tough 'uns,' said Josh, forcing himself to stay positive for his mother's sake. 'I'll get in there in no time. Have you called nine-nine-nine?'

'No,' replied Hattie. 'We didn't realise . . . we couldn't hear what you were saying.'

'Can you do it now then?' he urged. 'We need professional help, and fast.'

Hattie tore towards the house in the driving rain.

As soon as she was out of earshot, Josh said to Molly, 'I've been calling to Billy and Dan but there's not a sound. I didn't want to worry Mum even more by pointing it out. Don't say anything when she comes back.'

'OK.' Molly dropped to her knees beside Josh on the wet ground, picking up bricks and hurling them away.

254

Josh shouted again, 'Billy . . . Dan . . . can you hear me?'

But the only sound was the falling rain and the rumble of thunder.

Billy came to in a sitting position with something hard digging into his back. 'What the hell?' Dazed, he struggled to gather his wits. 'The kiln,' he muttered slowly, gradually remembering. 'It must have come down in the storm.' Dan, where was Dan?

Billy couldn't move his legs, and was pinned against the remaining wall by rubble that was packed against him almost up to his waist. One arm was trapped by a bont, an iron band that ran right around the circular oven to strengthen it as it expanded and contracted during firing. The pressure of the iron on his arm was agonising. Debris was piled perilously around him but looking up he could see a small patch of darkening sky through a gap. His head hurt. He ran his free hand over it and winced, feeling a lump, but there was no blood on his hand. He must have been knocked out by a falling brick or something. There was a horrible numb feeling in his ears.

Where the hell was Dan?

Turning carefully because of the pain, he saw Dan's head and shoulders; the rest of him was buried. He had a gash on the side of his head, which was sticky with blood. His eyes were closed and he wasn't moving. Billy couldn't tell if he was unconscious or dead, and couldn't get to him to find out.

Increasingly aware of a strange sensation in his ears, a sort of echoing silence, he realised that something must have happened to his hearing in the accident. He moved a brick with his free hand and carefully tapped it against another to test his hearing. All was silent. His ears must have got blocked with dust or something. His mouth was full of it. He moved his head to the side and spat, then raked his ears with his little finger to try to clear the eerie echo. It made no difference. He couldn't hear a thing, not even his own voice as he instinctively called for help.

Josh was talking to Molly and his mother near to the house, having taken them each by the arm and forcefully escorted them away from the ruins of the collapsed kiln. 'Will you both *please go* indoors and leave this to me,' he requested in a calm and authoritative tone, unprecedented in Josh. 'I don't want you anywhere near it in case it all comes down and you get hurt from flying bricks and metal.'

'You can't do it on your own,' stated Molly, eager to help.

'I can,' he insisted.

'Hattie can go indoors, I'm staying to give you a hand,' Molly insisted. 'It'll be quicker with two.'

'It'll be dangerous with more than one now that I'm getting deeper into it,' he informed her.

'I'll be very careful.'

'Let me spell it out for you, Molly,' he began in a commanding tone, 'the remaining bit of wall doesn't look any too safe and if we disturb the rubble too much the whole lot'll come down and wipe out anyone who's anywhere near it as well as those inside.'

'Oh . . . oh, I see. In that case I'd better leave it to you,' she finally conceded. 'I don't want to make things worse.'

'What about the danger for you, Josh?' his mother wanted to know.

'I'll take my chances,' he told her, without even realising he was putting the safety of others before his own. He wasn't afraid for his own life so much as what sort of a state he would find Billy and Dan in, given the lack of response to his calls; he wanted to spare his mother for as long as possible. 'I'm gonna do my damnedest to get them out so leave me to get on with it and go inside out of the rain.'

'I hate the idea of leaving you to do it alone,' Hattie told him.

'Me too,' added Molly, still reluctant to leave.

Seeing how worried they both were, he said, 'Look, you both have responsibilities; people who rely on you. Molly, you have a young child. Mum, you have a grandchild who's lost her mother, and her father is now in danger. You've got to think of them. There's no one depending on me – except Billy and Dan at this particular moment.'

'But, Josh—' began Hattie.

'I'm a big boy now, Mum, so do as I ask and go into the house and look after the others. I'll be all right. Help should be here soon.'

'I suppose you're right, son, we ought to go in – for a while, anyway,' Hattie said tearfully, giving him a wet hug; they were all soaked to the skin. 'I'm so proud of you, Josh.'

'Cut it out, Mum.' He turned and ran towards the kiln. Having a sudden thought he turned to see the back of the women going into the house. 'Mum, Molly,' he shouted with every last vestige of volume he could muster to make himself heard against the weather. The storm was moving away but it was still raining heavily, the thunder a distant rumble. 'Get on the blower again and see what's happened to the rescue services, will you?'

'Will do,' Hattie shrieked back.

'Tell 'em to get a move on.'

'OK.'

So now what? thought Billy, having tried unsuccessfully to free his arm. How the hell was he going to get Dan and himself out of here when he was pinned down by debris, his trapped arm under a lump of iron which was wedged and immovable? There was no point in hoping for rescue because no one knew they'd gone in to the kiln. No one ever came in here since they'd switched over to electric ovens. When they saw that the kiln had been brought down by the storm they would simply arrange to have the rubble cleared in due course.

256

They'd be worried when he and Dan couldn't be found, of course. Might the penny drop then? Possibly, but it could be too late for him and Dan then – if it wasn't already too late for Dan. The crumbled bricks and mortar around and above him looked extremely precarious. One wrong move and they'd be completely buried. Pointless to continue calling for help because they would all be indoors at Mum's party. No one would venture into the garden in this weather.

The echoing silence in his ears was scary and irritating. He shook his head and swallowed hard, his free hand pressed hard against his ear. Nothing happened. He tried again – and again, all to no avail. Then – after one more desperately vigorous attempt – there was a popping sensation in his head and sound rushed in, a startling blast of noise in contract to the silence. He could hear a man shouting. Someone was out there. Thank God!

'Help,' he called. 'Help.'

As his mother's voice died away and he got closer to the kiln, Josh heard a sound from inside the ruins: a cry for help.

'Billy?' he called.

'Is that you, Josh?'

'Yeah, it's me. I'm on my way in to get you.'

'Hurry up, mate. But mind how you go; it's very dodgy in here.'

'Are you badly hurt?' shouted Josh.

'No, I'm all right but Dan's in a bad way. I'm not sure if he's alive.'

'Bloody hell,' responded Josh. 'But I'm coming in, and help is on its way.'

Hearing the distant echo of voices as they were about to go into the house, the two women came rushing across the garden.

'It's Billy,' Josh told them breathlessly, on his knees clearing the rubble and crawling nearer. 'He's all right, but Dan's badly hurt.'

On the heels of relief that Billy was alive came fear for Dan that was so overpowering Molly felt as though the breath was sucked out of her. Her legs were weakened almost to the point of collapse but somehow she managed to remain vertical.

Hattie's voice echoed into the gathering dusk. 'Billy, it's Mum,' she called. 'Josh is coming in and the rescue people are on their way. Try and stay calm.'

'Is Sally there with you?'

'No, she's indoors with the children.'

'If I don't make it, make sure she gets home tonight.' His instructions were just audible. 'She can't stay overnight because of her insulin injection first thing in the morning.'

'You'll make it, son,' shouted Hattie, huge salty tears mingling with the rain running down her face. 'You're a Beckett, remember, and we're survivors.'

257

'Both of you go into the house,' ordered Josh. 'I'll call you if I need you.'

'We're going,' said Molly, realising that they were hindering his progress. She took Hattie's arm. 'Come on. Let's do as he says.'

As they walked towards the house, Hattie said in a strangled voice, 'I didn't know Josh had it in him.'

'Me neither,' was Molly's response. 'He's certainly shown us what he's really made of tonight.'

Back indoors, hugging her daughter, Molly felt physically ill with fear for Dan, and realised the full extent of her feelings for him.

'Ugh. You've made me all wet, Mummy,' complained Rosa.

'Sorry, darling.'

Turning to Hattie, Molly said, 'We need to get out of these wet clothes.'

But neither of them cared about her own physical discomfort. The only thing on their minds was what was happening outside.

Little by little, his hands raw and blistered, Josh crawled through the rubble until he finally reached his brother.

'Well done, mate,' praised Billy as Josh carefully removed some bricks and freed his arm from the iron band. Together they moved the debris from his legs.

'You should be able to get out now, if you take it steady,' said Josh. 'I've cleared a bit of a path on the way in. But you'll have to crawl and you'll have to be careful.'

'I'm not going without Dan,' Billy told him.

'I'll see to Dan.'

'Not without me, you won't,' insisted Billy. 'I don't think you're supposed to move someone when they're unconscious but we don't have a choice. We can't leave him here until medical help arrives with all that stuff likely to come down at any minute.'

'You really ought to leave it to me,' advised Josh, casting his eye over the cuts and bruises on his brother's face. 'You need to go and get yourself fixed up.'

'You'll never do it on your own,' Billy pointed out. 'It's a job for two.'

In all honesty, there wasn't a sensible argument against that so, working together, the brothers proceeded with caution towards Dan.

It had finally stopped raining, and Hattie and Molly were back outside, their eyes fixed on the collapsed kiln from a wise distance. Having been assured that Billy was safe, Sally had agreed to stay inside with the children. This was no place for them.

Now that the storm had passed the sky was lighter and, even though it was dusk, the women still had sufficient visibility to see the kiln ruins. Molly ached with tension; every nerve and muscle stretched to the limit.

258

They seemed to have been standing here for ever, waiting for news. Her heart beat even faster when she saw a figure emerge from the opening in the ruins made by Josh. It was Billy on all fours, moving slowly out backwards, then Josh came into view, the two of them half carrying, half dragging Dan. Such was Molly's relief that it was all she could do not to rush over to him.

'Where are the emergency services when you need them, eh?' muttered Hattie.

'The storm probably brought trees down and they're blocking the road.' Choked with emotion, Molly forced a calm tone so as not to betray her true feelings to Hattie.

Just then the sound of a clanging bell filled the air.

'About bloomin' time too,' declared Hattie as an ambulance pulled up outside, followed by a fire engine.

'Is he going to be all right?' Molly asked the ambulance men nervously as they carried Dan to the ambulance on a stretcher. She knew he must be alive because they hadn't covered his face with the blanket but he was very still and his hair was matted with blood.

'The doctors will be able to tell you that when they've had a look at him,' one of the men told her guardedly. 'But where there's life there's hope, and he'll be in good hands.' With professional care and skill, they lifted the stretcher into the ambulance, then one of the men turned to Billy.

'I think you need to come with us too, sir, just to let the doctors check you over. That's a nasty lump on your head.'

'There's no need for that,' he protested.

'I really think you should,' the man persisted.

'Do what the man says, Billy,' advised his mother. 'He's talking sense. We'll follow on in a taxi and see you at the hospital.'

'All right, I'll go, but I think you should stay here for the moment,' suggested Billy, wanting to spare them. 'The kids will be needing you. I'll give you a bell as soon as I know anything.' He looked towards Josh, who was standing back, soaking wet and covered in grime. 'Look after him too. He's been a bloody marvel tonight.'

'He has too,' agreed Hattie, taking her younger son's arm. 'I'm really proud of him.'

'If it hadn't been for him . . .' began Billy.

Just then there was a rumbling sound and they watched transfixed as the remaining wall of the kiln came crashing down, making Billy's comments all the more potent. Then the ambulance doors were closed and the vehicle rolled away down the street, the bell ringing and filling the air with a heart-stopping sense of urgency.

Molly's nerves were so raw as they waited for news from the hospital, she could hardly sit still in Hattie's living room. She'd only been this scared once before in her life and that was when Angie had had her fatal accident. The women were drinking tea. Josh – bathed, and changed out of his filthy clothes – was enjoying a glass of beer, well deserved in Molly's opinion. The children were in bed. At Hattie's suggestion Molly and Rosa were staying the night. This was no time to be on their own.

They'd turned on the television in an effort to ease the tension. There was a variety show on presented by Bernard Delfont but no one was watching it. The talk was spasmodic. They were all busy with their own thoughts.

'How did you know they were in the kiln, Josh?' wondered Hattie after a while, having had time to reflect on what had happened. 'And how come you were out there? I thought you were in your bedroom.'

There was a pause while he gathered his wits. The truth was too awful to admit and he saw no point in enlightening them as he didn't actually do the deed. 'I saw the whole thing from the bedroom window,' he lied. 'I was looking out at the storm and I saw them walking across the garden. When the rain suddenly started bucketing down they dashed into the kiln to shelter and a few minutes later it was struck by lightning.'

'Thank goodness you were looking out of the window,' said Hattie.

'I'll say,' added Molly. 'They'd be under that rubble now if you hadn't. I doubt if either of them would have survived.'

'Dan still might not,' Josh reminded her, unaware of her special sensitivity to the subject.

'I know. But at least he stands a chance, thanks to you.' Hattie paused thoughtfully. 'Why didn't you tell us what was going on as soon as you saw the kiln go down?'

A spot of intervention was needed here if he wasn't to give the game away as to the real reason he had been on hand to help. 'Dunno. I suppose I was so eager to help them I just didn't think of it,' he said, and that was partly true.

'Anyway, you've made us all proud,' praised his mother. 'You've been a real hero tonight.'

'Your mum's right,' added Molly.

'It was a close call,' Hattie went on, effusive in her praise of her son. 'That wall came down within seconds of your getting them out.'

'I think you've very brave,' put in Sally, looking at him with admiration. 'It takes a lot of bottle to do a thing like that. You could easily have been killed. You must have been terrified.'

'I don't think the danger registered,' he said, looking back on it and answering truthfully. 'I remember being scared for them. I expect if the risk had come home to me properly I'd have run a mile.'

In retrospect, the whole thing seemed unreal. It was all a bit of a blur; vivid in his memory but as though it had happened to someone else. It didn't seem possible that he could have done something like that. He wasn't courageous; never had been. How could Josh Beckett, the misfit who nobody liked, have put his own life at risk to save someone else's? That sort of thing wasn't his style at all. But it *had* happened. *He'd done it.* He'd actually saved someone's life. Getting Rosa out of the canal wasn't the same thing at all – his own life hadn't been at risk then. But it had been today. If anyone had told him yesterday that he would do this, he'd have laughed in their face. But the fact that he had done it felt very sweet. He'd done what he'd thought was impossible. He'd made his mother proud of him.

He felt different – not at all the same person who'd gone over to the workshop with revenge in his heart. Not normally the sort of person to analyse his feelings, he now found himself doing so and trying to identify the change. It was as though he was part of things now – instead of being an outsider – and it was a good feeling. Billy had said he was proud to be his brother when they were working together to rescue Dan. Josh would never ever forget how that had made him feel: warm inside; strong and capable of anything. He'd felt like Billy's pal, and that was something he'd always wanted even though he'd spent his whole life trying to deny it to himself.

He wanted the feeling of friendship between himself and Billy to last. He wanted his mum to stay proud of him; to feel respect in people's attitude towards him. Today was a one-off, of course. The chance to be a life-saving hero might never come his way again but he'd proved to himself that he wasn't entirely worthless and that had changed his perspective.

Now he felt like a man, not some miserable, whingeing boy. Surely there must be other more ordinary ways to earn respect. It certainly didn't come from stealing from his own family and planning revenge. Why had he wanted to do those things? What had it all been about? Where had all the anger come from? It had been there long before he'd been thrown out of the business.

The sound of the telephone ringing in the hall pierced into his thoughts and recalled him to the present. 'I'll get it,' he said, mouth dry and stomach churning as he picked up the receiver.

'Josh, it's Billy.'

'What's happening?'

There was a silence and Josh's heart beat so hard he thought it would stop.

'Dan's come round and they think he's going to pull through.'

'Oh, Billy, thank God for that.'

'It's too early to say the extent of any internal injuries but they're pretty certain that he doesn't have brain damage.'

'That's brilliant news,' said Josh, weak with relief. 'I'll tell the others.'

'Tell Sally I'll be back soon and I'll take her home on the bike.'

'Will do. See you later.'

261

'Oh . . . and, Josh . . .'

'Yeah.'

'You played a blinder tonight, mate. Well done!'

'Thanks.' He turned to see everyone had gathered in the hall. 'They're all waiting to hear the news so I'll have to go. See you later.'

'Sounds like good news,' said Hattie as he replaced the receiver.

He repeated what Billy had told him.

Hattie, characteristically, burst into tears. 'Oh, what a blessing,' she spluttered into her handkerchief. 'Dan's like a son to me.'

While Josh comforted his mother, Molly wiped her eyes and tried to stop her own tears falling too profusely so as not to reveal her feelings. None of them could possibly know the extent of her relief.

'Shall I make some tea?' suggested Sally. Naturally she was less emotional than the others because she didn't know Dan so well.

'That's kind of you, love,' replied Hattie. 'You know where everything is.'

'No tea for me, thanks,' said Josh, turning towards the kitchen. 'I'm gonna get myself something stronger.'

As Molly and Hattie went back into the living room, Hattie said, 'Phew, what a day. I wouldn't want too many like that, would you, Moll?'

'No I would not.'

It had been an emotional day for Molly in more ways than one. Not only had she been beside herself with worry for all the men, almost losing Dan had brought the strength of her love for him home to her with powerful clarity. From the first faint stirrings of awareness she'd tried to be sensible; had struggled not to fall; had clutched at her common sense and sanity, and fought with fierce determination to keep her grip on them. She couldn't count the times she'd reminded herself that she was married, and Dan wanted nothing more than friendship from her. But it had happened just the same. She could no longer pretend that his companionship was enough for her. Not to herself, anyway.

'Let me shake your hand, Josh,' were Dan's first words when the Beckett brothers arrived at his bedside the following evening at visiting time, bringing with them a large brown paper bag of grapes, which they put on his bedside locker, whereupon Billy proceeded to help himself. 'I've been told what you did last night. Billy and I both owe our lives to you.'

'I only did what anyone else would have done,' was Josh's modest reaction.

'It's a blessing you saw us go in to the kiln,' Dan continued. 'No one would have known we were under there otherwise since it isn't used any more. When Hattie came in just now with Patsy, she was telling me that you saw it all from your bedroom window.'

Josh felt hot with shame and hoped it didn't show. The decent thing would be to own up and tell the truth. But he was only human, and he hadn't become a saint just because he'd begun to see things more clearly. After all, there was no damage done to the pottery and no one would be hurt by him not coming clean.

'Yeah, that's right,' he said, shaking Dan's hand.

'Anyway, as soon as I get out of here I'll buy you a drink,' Dan added. 'It's the very least I can do.'

'I'll keep you to that,' replied Josh.

'You're looking all right, anyway,' observed Billy, running his eye over the patient, who was propped up with pillows and had a dressing on his head; the bedcovers were raised because of a badly bruised foot.

'I don't feel too bad really. I've got a stinking headache and my foot's sore as hell from where the rubble caught it but they're giving me painkillers so that's helping.'

'When do you think you'll be out of here?' enquired Billy.

'A few more days, I should think,' Dan speculated. 'They want to keep an eye on me because of the head wound, apparently.' He looked at Billy, who had some cuts and grazes on his face. 'You didn't get off scot-free either.'

'They're nothing mate,' Billy brushed aside. 'Just a few bruises here and there. All be gone by the end of the week.'

They talked for a while longer, then Billy said, 'Well, as they allow only two people at the bedside at a time, we'd better get out of here.'

'Is there a queue then?' Dan asked.

'Just Molly,' Billy told him. 'Hattie and your daughter will probably pop in again after Molly's finished but Hattie had just taken Patsy off to the cafeteria when we came in.'

'I'll see you then, lads,' said Dan. 'Thanks for coming.'

'We'll see you tomorrow.' Billy helped himself to some more grapes. 'And don't hang about in here too long. We need you at work.'

'I'd be in trouble if you didn't,' Dan laughed, wincing because his head hurt. 'Thanks for the grapes, by the way.' He gave Billy a wry grin. 'Nice of you to leave me a few.'

'I didn't want to be greedy, mate,' he joked. 'See you.'

'See you, and don't forget about that drink I owe you, Josh.'

'No chance of that,' he replied, and they headed off down the ward towards the exit.

'You've got quite a fan club,' remarked Molly, sitting down beside the bed and handing Dan a large bag of sweets. She was so full of joy and relief to see that he was all right. 'I've had to wait ages to see you.'

'Maybe I should get hurt more often if it's going to create this much attention.'

'Don't you dare give us all another scare.'

'Don't worry. I'm in no hurry to repeat it.' He peered into the bag.

263

'Ooh, chocolate toffees, my favourite. Thank you.'

'A pleasure.'

'So, what's going on in the outside world?'

'You've only been out of it for a day,' she smiled.

'Seems longer.'

'Probably because so much has happened to you, and being unconscious and everything,' she suggested. 'But things are much the same as always out there.' She paused, remembering. 'No they're not. There's one major change.'

'Oh?'

'Josh is smiling and being pleasant to everyone.'

'Really? I thought there was something odd when they were in here just now.'

'Oh, yeah, he's all sweetness and light now,' she went on. 'Being a hero seems to agree with him.'

'He was certainly a star yesterday.'

'I know.' He looked thoughtful. 'None of us know how we'd react if faced with a situation like that, but he was the last person I expected to show such mettle. I honestly didn't think he was capable.'

'Neither did he, I suspect,' she said with a wry grin. 'He's going about with a bemused expression on his face, as though he still can't quite believe it.'

'There's more to him than bad temper and light fingers, after all then.'

'I always knew there was, especially after he saved Rosa from drowning that time,' she told him. 'But I didn't think he would show us what he's made of in such a dramatic way.'

'I don't suppose anyone did.'

'Perhaps it was just what he needed to give him a sense of self-worth, knowing that he actually saved two people's lives, three if you count Rosa's,' she remarked. 'I think his problem has always been that he didn't think much of himself, despite his outward show of arrogance. Angie and Billy were so much older and so close, I think he always felt left out and that's why Hattie compensated by spoiling him – until she found out about the stealing, that is. He's been like a different person since the accident.'

'Let's hope it lasts.'

'I think it will,' Molly said. 'I've got a good feeling about that young man.'

He gave her a questioning look. 'So, who's looking after Rosa while you're here?'

'My mum,' she replied, adding, 'and on the subject of child-minding, I expect Hattie told you that she and I are looking after Patsy between us while you're laid up, so you've no need to worry about her.'

'She did tell me and I was about to mention it to you. I really do appreciate it, Molly. I'm powerless at the moment and I hate being stuck in here, leaving other people to look after my daughter, but it shouldn't be for long.'

'I'm sure it won't be, but while you are in here I should try and relax and enjoy having everything done for you,' she advised in a friendly manner. 'Patsy will be fine.'

'I'll try and do that, despite the hospital food.'

'That bad?'

'It isn't up to Hattie's standard, put it that way,' he explained. 'Still, they're catering on a mass scale so you can't expect home cooking.'

'No. The main thing is the medical treatment and they seem to know what they're doing.'

'Oh, yes.'

They lapsed into silence. Molly felt awkward suddenly and found herself staring at the floor. In the oddly strained atmosphere of the moment, a sudden worrying thought came into her mind. 'I hope you don't mind my coming to visit you,' she mentioned, looking up. 'I know I'm not family or anything.'

'Of course I don't mind.' He seemed astonished at the suggestion. 'I'd have been very disappointed if you hadn't come to see me.'

'That's all right then.'

'Anyway, I'm not sure if the others are my family now that Angie's gone.' He mulled it over for a moment. 'I mean, unlike Patsy, I don't have a blood tie, do I?'

'No, but whatever the legalities, they're family in your heart, and vice versa.'

'Yeah, of course they are, and I love them all to bits. Except Josh, of course, and I could probably even learn to like him after what he did yesterday.'

'I think that goes for the rest of us.'

She looked at his face; at the bruises and the bandaging. Her eyes filled with tears at the thought of how close he had come to losing his life.

Noticing her sudden distress, his warm eyes clouded with concern. 'Molly, what is it? Is something the matter?'

'Take no notice of me.' She bit back the tears. 'I'm just being ridiculously sentimental.'

'Come on, tell me what's worrying you. A trouble shared . . . as they say.'

In a burst of spontaneity, she blurted out, 'It's just that I was so scared yesterday when we didn't know if you would make it.' She took his hand in both of hers, her blue eyes resting on his face. 'I didn't think it was possible to be so terrified.' Tears were meandering down her cheeks and she mopped them with her handkerchief. 'I just don't know what I would have done if we'd lost you.'

'Hey, hey,' he said gently. 'I did make it so there's no need to be sad.'

265

'I know, like I said, I'm just being stupid.'

'Not at all. I'm flattered to know that you were so worried about me.'

She blew her nose. 'The truth is, Dan,' she began, unable to contain her feelings any longer, 'you've come to mean so much to me since we've been spending a lot of time together.'

Momentarily, he looked startled. 'And you mean a lot to me too, Molly,' he told her. 'Us being together with the girls is at the centre of my life.'

'But it's become more complicated than that for me now,' she confessed.

'Oh?'

'It's become more than just two single parents keeping each other company for the sake of the children for me, you see,' she went on to explain, her words tumbling out rapidly as if of their own volition. 'I never meant it to happen but it has and there's nothing I can do to change it. I've tried, believe me. I ought to stop seeing you outside of work but I can't do that because it wouldn't be fair to the children.'

'Oh, Molly . . .'

Finally coming to her senses and mortified almost beyond feeling that she had embarrassed him in this way, she leaped up. 'Sorry,' she mumbled thickly. 'None of that was meant to come out.'

'There's no need to apologise.'

'I don't know what's the matter with me.' Noticing that he was smiling, she added, 'Don't take the mick, Dan. I feel bad enough about it already.'

'I'm not . . .'

'I'll be on my way now so that Hattie and Patsy can come back in.'

'There's no need to rush off.'

'There's every need,' she corrected.

'No—'

'Get better soon,' she cut in quickly, and turned and hurried towards the exit.

At the ward doors she paused, taking a deep breath and arranging her face into a smile before she pushed them open. 'He's all yours, Hattie,' she said with feigned cheeriness. 'Your daddy is waiting for you, Patsy.'

'Billy and Josh have already left,' Hattie explained, oblivious of Molly's turmoil.

'OK,' she said absently.

'As they came here on Billy's motorbike they don't need to wait for the bus with us.'

'I'll wait for you downstairs in the reception area then,' said Molly, and made her way along the corridor, smarting with humiliation.

What on earth had possessed her to make a total idiot of herself and cause him to cringe with embarrassment? He hadn't known where to put himself. Well, you've certainly got a lot to learn about timing, you silly cow, she admonished herself. The poor man's laid up in a hospital bed after a dreadful ordeal, with no easy means of escape, and you force yourself on him by telling him in so many words that you're in love with him. How must that have made him feel – his so-called pal going all complicated on him when it's obviously the last thing on earth he wants. Her behaviour had been nothing short of pathetic.

It wasn't even as though he'd ever given her the slightest encouragement. Never so much as a word. Just an occasional look, and a few sparky moments that had probably just been wishful thinking on her part. She'd really blown it now. How could she ever face him again?

Chapter Eighteen

The relentless drone of the children's bickering was testing Molly's patience to the limit. Best friends or not, there were times when the claws came out and they sniped at one another over every little thing.

'Mum, Patsy won't give me my comic back,' complained Rosa coming into the kitchen where Molly was chipping potatoes to go with ham for their tea.

'She said I could borrow it to have a look, Auntie Molly,' was Patsy's side of the story.

'I said you could have a look,' retorted Rosa, blue eyes flashing at her enemy. 'I didn't say you could keep it.'

'I don't wanna keep it,' declared Patsy. 'I've got my own at my gran's house.' She thrust the comic at Rosa, her dark eyes hot with rage. 'Here, have your smelly comic.'

'If it's smelly it's only because you've touched it,' Rosa retaliated. 'Anyway, I don't want it back now that you've creased it and made it dirty.'

'Oh, for goodness' sake, give it a rest, the pair of you,' intervened Molly in exasperation. 'You've done nothing but squabble since I collected you from school. You're behaving like a couple of spoiled brats.'

'She started it.' This was Rosa.

'It was her . . .'

'Wasn't . . .'

'Was . . .'

'It's both of you,' cut in Molly, her voice rising, 'and I'm fed up with listening to it. Why don't you go out to play while I get the tea ready? It's a lovely evening.'

'I'm not going out with *her*,' scowled Rosa.

'And I'm not going out with *her*,' said the other.

'Right. That's enough!' yelled Molly. 'As you can't get along together, I'm going to split you up. Rosa, you stay in the kitchen with me; Patsy, you go into the living room.'

Neither moved.

'Go on then, chop chop,' urged Molly.

Slowly Patsy turned and left the room, slouching with sulkiness.

Rosa made to go after her. 'Oh no, madam, I told you to stay here and I meant it,' asserted her mother.

'But, Mu-um,' she pouted, 'I want to go with her.'

'So that you can carry on quarrelling until my nerves eventually snap,' was her mother's firm response. 'Not likely. I'm not having it, Rosa, so sit down at the table. *Now!*'

Simmering with umbrage, the child pulled out a chair and sat down heavily.

'You can both stay where you are until I say different,' said Molly, knowing that within minutes they would be begging to be together.

Wrapping the potato peelings in newspaper and putting them into the bin, Molly thought back over the week. She hadn't been back to the hospital to see Dan. After that last fiasco she couldn't face it. The memory of it still made her smart.

According to Hattie he was expecting to be discharged at the weekend and it was now Friday evening, so Molly's nerves were already jangling at the thought of seeing him for the first time since then. Hattie and the others didn't seem to have found it in the least odd that she hadn't visited him again. But why should they? As far as they were concerned she was simply someone who kept him company because their daughters were friends.

As arranged, she and Hattie had taken care of Patsy between them. She was staying with Hattie, who took her to school in the morning. Molly collected her as usual with Rosa and took her to The Hawthorns later on, in time for bed.

The big Beckett news this week was the new, affable Josh. Hattie was delighted with the change in him.

'He really does seem to have turned over a new leaf,' she had confided to Molly the other day in the office. 'He's a changed man. I'll even go so far as to say that it's a pleasure to have him around the house now. He and Billy are getting on better too. They even went out together for a pint the other night. And – wait till you hear this, Moll – he went across to the pottery last night after work at the factory to give Billy a hand because he's having to work late with Dan being away. Josh isn't an experienced thrower, of course, but there are plenty of ways he can make himself useful.'

'A reformed character, eh?' had been Molly's response.

'Well, yes, that does seem to be the case. Oh, it's such a treat to see him smiling,' Hattie had said. 'And what a relief not having him fly into a rage over nothing at all. I can relax in my own home for the first time in ages.'

'So the accident proved to be a life-changing experience for him then,' Molly had suggested.

'It seems that way. It seems too good to be true so I'm hoping it isn't just a five-minute wonder.'

'Somehow I don't think it will be,' Molly had reassured. 'I've got a good feeling about this.'

But now she was recalled to the present by the sound of Rosa's voice. 'Mum, please can I go in the other room with Patsy?' she wheedled. 'She can have a look at the comic and I won't quarrel with her, I promise.'

Following her daughter's gaze towards the door, Molly saw Patsy standing there, looking equally contrite. 'Can she come in please, Auntie Molly?' she entreated. 'We won't argue.'

'You didn't last long without each other, did you?' Molly looked from one to the other slowly. 'All right, but if I hear so much as a voice raised by either of you, I shall separate you until it's time for Patsy to go to her gran's,' she warned. 'I'm not messing around, I mean it.'

Rosa slid off her chair and headed for the door. All was quiet in the other room, Molly noticed a few minutes later as she put a packet of lard into the chip pan. But for how long when they were in this mood was anyone's guess.

'We'll have to make it a quick one,' Billy said to Josh that same evening at the bar of The Fox. They'd both just finished work. 'Mum will have our meal on the table soon, and I'm seeing Sally later on.'

'A pint?' asked Josh.

'I'll get these,' insisted Billy. 'I reckon I owe you one after the help you've given me at the pottery. Thanks for giving me a hand last night.'

Josh gave a casual shrug. 'I didn't have anything else to do.'

Billy ordered the drinks and turned to his brother. 'You're not a bad sort of a bloke when you're like this, you know,' he told him. 'In fact, I'd even go so far as to say that you're almost human.'

'Only almost? What do I have to do to get the full status?' was Josh's light response.

'Just stay the way you are. And don't go back to your old ways.'

'Was I really that bad?'

'Yeah, you were awful.' Billy saw no reason to hold back. 'You were a complete pain in the arse. As well as being a thief, you were rude, lazy and downright unhelpful.'

'Charming,' was Josh's spirited reaction.

'You did ask.'

'Yeah, I know.' He lowered his eyes. For the first time in his life he felt able to apologise. 'I'm sorry about everything, mate, especially the nicking.'

'If you'd really needed extra money, you should have asked for it.'

'Oh, yeah.' Josh looked up. 'You'd have soon sent me off with a flea in my ear.'

'Not necessarily,' Billy disagreed mildly. 'It depends how you were behaving at the time.'

''Well, anyway,' continued Josh, 'I didn't only do it for the money.'

'So you got a thrill from it then?'

'I got a buzz from stealing from the family, yeah,' he confessed, reflecting on the whole dreadful business. 'I've never felt the slightest urge to take anything from anyone else.'

'Why did you want to steal from your own flesh and blood, for Pete's sake?'

'Getting my own back on you all, I suppose.'

'For what?'

'Making me into the family fool,' he explained.

'You don't half exaggerate.'

'I'm just telling you how I felt. I was always the butt of the family jokes,' he reminded him.

'Par for the course for the baby of the family,' Billy replied.

'Yeah, I suppose so, but it seemed as though you were all against me,' Josh tried to explain. 'I always felt like some sort of a freak.'

'And you don't feel like that now?'

'No, I don't.' He looked thoughtfully into space. 'Dunno what's happened to me exactly but something has.'

'You've learned how to smile and be pleasant, that's what's happened.'

'It goes deeper than that, though. I feel different inside,' Josh told him. 'I'm not the sort of bloke to work out what makes me tick. But the accident changed me. Up until then I thought I was useless; an incompetent who couldn't do anything properly. Now I know that I can and I like the feeling. Looking back, I can see that I was caught in a trap before. I hated you all because you seemed to hate me, so I was stroppy and bigheaded, and you hated me even more.'

'You had more than your fair share of care and attention from Mum, though,' Billy reminded him. 'She's always taken your side about practically everything.'

'I know. She's been a real diamond,' Josh agreed. 'But it wasn't special attention from her that I needed. Her spoiling me just alienated me from you and Angie even more. What I wanted was to be included in things. To feel part of it all.'

'But you were such an obnoxious git,' Billy reminded him. 'That was why you weren't included. We got fed up with trying because you gave us such a hard time.'

'Yeah, I can see that now.' He paused, trying to make sense of it all. 'I don't know exactly when it started but for as far back as I can remember I've been angry. After the accident on Sunday, the anger just sort of went away.'

'Maybe we have been a bit hard on you over the years,' conceded Billy. 'But none of it was meant maliciously, you know. Well, not when you were a kid, anyway, and never by Angie. But when you came to work in the firm and got sulkier and ruder, there were times when I could have cheerfully throttled you. The stealing was the last straw.'

'Yeah, I know.' Josh made a face. 'I'm really ashamed. It's only now I can admit it. Before, the anger dominated my whole life. I knew I was going from bad to worse, and I couldn't stop doing it, even though it was making me miserable.'

'And now you're wallowing in the glory of being a hero?'

'S'pose so.'

'You're entitled to feel proud.' Billy drank his beer and studied his brother over the rim of the glass. 'But all the praise and fuss will die down as soon as the accident fades into the past. People won't forget but they'll move on to other things. What then? Are you going to revert back to your old ways because you're not getting enough attention?'

'It isn't just the praise that's making me feel different...' Josh struggled for the words to express his feelings, still not completely sure what had happened to him. 'It's as though a great black cloud has lifted and I'm more in control now. I can't promise that I'll never get stroppy again but I'm fairly certain I won't go back to how I was before. I'm determined not to.'

Billy took a long swig from his glass, mulling something over. 'If I can persuade the others to give you another chance, would you fancy coming back to work at the family firm?' he asked.

This was the last thing Josh had expected. He hadn't realised he was that much in favour. 'Are you serious? You're not just having me on?'

'I wouldn't joke about a thing like that,' confirmed Billy. 'I reckon you deserve another chance after what you did on Sunday night.'

'I'm all for it,' was Josh's eager response.

'You'll have to get to grips with the actual craft, though,' Billy told him seriously. 'You're eighteen now; it's time you progressed. Anyway, we've already got one workshop boy; we don't need another.'

'Suits me.'

'If this does come to be, you'll have to put your mind to it and work hard,' Billy warned, giving him a shrewd look. 'Don't mess us about.'

'I won't, don't worry,' Josh assured him. 'Working in a factory all day has taught me a few things – what I threw away being the main one. So, can I take this as a definite?'

'As far as I'm concerned, you can. But it isn't only up to me. I'll have to put it to the others, though you're very much the golden boy at the moment so I should think you stand a good chance.' His dark eyes hardened slightly. 'Before we go any further, Josh, if you start giving us trouble, you'll be out and it'll be for good. There'll be no going back if you let us down again.'

'I won't do that.' He was adamant. 'I can promise you.'

'Fair enough. I'll talk to the others as soon as I get the chance. I'll let you know.'

'Thanks, Billy.'

They drank their beer, easy in each other's company. 'There's a pre-season soccer match at Brentford next Saturday,' Billy mentioned casually after a while. 'Fancy coming?'

'Ooh, yeah,' enthused Josh.

'We'll go together then. But now we'd better drink up, or Mum'll give us a roasting for making her keep our food warm.'

The brothers finished their beer and left the pub, chatting companionably.

Molly had just finished washing the dishes after Saturday lunch when there was a knock at the door.

'Dan,' she said, her cheeks burning as she ushered him and Patsy inside, whereupon the latter rushed off to find Rosa. 'I wasn't expecting to see you. Come and sit down.' She led him into the living room and waved a hand towards an easy chair. Her nerves were taut, despite her casual air. 'When did you come out of hospital?'

'This morning.'

'How are you feeling?'

'I'll live.' The large dressing that had adorned his head when she'd visited him in hospital had been replaced by a much smaller one. 'Seriously, though, I'm fine. Everything's healing up as it should be.'

'Good.' She bit her lip. 'Actually, I intended to pop over to see you once I knew for definite that you were home.'

'I looked out for you at visiting time every day,' he told her with a meaningful look.

'Yeah, about that . . .' She turned towards the girls, who were chattering nearby. 'Can you go out and play so that us grown-ups can talk?'

'There's nothing to do out there,' said Rosa, choosing to be awkward.

'You don't usually have any trouble, especially when it's time to come in,' her mother pointed out. 'It's a nice day, too nice to be stuck indoors. So off you go.'

'Don't fancy it out there today, do we, Pats?'

'We're not in the mood,' said her friend, united against authority.

'What about us all going over to my place?' intervened Dan artfully, exchanging a glance with Molly. 'You can play outside in the garden there. Maybe even have tea out there as it's such a lovely sunny day.'

Rosa's eyes lit up. Even though she went to Patsy's quite often, a garden was still a novelty to a child who lived in a flat, especially a garden with a swing. 'That would be smashing,' she enthused.

'We've got some lovely chocolate cakes that Gran made for us,' added Patsy.

'Let's go then,' urged Rosa, eager to be on the way.

'We'd better check with your mum first,' Dan said, realising that he might have been too presumptuous. 'She might have other plans.'

'Nothing special,' Molly told him. 'Mum's working an extra shift so she won't need my company.' She smiled, though she was still feeling painfully tense. 'Give me a minute to powder my nose and I'll be with you.'

'We'll wait in the car,' he told her. 'Come on, kids.'

'About the other day at the hospital,' began Molly when she and Dan were finally alone, the children having departed to the sunshine. 'It was very rude to me to rush off like that.' She shook her head. 'I'm sure you understood why.' She put her hand to her brow. 'The whole thing was so awful I just had to get away.'

They were sitting in the lounge near the open French doors overlooking the lawn in the back garden. There was tea and biscuits on the coffee table between them.

'I didn't find it awful.'

'I think I must have been overemotional because of the accident,' she went on, keen to say her piece. 'It made me realise just how short life is. First we lost Angie, then we almost lost you. I said things I shouldn't have in the heat of the moment. I'm so sorry I embarrassed you.'

'You didn't.'

She looked at him with a half-smile. 'Oh, Dan, you're such a gentleman but there's no need to be kind,' she told him in a gentle tone. 'It was written all over your face. You were scared to death when I started coming out with all that stuff.'

'No I wasn't,' he denied.

'I was there, I saw you.'

'I admit I was a bit taken aback when you blurted it out at that particular moment because I wasn't expecting it,' he explained. 'But once I recovered I was pleased. Very pleased. Let's face it, it would have come out sooner or later because we both know that things have changed between us, even though I've been refusing to admit it to myself. All you did was bring things to a head.'

'Oh.' Now it was her turn to be taken aback. 'So . . . I hadn't imagined something in you then?'

'No, you didn't imagine anything,' he confirmed. 'It's become much more than just a matey thing for me too.'

The room seemed to fill with sunshine, the air was sweet with joy. 'You didn't want to admit it because you still feel married to Angie? Am I right?'

'Yes, you're dead right.' There was a thoughtful pause. 'I have had a problem with that.'

'So, you still feel married to Angie and you're not, and I don't feel married to Brian but I am.' She grinned. 'What a pair, eh? Between the two of us, there's not much hope of a future together.'

'Nonsense,' Dan said, making her blue eyes shine with hope. 'I had plenty of time to think while I was in hospital, and I finally admitted

275

what I've known all along in my heart: that Angie would want me to live life to the full, not just skirt around the edges. She's been gone nearly a year and a half now and I'll love her till I die. I'll *never ever* forget her. But it's time to start living again.'

Molly looked at him, waiting for him to continue.

'I want to live my life with you, Molly,' he went on, standing up and going towards her. 'I never thought it would happen to me again but I've fallen in love – with you.'

'Oh, Dan,' she sighed, rising and sinking into his arms.

'There is one major complication,' said Molly a little later when they finally got around to pouring the tea and eating the biscuits, seated together now on the sofa.

'Which is?'

'I may not feel it but I am actually married to Brian.'

'But you told me ages ago that your marriage didn't work,' he reminded her. 'He's never around to be a husband to you.'

'I know all that. But, for all his faults, he is my husband and I must respect that.'

'So what are you saying?' He looked worried. 'Are you telling me that you and I can't have a life together because you're legally bound to a man you rarely see and don't love?'

She pushed her blonde hair back from her brow, her face flushed. 'No, of course I'm not saying that. I want to be with you more than anything, and my marriage to Brian was over long before I fell in love with you – not that it was ever a marriage in the true sense of the word anyway. But Brian did come to my rescue when I was pregnant with Rosa and I can't just disregard his feelings.'

'He married you because it was what he wanted,' was Dan's opinion. 'He wouldn't have done it otherwise. Brian isn't a natural Good Samaritan.'

'True but that doesn't alter the fact he gave Rosa and me respectability.'

'And he got plenty back in return,' he reminded her firmly. 'The woman he'd always wanted in a permanent state of gratitude to him. He must have been jumping for joy.'

'Yes, I expect he was,' she agreed. 'All I ask of you is that we keep what you and I have between ourselves until after I've told him about it. I don't want him to come home and hear about it from someone else. It's probably only a matter of time before he tells me he wants to end the marriage formally, anyway. He wouldn't stay away so much if he hadn't found someone else.'

'How long will we have to wait, since he hardly ever comes home?' Dan asked.

'I'll write and ask him to come home for a weekend as soon as he can,' she decided. 'I'd rather not tell him about us in a letter. That really wouldn't be fair.'

'Mm, I can understand that.'

'Mind you, he can be an awkward so-and-so.' She put her tea cup down on the table. 'If he knows I want him to come home for a particular reason, he'll deliberately stay away to annoy me, so I'll have to play it down.'

'And, knowing that, you still want to consider his feelings?'

'Afraid so.' She gave him a tender look. 'Bear with me on this one, please, Dan.'

'OK.' He glanced towards the garden where the children were playing on the lawn. 'It won't be easy keeping it to ourselves with those two around. If they spot so much as a cuddle, the news will spread like wildfire.'

'Yes, we will have to be especially discreet.' Deciding to make a joke of it, Molly grinned and said, 'Still, the risk element might add spice and keep you interested.'

'I don't need risk to do that,' he assured her. 'All it will do is turn me into a nervous wreck.'

'How about us trying a little risk right now?' she suggested, turning towards him. 'I'll be careful not to hurt your bad head.'

'You can forget about that,' he murmured. 'I've forgotten it already.'

A minute or so later, the sound of young voices approaching caused them to spring apart.

'Can we have a biscuit please, Dad?' asked Patsy, bounding into the room with her pal in tow.

'Yes, go on then,' he said, unable to stifle a chuckle and adding from habit, 'But only one or you'll spoil your tea.'

His daughter gave him a steady look. 'What are you laughing at?'

'Nothing.'

'You're both giggling,' she observed, looking at Molly. 'What's so funny?'

'We're just happy that your dad is home from hospital and feeling better,' Molly told her.

'Oh, yeah, of course,' said Patsy, seeming satisfied. 'That's made me happy too.'

The little girls helped themselves to a biscuit each and went back out outside. As soon as they were out of earshot, the adults burst out laughing.

'I hope that husband of yours doesn't keep us waiting too long,' Dan smiled. 'My nerves are already in tatters.'

'I'm worth it, aren't I?'

'Oh, yes, you're worth it all right,' he said, continuing from where they'd left off.

★ ★ ★

277

The weeks that followed were the happiest Molly had ever known. She and Dan had only stolen moments alone together, but the times they spent with the children were even more enjoyable now for Molly. His love enriched the whole of her life, not just the bits when they were able to be romantic. In these first heady days she felt permanently light-hearted and excited, looking forward to each day with added zest. Her senses heightened by the knowledge that he loved her, everything seemed to shine. She'd never experienced anything like this before; not during her youthful love affair with Rosa's father, and certainly never with Brian. Rather than come between them, Dan's love for Angie brought them even closer because Molly had loved her too and wanted to feel she was with them in spirit.

Molly and Dan became extremely adept at seizing the moment when the children were occupied, and continued to go on weekend outings as before. They spent time at the Becketts as always; arriving independently and making sure their behaviour never hinted at anything beyond friendship. They spent more time in each other's homes in the evenings at weekends, but never spent the night together. That really would set tongues wagging before they were ready.

At work they became practised at behaving normally, though everyone was too busy to notice anyway. They were all taken up with the new-style Josh on his return to work at the pottery. The impossible youth had become a reasonable young man. Whether or not it would last still remained to be seen, but there was a general feeling of cautious optimism.

Mulling over the situation between herself and Dan one night in bed, Molly admitted that she was increasingly frustrated with the hole-and-corner way they had to conduct their relationship. She wanted to tell the world. But it had to remain a secret until after Brian had been told. Until then the subterfuge must continue.

Brian hadn't responded to her letter asking him to come home. It was typical of him to keep her waiting. He was probably doing it out of spite. She hoped she heard from him soon because the deception was becoming a strain. Maybe tomorrow she would get a letter telling her when to expect him, she thought hopefully, as she turned over to go to sleep.

'So you've got your feet under the table with that girl who works in the café, then,' said one of Brian's workmates on the building site.

'Not half,' Brian confirmed. 'She's eating out of my hand. She's a right little cracker, an' all.'

'I know that as we go there every day for our dinner,' pointed out the mate, a large ginger-haired man with huge, muscular arms liberally spread with tattoos. 'I dunno how you do it.'

'It's my sex appeal, innit?' grinned Brian. 'Women just can't resist me.'

'I think you're an ugly-looking bugger meself,' said Ginger. 'I don't know what they see in you.'

'I should hope you don't,' laughed Brian. 'I'd be really worried if you fancied me.'

'Not as worried as I'd be, mate,' guffawed Ginger.

The men were having a break and were sitting on a small pile of neatly stacked bricks in the sunshine, drinking tea; they were both stripped to the waist. As they sank their teeth into jam doughnuts and fell silent while they ate, Brian thought about the letter he'd received from Molly a few weeks ago, asking him to go home for a weekend. She could whistle for that. He was far too busy with Annie from the café to go to London.

Annie was twenty-five and separated from her husband. Absolutely ideal for Brian. The fact that she had a husband and wasn't free to marry would stop her getting any ideas in that direction as far as he was concerned. Even better, she didn't have any kids so was free to see him whenever he wanted. Uninhibited and experienced in the bedroom, she was also partial to a tipple so they got pleasantly drunk together, then did what came naturally.

She'd certainly taken his mind off Beryl, who seemed to have disappeared altogether. She hadn't been seen around for months. He'd tried to get her back often enough and got nowhere. So if she still wanted to play hard to get she could get on with it. He was fixed up elsewhere now.

With his social life on the up, he certainly had no intention of missing a weekend of booze and passion to go home to Molly and her brat. Come to think of it, he felt removed altogether from that whole setup now. He couldn't imagine himself ever letting Molly go – she was too much a part of him – but he didn't actually want to be with her any more.

He was brought out of his reverie by the foreman telling the men to get off their arses and go back to work. They finished their tea, ground out their cigarette ends under their shoes and stood up. One of the bricklayers was shouting something down from the scaffolding of a building in progress. The foreman went over to find out what he wanted.

'He's broken his trowel and wants another,' the foreman called over to Brian. 'Get it out of his tool box and take it up to him, will you, mate?'

Nodding, Brian got the trowel and walked over to the building, thinking ahead excitedly to tonight and his date with Annie. Luxuriating in the glorious anticipation, he climbed the ladder and handed the trowel to the bricklayer. Too preoccupied with his thoughts to take proper notice of what he was doing, he took the first step down, missed and slipped.

Clinging desperately to a rung of the ladder, his hands were sweating and burning with the pressure. Vaguely he was aware of someone below telling him that help was on its way. But his hands were slippery and it was hard to hold on. Finally his grip slithered away and he fell to the ground, landing in a heap. There was a stab of intense pain before he lost consciousness.

Hattie seemed to be in a strange mood, Molly noticed one day in the office. She seemed quiet and offhand.

'Anything wrong, Hat?' she enquired, standing by the other woman's desk where she was busy working out the wages.

'No.' She didn't look up. 'Is there any reason why there should be?'

'You seem a bit . . . well, more subdued than usual, that's all,' she told her.

'I'm the same as I always am.'

'Are you sure there's nothing worrying you?'

'Quite sure.'

'Hattie, this is me you're talking to,' Molly persisted. 'We're friends, we talk about things.'

'There's nothing to talk about,' Hattie insisted, still looking at Molly. 'I'm absolutely fine.'

Molly wasn't convinced, and wondered if perhaps Hattie was finding it all a bit too much, working full time and running that big house with Billy and Josh to look after as well, especially as she did everything for them. Vi came in to clean for her once a week, but it was still a lot for someone of any age and Hattie wasn't a young woman.

She didn't take short cuts to make things easier for herself either; she still made all her own cakes and cooked elaborate meals. None of the new frozen convenience foods was ever on the menu at Hattie's table. Mulling it over, Molly reminded herself of the need to be sensitive to her feelings. If she suggested that Hattie take it a bit easier, she might think she was implying that she was too old to cope and be deeply offended.

So, 'That's all right then,' was about all she could say.

At last Hattie looked up. 'It's nice of you to be concerned,' she said with a half-smile that was obviously forced. 'But there's nothing wrong. You know how hard I have to concentrate to get to grips with this damned PAYE system.'

'I'll leave you to get on with it then,' said Molly, and went back to her own desk.

On reflection, this wasn't the first time Hattie had seemed odd lately, and if Molly didn't know her better she would say she was miffed about something. But if that was the case she would come right out and say so – she wasn't the type to hold back – and the strained, rather cold moods never lasted long, and she always seemed perfectly all right for the rest of the time. Maybe she wasn't feeling well, Molly thought with a stab of alarm. But the more likely explanation was that things were getting to be too much for her.

Molly told herself she was probably worrying unnecessarily. Anyway, as Hattie insisted that everything was fine, about the only way in which Molly could help was to make sure the older woman wasn't burdened by having to look after Patsy too often. The long summer holidays had arrived, bringing with them the usual childcare problems.

Molly's mum helped out when she could, Vi was an absolute godsend, and Molly took as much time off work as she possibly could to be with Rosa. She also looked after Patsy, who always wanted to be with Rosa anyway. This meant Hattie didn't have to worry about her granddaughter. Being on the production side of the pottery, it was difficult for Dan to take time off work to look after his daughter for six weeks in the summer.

But now Molly got on with some typing, still feeling uneasy about her friend.

About half an hour later, Hattie appeared by her desk. 'Fancy a cuppa, love?' she asked, her mood seeming to have reverted to normal. 'I know it isn't time yet, strictly speaking, but I'm dying for a brew.'

Molly smiled, sighing with relief that all now seemed to be well. 'Yes, please,' she said. 'I'd love one.'

'I'll put the kettle on then.'

As Hattie disappeared to the tiny kitchen behind the office, Molly thought she must have been imagining things. Hattie was just like her usual self now. Everyone feels a bit off at times, she reminded herself, and Hattie is no exception.

Molly came to from a deep sleep with a start, her nerves tingling. What had woken her? Something must have disturbed her. She shot up, listening, her heart racing even faster when she heard a noise. There was someone moving about; someone was in the flat.

Her first thoughts were for Rosa and the need to protect her. Turning on the bedside lamp and getting out of bed, she picked up the first thing that came to hand as a defence weapon – a long-handled mirror from the dressing table. She crept warily towards the bedroom door and opened it with extreme caution. Whoever it was had a nerve, she thought, seeing a light coming from under the kitchen door. Didn't burglars usually creep around in the dark with a torch?

Inching towards the light with her mirror poised, she took a deep breath and opened the door, raising the mirror, ready to strike the intruder.

'Brian,' she gasped. He was sitting at the kitchen table drinking a cup of tea.

'Wotcha.'

'You frightened the living daylights out of me,' she told him shakily.

281

'Did I?'

'Yes, you bloomin' well did. I thought someone had broken in. Fancy just coming in like that without letting me know.'

'In case you've forgotten, I'm your husband and my name is on the rentbook,' he reminded her in an aggressive tone. 'I have a key to the door and I can use it whenever I choose.'

'Of course you can, but in the early hours of the morning in the middle of the week, you were the last person I expected to see.' She was still trembling from the scare he'd given her.

'And there was me being all considerate,' he came back at her. 'I avoided knocking at the front door so that I wouldn't disturb you.'

'Oh, oh, I see.' The power was still there; the ability to make her feel as though she was in the wrong. 'But you could still have let me know.'

'So I didn't get around to it, it isn't the end of the world,' he said. 'And now that you are up and about you can get me something to eat.'

'It's one o'clock in the morning . . .'

Before she had a chance to say more, he swivelled round so that she could see his lower half, and pointed to his foot, which she could now see was in plaster of paris. He picked up a pair of crutches that were lying across the chair, out of sight until now. 'I fell off a ladder on the site and broke my foot so I'll need plenty of looking after. And you can start by getting me some food. Egg and bacon'll do. Bung in a few sausages as well if you've got any. And plenty of bread and butter with the butter spread thick.'

His eyes rested on her with amusement as he lifted the crutches and waved them at her in a taunting gesture. He had the upper hand and was loving every moment. And she was expected to feel sympathy for him. 'I'll see what I've got,' she said through gritted teeth.

'Oh, and by the way,' he began as she went over to the larder, 'you wrote and asked me to come home for a weekend. What was that about?'

How could she tell him about her and Dan while he was laid up? 'Oh, nothing in particular,' she fibbed. 'You hadn't been back for a while, that's all.'

Chapter Nineteen

'He was laughing at me.' Molly told Dan the whole story the following lunchtime when the others were out. They were talking near Molly's desk. 'Waving the crutches at me like symbols of power. I know what he's like; he'll milk this broken foot for all it's worth. He'll have me dancing to his tune and there's not a thing I can do about it.'

'You can be firm,' he suggested. 'You mustn't let him run you ragged.'

'Easier said than done when you're dealing with Brian,' she pointed out. 'Anyway, I can't let him fend for himself when he's injured. I wouldn't want to, anyway. It's just that he can be so difficult.'

'Obviously you must help him but you don't have to be his slave.'

'He has a way of making me do things.'

'You're a soft touch where he's concerned.'

'Maybe.'

'How long will he be staying?'

'Until he's fit enough to go back to work, I suppose,' Molly replied. 'He's been forced to come home because he can't work so isn't earning and isn't able to pay for lodgings. He stayed on where he was for a while after his fall because he'd paid some rent in advance, apparently. But when that ran out the landlady had to relet his room to someone else.'

'He wouldn't get sick pay in the sort of job he does, I suppose?' Dan assumed.

'Oh, no. Casual labourers don't get anything like that. It's strictly cash in hand.'

'Isn't he eligible to claim from the state?'

'He won't go near officialdom because he hasn't paid any tax or insurance stamps for years, apparently.'

'So he's come home to sponge on you.'

'In a word, yes. But I don't mind that aspect of it in the least. As long as I'm earning he's welcome. Provided it doesn't go on for too long, I should just about be able to manage with an extra mouth to feed. Rosa and I live simply anyway.' She tapped her thumbnail on her chin, mulling things over. 'Trouble is, Brian's extravagant; he likes plenty of pocket money, so that could be a problem if I'm expected to supply it.'

'You'll have to tell him straight that you can't.'

'Oh, I will, don't worry.' She paused. 'But thinking about it, he won't stay longer than he has to because he won't like having to rely on me for money. It'll be too damaging to his pride,' she went on. 'My going out to work has always annoyed him.'

'It probably suits his pocket, though.'

'No doubt about that,' she agreed. 'He doesn't like the idea but he likes the reality. He stopped supporting me financially ages ago. Didn't feel under any obligation once I had an income.' She paused, absently studying her fingernails. 'Knowing Brian, he'll have some cash stashed away for his beer and cigarettes. He wouldn't risk being without those so he'll have come home before his money ran out altogether.'

'Sounds likely.'

'As I said, the money side of it doesn't worry me nearly as much as the misery of having him around. But there's not a bloomin' thing I can do about it, is there? He's my husband and I can't put him out on the street.'

'Of course you can't. Aand there is an up side to it, remember.' Dan was trying to stay positive.

'I'm blowed if I can see one.'

'We've been waiting for him to come home so that you can tell him about us, haven't we?' he reminded her. 'So now's your chance.'

'I can't tell him now.' She was shocked at the suggestion. 'Not while he's down.'

'But he isn't down, is he? You said yourself that he's enjoying every minute.'

'He'll enjoy having me running around after him, yes, and the power he has over me because of his current situation, but that doesn't alter the fact that he does have a broken foot and is incapacitated.'

'Only up to a point,' was Dan's opinion. 'I bet he'll manage to hobble down the pub whenever he fancies it.'

'You can bet your sweet life on it.'

'So, if he's well enough to do that he's well enough to be told the truth.'

'It's more complicated than that, Dan.'

'Oh?'

She stroked her chin meditatively. 'It wouldn't be wise to tell him now – when he's going to be living in the flat for a while – because he'll make life hell for Rosa as well as for me,' she explained. 'He'll turn the place into a battleground and have a go at me at every opportunity. He isn't physically violent but he does get very loud-mouthed when he's angry and it upsets her terribly. So you can see why I daren't make waves at this stage. It isn't as though I can ask him to leave because he has nowhere else to go, not until he's working again and can pay for lodgings. The time to tell him is when he's better and ready to go back to Norfolk.'

'I suppose you're right,' Dan agreed with reluctance. 'But I don't like the idea of your being there, with him making your life a misery.'

284

'I'll be all right. I'm used to him.'

'Well, if things gets too difficult for you, you'll just have to leave.' He was very concerned. 'You and Rosa can come and stay at my place.'

'I couldn't do that to Brian, not while he isn't one hundred per cent.'

'It could be weeks.'

'It shouldn't be for too long as the plaster had already been on for a while before he arrived home. So, we'll just have to be patient and remember that it won't be for ever. As soon as his foot is better, I'll tell him about us and we can come out in the open with it to everyone else.' She paused, making a face. 'Until then I won't be able to see so much of you.'

'Surely he won't stop you from going out, taking Rosa out,' he said worriedly.

'Of course not. But if he gets so much as a whiff of anything between you and me, he'll go berserk and I just can't risk the upset for Rosa,' Molly explained. 'So we'll have to cool it for the moment. We'll meet when we need to because of the girls, and I'll see you at work, but that'll be about it until he's been put in the picture.'

'I can see that it has to be this way but I'm not happy about it,' he said miserably.

'We'll manage to snatch a few moments now and then, like we do now.'

'Even so . . .'

'Look, I know it's asking a lot but please bear with me. It won't be for long.' She gave him a close look. 'Brian doesn't come near me any more, so there'll be nothing like that.

His relief was obvious. 'All right,' he sighed. 'You can rely on me. But as soon as he's fit again, he has to be told.'

'He will be, I promise,' Molly said, slipping her arms round him. 'But don't let's waste these few precious moments arguing. The others will be back soon.'

'You are so right,' Dan said, drawing her close.

'You finally decided to come home then,' was the gruff greeting Molly received when she stepped in the door, the girls having lingered outside to talk to some neighbourhood children. 'It took you long enough. I could have died of thirst waiting for you to get back.'

Brian had been home for two weeks, fourteen days of sheer hell for Molly. He'd never been an easy man but was currently impossible. He complained about every little thing, from the plaster on his foot to the meals she provided to the noise the children made when they were playing indoors. He was demanding to the nth degree and created such a tense atmosphere in the home, the children avoided the living room – where he sat in judgement in his armchair – even missing their favourite TV programmes so they wouldn't have to be near him. His dark

285

hostility was chilling for those of tender years.

Fortunately, the holidays were over and they were back at school so out of his way all day. The weather was still quite mild and it stayed light until after Patsy had gone home so they were able to play outside.

'Sorry.' Molly was breathless from hurrying. 'I had to go to the shops on the way home.'

'And never mind about me,' Brian grumbled. 'I can waste away here for all you care.'

'I was shopping for food so that you won't do that,' she pointed out.

'Hmmph.'

'Anyway, you're perfectly able to make yourself a cup of tea.'

'I have got a bad foot, you know,' he reminded her.

'I do know that, Brian.' She hurried through to the kitchen, put her shopping down and went straight back into the living room. 'By the look of the dirty dishes piled up in the sink you've gone neither hungry nor thirsty while I've been out.'

'I had to do something to keep starvation at bay, didn't I?' he complained. 'Those sandwiches you left for me weren't nearly enough.'

'I made plenty.' She'd left him enough to feed an army.

'They weren't enough for me,' he insisted. 'So I fried myself some sausages.'

'So why wait for me to come home to make you a cup of tea then?' she asked.

'Because you're my wife and it's your duty to get home as soon as you can to look after me. Not to stop off for shopping. You should organise yourself better.'

She took a deep breath to calm herself. 'Normally I'm very organised,' she defended. 'I had to go to the shops because you're eating me out of house and home so I had to go and buy more food.'

This silenced him; but not for long. 'I'm a strong man with a healthy appetite. I've got to do something to cheer myself up when I'm stuck here all day on my own.'

'You're not stuck here all day,' she felt compelled to point out. 'You go down to the pub every lunchtime. And don't deny it because I can smell the booze on your breath when I get in and you've been seen going in there by the neighbours.'

'A man's got to have some pleasure,' he pointed out gloomily. 'Surely you don't begrudge me that.'

'Of course I don't,' was her heated response. 'But as you seem to have endless money to spend on beer maybe you could help out by paying for your own cigarettes as well. I don't earn a fortune, you know.'

'Ooh, not much,' he argued.

She threw him a look. 'What's that supposed to mean?'

'You do all right for yourself,' he stated categorically. 'You only have to look round this place to see that. You've got a telly and one of those dryer things. You've even bought a fridge since I was here last.'

'Only a little one, and I saved up for it,' she informed him. 'Everything I earn goes into the household budget and I'm careful with money. I have to be with a child to bring up on my own.'

'You're not on your own. I send money . . .' Even he could see that he didn't have a leg to stand on with that one. 'Well, I used to.'

'Not for ages, and that's absolutely fine with me,' she assured him. 'I can manage when there's just Rosa and myself. But what I earn has to cover everything, including Rosa's clothes, and I'm not prepared for her to go without because I have to fund your chain-smoking habit.'

'You even resent me having a smoke . . .'

'I don't, I really don't.' She was almost begging him to understand. 'You know I'm not like that. But it would help me if you could pay for your own cigarettes as you've obviously got some money tucked away.'

'I kept you for long enough, now it's your turn to keep me,' was how he dealt with that.

'And happily will I do so for as long as I can,' she told him. 'But my wages don't run to fifty or sixty cigarettes a day. Anyway, you've changed your tune, haven't you? You used to hate the idea of being kept by a woman.'

'Yeah, well, I'm injured so I can't do anything else, can I?'

'There is that,' she agreed, compunction creeping in now for having stood her ground with him. 'I am trying to do my best for you, Brian.'

He looked at her and for a moment his face seemed to soften. But it was only fleeting. 'You should try a bit harder instead of resenting having to buy me a few cigarettes,' he said nastily.

Molly bit back a retort and said instead, 'I'll make some tea,' and left the room.

In the kitchen, she felt giddy with tension and had to steady herself by leaning on the worktop. Despite his hatefulness, some part of her felt desperately sorry for him. There was something pitiful about him. Would he have become such a monster if she'd been able to return his love when he'd wanted her to, she wondered. Those days were long gone. He didn't want that now; he didn't want to be with her any more than she wanted to be with him. But he would never admit it. Partly, she suspected, because he couldn't let go of a youthful obsession and also because she was useful to keep in the background when he needed someone to fall back on.

Her pity changed to anger at the thought that he was using her as a convenience. His woman in Norfolk – who she was sure must exist – obviously wasn't prepared to keep him while he wasn't working. But Molly was obliged to because she was his wife and she owed him, was the way he would see it. Thinking back to the time before they got married when he'd been quite a nice bloke, she wondered how they could have reached a state where reasonable communication just wasn't possible.

Ensconced in the armchair drinking his tea, with his foot resting on a footstool Molly had borrowed for him from a neighbour, Brian was simmering with umbrage for the world in general and particularly the female of the species. Women – you couldn't trust any one of them. After all he'd done for Molly and her kid, she had the cheek to say she didn't want to pay for his ciggies, the greedy cow. She'd insisted on going out to work against his wishes, so now she could pay up and look happy about it.

Then there was Annie. What a heartless bitch she'd turned out to be. As soon as he didn't have money to lavish on her, she ditched him without a second thought. It wasn't that he was bothered about Annie, as such – she'd never meant as much to him as Beryl had – but he would have liked to have been the one to give the marching orders.

And as for Beryl . . . well, maybe her reaction on finding out that he was married had been understandable, but refusing to have him back and then disappearing completely, that really was going too far. He'd got short shrift from her mother when he'd called at the house recently; she told him that Beryl had gone away and slammed the door in his face.

It was only the absence of an alternative that had driven him back to Molly. He didn't want to be here with a woman who didn't love him but his bed and board were free so it suited him for the moment. It was true, he did have a beer fund put by – due to a win on the horses just before his accident – but Molly wasn't going to get her hot little hands on that as a contribution towards his keep.

There had been a time when he'd had Molly exactly where he'd wanted her: grateful and eager to please him. Where was her gratitude now? She didn't even want to pay for his fags.

Beryl would have, he thought wistfully. She'd have done anything for him when they were together. He still couldn't believe that she wouldn't give him another chance. They could have worked something out. As loath as he was to admit it, he missed her.

Oh well, only a couple more weeks and he'd go down the hospital and get his plaster off. He'd be free to do as he pleased then. But while he was stuck here he may as well make the most of it.

'Molly,' he bawled at the top of his voice.

After a few seconds she poked her head around the door. 'Yes, what is it?'

'Get me some biscuits, will yer?'

There was only the slightest hesitation before she said, 'Yeah, sure,' and turned and went into the kitchen to get them.

'So he's getting his plaster off today then?' said Dan.

'Yes, that's right,' Molly replied. 'I ordered him a taxi to take him to the hospital.'

'Good.'

'He'll be relieved to get it done, understandably,' she mentioned. 'The itching's been driving him mad. He's fed up with being restricted too.'

'Aren't we all?' was his meaningful reaction.

'You can say that again,' she agreed with a wry grin.

'Thank God it's almost over for all of us.'

She nodded. 'Brian's always been a skiver but I think he actually wants to get back to Norfolk and work,' she told him. 'He makes no secret of the fact that Rosa and I irritate the pants off him.'

'Oh well, he'll soon be free to do as he pleases.'

It was lunchtime and they were alone in the pottery. She was sitting at her desk; he was perched on the edge. They were drinking coffee.

'I bet he'll go berserk when I tell him about us, even though he can't wait to get away,' she mentioned ruefully. 'I'm really dreading it.'

'Would you like me to do it for you?'

'Oh no,' she said at once. 'I must do it myself.'

'Can I be there to give you moral support then?'

'Thanks for offering but I'd rather be on my own.' She paused thoughtfully. 'But I don't want Rosa to be in the flat at the time so perhaps you can help me out on that one.'

'Of course. When will you do it?'

'It depends,' she replied. 'I'll have to see how his foot is with the plaster off.'

'As long as you don't let him slip off to Norfolk without saying anything.'

'Not a chance.' She gave this more thought as she finished her coffee and screwed her greaseproof sandwich paper into a ball and threw it into the waste-paper basket. 'Mind you, knowing him he'll just go when he feels like it without letting me know, once he's fully functional again. I might get home from work one day to find him gone.'

'Oh, Molly, we can't let that happen, so the sooner you do it the better.'

'Mm, I know,' she agreed. 'But I do want to make sure he's better before I spring it on him.' She sighed. 'It'll be such a relief to have it out in the open but, even after everything he's done, I can't bring myself to be too hard on him. It won't break his heart but it will hurt his pride.'

'I can understand that it won't be easy for you,' Dan said kindly. 'But it has to be done. If you wait for him to end it to protect his ego, we might have a very long wait. Brian strikes me as the sort of person to let things drift on.'

'Yes, he is.'

Dan stood up and opened his arms to her. 'Come here,' he said tenderly.

289

He kissed her and stroked her hair. They were totally engrossed in each other; much too deeply immersed to notice someone in the workshop watching them through the office window . . .

'Oh, very cosy,' said Hattie, her voice breaking with emotion as Molly and Dan sprang apart and stood facing her, both looking flushed and startled. 'Good job I happened to come back early. At least I know what's going on now.'

'We were going to tell you—' began Molly.

'Very soon,' Dan cut in.

Hattie looked at Molly with bitter disappointment. 'So, not content with stealing my granddaughter away from me, now you want her father as well, you slut.'

'What!'

'Got plans to be her stepmother, have you?' snapped Hattie, close to tears. 'Well, it's obviously time you were reminded that you are already married to someone else.'

'Stealing your granddaughter?' Molly was astonished.

'That's right.'

'What on earth are you talking about?'

'Yeah, what are you getting at?' Dan also wanted to know.

'Don't come the innocent with me, Molly Hawkins,' Hattie ranted, directing her comments to Molly. 'You've made sure it's you Patsy wants to be with and not me.'

'Rosa is the attraction,' said the staggered Molly.

'You've encouraged it,' accused Hattie. 'Always taking her off my hands. Always offering to baby-sit and worming your way into her affections.'

'I thought I was helping by looking after her a bit more often; thought I was taking the burden off you.'

'Burden?' Hattie raged. 'As if my granddaughter could ever be a burden to me.'

'I didn't mean that . . .'

'Of course she doesn't,' Dan backed her up.

'And as for you,' said Hattie, turning to Dan as though Molly hadn't spoken. 'Men like you never change.'

'Men like me?'

'You couldn't leave the women alone when you were a lad, and you still can't.'

'That just isn't true,' he defended, trying to be patient because he could see how upset she was.

'How could you?' Hattie was beside herself. 'How could you be unfaithful to Angie?'

'I have never done that, Hattie,' he replied. 'Surely you must know that of me.'

'I've just seen you with my own eyes.'

He hesitated before replying because he didn't want to hurt her any more than she was hurt already. But she'd put him a position whereby the truth couldn't be avoided. 'Angie's been dead for a year and a half now, Hattie. So in no way am I being unfaithful to her.'

'I don't know why I didn't guess what was going on; it should have been obvious with the two of you spending so much time together.' Hattie was far too distraught to listen to reason. 'I suppose I was too busy watching my granddaughter being taken away from me to notice much else.'

All became clear to Molly now: the intermittent coldness; the strange moods. 'I would never knowingly do anything to hurt you, Hattie,' she said ardently. 'I genuinely believed I was helping you by having Patsy as often as I could. She and Rosa always want to be together anyway, so it seemed the logical thing to do, especially as you have a lot on your plate already with a full-time job and the boys to look after. If only you'd told me how you were feeling instead of letting it simmer away inside you, building up and making you unhappy—'

'How could I spoil things for Patsy?' Hattie cut her short. 'You made sure she wanted to be at your place and not mine.'

'With Rosa, not me,' Molly told her again.

'It was all at your instigation,' Hattie insisted.

'Children need each other, Hattie, that's an indisputable fact,' Molly pointed out. 'It's only natural she wants to be with a friend of her own age. That doesn't mean she loves you any the less. She adores you. But she wants to be with Rosa and I couldn't very well dump my daughter on you as well, could I? That wouldn't have been fair.'

'I wouldn't have minded.'

'Oh, Hattie, I really did think I was helping—'

'Liar,' she shouted, and Molly didn't recognise the woman from whose mouth these words were pouring. Her face was taut with rage; the brown eyes, usually so full of warmth and generosity, were hard and accusing. Red blotches suffused her face and neck and her mouth was set in a grim line. 'I'm really disappointed in you. You're the last person on earth I expected to be promiscuous. I know that your Brian isn't much of a husband to you but you *are* married to him.'

'There's no need to be insulting, Hattie,' objected Dan, his arm around Molly protectively. 'Neither of us meant to hurt you. We were hoping for your blessing.'

'You must be joking,' came her withering response. 'I never want to see either of you again.'

'Hattie,' cried Molly, moving towards her, only to have her shrink away. 'You don't mean that.'

'I've never meant anything more in my life,' she confirmed. 'I'll leave my job here rather than have to work with you.'

'If anyone has to go it'll be me,' said Molly.

'And me,' added Dan.

'Oh, yes, and make me feel guilty because you both have children to feed,' she came back at them with venom. 'Not likely! George left me well provided for. I can manage without the salary.'

'But you can't leave.' Molly was frantic.

'Just watch me.'

'But you're needed here,' Molly tried to persuade. 'I can't manage in the office without you. You know that.'

Hattie considered the matter briefly. 'All right. I'll stay until you've found a replacement for me,' she informed them briskly. 'But only for the sake of the firm. I wouldn't want it to suffer on my account after all the work George put in building it up. But you must get someone for my job as soon as possible. I don't want to stay a moment longer than is absolutely necessary.'

The office door was open. Billy had come back from the house and heard raised voices.

'What's going on?' he wanted to know.

'These two have been at it behind our backs. I just came in and caught them,' Hattie informed him, her voice high and shaky.

'Oh,' muttered Billy, looking at his mother anxiously.

'The whole thing has made me feel so queer I'm going home and I won't be back this afternoon.' Hattie marched from the room, leaving them all staring after her through the office window as she crossed the workshop and left the premises.

'You should have told her, you know,' admonished Billy, 'rather than let her find out this way.'

'We were waiting until we'd told Brian.' Molly gave him a quizzical look. 'You don't seem very shocked.'

'That's because I'm not.'

'I thought we'd been careful to hide it.'

'You can hide what you do but it isn't so easy to hide how you feel,' he told them. 'I don't know why Mum didn't spot it.'

'She's been too preoccupied with something else,' said Molly, feeling tears well up now that the shock was wearing off and the reality sinking in.

'So are you going to turn on us too?' Dan enquired miserably.

'No, not me. My sister isn't ever coming back and you both deserve a chance of happiness, which Molly will never get with that waste of space of a husband of hers. Angie would be the first to agree about that.' His tone hardened. 'But I could kill you for upsetting my mum.'

'I'm devastated about that too. It was the last thing we intended,' Molly made clear. 'I'll give her a while to calm down then go over to the house and try to put things right.'

'You can try,' said Billy grimly. 'But I don't fancy your chances.'

At least now that it was out in the open Molly and Dan could have a conversation at work without the fear of appearing to be too friendly.

'I shall have to tell Brian tonight now, whatever happens,' Molly told Dan later when he came into the office. 'Now that the secret's out, it'll soon get around and I don't want him hearing about it from someone else.'

'Yes, you will have to tell him,' he agreed. 'But I really think I should be with you when you do it just in case it gets rough.'

'Your presence will only inflame the situation,' she told him quickly. 'Anyway, I need you to keep Rosa out of the way.'

'That's true. Well, if you're absolutely sure . . .'

'I am.' She shook her head sadly. 'Nothing could be worse than having Hattie turn on us. I'll never ever forgive myself for hurting her.'

'I feel terrible about that too,' Dan said. 'Maybe I should have a word with her.'

'She won't speak to you; she doesn't want to speak to either of us – ever again,' she reminded him. 'As I told you, she made that very clear when I went over there to see her earlier. She looked so sad when she opened the door, then told me to go away and never come back before she shut the door in my face.' She looked grave. 'It's breaking my heart, Dan. Hattie and I have grown so close since Angie died; I can't bear the idea of not having her in my life.'

'She'll come round – eventually.'

'I'm not so sure. She's been feeling so hurt about Patsy wanting to be at mine more than hers. And it's obviously been bothering her for a while. I should have been sensitive enough to realise.'

'You can't see into her mind.'

'I was given a clue, though, because she's been a bit off with me quite a few times lately,' Molly said. 'I thought it was because she'd got too much to do and offered to have Patsy even more.' Her eyes rolled heavenwards and she sighed. 'Talk about the mother of all misunderstandings. How could I have got it so wrong?'

'Because you're human, like everyone else,' Dan reminded her. 'Anyway, I'm as much to blame as you are. Patsy's my daughter, after all. And I didn't realise her grandmother was being hurt either.'

The conversation was interrupted by Billy passing the office door on his way somewhere and calling out, 'Oi, you two, cut it out will you? You're making the rest of us jealous.'

This was Billy's way of confirming that he'd fully accepted the situation between them. That was something, thought Molly. At least it wasn't quite just her and Dan against the rest of the world. It felt very lonely, though, being cast out of Hattie's life.

That evening – for the second time in a matter of hours – Molly had to hear herself described as a slut, though that was one of Brian's milder insults.

'Bitch, you evil bitch,' he roared after uttering a stream of invective that was foul even for him and made Molly very glad that Rosa wasn't there. 'After all I've done for you, you've made a fool of me.'

Her emotions still raw from the set-to with Hattie, remorse came easily. 'Sorry, Brian—'

'Sorry . . . what good is sorry to me?' he ranted.

'What more can I say?'

'Ugh, it turns my stomach to look at you,' he growled as though she hadn't spoken. 'You're soiled goods . . .' His eyes rested on her maliciously. 'Still, that's what you were when I married you, isn't it? You were then and you are now. You're nothing but a dirty little tart.'

She let him rant on; just stood there taking it. She was in the centre of the living room. He was standing by the fireplace, his bad foot out of plaster and encased in a slipper. When he paused to light a cigarette, she said, 'Don't tell me you haven't found someone else, Brian.'

'We're not all tarred with the same brush as you, you know,' he replied bitterly. 'I've never even looked at another woman.'

'Surely you're not expecting me to believe that there hasn't been anyone in all of this time,' she challenged. 'I mean, it isn't as if you and I . . . I mean, we haven't, not for ages.'

Such was his outrage, he could easily have fooled a stranger. 'You're disgusting,' he bellowed. 'While I'm away, working hard and staying in miserable digs, you're having a cheap affair with another bloke and you've got the bloody cheek to accuse me of doing the same.'

'It isn't a cheap affair,' she denied. 'Anyway, our marriage being finished has nothing to do with Dan. It was over years ago but you and I both let it drift on. You certainly didn't seem eager to come home.'

'It's a long way.'

'And you had more interesting things to do?'

A liar to the end, he said, 'No, not really. I might have had a few beers with the lads on a Saturday night and a bit of a laugh but that's all. The rest of the time I was working or stuck in the lodgings on my own.'

And the Queen does her shopping at the Co-op, was her ironic thought, but it was futile to argue so she returned to the purpose of this conversation. 'As you and I rarely saw each other, ending our marriage didn't seem important because you were never here anyway, and there was no other man in my life. But now that I want to make a new start with Dan, we need to tidy things up properly.

'You're not getting a divorce, if that's what you're suggesting,' he declared. 'I'm not having my name dragged through the courts.'

'But, Brian—'

'There'll be no divorce,' he cut in, 'so you can forget that right away.'

'Why not?' she wanted to know. 'You don't enjoy being with me. You can't wait to get away.'

'Why should I do what you want?' he barked. 'You've betrayed me.'

He paused, looking at her, his eyes narrowed to slits. 'After all I've done for you too.'

'I'll always be grateful to you for giving Rosa respectability, honestly Brian.' Forcing herself to stand her ground against his crushing insults, Molly added, 'But I think I've more than paid off that debt with years of dedicated slavery to you. You've had more than your money's worth out of me and now it's time for us both to move on.'

'Never.'

'What's the point of hanging on to something that doesn't make either of us happy?'

'We're married, that's the point – for better or worse, till death us do part, remember,' he said because it suited him. 'And don't think you're getting me to move out of this flat because I'm not going anywhere. I'll come back to London to work rather than let you have it.'

'I'll leave then,' she told him straight. 'One of us has to go. It isn't good for Rosa to live in the atmosphere you create when you and I are together, the constant arguments and feeling of general hostility.'

'Suit yourself,' he shrugged.

'You're welcome to the flat, as long as you don't mind paying the bills that go with it.' She paused, watching his face. 'Yeah, you'd forgotten about those, hadn't you? It's been such a long time since you had anything like that to deal with. Living in lodgings is cheap in comparison with running a home.'

'So you'd walk out on me when I've got a bad foot,' he said, changing his tack slightly. 'You'd leave me to fend for myself while you go off with your fancy man.'

'But your foot's better,' she said, looking down. 'You've had the plaster taken off.'

'I've got to take it easy for a week or so, though,' he told her. 'I won't be going back to work just yet because what I do is so physically demanding.'

He still managed to make her feel compelled to do what he wanted. 'All right, I'll stay until you're properly back on your feet again,' she conceded. 'But one of us has to go then. And could you please be a bit more patient with Rosa while we are all living in this flat?'

'I don't do her any harm.'

'You don't do her much good either, with your short temper,' was her tart reply.

'I've had a bad foot. You can't expect sweetness and light from a man in pain.'

There was no point in discussing the subject further because he would never admit to being in the wrong about anything. 'OK. Now that you know where you stand with me, I'll go and get Rosa. It's past her bedtime.'

'What about my tea?' Brian demanded, settling down in the armchair.

Such was the dominance of his personality, she almost stopped to make something for him, but her priorities finally prevailed. 'I have to collect Rosa first. She'll be tired and she's got school in the morning. I'll get you something when I get back if you don't want to do it yourself,' she said, and hurried from the room.

The next day it seemed to Molly as though she went from one battleground to another. She left the hostile atmosphere at home only to walk into another at the office with Hattie back at her desk, giving Molly the cold shoulder and speaking to her only when it couldn't be avoided.

As for Molly being able to explain her side of the story, there was absolutely no chance. Hattie's mind was made up.

'The subject is closed,' she stated when Molly begged her to listen.

'You're wrong about my motives towards Patsy—'

'Stop,' barked Hattie in a tone that Molly didn't recognise. She looked at Molly coldly, though a slight puffiness around her eyes indicated that she wasn't quite as hard as she was trying to make out. 'I'm only here because I don't want to upset the running of my husband's firm. As soon as you get fixed up with a replacement, you won't see me again.' She paused before adding, 'Not if I see you first anyway.'

With these painful words still echoing in her head, Molly left work early to call on her mother, already bracing herself for another attack. But it couldn't be put off. If her mother heard about Molly and Dan through other means there would be hell to pay.

'Trust you to get yourself into a mess,' was Joan's reaction after Molly had poured out the whole story over a cup of tea at the kitchen table. 'By God, you don't do things by halves, do you, girl? You've all but ended your marriage to Brian, you've alienated Hattie Beckett—'

'And now I've alienated you, I suppose,' Molly assumed miserably.

'You can't expect me to do cartwheels about what you've been getting up to, can you?' was Joan's curt reply. 'Everyone will be talking about you, and giving me funny looks. That sort of gossip reflects on me, you know.'

'I'm sorry, Mum,' Molly sighed. 'I know I've been a big disappointment to you. But I really do love Dan.'

'Love,' Joan sniffed. 'You're a married woman with a child to think of.'

'Dan's a good man. He'll be good to Rosa.'

Joan shrugged. 'Only time will tell.' A thoughtful pause. 'You say that Hattie Beckett's more concerned about you taking her granddaughter away from her than your carrying on with Dan Plater?'

'We haven't been "carrying on", as such. You're making it sound sordid,' corrected Molly.

'You're a married woman seeing another man,' declared Joan. 'That's sordid enough for me.'

'If you say so,' she sighed. 'But, yes, Hattie did get the wrong end of the stick about Patsy. I really did think I was helping.' Her eyes became hot with tears. 'First I lose Angie; now Hattie. And all because I was too insensitive to realise the effect of what I was doing. It's all my own fault.'

Joan leaned towards her daughter as though to comfort her, hesitated then drew back quickly. 'Another cup of tea?' she invited crisply.

'Yes, please. Then I'll have to go; it's nearly time to collect the kids from school.'

Looking at the clock on the wall, Joan said. 'You've got a few minutes yet before you need leave.'

'Hello, Mrs Rawlings,' said Billy, opening the front door on the evening of the same day. 'What brings you here?'

'Is your mother in?'

'She is but I don't know if—'

'Tell her I'll stay here ringing the bell until she does see me, so she might as well get it over with now and save us both some time.'

Hattie appeared behind him. 'Joan Rawlings,' she said coldly, 'what do you want?'

'A few words.' Looking towards Billy, she added with emphasis, 'In private, if you please.'

'You'd better come in then, hadn't you?' Hattie said ungraciously, but opening the door wider and leading Joan through to the living room.

As soon as the door closed behind them, Joan came straight to the point. She wasn't offered a seat so faced Hattie standing up. 'I hear you've been accusing my Molly of trying to steal the affections of your granddaughter?'

'That's right,' she readily admitted. 'It is what she's been doing.'

'Have you lost your mind or something?' blasted Joan. 'You know Molly well enough to know that she would never do a thing like that.'

'I used to think I knew her,' replied Hattie with a sour expression.

'You still do.'

'I trusted that girl with my life,' Hattie told her in a tight voice. 'And all the time she's been carrying on with my daughter's husband and leaving me out in the cold with my own granddaughter.'

'For one thing Dan Plater is your daughter's widower now,' Joan corrected firmly. 'And for another, Molly really did think she was helping by offering to have Patsy more often. She was being considerate. And you repay her by breaking her heart. You ought to be damned well ashamed of yourself.'

Hattie gave her a shrewd look. 'What's comes over you all of a sudden?' she asked, her eyes narrowed suspiciously. 'You don't usually have a kind word to say to her. You're always too busy singing Peggy's praises.'

Joan's face worked but she quickly composed herself. 'That's between me and my daughter and none of your business, as I told you the last time you tried to interfere. I won't have you upsetting Molly. She doesn't deserve it. She has quite enough to do, working and raising a child with no help at all from her waster of a husband. But she's bent over backwards to help out with young Patsy since Angie died, looking after her every day after school and offering her services more often lately, to save you from having to do it.'

'And managing to find the time to canoodle with my son-in-law as well.'

'Molly and Dan are adults, for goodness' sake,' Joan pointed out brusquely. 'What they do in their private life is their own business. It isn't for us to judge them, no matter what our personal feelings are. Anyway, surely you didn't expect Dan to stay single for ever. He's a young man with a lot of living ahead of him. It wouldn't be right for him to be lonely for the rest of his days. And Molly might as well not have a husband for all the use Brian is to her.'

Hattie stood with her arms folded, looking at Joan with a grim expression.

'Molly and Dan both loved your daughter and they'll make sure she's never forgotten,' Joan went on.

'What's that got to do with it?'

'I should have thought that was obvious. It'll be a damned sight better from your point of view than Dan getting together with some stranger who'll be only too pleased to erase Angie from his memory, and little Patsy from yours. A stranger might object to him staying in touch with his late wife's family. Some women see the first wife as a threat.'

'Oh, I'm not listening to any more of this rubbish,' pronounced Hattie. 'So get out of my house. Go on – *out*.'

Joan didn't move. 'I haven't quite finished yet.' Her tone became softer. 'Look, Hattie, you've been through a lot these past few years, losing your husband then your daughter. God knows what it must be like to lose a daughter.'

The other woman stared at her in stony silence.

'You and I have never been friends but you're a good woman. I can't deny that,' she went on. 'And I know you well enough to know that this isn't the real Hattie Beckett saying all these horrible things about my Molly. It's the lingering grief talking. It's colouring your judgement. You need to calm down and get things into perspective.'

It was as though Hattie had turned to stone; she just stood there without saying a word. Then: 'Please go,' she said at last in a weary tone. 'I don't want to listen to any more.'

'Fair enough,' said Joan with a sigh of resignation. 'If you won't listen to reason I'll go, but I don't know how you can sleep at night, hurting Molly like this. The poor girl's distraught. She thinks the world of you.'

With that she turned and walked away with a heavy step. Billy and Josh – who were outside the room with their ears pressed against the door – hurried out of sight.

Chapter Twenty

The next day Molly had a welcome respite from the toxic atmosphere at the office because she needed to go to Notting Hill Gate to the shop.

'See you later then,' she said to Hattie. 'I'll be back as soon as I can.'

'Right.' She didn't even look up from the work she was doing at her desk.

Molly was walking towards the bus stop when Billy caught her up.

'I need to talk to you on your own without Mum knowing,' he explained, falling into step beside her. 'I don't want her to think that there's a conspiracy.'

'We're on our own now so fire away.'

'She's eating her heart out over this thing between you and her, and I'm really worried about her.'

'Me too.'

'I've never known her to be like this before,' he went on, his dark eyes solemn. 'You know Mum – she's usually so fair and straightforward. If she's angry about something she'll come right out and say so, and it's over and done with. She doesn't normally have a sulky bone in her body and I've never known her to bear a grudge before.'

'It's very out of character,' Molly agreed. 'Which just goes to show how deeply I must have hurt her.' She sighed. 'Honestly, Billy, I really wasn't trying to steal Patsy away from her. And as for Dan and me, our friendship just developed into love. It wasn't something we planned. And neither of us feels we are being disloyal to Angie.'

'There's no reason why you should, and Mum would see it that way if she was thinking straight, but she isn't, and the situation needs sorting sharpish before it gets a chance to take root. I was wondering if there's anything at all you can do to patch things up between you. I can't bear to see her so unhappy.'

'I'd do anything to put things right but she won't let me near her,' Molly told him. 'She's got this idea into her head and there's no shifting her.'

'I've tried talking to her about it too but she won't have it.' He paused thoughtfully. 'The fact of the matter is, Molly, she needs you. Josh and I can only give her so much in the way of support. We can't give her what a woman friend can. And if she does go ahead and leave her job at the

301

pottery she'll be lost. She doesn't have any other close women friends that I know of.'

'I need her too.' Molly's tone was grave. 'We turned to each other after Angie died. She'd lost her only daughter; I'd lost my closest friend. We filled a gap in each other's lives then but it grew into friendship that we both came to value.'

'Which is why we've got to get things back to normal.'

'All I can do is keep trying to persuade her to listen to me,' Molly told him. 'I'll get down on my knees if I have to. I won't give up, I promise.'

'I knew I could rely on you.' He slowed his step, ready to turn back. 'It's a worry all right.' He shook his head slowly, puffing out his lips. 'I really thought it was going to get sorted last night when your mum came round to see her,' he mentioned almost as an afterthought. 'I had high hopes that she'd talk her round. But no such luck.'

Molly stopped dead in her tracks, staring at him. '*My mum went to see Hattie?*' She was astonished.

'You didn't know?'

'No. I didn't.'

'Well, she was there; turned up out of the blue at the house and demanded to see Mum in private,' he informed her. 'She gave her a real trouncing on your behalf, an' all. You should have heard her. Josh and I were earwigging outside the door.'

'Are you saying that my mother was sticking up for me?' Molly couldn't believe it.

'Phew, not half,' Billy confirmed. 'She was praising you to the heavens. She told Mum how you were only trying to help by looking after Patsy, and how wonderful you've been with her since Angie died, even though you've got more than enough on your plate already. Said you didn't deserve to be treated like this and she ought to be ashamed of herself, or words to that effect. But our mum was having none of it. Told her to get out. Your mum didn't leave without saying her piece, though. She really went to town.'

'Well, well . . .'

'I was hoping that when Mum had calmed down after the visit, she might have thought about it and seen the sense in what she said. But apparently not.'

'I'll keep trying, don't worry, Billy.' They had reached the Uxbridge Road and the 607 came into sight. 'But there's my bus so I'll have to go. See you later.'

'See you, Molly.'

As Molly tore towards the bus stop, she was still in a state of shock. Her mother defending her? What a turn-up for the books!

That evening Molly left Rosa with Dan and Patsy, and went to visit the lady in question.

'Those Beckett boys had no business to listen outside the door,' was Joan's reaction to what Molly had to say. They were sitting either side of the fire. 'I made it quite clear that it was a private matter.'

'It's understandable, I suppose,' defended Molly. 'They're worried about their mum and were hoping you might have made her see things more clearly.'

'No chance. She can be really stubborn when she likes, that one.'

'Thanks for taking my side, anyway, Mum,' said Molly. 'I must admit I'm surprised.'

Joan threw her a look. 'I don't know why you should be,' she pronounced. 'You're my daughter; of course I'll stick up for you. The woman's upset you. I'm not going to let her get away with that, am I?'

'Thanks, Mum. I'm touched that you did that for me,' Molly told her.

Molly's reaction of surprise to Joan's defence of her brought Hattie's harsh criticism of Joan herself back into her mind, making her smart. 'Look, Molly, I know I go on at you a bit sometimes but that doesn't mean I don't care about you, you know.'

Molly was even more shocked to hear this, since such an admission had never come her way before. 'Oh, that's nice,' was her response.

'As long as you do know that.'

Seizing this unexpected opportunity to get certain things off her chest, Molly said, 'Peggy has always been the favourite though, hasn't she?'

'Peggy has always had a very persuasive personality and was a very difficult child,' Joan explained. 'She's always been able to pull my strings; she bullied me from a very young age. She could get her own way because I was always – and I know this is a strange thing for a mother to say – but I was rather frightened of her. I was weak, I suppose. The tantrums she threw if she couldn't get her own way were exhausting and I could only take so much. Whereas you were always sweet-natured and easy-going.' Joan looked at her daughter across the hearth. 'I've not been fair to you, have I?'

'Coming second to Peggy has hurt, I won't deny it.'

'You never came second.'

'That's what it feels like.'

'That isn't how it is. It's just that . . .'

'She's always got everything right and I got it all wrong,' Molly finished for her as her mother struggled to find the right words.

'I suppose there was something of that in it,' Joan confessed. 'I wanted the best for you both but it never seemed to come off for you, what with you having to get married, and then Brian not coming up to scratch as a husband and provider. And now your marriage breaking up.' She stroked her chin, thinking. 'I was disappointed *for* you – not *in* you. You deserved better and I was powerless to do anything about it. It made me angry and I took it out on you. I couldn't seem to stop myself.'

'I've always felt in Peggy's shadow.'

'I can see now that you would have done.' Joan sighed. 'It's all too easy to hurt someone without realising that you're doing it,' she said sadly. 'Like I have with you, and you have with Hattie, and Peggy has with me.'

'Peggy's hurt you?'

'She does it all the time,' Joan confirmed. 'She thinks I don't feel it when she sneers at me and jumps down my throat every time I open my mouth.'

'I've had a go at her about that,' Molly told her, 'but you never seemed to notice she was doing it.'

'It's easier to let it all go over my head than stand up to her,' she explained. 'But I notice all right. You'd have to have a skin like a rhino not to. Subtlety isn't exactly Peggy's strong point.'

'You shouldn't let her get away with it,' advised Molly. 'It isn't right, the way she treats you. Stand up for yourself, Mum.'

'It isn't as easy as it might seem and you'll realise that when Rosa grows up,' Joan told her. 'You don't want to lose your children so you go along with them.'

'Not with me, you don't,' Molly couldn't help pointing out.

'Probably because I know I'll never lose you,' was her thoughtful response. 'I trust you always to be there for me so I don't have to watch every word I say. You always have been there, always calling in, always there when I'm ill. I might not seem to appreciate it but I do.'

'Oh, Mum.' Molly's throat was beginning to tighten. 'Hearing you say that means so much to me.'

In her own blunt way her mother had always been there for her too, she now realised. She might not have been outwardly caring or always given the best advice; encouraging Molly to marry Brian hadn't been one of her better ideas. But she'd done what had seemed the best thing for Molly at the time and it had protected Molly and Rosa from public abuse. She'd never given praise or shown affection but she'd never deserted her either. She'd taken her and Brian in when they couldn't find anywhere to live. She'd helped out with Rosa when she could, given that she had a job of her own. And last night she'd shown her true colours by defending Molly against Hattie.

'I don't find it easy to show my feelings,' Joan explained, her face flushed, lips dry. 'But that doesn't mean that they aren't there.'

Molly's constricted throat finally got the better of her. 'Oh, Mum, you've always been there for me too,' she choked out, hot, salty tears stinging her eyes.

'I know I've got a sharp tongue . . .'

'Gillettes have nothing on you at times.'

'A real old battleaxe, eh?'

'Maybe.' Molly stood up and held her arms out to her. 'Come here,' she said.

At first Joan didn't move. Then slowly she got up and went to her daughter, stiff and restrained. But as Molly threw her arms around her with genuine affection, her inhibition gradually lessened and the two women embraced. Molly couldn't remember the last time this had happened. 'It'll be better between us now, battleaxe or not,' sobbed Molly, 'because now I understand you a little better.'

The next day Brian was standing at the bar of his local pub on his own, towards the end of the lunchtime session. The blokes who'd popped in for a quick one in their dinner hour had all left to go back to work. He wasn't in the mood for company anyway. He'd been drinking steadily since opening time so was well past pleasantly tiddly, and deep into maudlin.

How had he ended up in such a mess? He asked himself, brimming over with self-pity. He had no woman in his life, no proper home and no kids of his own. The answer was simple. Molly. She'd ruined his life. If he hadn't married her to get her out of trouble, he might have met someone who would have doted on him. Someone like Beryl, who he'd lost because he was already married to Molly.

Admittedly, he'd been besotted with Molly at the beginning and glad to marry her under any circumstances. And yes, maybe he had seized the opportunity and pushed her into it when she was desperate. She'd been the girl of his dreams in those days. How was he to know that he'd end up hating her because she wouldn't love him back? It had all seemed so simple then. And now she'd found someone else.

He ordered another whisky but the barman refused to serve him; said he'd had enough. Bloody cheek, Brian thought, as he staggered out of the pub in a drunken rage. What's the world coming to when you can't even have a quiet drink in your own local?

Now all he had to look forward to was going home to an empty flat because his wife was out working instead of being indoors looking after him. The matter of how they would live if she wasn't out working conveniently slipped his mind.

He halted in his step, swaying slightly. Why was he going home instead of fighting back? He'd been a fool. He'd let her off too easily; just laid down and let her trample all over him. Well, she wasn't going to get away with it. He was going to see to that.

'Can you get on the phone to our clay suppliers, please, Molly?' requested Billy, coming into the office. 'Tell them to get a move on with our order. We're getting really low in the store.' He gave her a shrewd look. 'You did order it, didn't you?'

'Yeah, course I did; well over a week ago.' She reached for the suppliers' order book and flicked through the pages. 'Yes, here it is. It was ten days ago. I'll get on to them right away.'

'Thanks, love.' He looked across at his mother who was at the filing cabinet. 'You all right, Mum?'

'I'm fine,' was her dull reply.

'You look busy.' He was hoping to get some sort of dialogue going that would draw both women in.

'I am extremely busy. I need to keep on top of things,' she told him in the flat tone she had adopted since the trouble. 'I want to leave everything up to date for my successor.'

Her words rang in the air followed by a tense silence. It sounded so definite; so final. Hoping she could somehow persuade Hattie to change her mind and stay on, Molly hadn't done anything about trying to find her replacement. But the other woman didn't know that.

'None of us wants you to go, Mum . . .'

'We don't,' ventured Molly.

'My decision is irreversible . . .'

The sound of a disturbance in the workshop stopped her in mid-sentence and they all turned towards the window.

'What the hell . . .?' began Billy.

'Oh no,' wailed Molly as she saw who was there.

'Brian Hawkins and he's as drunk as a skunk by the look of him,' said Billy.

He rushed out of the office followed by the two women.

'Wotcha, Billy, me old mate,' greeted Brian in a slurred tone.

'What are you doing here?' demanded Billy.

'I've come to have a few . . . a few words with Dan here,' he muttered slowly, turning his bleary eyes towards the other man. 'Come to put him wise about a few things.'

'Go home and sober up,' ordered Billy.

'The man's got a right to know the sort of woman he's got mixed up with.' Brian wasn't to be deterred.

'Brian, please . . .' began Molly.

'Worried now, are you, you old slag?' he challenged her drunkenly. 'Worried he won't wanna know when he finds out what you're really like.'

'Out,' ordered Dan, moving towards him and grabbing his arm. 'Don't you dare come here calling her names.'

'Yeah, clear off,' added Billy, taking his other arm.

'Right now,' said Josh, adding his support.

'Not until I've had my say,' mumbled Brian, trying to shrug them off only to have their grip on him tighten.

'Let him say what he has to,' Molly urged them. 'I'm not afraid of what he has to say. Go on, Brian. Do your worst.'

The men released their hold on him but stood close by.

Unsteady on his feet, Brian turned to Dan. 'She was soiled goods when I married her, you know,' he drawled. 'She was already up the spout with some other bloke's kid.'

306

'Is that all? You're not telling me anything I don't already know,' said Dan.

Brian was too far gone to pay any attention to what Dan had to say. 'I saved her reputation and what does she do? She starts carrying on behind my back.' His speech was slow and thick with inebriation. 'She used me, then, after all I've done for her, she does the dirty on me, and she'll do the same to you. I should have left her in the gutter where she belongs. She's a disgusting little tramp and you'd do well to steer clear. Don't touch her with a barge pole, mate.'

'That's enough.' Dan squared up to him.

He was about to land him one on the jaw when there was an interruption from a most unexpected source.

Hattie pushed Dan aside and stood between the two men, facing Brian. 'You're not fit to breathe the same air as your wife,' she stated categorically. 'You talk about everything you've done for her. You saved her reputation, yes, but that's about the only good thing. And, my God, did you make her pay.'

'Been running to you with lies about me, has she?' Brian sneered.

'No, she's never said a word to me about her marriage but my senses are all in good working order and I can read between the lines. You've bullied her and kept her grateful; you've been living away from home, giving her no support and getting up to God knows what. So don't come here telling us what you've done for her. She's the salt of the earth and far too good for you. She's a wonderful mother, and she's been a marvellous wife to you, waiting on you hand and foot and letting you get your own way about everything. You've never made her happy. Now she's found someone who will. So go away and leave her alone.'

'You old bag,' muttered Brian, swaying.

'Now you've gone too far,' Billy ground out, and he and Dan escorted Brian forcefully from the premises, followed by Josh. Frankie was out on an errand so the two women were then alone in the workshop.

'Thank you for standing up for me, Hattie,' said Molly, feeling tearful and shaky in the aftermath of Brian's attack.

Hattie looked bewildered, as though emerging from a far-off place in her mind. 'Oh, Molly,' she said thickly, her lips trembling, 'how can you ever forgive me?'

They went into the office and shut the door. The others respected their need to be alone so left them to it.

'I've been so stupid,' Hattie readily admitted. 'All that stuff about you stealing Patsy.' She held her head. 'I don't know what got into me because I know you would never knowingly do such a thing.'

'It doesn't matter—' Molly began.

'It does matter,' Hattie interrupted forcefully. 'I'm a mature woman and I should have known better. I want my granddaughter to be happy.

How could I have been so small-minded?'

'It was a misunderstanding—'

'I had no right to hurt you that way.' She looked into the distance as though trying to make sense of it all. 'All those awful things I said about you and Dan too.'

'You were upset—'

'I must have been out of my mind. It was as if that person saying those things when I found you together wasn't me. I could hear the words but not feel them coming out of my mouth. I was hurting so much, I just hit out about anything.'

'You'd been hurt for a while about my looking after Patsy so much, hadn't you?'

'Yeah. I felt as though I was losing her and it was just one loss too many.' She shook her head. 'Heaven knows what came over me to get such an idea.'

'Too much grief,' was Molly's opinion. 'It's left you feeling insecure.'

Hattie bit her lip, smarting at the memory. 'All those things I said—'

'Forget it—'

'I can't,' said Hattie. 'I insulted you, I insulted Dan. Whatever was I thinking of?'

'Don't be too hard on yourself. It wasn't all your fault,' Molly urged her to realise. 'I should have been more sensitive to your feelings. I shouldn't have taken it on myself to have Patsy more often without discussing it with you first. If you hadn't been so upset about that you probably wouldn't have blown your top about Dan and me.'

Hattie thought about this. 'Maybe you're right. It all kind of built up and the slightest thing seemed to cause me pain.'

'It's all sorted out now,' soothed Molly. 'And there's no real harm done. In fact, some good has come out of it because it's taught me not to take other people's feelings for granted in future.'

Hattie took her hand. 'Can we end the post-mortem and put it behind us?'

Warm and tearful with relief, Molly hugged her. 'Yes, please.'

'Oh, thank goodness for that.'

'I must get on to the suppliers,' said Molly shakily, when they drew back, 'or I'll have Billy on my back.'

'And I must go and put things right with Dan.' Hattie thought for a moment. 'You and Rosa are welcome to stay at my place, you know,' she offered. 'I don't like the idea of the two of you being in the flat with Brian while he's in this mood.'

'Thanks, Hattie, and I might take you up on it later but I need to be there when he sobers up, to clear up a few things.' She paused. 'Though it might be best if Rosa isn't there.'

'She's welcome to stay with me,' said Hattie again, adding quickly, 'but I expect she'll be happier with Patsy at Dan's.'

'I appreciate the offer, though.'

'I know, dear.'

Molly groaned, biting her lip. 'When I've made that phone call to the suppliers, I think I'd better go home to make sure Brian got there safely. The state he was in when he left, he could have fallen and hurt himself, or got arrested for being drunk and disorderly.'

'After what he's just done it's a wonder you don't want to just leave him to rot.'

'I could never do that,' Molly told her. 'It just isn't in my nature.'

It was almost midnight when Brian finally emerged from the bedroom, groaning and holding his head. He'd collapsed in a drunken heap on the bed fully dressed when he got home from the pottery; this was where Molly had found him. Rosa was staying at Dan's for the night. Molly was in her dressing gown in the armchair waiting for Brian to wake up. She made him black coffee, gave him some Alka-Seltzer and told him she wanted to talk to him.

'Not now,' he objected, sinking into an armchair, wincing. 'Can't you see that I'm suffering?'

'It can't wait, I'm afraid,' she stated firmly. 'Anyway, I'm not feeling my best either after what you put me through this afternoon.'

He peered at her, screwing up his eyes as though he didn't know what she was talking about.

'I know you were drunk and probably don't remember much about it,' she went on, 'but you can take it from me that your behaviour at the pottery was disgraceful.'

'Oh, that,' he mumbled, falling silent as though struggling to recall. 'You're right, I don't remember much about it but I do know that I wanted to put lover boy straight about the woman he's got mixed up with.'

'Anyway, your disgusting performance has brought me to a decision,' Molly said quickly.

'Oh yeah?' His attitude was one of indifference.

'Either you move out of the flat right away or I will,' she announced. 'We can't be under the same roof any longer. It isn't healthy for any of us.'

'That's right, kick a man when he's down,' he accused. 'You know I'm not working.'

'I said I'd give you a couple of weeks to get back to work and I'll stand by that,' Molly made clear. 'If you want to stay on here for a while longer I'll pay the bills and supply you with food but I won't stay if you're here, Brian. There's too much bad feeling and it isn't good for Rosa or me. I'll stay with Hattie until you've gone back to Norfolk.'

'I might not go back,' he informed her. 'I might get a job here in London.'

'In that case you take over the bills of the flat and I'll make arrangements for alternative accommodation on a permanent basis,' she told him. 'But either way this is the last night we'll spend under the same roof. I'm determined about that.'

'I'm going nowhere,' he declared.

'In that case I'll be gone by tomorrow night. If it wasn't so late I'd go now.'

'Suit yourself,' he shrugged.

Molly was at Dan's early the next morning to collect her daughter. She took both the children to school and went into the office as usual, but left early, having arranged to stay at Hattie's temporarily. Dan suggested that she and Rosa move in with him but Molly didn't want to add fuel to the scandalmongers' fire just yet. There would be quite enough of that later on. Hattie's was her best bet for now. She wasn't to know then the dramatic events about to unfold . . .

'You're just being overdramatic,' grumbled Brian as Molly packed a suitcase with clothes for herself and Rosa. 'There's no need for this, no need at all.'

'There's every need,' she insisted, folding a jumper and putting it into the case. 'You and I can't stay together. I can't take any more and, although you won't admit it, I don't think you can either.'

'All right, I admit I shouldn't have got drunk and gone to the pottery yesterday,' he conceded. 'I won't do anything like that again. I'll change, I promise.'

'You can't,' was her genuine belief. 'Not while you're with me, anyway. We just make each other miserable. We're not right for each other and we never have been.' She looked at him gravely. 'Can you honestly remember the last time you got any pleasure from being with me?'

He didn't reply at first. Then: 'You don't expect it to be all roses when you've been married for a while.'

'No, but you should be able to live in some sort of harmony.'

'So I'm to be left high and dry while you go off with your fancy man.'

'I'm not going to live with Dan, not just yet anyway,' she corrected. 'Rosa and I are going to stay with Hattie for the time being.'

'Bitch. You two-timing bitch.'

She looked at him. The extra weight he'd put on from too little exercise and too much food, while he'd been laid up, made his face look puffy, his little eyes seeming even more deepset as they regarded her with contempt. 'Are you still expecting me to believe that you haven't found someone else in all the time you've been away?' she asked.

'How many more times must I tell you,' he replied, his voice rising angrily. 'The answer is no, *I am not a liar.*'

310

There was no point in pursuing it so she said, 'OK, if you say so.'

Turning back to packing, she put Rosa's underwear neatly into the case while Brian wandered off into the other room. She was just fastening the suitcase when the doorbell rang. As usual he ignored it and waited for her to answer it.

'Yes?' she asked, faced with a stranger on the doorstep, a middle-aged woman with a round face and a healthy complexion.

'Mrs Hawkins?' She peered enquiringly at Molly through spectacles.

'That's right.'

'Is your husband in?'

She nodded.

'Could you tell him that Flo Brown wants to see him urgently, please?'

'Why not come in and tell him yourself?' invited Molly, intrigued. If Brian was going in for maturity these days, he'd certainly done it in a big way. The woman looked more than old enough to be his mother.

'Flo,' gasped Brian as Molly showed the visitor in the living room.

'Surprised to see me, eh, Brian?'

'What the hell are you doing here? How . . .?'

'I got your address from the site office,' she explained briskly. 'You'd have heard from me a damned sight sooner if I'd had my way. But Beryl made me promise not to contact you.'

He looked sheepishly at Molly, then back at Flo. 'Look, we can't talk here,' he said.

'Don't mind me,' Molly told them, looking from one to the other.

'Here will do just fine,' announced Flo. 'Your wife needs to know what's been going on.' She turned to Molly. 'Sorry to burst in on you like this, love. But I had to come. It's important.'

'Carry on,' invited Molly.

Turning her attention to Brian, Flo made an announcement. 'Beryl's had a baby. Your baby. A little boy.'

Molly couldn't stifle a gasp, the blood draining from her face.

Brian turned bright red, then deathly white. 'Bloody 'ell,' he blurted out, his voice shaking. 'What did you say?'

'You 'eard.'

'I can't believe it.'

'It can't be that much of a shock.' She gave him a hard look. 'I know you're not the brightest button in the box but even you must know how babies are made.'

'Why . . . why didn't she tell me?'

'Because she didn't want you to know, seeing that you're married to someone else,' Flo informed him. 'She went away to stay at my sister's in Margate to avoid the scandal.'

'So that's why she disappeared.' He still looked pale and bewildered.

'That's right. The idea was for her to give the baby up for adoption

311

straight away and no one in Boxham would have been any wiser,' she went on. 'But she won't go through with it now. She's determined to keep him so we're going to have to put up with the scandal after all. But it's gonna be hard, *very hard*, which is why I'm here.'

Molly had never seen Brian lost for words before but he was now. He just stared at the woman with a bemused expression.

'I've come to demand that you face up to your responsibilities and give Beryl some financial support,' she informed him. 'She doesn't know I'm here. She'd sooner die than ask you for anything, the way you treated her. But I'm not prepared to see her struggle and let you get off scot-free.' She turned to Molly. 'He got engaged to my daughter, you know. Bought her an engagement ring and everything. They even had the wedding planned. Then one of his mates grassed on him. It broke my Beryl's heart when she found out he was married. She broke it off right away.'

'The poor girl.' Molly turned to Brian. 'What was that you were saying just now about never being unfaithful to your wife? And all that rubbish about not being a liar?'

'Well, I . . .'

'There's been a change of plan,' Molly informed him brusquely. 'I'm not leaving, you are. Pack your things and get out. *Now.* You can use the money you've got stashed away for beer for the fare to Norfolk. Go and look after your son and his mother. I'm sure you'll feel fit enough to go back to work now that there isn't an alternative.' She looked at Flo. 'Tell your daughter she's welcome to him. Now if you'll both excuse me I'm going to unpack.'

And she left the room.

It was a fine June day in 1959. A perfect day for a wedding, the sun shining from a clear blue sky and just a whisper of a breeze keeping things cool. The service was over and the bride and groom were posing for photographs outside the church. Sally was radiant in a long white dress with a frothy veil. Bridesmaids Rosa and Patsy were sweet and pretty in pale lemon dresses and flowers in their hair; a friend of Sally's was the only adult bridesmaid. Billy looked handsome and proud with best man Josh beside him.

'Don't they make a lovely couple?' said Hattie.

'They certainly do,' agreed Molly.

'It'll be your turn next,' Hattie suggested.

'I hope so,' replied Molly dreamily.

'It can't come quick enough for me,' added Dan.

'It'll be a while, though.' Molly was being realistic. 'Divorce takes ages.'

'What's worth having is worth waiting for,' put in Joan, who'd been invited to the wedding as a Beckett family friend. She and Hattie were getting on much better these days. Joan was easier company now that she was happier in herself. Having a better relationship with Molly had made a big difference.

'Exactly,' agreed Molly.

Brian had admitted to adultery and wanted a divorce so that he could marry Beryl, with whom he was now living at her mother's house in Norfolk. When he'd come back to collect the last of his things from the flat, he'd been full of his new life, boasting about being a dad and claiming that his son was handsome like his father. He would never admit it, but Molly suspected that Beryl had laid down a few ground rules when she'd taken him back. Still, this was the happiest Molly had ever seen him, and she was glad he'd found someone to really love him and give him a child of his own.

Divorce was an extremely lengthy process, so Molly and Rosa had moved into Dan's place and were living as a family. Both the children's grandmothers played a large part in their lives. Molly made sure of that.

'You're wanted, Hattie,' said Dan now as the photographer asked for the parents of the bride and groom to be included in the picture.

Looking elegant in a pale blue suit and fancy hat, Hattie moved into the wedding group. Joan slipped to the front of the crowd to get a better view, leaving Molly and Dan alone.

'I've been thinking about Angie a lot today,' Molly told him. 'How proud she'd have been to see her brother married and her daughter up there in all her bridesmaid finery.'

'I've been thinking the same thing myself,' he confessed. 'Angie feels very close today.'

'To me too.'

The constant presence in their lives of his late wife's memory created a bond between them rather than a division. It was something they both valued and didn't want to lose. He slipped his arm around her and they stood there for a few moments watching the scene in front of them.

'Look at the girls,' said Molly, pointing towards Rosa and Patsy, who were making faces at the anxious-looking photographer. 'When I told Rosa that Patsy couldn't be her friend any more she was worried to death. You should have seen her face when I explained it was only because they were going to be sisters.'

'Patsy's thrilled to bits as well,' said Dan.

Molly looked at the man she would soon marry. 'I never believed I could be so happy, Dan.'

'That goes for me too.' He kissed her forehead with infinite tenderness. 'We're lucky, Mrs soon-to-be Plater. We've both been given a second chance of love. Come on, we'd better grab our little horrors before the photographer is driven to do something he'll regret.'

He took her hand and they walked forward in the sunshine.